PRIZED POSSESSIONS

Also by Jessica Stirling

The Spoiled Earth
The Hiring Fair
The Dark Pasture
The Deep Well at Noon
The Blue Evening Gone
The Gates of Midnight
Treasures on Earth
Creature Comforts
Hearts of Gold
The Good Provider
The Asking Price
The Wise Child
The Welcome Light
A Lantern for the Dark
Shadows on the Shore
The Penny Wedding
The Marrying Kind
The Workhouse Girl
The Island Wife
The Wind from the Hills
The Strawberry Season

as Caroline Crosby

The Haldanes

PRIZED POSSESSIONS

Jessica Stirling

St. Martin's Press
New York

WWW.STMARTINS.COM

ISBN 0-312-28057-2

FIRST PUBLISHED IN GREAT BRITAIN BY HODDER AND STOUGHTON
A DIVISION OF HODDER HEADLINE PLC

FIRST U.S. EDITION: AUGUST 2001

10 9 8 7 6 5 4 3 2 1

Chapter One

Friday night had never been Bernard Peabody's favourite time of the week, for then, rain or shine, sleet, hail or howling gale, he would be sent out into the streets of the Gorbals to collect what he could of the rents. This was the price he had to pay for being a humble factor in Shannon, Peters & Dean, the estate agents, who had been kind enough to employ him back in 1919 and who had rewarded eleven years of unstinting service by piling more and more responsibilities on to his narrow shoulders.

Mr Peabody did not complain. In fact if these little 'promotions' hadn't come his way he would have been disappointed. Every additional name in the tenants' book meant another tiny increment in his tiny wage and gave him – so he fondly imagined – a wee bit more status in the office. Not for him the genteel stairways of Shannon, Peters & Dean's West End apartments, the hot commercial properties of Glasgow's city centre or the leafy suburban estates that Mr Shannon had recently added to the books: the bungalows, the de-luxe apartment blocks that were springing up, arms akimbo, south and west of the river. His territory remained as it had always been, the vigorous old route that ran from Glasgow Cross through the Saltmarket and – holding on to its hat – across the Clyde by the Albert Bridge and into the district known as the Gorbals; or, to be a shade more precise, into that unpicturesque part of the Gorbals that everyone referred to as the Calcutta Road.

Nobody, least of all Mr Peabody, knew why the stubby thoroughfare that linked Keane Street and the infamous Lavender Court had been named after a city in India. No Indians, give or take the odd Lascar, resided in the area. Poles, yes, Italians, yes, Jews, certainly; plus a multitude of the Irish-Scots who had been left behind when the nineteenth century ran out of steam. All of those and even the odd Englishman, but not an Asian in sight.

Why then *Calcutta* Road? Only old Mr Dean could have provided Bernard Peabody with an explanation – 'Called after a clipper ship, laddie' – but Mr Dean was far too venerable to be approached by a mere clerk in whom curiosity would not be regarded as a virtue.

Names were not uppermost in Mr Peabody's mind as he trudged into the Gorbals, however. For the past five months no mental games or conundrums had soothed the agent's apprehension as he crossed the Albert Bridge and headed towards No. 10 Lavender Court, where the widow Conway and her three unmarried daughters lived.

It wasn't the girls who made him nervous so much as the widow herself. Although she seemed friendly, certainly to Mr Peabody, Mrs Conway had a reputation for scaring the breeks off every tallyman, tinker and tout who set foot in her close or knocked upon her big glossy brown door.

Why, Mr Peabody wondered, as he passed the window of Brady's pub, did Mrs Conway's door seem so much larger than anyone else's? It was, he knew, exactly the same size as all the others in the building. He could only put it down to the fact that within days of taking occupancy she'd not only changed the mortice-lock for a Chubb but had painted the woodwork a rich chocolate brown and embellished the surface with a series of wavy little lines that reminded him, for some reason, of maidenhair.

Strictly speaking she wasn't allowed to make alterations to the property without written permission from the factor. Therefore he could have exercised his authority and had her grovelling. But he could not imagine Mrs Conway grovelling to anyone, let alone a mere rent-collector. So he had said nothing except, 'Very nice. Aye, very nice, Mrs Conway,' when she'd drawn his attention to the luminous oblong that added such distinction to the third-floor landing.

It had been on the tip of his tongue to enquire where she'd found the money to pay for such expensive luxuries as gloss paint and Chubb locks when she was for ever complaining how hard it was for her to make ends meet. He had put that question to one side too, however, for the eyes of the girls had been upon him, so sleek and speculative that he'd been only too anxious to scoop up the coins that Lizzie Conway had counted from her purse and beat a hasty retreat across the landing to the Gowers.

Now it was Friday again, and cold.

In mid-afternoon the first of the November fogs had come snuffling up from the Clyde. Mr Peabody had peeked from the windows of the office in St Anne's Street in the touch-and-go hour between three o'clock and four nervously awaiting the onset of a real pea-souper. He disliked the Gorbals at the best of times, more for its reputation than its reality, but on foggy nights, when the boys of the neighbourhood appeared like wraiths out of the murk, his nervousness would bring on a stomach ache that not even a nip of brandy or a tot of rum could ease. But, thank God, the fog had not settled and by the time he had strapped on his collection pouch, buttoned his overcoat and adjusted his bowler, the wind had stiffened and the sky over the city was as clear as it ever got at this time of the year.

It was cold, though, very cold. You could feel it pinching your nostrils, the tips of your ears and all around your mouth. Mr Peabody regretted that he had not heeded his mother's advice and brought along his muffler, the long grey woollen protector that his mother had spent weeks knitting for him but that he, a

JESSICA STIRLING

dab hand with the needles himself, could have knocked off in a couple of nights. He hadn't brought the muffler, though; a kind of stubborn pride had prevented it, the feeling that he would be regarded as a weakling by the office juniors, though it was mainly in the hope of impressing his hardiness on the Conways that he strode out into the November twilight ungloved and unscarfed.

To poor Mr Peabody – a thirty-four-year-old virgin – any girl who lived in one of Shannon, Peters & Dean's slum properties had to be 'bad'.

Naturally that was part of the attraction that Polly – particularly Polly – and Babs Conway held for him: the notion that their flirtatiousness indicated the possibility, remote though it might be, of some form of sexual activity.

Small wonder then that he approached the close-mouth at No. 10 trembling with excitement as well as trepidation and, clutching his collection pouch tightly against his thighs, began a cautious ascent of the stairs.

Unlike most of the main streets of the Gorbals which, contrary to repute, were broad and airy and flanked by old but solidly built dwellings, Lavender Court had an overwhelming narrowness that made the tenements seem particularly menacing. It wasn't much of a street in any case, eight buildings, four on each side, racked together on a steep incline that ran up to the weeping brick wall of the shunting yards of the Kingston Iron Works above which, day and night, black smoke and white steam curled up into the slot of the sky.

The westward trek of affluent and aspiring citizens just after the war had created a vacuum into which had flocked the poor and shiftless. Overcrowding was rife, nowhere more so than in the region of Calcutta Road.

The Lavender Court tenements, for instance, were owned by a host of different landlords, many of whom were almost as poor

4

as their tenants and none too particular when it came to obeying the letter of the law in regard to health and safety, especially when infants, small children, itinerant lodgers and relatives were added into the equation.

Even with the best will in the world the good-wives of the close couldn't possibly cope with the rivers of sewage that leaked down the stairs from the half-landing lavatories. They had to endure choked drains, backed-up pipes, leaking eaves, smashed windows, and, unfortunately, puddles of urine and vomit that appeared mysteriously in the dark and noisy hour after the pubs got out. No amount of mopping and scrubbing could keep the common stair clean and after a time even the most fastidious soon gave up and accepted that if things weren't going to get any better they certainly couldn't get much worse.

Then one fine June forenoon, a rusty little motor van rounded the corner from Keane Street, bounced over the cobbles, braked to a halt in front of No. 10 and Lizzie Conway emerged from the passenger seat and, aided by her good-looking daughters, began unloading furniture.

Windows all up the front of the building, most of which had been propped open against the stifling heat, suddenly bloomed a crop of fat arms and fatter faces, while out of the back courts packs of small children appeared as if summoned by a piper.

The sight of a motor vehicle of any kind was unusual in Lavender Court — in this neighbourhood the horse and cart still held sway — and the sight of a motor vehicle, even a battered van, with four females inside was rare enough to be regarded as a phenomenon.

Polly, the oldest and most sensible of the Conway girls, was well aware of the neighbours' scrutiny. Even before she clambered out of the back of the van she sensed their disapproval. She leaned against the back of the worn seat and looked past Mr McIntosh's head. The van, in fact, had been temporarily borrowed from the Department of Sanitation's laundry and Mr McIntosh, the driver, was doing Lizzie a favour by transporting her family and her goods and chattels from one tenement to another.

Polly watched through the windscreen as her mother clambered from the van and came around to the rear.

'Not much of a place, is it?' Mr McIntosh murmured.

'Better than where we came from,' said Polly.

'Is this what your mam calls goin' up in the world?' Mr McIntosh said.

'It'll do us fine,' Polly said, 'until something better comes our way.'

'If it ever does,' said Mr McIntosh.

'It will,' said Polly, cheerfully. 'You'll see, it will.'

Lizzie opened the rear door and eased a small chest of drawers from the van while Mr McIntosh kept the engine running in case, for some reason, a fast getaway was required.

'You comin' here for t' stay, missus?'

Lizzie lowered the chest to the pavement and leaned an elbow on top.

She had a manner to her, not hoity-toity exactly but so confident and assured that the youngster who had asked the question backed away even before the woman opened her mouth.

'Oh, no,' Polly whispered to her sister, Babs, 'Mammy's going to get us off on the wrong foot again.'

'Rubbish!' Babs said. 'She's just makin' her presence felt.'

'What's *your* name then?' Polly heard her mother say, in precisely the same tone a copper might use to interrogate a murder suspect.

'Me? I never said nothin',' little Billy Hallop declared and, though he was all of ten years old and built like a small tank engine, turned on his heel and raced away into the close, yelling, 'Mammy, Mammy, Mammy.'

A split second later Polly saw a male face appear in the window of a ground-floor bedroom, a small, round, squashed sort of face with features so flat that they might have been pressed in a vice. There was no curiosity in the young man's watery blue eyes, only annoyance.

He barked, 'What are you doin' then, scarin' oor Billy?'

Lizzie Conway ignored the young man and, with a little smile, drew a long length of carpet from the van.

'Right, girls,' she said. 'You can get out now.'

Polly followed her sisters as they scrambled out of the hot, uncomfortable interior of the van where they had been packed behind the chairs. Without further instruction she began to extract huge cardboard boxes and small items of furniture, handing them to Rosie who passed them in turn to Babs who piled them up on the pavement.

In the ground-floor window Jackie Hallop's head protruded from the shell of the bedroom. He wore a grubby cotton undervest and in the dusty June sunlight his chest and shoulders were white enough to suggest that he seldom emerged from the bedroom in daylight.

His bark this time had a shrillness that made it sound more like a yap.

'Hoi, you. I'm talkin' t' you.' He singled out Babs. 'You, blondie.'

Still with that odd little smile on her lips Lizzie Conway turned and stared. Polly followed the line of her mother's gaze.

All up the height of the tenement, windows were filled with arms and faces, with bosoms large and small. A strange silence descended upon the onlookers, even upon the ring of children who had gathered round, a silence pierced only by the shrieking of an infant and, like an echo, the hoot of a shunting engine behind the iron works wall. Then with a wonderfully deliberate swagger, Polly's mother strolled over to the window and, leaning forward from the waist, whispered to young Mr Hallop.

'*What* did you call her?' Lizzie asked.

'Blondie?'

'Her name's Babs,' Lizzie said. 'But it wouldn't matter if

she was the Queen of Sheba, that'll be the first an' last time you'll talk to one o' my girls without talkin' to me first. Do I make myself clear?'

'I'll talk t' who I like,' the young man mumbled.

Lizzie leaned closer still.

She bent her arm and closed her fingers, making a fist, a rather large fist, which she placed one inch from Jackie Hallop's nose.

'Oh, *will* you?' Polly heard her mother say in a dangerously affable tone. 'How'd you like to be talkin' through a mouthful o' broken teeth?'

'You,' Jackie said, swallowing hard, 'an' what army?'

Polly saw her mother lean closer, so close to the young man that there was no more than the breadth of the fist between then. She could not hear which of the choice threats her mother used, which of the unladylike pieces of local jargon that would indicate to the young man, and to the neighbourhood, that she, Lizzie Conway, had the sort of connections that demanded if not respect at least a modicum of caution. Whichever one it was, whichever name Mammy Conway invoked, the effect on Jackie Hallop was startling.

Polly watched his pale face turn even paler. He jerked backward, bumped his head on the frame, vanished. A moment later, like the blade of a guillotine, the window slammed shut.

Mammy walked back to join her girls, her round hips rolling under the skimpy floral-print dress, that odd little smile still on her lips, a smile that seemed to signify not triumph but contempt.

'God, you've done it again, Mammy,' Babs hissed.

'Done what?' said Lizzie.

'Got us off on the wrong foot,' said Babs. 'Who's gonna talk to us now?'

'You don't want to talk to the likes of him,' Lizzie said.

Just behind her ear, Polly heard Babs murmur, 'Oh, I dunno. He looked pretty tasty to me.'

'Polly, Babs,' Lizzie said, pointing a warning finger. 'No back-chat, please. Get this van unloaded. Mr McIntosh doesn't have all day.'

Polly sighed, followed Babs to the back of the van, took a two-handed grip on a kitchen table and carefully extricated it.

'Good,' Mammy said, smiling again. 'Good girls.'

Five minutes later the contents of the van were piled on the pavement. Boxes and battered hampers were built round the table and chest of drawers, with Polly and her sisters sitting on or among them while the vehicle, with Lizzie Conway in the passenger seat, sped down the hill and, tilted on two wheels, disappeared into Keane Street.

They sat back to back, Rosie, Babs and Polly, all bare legs and bare arms, and scowled at the crowd around them.

To those urchins who had larceny constantly in mind, Polly reckoned that the big walnut dome of a Mullard wireless set protruding from one of the boxes must surely represent temptation. But the sight of three alert, unintimidated girls was enough to put them off. They were impudent and bold, Polly decided, but not *that* impudent and bold, not daft enough to tamper with the possessions of a stranger who had already made one of the local hard men back down.

She sat back a little, quite unafraid now. She had been reared in worse places than this and had gone to school, at least for a time, with kids who made this lot look like angels. They watched from a safe distance, watched and speculated with the unrevealing expressions of savages who do not know quite what the tide has washed in, while on the corner a little group of adult layabouts gathered, attracted no doubt by the smell of thievable property and three fresh young skirts.

'Don't look in that direction, Babs,' Polly said, under her breath.

'Why not?' said Babs, looking in that direction.

'We don't want to bring them down on us, do we?'

'Maybe *you* don't,' Babs said. 'Personally I wouldn't mind.'

'It'll only cause trouble when Mammy gets back.'

'Yeah, I suppose you're right.'

Polly was by no means unaware how magnetic she and her sisters looked, seated there on top of the furniture. She was a shade less vain than either Rosie or Babs, but she was not so modest as to consider herself unattractive. She was tall and had long chestnut hair pulled back into a bunch behind her head, and a sharp little chin and, though she was still short of her twentieth birthday, had good legs, especially when, as now, she wore rayon stockings and a pair of patent leather shoes with half heels.

She lit a cigarette and took several long fulfilling drags before she passed it to her sister Babs, mouse-coloured but not mousy, short but not stocky, who when she inhaled showed off a figure that Jean Harlow herself might have envied. Finally, because Mammy wasn't around, Babs carefully passed the last half-inch of the Woodbine to Rosie who, at sixteen, looked dainty and cool in spite of being clad in a woollen jumper and a grey pleated skirt.

Even Rosie knew how to smoke, opening and closing her mouth over the cloud of tobacco smoke, toying with it until, at last, one perfect ring was formed, a transient O that floated up on the heat wave from the pavement and dissolved overhead while everyone, except Polly, watched in fascination.

'Give's a drag on that, then, eh?' said one young reprobate who, even at twelve, was well on the way to becoming a nicotine addict. 'G'an, give's a puff.'

Mouth still open and half filled with smoke, Rosie stared at him blankly. She shrugged and glanced at Babs who, kicking out one foot, snapped, 'Piss off, sonny,' and gave a slow, arrogant flick of the head that made her short-cropped hair toss and shine in the sunlight.

Ten minutes later Polly was relieved to see her mother hurrying on foot up the hill from Keane Street.

Five minutes after that Lizzie Conway turned the key in the

lock of the third-floor room-and-kitchen and the family without a man moved in.

Mr Peabody had never visited a bordello — well once, in Amiens, but he had only gone there for a beer — but when he thought of the word in its French form he imagined a place not a million miles removed from Mrs Conway's room-and-kitchen, which just goes to show how little Mr Peabody really knew of the world.

Perhaps it was the fragrance of perfume, nail varnish and setting lotion that lent a sinful air to the house, or the quantity of clothing that was scattered about, intimate female garments of all sorts draped from the drying pulley or over clothes-horses in front of the range.

Even in the narrow hall just behind the front door there were items that seemed calculated to take a man's mind off his rent book. A fancy china doll with painted cheeks and arms stretched out to welcome you sat on top of the coal bunker. On an upright table shaped like a Greek column, a lamp with a round pink globe poised on the fingertips of a lady whose nude body was curved into a position so supple and inviting that Mr Peabody could hardly take his eyes off it; unless, that is, Polly happened to open the landing door to his tentative knock, for then he would be unable to take his eyes off Polly and would wonder if she, lithe and slim as a willow, might be able to achieve such an extreme position if *she* wasn't wearing any clothes.

Left of the tiny hallway lay the girls' bedroom, the door never quite open, never quite closed; a mysterious haven from within which, some Friday nights, he could detect silky little sounds or faint strains of dance music or, once, a girl's unaccompanied voice dreamily crooning 'One Alone'.

To the right lay the kitchen into which he was admitted or, to be more accurate, into which he was dragged, for his shyness was such that he could hardly bring himself to cross the threshold even although he had every right to be there. The kitchen was totally unlike any tenement kitchen that Mr Peabody had ever entered before.

It had a cluttered, overstuffed feel to it, less cosy than claustrophobic. There were cushions everywhere, even on the kitchen chairs, and thick quilted blankets that reminded Mr Peabody of Mexican bandits in cowboy films. And a smell not of gas or paraffin, of Brasso or black lead, kippers or burned toast but a sweet flowery fragrance laced with cigarette smoke that seemed to poor Mr Peabody like the very essence of decadence.

It was, in fact, soap, for, overstuffed or not, there was no cleaner kitchen in the whole of the Gorbals than Lizzie Conway's and none on his route more welcoming.

'Will you not be taking your coat off then, Mr Peabody?' Lizzie said.

'No, I think ...'

Babs said, 'Go on, Mr Peabody, take your coat off.'

Polly said, more politely, 'Stay and have a cup of tea.'

'No, really. I've only just started the round. I'll need to be gettin' on.'

'At least sit yourself down,' Lizzie said. 'Take the weight off your feet for a minute while I go an' find my purse.'

'Is it all right?'

'Is what all right, Mr Peabody?'

'I mean, do you have the ...'

'The rent money? Aye, of course I have the rent money,' Lizzie said and went rolling out of the kitchen into the bedroom across the hall.

She was gone for several minutes, during which time Mr Peabody perched himself on one of the heavy cushions on one of the kitchen chairs and unbuttoned his overcoat just enough to bring his pouch into his lap, for although the pouch was still empty – Mrs Conway's was indeed his first port of call – he was wary of letting the money bag be seen.

'What are you fiddlin' with down there, Mr Peabody?' Babs said.

'I'm – I'm getting out my pencil.'

A very straight-faced question: 'Is there lead in it?'

'I sharpened it before I left the office.'

'Oh, that's nice,' said Babs. 'I prefer a really *sharp* pencil m'self.'

Mr Peabody failed to pick up on the innuendo or even to credit the girls with sufficient worldly experience to know what sex was about. He imagined that their seductive poses were entirely unconscious and so, to protect their innocence, tried not to stare but concentrated on arranging the rent books on the table. No plain pine for Lizzie Conway's table, no cork matting or chequered oilcloth; a genuine tablecloth, a good, whole piece of Irish linen embroidered with forget-me-nots and trimmed with lace.

It had a sleek, smooth feel to it, the sort of texture that invited stroking. Mr Peabody resisted. He closed his fist over the pencil, peered at the page, at the name *Mrs Elizabeth M. Conway* and wondered, in a vague way, what, if anything, the *M* stood for, who her husband had been and what had become of him.

He didn't have the temerity to put the question or request any sort of confidence that might be construed as special interest.

The golden rule for rent-collectors – 'Never have a tenant for a friend and never have a friend for a tenant' – was one to which Mr Peabody subscribed. It seemed to him a sensible philosophy, given the sort of liberties that some clients tried to take to wriggle out of paying their dues.

Purse in hand, Lizzie returned.

Mr Peabody glanced guiltily over his shoulder.

She stood close to the chair, pressing her stomach lightly against the crown of his shoulder. She still had her figure which, given that she had borne three children and must be all of thirty-seven or -eight years old, Mr Peabody found remarkable in itself. She was hardly a sylph, of course, but the curves of her bosom and stomach were generous rather than ponderous.

She touched his shoulder.

'Are you sure you it's money you want, Mr Peabody?' she said.

It was a clumsy joke that he'd heard a hundred times before. Usually he managed to laugh it off, say something jokey in return. But there was nothing humorous about Mrs Conway.

'I'm afraid I have to insist that ...' Bernard Peabody began.

'I know you do. Aye, I know,' said Mrs Conway. 'We wouldn't be wanting Shannon and Whatsit to be out of pocket, would we?'

Mr Peabody experienced an automatic dart of loyalty to the firm that paid his wages and, confusingly, a simultaneous tweak of sympathy for the woman with the open purse in her hand.

Lizzie Conway placed the coins upon the table.

Ten single shillings. Eight brown pennies. He counted them where they lay, not daring to insult her by scooping them swiftly into the bag. He pencilled the sum in the appropriate column in his book, filled out a receipt, initialled it, licked the gummed tab with the tip of his tongue and stuck it into the green linen-backed booklet that Mrs Conway passed to him.

She said, 'I don't suppose you'd ever let me off?'

'I wish I could,' Mr Peabody said. 'But I can't.'

'Never?'

'No. Never.'

The girls were still watching him. Motionless. Solemn, but not sour.

'More than your job's worth, I suppose,' Lizzie Conway said.

He got to his feet, the lid of the pouch snagging on the edge of the table, the tiny brass stud catching on the cloth as he tried to step back.

He felt ashamed of himself. It was as if she'd forced him into admitting his selfishness, as if he were betraying his own kind. She wasn't his kind, though. He struggled to remind himself that she was *not* his kind at all. If she had been his kind she wouldn't be living off the Calcutta Road in a property that, if the Department of Health and Sanitation had its way, would soon be condemned.

The rugs, the cushions, the tablecloth, the fancy ornaments, the new lock in the newly painted door could not disguise the fact that Mrs Elizabeth Conway lived in a slum and that he, Albert Bernard Peabody, did not. He lived far across the river in the new garden suburb of Knightswood which, he thought, gave him a certain distinction.

He put the coins into the empty pouch, fastened it, buttoned his coat and reached to the table for his bowler hat and rent book.

She covered his hand with hers. The taunting little smile had gone from her lips. Her brown eyes were calm and compassionate. She looked more striking than ever, Mr Peabody thought, not pretty the way her daughters were but with that long-chinned face, candid brow and curly brown hair caught above her ears with two tiny velvet ribbons, undoubtedly attractive.

'I shouldn't have said that,' she murmured, squeezing his knuckles. 'These days a man has to take what he can get to keep body and soul together. Besides' – another gentle squeeze before she released him – 'I've got nothing but respect for what you do, Mr Peabody, nothing but the greatest respect.'

'What *I* do? What do I do?'

'Collecting rents from the likes of us can't be easy.' She handed him his hat. 'It's a manly art, in my opinion.'

'I'm not sure I see what's ma—'

'No, it is. A manly art. Right, girls?'

'Too true,' said Babs.

'Absolutely,' said Polly.

For a moment Bernard Peabody thought they might be ribbing him. He glanced from one to the other in search of a telltale smirk but found nothing to indicate that Mrs Conway's compliment had not been sincere.

All three were looking at him now with something bordering admiration. He felt himself swell up. He straightened, pulled back his shoulders the way he'd done on the parade ground or, more especially, that morning when the battalion had marched through the streets of Glasgow to entrain for Flanders.

He cleared his throat. 'Well, thank you, Mrs Conway,' he said. 'I do my best. The times are hard for all of us, I know, but – well, I do my best.'

A minute or so later he stepped across the landing to confront old Mrs Gower and her alcoholic brother while Babs Conway waved bye-bye from the pink-lit hallway and then, to his regret, closed the glossy brown door.

Behind the glossy brown door Babs and Polly lingered in the glow of the lady-lamp. Babs laughed aloud and even Polly could not help but smile at the poor man's bashful confusion.

'What do you think then, girls?' Lizzie asked as she herded her daughters back into the kitchen.

'He's an idiot,' Babs declared. 'A complete bloody idiot.'

'No, he's not,' Polly said. 'I rather like him.'

'Aye,' Lizzie Conway said, 'and if push comes to shove, will he do?'

And Polly, not laughing, said, 'Yes, Mammy. He'll do.'

Chapter Two

It was a long road for a wee girl to walk from Gorbals Cross but Rosie reminded herself that she was no longer a wee girl. She was a woman, or nearly so.

If it hadn't been that she couldn't hear very well she'd have been out of school and earning good money like her sisters. It was largely her own fault she'd got stuck with the Saturday chore, however. She was the one who'd learned the ropes, in a manner of speaking, since that time a year ago when Mammy had come down with a chill in the kidneys and Babs, who pretended to be scared of Alex O'Hara, had dug in her heels and turned on the waterworks and Polly, who was in charge when Mammy was sick, had nabbed her, wee Rosalind, and said, '*You'll* just have to do it,' by which Polly meant go and pay O'Hara his money at the Rowing Club in Molliston Street.

And Rosie had nodded. 'Okay.'

She *had* been a wee girl then – a year had made all the difference – and consequently she hadn't been afraid of O'Hara.

Besides, she couldn't hear his nasty voice, not unless he roared. Even then it sounded just faintly annoying, like the wail of the whistle from the UCBS bakery that made everybody else jump if they happened to be in the vicinity.

That first time, she'd been dressed in bits of the uniform that had recently become mandatory apparel – how she loved the look of that phrase — for pupils at the Institute: a neat little grey skirt that didn't even cover your knees, ankle socks, one-bar shoes, a blouse with a yoke collar and a greeny-grey cardigan, all of which Mammy had purchased without protest, though Babs had gone hysterical at the amount of money it had cost. Mr Feldman had offered to find a benefactor but Mammy wouldn't hear of it and had gone to Mr Manone again and he, apparently, had come through with the goods.

Then, rather ironically, she, Rosie, had been the one who'd had to make the trip to the Rowing Club, down among the warehouses and sheds at that point where the Clyde starts to turn back on itself and you don't know whether you're in Kingston, Kinning Park or Govan. All she knew, that first day, was that Molliston Street wasn't near the room above Denzil's public house or the basement in Grove Street or the unnameable place by the railway that she was just barely old enough to remember but that still gave Polly the creeps.

Pint glass in hand, a cigarette sticking out of the corner of his mouth, Alex O'Hara had peered at her, then, twigging what was wrong, had made the sort of kissing motions that you make to a baby or a budgerigar before she'd had a chance to take the fiver from her top pocket and offer it to him; a gesture that had caused Mr O'Hara great consternation and made the men in the background hoot with laughter.

He'd pushed her away, finger prodding into her shoulder, pushed her out of the lobby of the Rowing Club and into the alcove where the men's lavatory was. He'd raged at her for a second or two, then, relenting, he'd put the fiver in one pocket of his long overcoat, had fished a sixpence from another and had offered it to her.

She'd shaken her head.

'Wha-aat?' he'd said, making his lips move properly for the first time. 'Ta-aake it, da-aarlin'. It's for you.'

She'd pointed at the cigarette in his mouth and with an extravagant wave of the hand, cribbed from Gloria Swanson, had indicated that she wanted a smoke. Mr O'Hara had laughed, had taken a packet from his pocket – Gold Flake, not Woodbine – had counted out three cigarettes and had given them to her. She'd tucked them safe away in her pocket. Then he'd taken another ciggie from the packet and had pushed it against her lips. Then he'd put the pint glass carefully down on the floor and had fumbled for and found a matchbox and had struck a match and had lit the cigarette in her mouth.

She'd inhaled deeply, throwing her head back and blowing out smoke in a long, moist, vampy plume the way she and Babs rehearsed in the bedroom when Mammy was out and they could find nothing better to do with themselves.

Mr O'Hara had uttered a naughty word – she could always lip-read the naughty words – and red-faced and flustered had shoved her out of the front door into Molliston Street.

She hadn't told Polly or Mammy what had happened but, even when Mammy was well again, she volunteered for the job and, once a month thereafter, dressed in her Institute uniform, had walked all the way to Molliston Street to pay Alex O'Hara his blood money.

Rosalind Conway might be deaf, but she certainly wasn't daft. She knew who Alex O'Hara was, how he made his dough and why everyone was afraid of him. He was the man you saw about borrowing money when you had nothing left to pawn. He was the man who would come after you if you didn't shell out. He was the man who would cut your face open with the cut-throat razor he kept in the pocket of his double-breasted suit.

He was the Collector.

And she had him under her thumb.

Polly explained it to her on the day she turned sixteen. Polly took her out to the Black Cat Café as a birthday treat, just the two of them. She bought ice-cream and, using the mixture of signs and round vowels by which they communicated when she, Rosie, didn't want to use the little tin-plated trumpet, told her that it wasn't Mammy who'd gone into hock with O'Hara but their old man, Daddy, long gone now and probably dead.

Rosie asked why the debt hadn't died with Daddy. Polly shook her head, and told her it wasn't like that with the crowd O'Hara worked for and that Daddy had also worked for, a long time ago.

'Daddy did die in the war, didn't he?' Rosie asked.

'Missing,' Polly answered. 'Believed killed.'

'He was a Highlander, wasn't he – a kiltie?'

She wasn't able to get her tongue around the words. They felt flat and quacky in her mouth. When she spoke like this to anyone who didn't know her they thought she was weak in the head. But Polly was used to it. Polly still worked with her sometimes, though less patiently than Mr Feldman or Miss Fyfe, teaching her to blow and suck, *ta-ta* and *la-la* so that she could feel the resonance of the words in her throat.

The tin-plated hearing trumpet that Mr Feldman had finally managed to obtain for her had helped a little, for then, when she spoke slowly and softly, she could hear where she was going wrong.

She hated the trumpet, though. It seemed to anounce her deficiency, make her visibly different from everyone else. She never used the trumpet with Alex O'Hara and had already vowed to herself that she never would. In any case, after her third or fourth visit to the Ferryhead Rowing Club, she could make out what he was saying well enough, even although he hardly moved his lips.

None of the things that Polly told her that day in the Black Cat Café came as much of a surprise.

She might have missed most of the family conversations that went on but she was blessed with sharp eyes and an ability to concentrate and had already guessed that Alex O'Hara, with his long overcoat, soft felt hat and scar like a tribal mark, was part of a shadowy nether world to which her mother remained connected by dint of that long-ago marriage to Frank Conway.

'Yes, honey,' Polly told her. 'Daddy was a kiltie. He fought at the Western Front and we never found out what happened to him.'

'Did he steal money from Alex O'Hara?'

'No, from old Mr Manone.'

'Is that what Mammy's still paying for?'

'Yes, it is.'

'When will it all be paid back?'

Polly pulled a face. 'I don't know.'

'Would you like me to ask Mr O'Hara?'

'No,' Polly shouted, then, embarrassed, leaned across the empty ice-cream dishes and, articulating very precisely, said, 'No. You must not say anything to Alex O'Hara. Do you understand me, Rosie? You must not go asking questions.'

'He would tell me, you know.'

'He would cut your throat as quick as look at you.'

'No. He likes me.'

'Has he told you he likes you?'

'He gives me ciggies and chocolate.'

'Has he . . .' For an instant Polly was at a loss for the right word or sign. 'Has he – tried to touch you?'

'I wouldn't let him.'

And that was the truth.

Mr O'Hara just grinned when she played up to him, when she put on the airs and graces that Babs had taught her. He seemed pleased that she wasn't afraid of him in spite of his line of work, in spite of the evidence of the thin white scar on his cheekbone. In any case she was never with him for long, ten minutes at most, either out on the pavement in the quiet Saturday evening street or, if it was pouring, just inside the lobby near the lavatory.

'Are you sure he hasn't tried to touch you?'

'No-ope.'

She stared into Polly's eyes and put on a weak, pouting expression as if she really were half daft. It was a look she could do to perfection, a look that made people think twice – practically everyone, except Mr Feldman who got riled whenever she tried it on with him.

'If he does,' Polly said, 'if O'Hara ever does ...'

'Tell you.'

'Aye, not Mammy.' A finger to the breastbone. 'Tell me first.'

There were times when Rosie thought it might be fun to have Alex O'Hara touch her.

She'd been touched once before – by Gordon Porlock, who was a full mute and had been at the Institute with her since they were both eight years old.

Gordon Porlock had gone all odd this past year or so, angry and odd. He had caught her by the arm one day in the back corridor, had tried to kiss her, had rubbed himself against her and had groped up her skirt. She had kicked him, screamed at him soundlessly, mouth wide open, registering not fright or horror but pure indignation. He had backed away, had turned and fled down the corridor, holding not his shin but his crotch. From that day on Gordon had avoided her like the plague, and she had watched Polly and Babs talk with renewed interest, and had kidded herself that she knew how to handle men.

Besides, she was beginning to like the way Mr O'Hara treated her. How he would be out on the pavement waiting for her to turn the corner at the top of Molliston Street. How he would wave a welcome, removing one hand from his pocket and fashioning a sign, like someone swearing an oath.

As soon as she'd parted with the fiver he would smile and when he stood close to her, pint glass in hand, she would feel quite safe and protected.

Alex O'Hara was much older than she was, of course. Ten years at least. That didn't matter. In fact it was better. She'd

seen what happened to girls who wedded young chaps. Two
or three years, two or three bairns into the marriage and you
would be struggling to make do on dole money and your figure
would be gone for good. And hubby would be down the pub
every night, scrounging drink while you were stuck in Lavender
Court or Keane Street trying to stop the rot. Rosie knew that
Babs had nothing but scorn for girls who jumped into marriage.
Babs was for ever shouting that she wasn't going to get caught
in that trap, not her, would never go out with boys who didn't
have money to spend or let any boys she did go out with have
more than a 'nibble', whatever that meant.

Because Rosie was still attending the Institute and wore its
uniform she had never had a boyfriend. You didn't meet proper
boyfriends in the Institute. You met boyfriends at the corner
up by Gorbals Cross where she was forbidden to loiter or in
the Black Cat Café late at night or, best of all, up town at the
roller-skating rink. You could meet them too at Socialist Sunday
School dances or on Jewish pipe band picnics but Mammy would
have had a fit if any of her girls, any of her prized possessions,
had suggested consorting with Jews or Communists, though as
far as Rosie could make out Jews and Communists were among
the nicest people you could meet.

Alex O'Hara, then, was her very first boyfriend.

He met her by arrangement every fourth of fifth Saturday
down in Molliston Street, in the deserted cul-de-sac away from
the Ibrox football crowd and the bedlam of the Paisley Road.
He never suggested making a date with her. Rosie reckoned he
was just shy or, more likely, that he'd encountered Mammy and
was as wary of crossing her mother as most other chaps seemed
to be, even if Alex was a bigwig and had a bad reputation.

Anyway it was simpler to *pretend* that he was her boyfriend.

It made the walk from Gorbals Cross seem purposeful and
exciting. She even kidded herself that Alex wouldn't mind if she
turned up without the fiver some Saturday, that perhaps then he
would draw her gently into the doorway or walk hand in hand

with her down towards the river and there on the ash pad –
where horses had been kept to pull the ferry in the olden days
– there he would kiss her. She speculated on what his pinched,
rather frozen mouth would feel like, if it would be as cold as
it looked or if the touch of her lips would instantly ignite the
flames of passion.

Now and then, not often, she saw Alex in the Gorbals or
Laurieston.

Unplanned and unexpected, the encounters gave her a start
and reminded her that Alex didn't spend his entire life waiting
for her on the pavement outside the Ferryhead Rowing Club.
When they met by chance Alex would pretend not to notice
her or, if she waved, would lower his head and nod reluctantly.
Only once had he spoken. 'What're you doin' at Gorbals Cross?'
he'd said. 'Is it not past your bedtime, a wee girl like you?' She
hadn't made him out clearly, though, and had given him a big
beaming smile in lieu of an answer. And he had shrugged and
gone strolling on about his business.

It was easy to foster the illusion that Alex O'Hara, the
Collector, was her boyfriend, to convince herself that when she
knew him better she would be able to wheedle out of him what
she wanted: not cigarettes, not bars of Five Boys chocolate, not
even stolen kisses by the riverside but the sort of information
that Polly and Babs refused to share with her.

So she came striding briskly down Paisley Road in the
witching hour between twilight and full dark, extra careful of
tramcars laden with football supporters and buses that swept
too close to the pavements.

She dodged nimbly among the shoppers until the two big
arc-lamps that lit up the front of Gerber's clothing factory came
in sight. Then she switched her concentration up to full blast
and sped across the thoroughfare, holding her hat with one
hand and cupping the other round her left ear to separate the
clash and clatter of trams from the dangerous hiss of motorcars
and buses.

She darted into Congleton Street, turned into the top of Molliston Street and saw Alex in the distance, waiting for her, same as he always was — only different. It wasn't a subtle difference. Oh, no. A blind man could have spotted it. Rosie let out a throaty little squeal of delight.

She came up to him and looked him up and down.

'Are you going to a wedding then?' she asked, as distinctly as possible.

He shook his head. Her appraisal disconcerted him. He was, Rosie thought, very easily disconcerted.

She said, 'You look real nice. I have never seen a man in a monkey suit before, not outside a tailor's window.'

'Got the money?'

'Yes,' she said.

She took the banknote from her pocket and held it up. It was folded into the shape of a taper, longer than it was broad. He suited the suit, and the suit suited him. She would have told him that too if she could have got her tongue around the words without fumbling.

Mischievously, she waved the banknote before him.

He snatched at it with his left hand. He wore a wristlet watch on an expanding band. Cuff-links. He had shaved very cleanly and the dark shadow of stubble was all beneath the skin. His jet black hair was slicked back and his features seemed less prominent, less rapacious. He appeared comfortable in the formal outfit, as if he had been born into silver-spoon society and had somehow become misplaced.

In fact, he looked almost harmless.

She wafted the note about.

He was not a large man and looked as if he should be nippy on his feet but he flapped ineffectually, his reactions slower than she would have anticipated. Momentarily intoxicated by her superiority, she giggled. Then he snatched at her, not the note. He grabbed her arms first then her forearm and hip, fingers digging into her thigh through her school skirt.

25

'I was only teasing,' Rosie got out, the words clumsy with dismay.

'Don't,' he said. 'Don't come it wi' me, not where money's concerned.'

He plucked the banknote from her fingers, released her and stepped back.

She could still feel his fingers squeezing her hip. She wriggled, straightened her knickers, adjusted her skirt.

She didn't know whether to be indignant or tearful. It hadn't occurred to her to treat him roughly as she'd treated Gordon Porlock, and it dawned on her at that moment that she really knew nothing about men after all.

She said, 'I am sorry.'

He eyed her, head back.

The fiver had already vanished into one of his pockets and a small, hesitant smile seemed to be hovering on the corner of his lips.

She felt hot all over.

'Is it a wedding you're dressed up for?' she said, at length.

'Nah.' He seemed not just reluctant but almost incapable of answering an innocent question. He glanced over his shoulder at the doors of the Rowing Club – propped wide open tonight – then forced himself to admit, 'Dinner, a testimonial dinner. Know what that means, kid?'

Inside the club she could make out other men in monkey suits, black and bulky against the whisky-coloured light that filtered from the bar. It looked secretive beyond the lobby but solemn too.

'Is it a testimonial for somebody important?'

He shook his head. 'You shouldn't ask so many questions, Rosie.'

It was the first time that he had used her name. It seemed more intimate and romantic than any of the standard terms of endearment that tabbed the end of his conversations, the 'dears' and 'darlings' that were so devoid of sentiment that they sounded like insults. Now he had called her by her name and had recognised her right to an identity. She felt the heat go out of her and, pleased and flattered, gave him a cheesy smile.

He shook his head again, took her arm and led her two or three steps away from the doorway. He glanced bleakly up the street and then, squinting a little, down the long empty stretch that ended at the river.

On the far bank the lights of Anderston and the Finnieston docks glimmered in the dank haze and Rosie watched a little tug or puffer carve across the plane of the Clyde, silent as a phantom.

'Mr O'Hara?'

'What? What now, Rosie, for Christ's sake?'

'Did you know my daddy?'

Whatever might be said against Lizzie Conway nobody could ever accuse her of laziness. She'd always been a demon for hard work. Her detractors might argue that she'd never held on to a job for long and that her progress in the labour market had been erratic at best.

They might have said that if she'd been less voluble in sticking up for her rights she might have made something of herself. What that 'something' might be was left unspecified, for somehow familiar comforting homilies didn't apply to a woman like Lizzie Conway who had clambered out of poverty with three young children and an insupportable burden of debt hanging round her neck.

If it hadn't been for the children and the fact that she needed a permanent address from which to apply – unsuccessfully – for a war widow's pension, she would simply have vanished into the blue. That, at least, was the fairytale Lizzie had put about, the lie that her ailing mother and spinster sister had been persuaded to swallow.

No one had wanted to believe that indomitable, bull-in-a-china-shop Lizzie would be stupid enough to stay on in the Gorbals simply to await the return of a husband who, if he wasn't actually rotting in a field in Flanders, certainly didn't intend to hot-foot it back to Glasgow.

The debt with which Frank had saddled her had committed her to sixty hours a week grafting at a machine in Gerber's factory or cleaning for the Corporation Tramways Department, among other employments. Hard work had turned out to be the stuff of life for Lizzie, though. Hopelessness, exhaustion and despair were held at bay not just by strength of will but by devotion to her daughters and a steely determination to see them, and everyone else for whom she felt responsible, fare better than she had done.

For four years now she'd been employed by the Public Health Department and worked ten-hour days in the laundry of the Sanitary Wash-house at Balmain Park where bedding and body clothing from the victims of infectious diseases were labelled, disinfected, washed, dried and returned, irrespective of whether the poor patient died or recovered.

Sometimes Lizzie plied the rakes in the disinfecting tanks. Sometimes she took her turn rinsing frail items at stone wash-tubs. But usually she was put to labelling in the room next door to the main hall where the noise of the dash wheels and the incessant clack of the carpet-beating machine were so wearing that she would come home half deaf and would have to use Rosie's special syringe to ease the ringing in her ears.

None the less, Lizzie was proud to be part of a procedure that had all but rid the city of typhus and cholera and that had diphtheria, phthisis and scarlet fever well on the run; proud of the fact that all the goods and chattels hauled in for cleansing in the morning were always returned before midnight. Property, after all, was property.

The Public Health authorities weren't thieves; which was more than could be said for Frank Conway, her dear departed husband, who had been a thief born and bred and who, if he hadn't vanished in the smoke of battle somewhere north of Baupaume, would probably have wound up floating face down in the Clyde or, if luck had been on his side, serving a twenty-year stretch in Barlinnie.

She still thought of Frank from time to time.

Memories of good times as well as bad would steal upon her as she settled her head on the pillow or, more often, cat-napped in the chair by the fire.

She imagined that she could hear his voice, the persuasive, arrogant murmur that had made every daft dream he chose to peddle seem practical.

She recalled how he'd looked the first time she'd clapped eyes on him, just before he went to work for the Eye-tie. All glammed up in a trilby, hand-sewn boots and an embroidered waistcoat. Black curls bobbing. More Italian in appearance than any of old Carlo Manone's mob, though Frank was the errant son of a dirt farmer from Armagh, and as Irish as the pigs of Docherty.

She had loved him and hated him in equal measure. Though he had never raised his hand to her in the six years they were married he'd been callous in other ways. The hand-sewn boots and embroidered waistcoat had been no more real and lasting than his declarations of undying passion; mere trophies of a successful housebreaking, pawned before the marriage was three weeks old.

Even although Frank was a staunch Protestant, worry about his unsuitability had done for Lizzie's father, so her mother claimed. The truth was that Charlie McKerlie had chalked up more hours in Brady's public house than any man in the barony and had died right there at the bar, a pickled egg in one hand, a glass of whisky in the other.

Naturally it had been left to Frank to scrape up the money to bury the old bugger, with black horses, black plumes, and a cortège half a mile long with free booze at the end of it.

Lizzie's mother had declared herself too ill to face the rigours of a funeral service but had recovered sufficiently to be carried downstairs and placed in the open carriage that Frank had hired from Carlo Manone and had ridden in style to the wake in the Orange Halls, acknowledging condolences with a wave of her gloved hand.

On that Saturday evening, however, Lizzie wasn't thinking of Frank Conway, or of times past.

She sprawled in the battered armchair by the fire, head on a cushion, garters unloosened and legs stuck out, not quite asleep and not quite awake, mulling over the pilgrimage that she must make to Dominic Manone's house, and the manoeuvres that would follow; not a plan yet, nothing so ordered as a plan, but the nucleus of one, the first foetal stirrings of a plan to shake the dust of the Gorbals from her feet once and for all.

She heard a key scratch in the Chubb lock, and opened one eye.

She waited for the babble that would signal that Polly and Babs had returned from window-shopping in town; or – Lizzie opened both eyes – it could be Rosie back from Molliston Street.

Rosie was never clumsy, never noisy. She could slip into the house quiet as a mouse when she wanted to.

She might not even enter the kitchen at all but go straight into the bedroom to peel off her Institute skirt and jacket, brush them, hang them up on the wire and, if she wasn't in a mood for conversation, would lie on the floor, switch on the wireless and, with her better ear – the left – pressed tightly against the set, scan the dial for dance-band music.

'Mammy?'

'Yes, dear.'

In spite of the daft hat and blazer Rosie no longer resembled a child.

She had the same air of precocity that Polly had developed soon after she went to work as an office junior in the Burgh

Hall, a job that she had secured through the intervention of the Italian whose influence, it seemed, was everywhere. He had got Babs her job too, clerking with Central Warehouse Company. But Lizzie doubted if even Mr Manone would be able to find work for Rosie, not with her disability.

'Mammy?'

'What? What's wrong?'

She resisted an urge to lunge from the armchair and demand to be told what her youngest had been up to and why she was so flushed. She remained where she was, head against the cushion, and squeezed her knees together to relieve the cramp that had suddenly affected her stomach.

Rosie shook her head. 'Nothing.'

Lizzie raised herself on an elbow, faced her daughter squarely and said loudly, 'You did not lose the money, did you?'

'I gave Alex the money,' Rosie answered.

'Did he say somethin' to upset you?'

Rosie shook her head again.

At that moment Lizzie realised that her youngest wasn't going to tell her the truth, no matter what.

Cramp tightened its grip. She didn't dare thrust herself out of the armchair. If she did she would surely grab Rosie by the shoulders and shake her like an old doormat. She had seldom struck any of the girls in temper, not even when things were at their worst.

Rosie's eyes widened.

Feigned innocence, Lizzie thought.

Something *had* happened. Something to do with O'Hara. By God, she promised herself, if that wee bastard has laid a finger on my Rosie I'll cut his damned ears off, aye, and not just his damned ears either.

Rosie said, 'What's for tea?'

Automatically Lizzie made a swimming motion.

'Fish,' said Rosie. 'Lovely. What kind of fish, Mammy?'

Never mind the bloody fish, Lizzie thought. Tell me what's

brought that flush to your cheek. Tell me what's upset you. Don't shut me out, Rosie. Please, don't shut me out.

'Cod,' she said aloud. 'Just cod.'

The baked cod had been devoured and, since it was Saturday, one slice of pineapple cake each. Then the girls had whipped through the washing-up. As soon as the last plate had been racked and the tablecloth brushed and put away, though, there had been the usual free-for-all with Babs and Polly squabbling over make-up and fighting to be first to grab the curling tongs from the gas ring.

Then they were off, breezing away, chirruping to Rosie and blowing kisses to Mammy as they dived for the door, leaving behind a clean kitchen, a breathless silence and the cloying odour of face powder.

Lizzie was always surprised to find herself alone; not quite alone, of course, for Rosie was still with her, lying low in the bedroom.

It had been twenty years, near enough, since Lizzie had gone on the randan on a Saturday night. Back in the old days it had been dances at the Orange Halls. Concerts. Variety shows. Plays and pantomimes under the spluttering carbon-arc lamps of the Princess Theatre. Great days. Wonderful times.

Her mother had girned at her precocity, her father had grumbled that she was never at home. Her sister Janet, who'd never had any sort of life, had put on a prim, acid-drop expression and warned her that if she didn't mend her ways she would be damned and go to hell.

Janet had been dead right. She had gone to hell. They'd all gone to hell one way or another soon after the war got under way.

Now, in just eighteen months she would be forty years old. She was still presentable in appearance but the years had laid their mark on her in subtle ways and, like many 'busy' people, she was afraid of being left alone.

She slumped in the chair by the fire, listening to the *tick-tock-tick* of the little metal clock on the mantelshelf, and to the silence within the house. She had no inclination to lift a newspaper or read a book or go into the bedroom and listen to the wireless. She had never acquired the habit of leisure. And she wouldn't be at ease for long.

On Saturday nights she was committed to trudging a half-mile to the backlands tenement in Laurieston where her mother and sister lived; to help Janet lift the old woman from her chair, untangle her from her clothes, sponge her, dry her, put on her nightgown and heave her up into the wall-bed, while her mother moaned at their clumsiness and Janet apologised, endlessly.

Lizzie got to her feet, gave herself a shake and, telling herself not to be daft, went into the lobby to find her coat and hat.

God, what was happening to her? Now she had nothing much to worry about she worried about every little thing.

Forcing on a cheery smile, she pushed open the door of the bedroom.

The room was lit by the glow of the gas fire that Rosie, without permission, had turned on.

The drab curtain that screened the street had not been closed and a faint, wan glow from a lamp outside penetrated the glass. The broad bed in which the girls slept together filled the alcove, its heavy cotton bedspread unruffled. A battered old wardrobe with broken hinges almost barred access and the room seemed so compressed that Rosie, on the floor, was almost invisible.

She lay with legs drawn up, an arm folded across her breast.

The Mullard wireless set, the family's pride and joy, stood mute upon the chest of drawers but the second-hand gramophone that Polly had bought last Christmas was placed on the floor by Rosie's head.

Music played softly, so softly that Lizzie could barely hear it.

She stepped forward and peered down at her youngest who, chin cradled on her fist, was suspended over the turntable, her left ear a half-inch from the sound-box on the end of the gramophone's metallic arm.

Rosie's eyes were closed. Caught up in the sentimental ballad, she was oblivious to her mother's presence.

'One Alone,' Lizzie murmured. 'Dear God!' then, shaking her head, left Rosie to her love songs and slipped out of the house to go up to Laurieston and tuck her arthritic old bitch of a mother into bed for the night.

Chapter Three

Whatever faith Lizzie Conway had once possessed had been lost long ago. She couldn't say for sure just when she'd grown disillusioned with the platitudes dispensed by old Mr Wylie, minister of St Margaret's Church in the Calcutta Road, or when his weary promises of a better day tomorrow had grown stale.

One thing was for sure: she no longer subscribed to a gospel of exalted poverty or the retribution that the Socialist preachers called down upon the heads of the unworthy – by which they meant the capitalist swine who had industry and commerce sewn into their pockets and who cared not a fig for the plight of the common man provided their annual dividends kept rolling in.

For Lizzie, as for many Glaswegians, religion had become a matter of racial and social divisions too deep to fathom yet too shallow to explain. Slogans painted on walls and hoardings, the public communiqués of the city's twisted zealots, were a constant reminder that not all wars were economic and that historical differences were just as enduring as the class struggle itself. Orangemen marched, Catholics trotted off to mass, Jews got on with business and bothered no one. Out in the streets young men formed gangs. Bully Boys fought with Tongs and Tongs with Neds and they all, or nearly all, queued up together at the Labour Exchange when Fairfield's shipyard, Dixon's Blazes or the Kingston Iron Works paid off another two or three hundred men.

She lived, did Lizzie, in a neighbourhood where rage, ignorance and fear bubbled just beneath the surface, and a hunger march or a Jewish picnic or one of the great sprawling gang fights that happened after football matches all began to seem like part of the same event, an event, as far as Lizzie could make out, that had no relevance to pulpit preaching or priestly consolations. She was a Protestant. She was in work. She kept her nose and her house clean. She loved her children and tended to the welfare of her elderly mother. She planned for the future, and paid for the past. That was all that really mattered. That was life in the here-and-now. The hereafter could take care of itself.

Once in a blue moon, though, she would put on her Sunday best and catch a tram along the Paisley Road to visit a man who some folk south of the river regarded as a sort of a god.

His name was Dominic Manone. He was the second son of an immigrant who had come to Glasgow thirty years ago from a village near Genoa. The first son, Carlo, had died, along with one hundred and thirty thousand of his countrymen, fighting the Austrians at a place called Monfalcone in the early summer of 1917. The other boys, Dominic included, had been young enough to be spared the war. Soon after the Armistice old Carlo Manone had taken most of the family away, God knew where, leaving only Dominic in residence in the tall house in Manor Park Avenue with an aunt and uncle to look after him.

Little more than a boy then, young Dominic had been round-faced, smooth-skinned and sallow and looked as if butter wouldn't melt in his mouth. He had the uncle behind him, though, Uncle Guido, and eight or ten henchmen of various persuasions, mainly Scots and Irish, to handle the business, legal and otherwise. Over the next few years young Dominic had learned how to run the family's affairs and had brought a strange sort of order to the untameable fraternity of hooligans and thugs who ran wild about his territory.

His territory, and his influence, seemed boundless, though few honest, hard-working citizens had ever heard of him. He put in an appearance now and then at *Comunità* meetings but did not show face at any of the religious ceremonies that graced the Italian calendar. Not only did he come from the north, he was, by all accounts, anti-clerical in his views, more Communist than Catholic and, worst of all, he refused to favour Italians when it came to dishing out employment and preferred to take on an Irishman or Scot to some solemn, big-eyed *contadino* from back in the old country.

In whole or in part, the Manones owned two restaurants, four cafés, an ice-cream factory, a warehouse, a firm that imported religious statuary and another that manufactured crockery.

Dominic Manone's other sources of income were less obvious and even more lucrative. Through agents he ran much of the off-course bookmaking south of the river. Purchased and resold certain pieces of jewellery, plus antiques and occasional *objets d'art*. Financed speculative excursions into the acquisition of large quantities of booze or hard currency or, indeed, anything that could be sold on before the coppers could trace it. He was also in a position to guarantee that this public house or that corner shop would remain unmolested by the Neds or the Bully Boys or some other pack of vandals to whom destruction was an end in itself. For this service he charged modest fees, collected on a regular basis by the likes of Alex O'Hara or little Tommy Bonnar.

If you wanted anything from Dominic you didn't approach him directly and you most certainly did not send him a letter. You 'had a word' with Alex O'Hara or Tony Lombard who were usually to be found hanging around the Ferryhead Rowing Club. There were other go-betweens too, including mean little Tommy Bonnar with his pinched bone-white face and graveyard cough.

Lizzie did not have to pass messages down the line and wait for an answer to return by the same unreliable route. She had Dominic Manone's ear whenever she wanted it, though she was careful not to abuse the privilege. However affable Dominic might appear if and when you encountered him, he was a force, a quite deadly force, to be reckoned with.

Lizzie was nervous as she walked along Belville Road and turned into the top of Manor Park Avenue. She felt like a fish out of water in the select neighbourhood, though it was no longer the apogee of upper-crust ambition to own one of the villas in the leafy streets off Belville Road. Progress and the passage of time had moved the frontier south and west, and for all their stateliness there was already a faintly neglected air to the houses about the park.

Lizzie was the brightest object on the horizon. She wasn't wilfully gaudy. She just preferred bright colours and loose-fitting clothes. Nothing expensive, not even the 'vagabond' hat. She was adept and imaginative with needle and thread, however, and could conjure something almost fashionable out of cast-offs by adding a half belt or trimming down on buttons.

She turned into the gate of Elvanfoot; the villas here still had names, not postal numbers. Stone posts, an unlocked wrought-iron gate, crunchy red gravel, borders of newly turned black earth, no flowers.

Lizzie approached the front door and, glancing surreptitiously into the window, saw a standard lamp lit in the big front parlour, a fire in the grate and Dominic Manone himself propped in a leather chair reading a newspaper.

She sucked in a deep breath and rang the doorbell.

Uncle Guido opened the door. He knew Lizzie by sight and did not have to enquire what she wanted at that hour of a Sunday morning.

Guido Manone was as different from his nephew as chalk is from cheese. He was tall, so tall that he had developed a little carpenter's stoop that served to press his long, horsey chin into his chest. He seemed to be all face and hands, features that were disproportionately large compared with his dainty feet and stick-like build. He did not smile but he did bow. In his heyday he had been quite a ladies' man and, even in his sixties, much of this courtliness remained.

'I — I've c-come to see Mr Manone,' Lizzie stammered. 'I — I wonder if this is a sort of convenient time.' Guido Manone stepped back and, with a sweep of his large hand, invited her in.

If there were servants in the house then they were not in evidence. Perhaps, Lizzie thought, they were all at chapel.

She followed Uncle Guido across a broad expanse of carpet to an oak-panelled door. The house had always struck her as gloomy, more like a museum than a dwelling. There were all sorts of strange smells in the atmosphere, spicy smells like cinnamon and clove and a waft of cigar smoke to add a hint of luxury.

Uncle Guido rapped upon the door, opened it and ushered Lizzie into the room she thought of as the parlour. Some parlour! You could have fitted four tenement kitchens into it and still have had room to spare. Massive marble fireplace. Old furniture. Oil paintings of saints and half-clad women on the walls. By the fireplace, standing, was young Dominic Manone. He wore a spotless white shirt, dark waistcoat and matching trousers; polished black shoes, not slippers, as if even at home on a Sunday morning a formal code had to be observed.

Lizzie was used to cocky little dandies with primrose socks, polka-dot bow ties and soft felt hats, the 'chancer' element who had run the rackets in Frank's day. They were dreary pretenders compared to Dominic Manone.

His solemn, olive-tinted face and black unsurprised eyebrows, so straight that they might have been inked in by a draughtsman, were daunting and appealing at one and the same time.

'What is it you want?' he asked in a slightly lisping accent that owed more to Glasgow than Genoa. 'Do you want coffee, or will I send for tea?'

'No,' she said. 'No, thank you, Mr Manone. I won't be stoppin' long. I just want a word with you about – about the matter between us.'

'What matter is that?' he said.

On a polished side table stood a china coffee pot, cup and saucer, a cigarette box and a tub of the long, blue-headed matches that you only saw in the very best restaurants. Dominic Manone did not offer Lizzie a cigarette or even a seat. He perched on the arm of the Georgian wing chair by the fire.

He looked as strong and compact as a street fighter, one of the bare-knuckle breed, not a cowardly razor king. If he had not been who he was he could have been a legend in the ring. Except that the Italians, like the Jews, seldom took part in the fierce gang fights that spilled blood for no purpose.

If he *had* been a fist fighter though, Lizzie thought, she would have bet on him every time.

She said, 'I need to know when I'll be paid up.'

'Why?'

'Because I do.'

Chin tucked in, head cocked, he glanced at her from the tops of his eyes. 'What's the matter? Don't you like your new house?'

'Who told you about my new house?' Lizzie said, then added, 'Anyway, it isn't a new house. It's just bigger than the last place.'

'Is it the girls, your daughters, you worry about?'

'What sort of a mother would I be if I didn't worry about my children? Please, Mr Manone, tell me when I'll be all paid up.'

'Never,' he said, softly. 'You haven't even cleared the interest on our eight hundred pounds. What was your first repayment – five shillings? Then ten shillings. Now it's twenty-five a week. We've always been accommodating, have we not? Never so much did we ask that you would be left penniless.' He shook his head.

'Find six hundred fins – no, find *five* hundred – and we'll call it square.'

'Where am I goin' to get five hundred pounds?'

'Do you see the position I'm in, Lizzie?' Dominic said. 'How can I let you off what you owe when it's so much? What would the other people who owe me money think? That Dominic Manone had gone soft in the head?'

'I didn't steal your damned money,' Lizzie said.

'Where did it go then? Where *is* my eight hundred pounds?'

'Frank spent it,' Lizzie said. 'Or took it with him. How do I know? I never saw a flamin' penny of it.'

'We have only your word on that.'

'Dear God!' Lizzie said. 'Do you think I'd have been livin' hand to mouth for the past ten years if I'd had eight hundred quid tucked away? I'd have been off out of here. Off like a shot.'

'Would you have taken your mama with you, and your sister too?'

'Meanin' if I'd left them behind you'd have had them carved up?' Lizzie said. 'For God's sake, what kind of a man are you?'

'You must not be so dramatic, Lizzie.' He got up, fetched a chair from a corner, placed it behind her. 'Haven't I done what I could for you? Have I not been helpful to your family?'

'You have,' Lizzie admitted. 'You found the girls jobs when there was no work about. I'm grateful for that but ...'

'What more do you need from me?'

'Supposin',' Lizzie said, 'I want to get married again?'

Surprised, he pursed his lips. 'You don't need my blessing for that.'

'How can I saddle a new husband with my last husband's debt?' Lizzie said. 'That wouldn't be fair, would it?'

'He isn't a rich man, this potential husband?'

'Far from it.'

'Is he from this part of the world?' Dominic asked.

'West End.'

'Have you told him anything about our arrangement?'

''Course I bloody haven't.'

'Do you wish me to talk with him? Explain the situation.'

'I can do that myself – if and when I have to.'

'Oh, I think that you *will* have to.' Dominic paused. 'Unless ...'

'Unless what?' said Lizzie, looking up.

'Your girls are working? Could they not take over your debt?'

'*What?*' Lizzie yelled. 'Land my girls with *my* debt. I'd die first. I'd let you cut my throat before I'd allow my daughters fall into your ...'

She tried to take control of herself. It didn't do to raise your voice to Dominic Manone, to treat him as if he were any Tom, Dick or Harry. His suggestion had been totally unexpected. It hadn't occurred to her that Frank Conway's debt might pass down through the generations like some disease of the blood. Cramp gripped her, making her wince.

Oddly enough, for a man in his position Dominic wasn't used to watching people suffer. Also, he had considerable sympathy for Lizzie Conway, more sympathy for her than for any other person, man or woman, with whom he did business. It wasn't her fault that she had been caught in the poverty trap. It wasn't her greed or stupidity that had put the albatross around her neck. She had inherited a crippling debt.

If Lizzie Conway thought that he could write it off, however, just eliminate it from the books at the stroke of a pen, she was much mistaken. No matter how much sympathy he had for her, no matter how much he admired her struggle to make something of herself, he couldn't go against nature. Everything had to be paid for in kind or in blood. That was his father's law, the law of nations. To flout it, even once, would be opening the door to anarchy.

He didn't know Lizzie Conway very well. He had never

clapped eyes on her daughters, except that one time three or four years ago when he'd driven down to Rutherglen Road to watch the arrival of the hunger marchers, to experience at first hand the palpable and stimulating rage that dripped like sweat from the legions of dockers, steel-workers, miners and shipwrights who came tramping down the high road, heading, so they said, for London.

Lizzie Conway had been stationed on the pavement at the end of the parkway, her arms about her girls, holding them tightly to her as if to prevent them being sucked into the floodtide of protest.

He had been hidden in the rear seat of the long-bodied Alfa Romeo with Uncle Guido and Tony Lombard and some skirt that Tony had brought along. He had looked out and had seen Frank Conway's widow, not waving, not cheering, showing none of the wild solidarity that activated the women around her. She'd had her arms around her girls, grown though they were, and he, Carlo Manone's son, had envied them not just their unity but their closeness, their resistance to the anarchic fever that was sweeping through the streets.

'I'm not going to do your girls any harm,' he said.

'If you do,' Lizzie said, 'I'll ...'

'What? Murder me?' He uttered a little *huh-huh* of laughter, not cynical but warm, as if the idea of being done in by this common, unglamorous woman was somehow amusing. 'You wouldn't murder me, Lizzie Conway. You wouldn't know how.' Then he was serious again. 'Who is this guy who wants to marry you? What's his name?'

'He's not one of your crowd.'

'Has he asked you?'

'Not yet; but he will.'

'Do you love him?'

'He's a good man,' Lizzie said. 'He'll look after me.'

'What about your daughters? Will he look after them too?'

'He'll take us all out of here.'

'I thought you liked living in the Gorbals.'

'I hate living in the Gorbals. It's no place for young girls.'

'They are not young girls. They are young women.'

'I don't want them marryin' any of your boys.'

Again the *huh-huh* of amusement. 'They could do worse.'

'Could they? Worse than Alex O'Hara?'

Dominic pushed himself to his feet. He adjusted his shirt cuffs and stared from the window at the plane trees that lofted their branches over the hedges.

'I can't help you,' he said. 'I can't rub out the debt. If you want to get married then you'll have to tell your husband the truth; or find some way to raise the wind behind his back.'

'How much would buy me out once and for all?'

'I told you five hundred.'

'All right,' Lizzie said.

Dominic turned from his contemplation of the trees. 'You will pay it?'

'Yes.'

He came forward, placed his hands on the chair and leaned towards her. His breath had the same smell as the house, dry and spicy, but not unpleasant. He touched her cheek, a soft little slap to make her raise her head and look at him. 'You've found the money, haven't you? The money Frank stole?'

'I haven't found the money. I've no idea where it is, or what Frank—'

'Don't lie to me, Lizzie Conway.'

'After ten bloody years – *twelve* bloody years – what chance have I got of findin' anythin'?' Lizzie said. 'If you ask me I don't think there is any money. I think Frank blewed it before he joined up.'

'Eight hundred fins? Come on!'

Lizzie drew in a breath. She touched Dominic's wrist with her fingertip and lightly pushed his hand away from the proximity of her face. Even that, she realised, was a daring thing to do.

He stepped back.

Lizzie got to her feet.

She brushed at her skirt, fiddled with the collar of her coat and straightened her hat before she looked up again. 'No, Mr Manone, I'm *not* goin' to pull a wad of banknotes from my purse. I *don't* have the money.'

'So why did you come here this morning?'

'To find out how much you'd settle for.'

'Well,' Dominic said, 'now you know.'

'Aye,' Lizzie said. 'Now I know.'

In the last tenement, and the tenement before that, all four Conways had been crowded into a single room. There had been a bed set into the wall and another had been dragged down out of a cupboard late every night and cranked back up early every morning. Before that, in the basement in the old weavers' row near the railway, there had been no bed at all and Mammy and the girls had slept all together on a straw-filled palliasse on a damp stone floor, among rat-dirt and cockroaches. Mercifully, Rosie couldn't remember that far back.

In the winter of 1920 Rosie had contracted a fever that had all but destroyed her hearing. The cause of the fever and just how close Rosie had come to death were matters that Lizzie refused to discuss with anyone except Mr Feldman. Only Polly could recall those dreadful days and nights when Rosie had been racked by crisis after crisis, when Mammy, solid, reliable, unfazeable Mammy, had wept with frustration when the doctor had refused to treat Rosie without payment in advance.

Finally Mammy had lifted Rosie from the mattress, had wrapped her in a blanket and had gone running out into icy darkness, leaving Polly – wide awake and scared, so scared – in charge of Babs. It had been mid-morning before Mammy had returned, haggard and hollow-eyed. Without Rosie. Rosie had been kept at the Victoria Infirmary where Mammy had carried her and where some kindly register had taken her in, in spite of the fact that Mammy had no insurance and couldn't pay the fees.

It had been a fortnight before Rosie had been returned to them, frail, fractious, and permanently deaf. And Mammy had never been quite the same afterwards, never easy, never relaxed.

She had taken night work on top of her day shifts. Polly had often been kept away from school to look after her ailing sister. Before the summer was out, though, they were up and off, quitting the damp, rat-infested basement for a tenement kitchen that was at least dry and there had been real beds to sleep in, enough coal to keep the place warm and just enough food on the table to nourish them. They had survived thus until Polly was old enough to leave school and find work and then, with an extra wage, however small, coming into the house, things had become marginally easier.

Bits and pieces of second-hand furniture had begun to fill up the spaces, ornaments to appear on the shelves, and rugs and blankets and cushions, purchased from market stalls, had created a cosy clutter. After Babs had been found work too there had even been enough to buy clothes that fitted, shoes that didn't let in the wet and an occasional luxury like the wireless or the gramophone.

Only Polly was old enough to realise just how much her mother had sacrificed to bring them up.

When Rosie grumbled or Babs moaned it was Polly, not Mammy, who would snap at them or give them a good hard slap and tell them to sit up and count their blessings.

Only Polly really understood her mother well enough to be sensitive to the changes that were taking place, those prickly little undercurrents of restlessness and brooding silences. So it was Polly who spotted the first white hairs, the first wrinkles, the first trace of night sweats and that – that *heaviness* that had begun to affect her mother. In themselves the signs meant little. She, Lizzie, had been 'down' before; a kidney infection had all but floored her for the best part of six weeks. But this was different, quite different.

'Are you feeling all right?'

'I'm feelin' fine.'

'You don't look quite yourself.'

'I'm fine, Polly. Stop botherin' me.'

They were sitting up together about half past nine o'clock, not an unusual hour for the family to retire on Sunday night. In the bedroom across the little hall Babs and Rosie would still be fiddling with the knobs of the wireless set in the hope of discovering dance music or something more cheerful than solemn-voiced Englishmen discussing politics or religion. Mammy was already in bed, Polly seated on a chair close by, her feet stretched out and resting on the quilt.

'I mean,' Polly said, 'if there *was* somethin' wrong, you'd tell me, right?'

Lizzie put down the tattered magazine, *Sea Breezes*, that she'd pinched from Tosh, the van driver at the laundry.

'Polly, for God's sake,' she said, 'nothin's wrong with me.'

A tubby lamp on a shelf overhead shed light upon them. There were no other lights in the kitchen but the fire still glowed in the grate, the uncurtained window above the sink caught the faint gaseous glow of arc-lamps from the shunting yard to the east, and patched on to the night sky were the lights of backland tenements.

The little metal clock ticked busily in the awkward silence.

Lizzie peered at her daughter, frowning.

Polly wore a cotton nightgown, had a shawl over her shoulders and six or eight little paper curlers screwed into her brown hair. Somehow she felt disadvantaged by the curlers. She pretended to be engrossed in the copy of *Breathless Surrender* that Mammy had also pinched from van driver McIntosh.

'Are you tellin' me I look ill?' Lizzie said.

'No, you don't look ill.'

'Hoi.' Lizzie nudged her daughter with a hefty elbow. 'Look at me, Poll?'

Polly spared her mother a darting glance. 'What?'

'You tell *me*. You started it.'

Polly sighed. 'You're just not yourself these days. Are you worried about something?'

'I'm always worried about somethin'.'

'I mean, particularly.' Polly hesitated. 'Has it started?'

'Has what started?'

'You know what I mean — the change?'

'God, I wish things *would* change.'

'*The* change,' said Polly. 'The time of life change.'

'Oh, that! No, though there are signs it mayn't be far away.'

Polly put *Breathless Surrender* to one side. 'Isn't it early?'

'It started with Gran McKerlie soon after I was born.'

'Gran was always sick,' Polly said. 'What about Auntie Janet?'

'God knows!' Mammy said. 'Janet never talks about these things.'

'Is that because she's still a virgin?'

'Polly!'

'Well — she is, isn't she?'

'Probably,' Lizzie said, warily.

'Is the change worse for virgins?'

'I doubt,' Mammy said, 'if you'll ever have to worry about that.'

'Thanks very much,' Polly said. 'I hope you're not implying—'

Mammy patted her arm. 'I know you'd never do anythin' stupid.'

Polly was not so sure, and prudently changed the subject.

'Did you go to talk to Mr Manone this morning?'

'Aye.'

'Thought as much,' Polly said. 'About our Rosie?'

'Rosie?' Mammy appeared puzzled. 'What does Mr Manone have to do with our Rosie?'

'I thought you might be trying to borrow money again. For Rosie, I mean. Or,' Polly added, hastily, 'that you were asking him to find her a job.'

'Time enough for that come June, when she leaves the Institute,' Mammy said. 'Anyway, Mr Feldman tells me he might be able to find somethin' suited to her abilities. She can type forty words a minute, you know.'

'Yeah,' Polly said, 'but she'll never be able to take dictation or answer a telephone.' She paused. 'What *did* you go to see Manone about?'

Mammy lay back against the pillow and looked up at the stained lace fringe of the miniature lampshade on the shelf above her head. 'I needed to find out how much we still owe him.'

'How much?'

'Eight hundred pounds.'

'Huh!' Polly said. 'You should've saved yourself the tram fare, Mam. I could have told you that Manone's never gonna let us off the hook. It's the way sharks like him work. You borrow something, not even very much, and wind up paying off the bloody interest for the rest of your life.' She inched closer to the bed and rested a hand against her mother's arm. 'I suppose the smarmy sod told you it was a debt of honour.'

'Oh, I knew that already. I've known it for years.'

'It's why he looks out for us,' Polly said. 'He looks after us the way you'd look after a herd of cows. He finds us jobs just so's he can milk us for money every month.'

'He says he'll settle for five.'

Polly drew back, shook her head. 'He knows you'll never be able to rake up five hundred. Anyhow he doesn't want you to pay him off. That's the last thing he wants. He just wants to keep the tap dripping.'

'I'm sick of it,' Mammy admitted.

'I know you are,' said Polly.

'What'll happen when you get married?'

'I've no intention of getting married,' Polly said.

'I don't want you to wind up like your Auntie Janet.'

'Don't even jest,' said Polly.

'See,' Mammy said, 'that's the trouble. I'd like you to get married. I'd like to see all of you married.' Polly had heard this song before. 'I'm frightened you get carried away by the wrong sort of chap. Don't tell me it can't happen. I've seen it happen. One minute you're nice sensible girls, next minute you're swept off your feet by some Ned in a fancy suit who rattles a bit of cash in his pocket.'

'Well' – Polly regretted it before the words were properly out of her mouth – 'well, if this mythical guy's rattling money in his pocket and he's mad enough to want to drag one of us to the altar he might even be willing to square your debt with Dominic Manone.'

'No.'

'Clean the slate,' said Polly, lamely.

'Never.'

Mammy heaved herself from the pillows. For an instant it seemed that she had been gripped by cramp again. She placed her chin on her knees and stared, scowling, at the pattern on the quilt. Polly saw the muscles of her mother's forearms flex, the contour of shoulder and back change as she stiffened her spine. There was nothing old, nothing aged about Mammy now, nothing in the pose to indicate that her determination was waning.

'I'll not hand it down to you, not to any of you,' she said. 'Frank Conway was my man. I took him on for all the wrong reasons an' I've had to pay the price ever since. But not you, Poll, or your sisters. Once you're all safely out of here then I'll do what I have to do.'

'And what's that?' Polly asked.

'Go and live with Gran and Janet, I suppose.'

'Is that the best you can dream up?'

'Or marry.' Mammy rubbed her cheek against her shoulder. 'Now wouldn't that be a turn-up, dearest, if your mammy went an' got married first.'

'Who is he?' Polly said. 'Hell's bells, Mam, it's not yon van driver, is it?'

'McIntosh? Nah, nah. He's already got a wife. Besides, he's too old for a sparky young thing like me.'

'What *are* you talkin' about?' Polly sat bolt upright. Stared at her mother. Blinked. Said, 'Good God, you *do* have some guy in mind. You've no intention of going to stay with Gran and Janet. Who is he? Does he fancy you?'

'I think he does – but he doesn't know it yet.'

'Who?' It was Polly's turn to nudge. 'Who? Who? Who?'

'Mr Peabody.'

'The factor's man?' Polly's mouth opened and closed in astonishment. 'Oh, Mammy, you can't be serious? I mean, I know you said you fancied him but I thought it was a joke.'

'No, it's no joke,' Mammy admitted. 'I haven't done anythin' about it yet – and perhaps I never will – but let's just say I wouldn't be averse to marryin' Bernard Peabody, or someone very like him.'

Polly swallowed, thickly. Her eyes grew hot. She felt less bewildered than betrayed by her mother's admission, as if the whole affair were cut and dried and the shabby little agent were already waiting in the wings to take her place in Mammy's affections. She stammered, 'Are – are you really in love with him?'

'Don't be so bloody daft,' said Mammy and, with a fruity little chuckle, rolled on to her side and drew the blankets firmly over her head.

Chapter Four

As Polly was for ever reminding her sister it was more than their lives were worth to be caught fraternising with the Hallops. For this reason Babs continued to treat Jackie and his brothers with disdain whenever she encountered them in Lavender Court, though she would nod to Jackie's mother now or bestow a haughty little smile on his small sisters just to show them that she wasn't entirely two-faced. What Polly said was true, of course: Mammy would have a purple fit if she suspected that one of her darling daughters and scruffy Jackie Hallop were on the way to becoming sweethearts or that Babs and Polly were frequent visitors to the Hallops' yard in Kingston Lane.

It was not exactly Polly's wish to spend two or three evenings a week consorting with Jackie Hallop and his friends but, as eldest, she felt a certain responsibility to her sister and at first she tagged along just to make sure that Babs did not get into trouble.

From the outside the Hallops' yard was unremarkable. Even the sign above the padlocked gate – *Sunbeam Garage & Repair Works* – was nothing more than a sheet of corrugated iron painted in faded letters.

Kingston Lane was one of those sneaky little alleys that linked nowhere to nowhere, a remnant of the days long gone when the Gorbals had been a village of cottages and market gardens. Back of the so-called 'repair shop' – another monument to corrugated iron – brambles still ripened in autumn, dog-roses still blossomed and a country-lover might have found evidence of the herbal beds that had flourished here a hundred years ago, a tiny clump of mint, a sprig of thyme or fennel clinging to the ashy soil below the disused railway tunnel.

The yard was strewn with bits and pieces of metal – Jackie got quite upset if you referred to it as 'junk' – most of it stripped from motorcars and motorcycles; an L-shaped necropolis of dented fenders and fretted wings, of bent axles, rusting sub-frames and side-cars eroded almost beyond redemption. There was no sign of sophisticated machinery, only one ancient wooden structure rather like a gibbet, topped by a pulley wheel that clicked and revolved all by itself even when the air was still.

When Mrs Hallop's boys were called upon to work, they worked hard. Jackie and his older brother Dennis could be busy little bees when it suited them. An expert mechanic, Jackie had a particular fondness for motorcycles. He could strip a machine in a matter of hours and, if there was urgency about it, reconstruct the damned thing and have it off the premises before the dawn patrol appeared on the horizon. In fact, three constables and one divisional sergeant were roaring around the county on bikes that had Jackie Hallop's fingerprints all over them – and nobody any the wiser.

Jackie believed that it paid to have friends in high places and was never less than civil when it came to dealing with coppers. Which was more than could be said for his honest, quite-above-board father whose fondness for a dram often had him struggling in the arms of the law on Friday nights and had come close to costing him his job as a railway porter.

If old Sandy Hallop had lost his job, however, it would hardly have mattered. His sons would see him right, for the Hallop lads were coining in more in a month than a railway porter earned in a year.

For Babs, however, money was not the main attraction.

Every Saturday night young Jackie Hallop shed his greasy overalls, donned a beautiful pale blue double-breasted lounge suit and turned up at the Calcutta Road Palais de Danse looking like a million dollars. It would take more than a length of lined flannel to transform Jackie into Prince Charming, of course, but the Calcutta Palais, though glittery, was hardly a royal palace and most of the girls there were impressed by gorgeous feathers.

Jackie had one or two other things going for him, too. He had escaped the plague of acne that affected so many of his peers and his complexion, though pale, was passing smooth. And he wasn't much of a one for the booze. Beer made him sick and spirits made his head spin so he was usually sober when most of those around him were falling down drunk, which was a big advantage when it came to getting off with girls.

Next to motorcycles, girls were Jackie Hallop's passion in life. He liked them even more than he liked money. If the ladies generally preferred money to Jackie then that was just dandy, for Jackie had acquired the knack of making the two things – Jackie and cash – seem indissoluble.

Pale blue suit, silk tie, wristlet watch, plump buffalo-hide wallet with its edging of fivers were advertising pure and simple, bait to sucker unwary victims into believing that Jackie Hallop was a gentleman in the making.

Even Babs Conway wasn't that daft.

She lived just three floors up from the Hallops and saw Jackie for what he really was, slight, scrofulous and almost indistinguishable from the Neds who lolled about the street corners. She knew that he slept four to a bed with his brothers and, when it suited him, wouldn't get up until noon.

Babs was also aware, however, that Jackie had money to burn and that he fancied her and that when he chatted her up there was a delicious undercurrent of opportunity running through the conversation. And, as if that wasn't enough, the Hallops' repair shop in Kingston Lane offered sanctuary when the prospect of another evening wasted at home became just too tedious for words.

The group that gathered round the stove in Hallops' repair shed were not all mercenaries. Occasionally – though not often – they talked of things other than money and the fun it could purchase.

Polly and Babs had escaped the poverty trap thanks to Mammy's efforts and the Hallop boys through their connection with Mr Manone. But others in the company hadn't shaken off their birthright and remained moral outcasts from the system and blamed capitalism for their descent into lawlessness. Such a one was Patsy Walsh. His aim was not to escape into the middle class but to overthrow that class, to destroy an exploitative *kultur* that deliberately robbed the workers of their will to fight.

Polly found this aspect of Patsy Walsh both interesting and, in its way, rather attractive. She was not in favour of what he did but she had been reared in a tough neighbourhood and some of that toughness had affected her too. How could it be otherwise? She was not put off by what Patsy did for a living and, if she had been more open about it, might even have confessed that she found the anomalies and paradoxes in his character intriguing.

Patsy was a house-breaker, a negotiator, a salesman, a voice in the wilderness; a wheedling, gentle honeycomb of a voice who, given the chance, could have argued intelligently with Baldwin or Beaverbrook. He was also a fellow traveller, a disciple of Marx and had confided in Polly that he'd been in Berlin that jolly day in May when the Communists had attacked the police stations and nine comrades had been martyred. He had seen things in Germany, he said, that made Glasgow's hunger marches look like a Christmas pantomime.

If Patsy had been less adept at breaking into houses and offices he might have been treated as a buffoon by the young men who met around the stove to share tea, toast and margarine, and talk of movie stars, football heroes, dancing – and money.

As it was, they all held him just a little in awe and even Polly was not immune to his rough charms.

She crouched on a bench by the stove with Babs and Patsy beside her.

Jackie straddled a motorcycle, his narrow thighs embracing the saddle, arms folded on the handlebars while Patsy discoursed on international injustice and the national disgrace of having in power a Labour Party that was too scared to do anything original or effective.

Polly listened intently, nodding now and then in agreement.

She had removed her Scotch tammy to expose her chestnut hair. She had a neat haircut now and the sort of look that she knew bothered Comrade Walsh, for he had already told her that she was close to becoming middle class; a comment that Polly thought rather flattering in a back-handed way.

Tommy Bonnar had also turned up at the yard that evening.

Polly wasn't sure why he had come and he did not explain his reason. She didn't like or trust wee Tommy, with his skeletal features, graveyard cough and those dead, zinc-coloured eyes that seemed to see nothing yet missed nothing.

'If I had money, real money, big money,' Patsy said, 'I'd be puttin' it into building, so I would.'

'What sorta buildin'?' said Dennis Hallop, who was out in the shadows under the beams filing something in a vice. 'A bank, like?'

'Hell no, man,' said Patsy. 'Construction. The fathers of this fair city of ours will soon have no choice but to be knockin' most of it down. Then the ones who'll make money, real money, will be those who can lay drains an' pile bricks an' slate roofs.'

'Tradesmen!' said Babs, not quite critically.

'If this government stays in power long enough, the municipal borrowin' rate will be allowed to rise to six quid in twenty', Patsy went on. 'Then the steam hammers'll cut a swathe through

Glasgow like you wouldn't believe. Everythin' from the Carlton to the Calcutta Road will be swept away.'

'I hope they give us some warnin',' Babs said. 'I mean, I wouldn't want to get tossed out on t' the street in my nightie-nite.'

Jackie grinned and massaged the rubber grips of the motorcycle as if he were kneading flesh. 'I'll be there t' save you, darlin'. 'Specially if you're only wearin' your nightie-nite.'

'Look what they've done already.' Patsy ignored Jackie's attempt to sabotage a serious conversation. 'Three thousand suburban cottages in Knightswood. Three thousand's a flea-bite. We need sixty thousand, seventy thousand new homes to rehouse the Clydeside wards. Where's that money gonna come from, these days?'

'And where's it going to go?' said Polly.

Patsy gave her a brusque nod.

'Have a guess, sweetheart,' he said.

'The building trades, like you say,' Polly answered. 'They've started developments already in Mosspark and Anniesland.'

'How do you know?' said Babs.

'I've seen the plans,' said Polly.

'What plans?'

'In the burgh council offices. Where I work.'

'They let you see the plans?' Dennis was impressed.

'Aye, sure.'

'What're you then, an archy-tect?'

'I've access to architectural files when I need them,' said Polly.

'Do you now?' said Tommy Bonnar, and coughed.

'What's *our* burgh council got to do with buildin' programmes in Mosspark?' said Jackie.

'Transportation,' said Polly. 'Tramcar routes, that sort of thing.'

'Never thought o' that,' Jackie admitted.

'Other people have,' said Patsy.

'Like who?' said Babs.

'Like the landlords an' factors who're already buyin' up every strip of private land they can get their grubby paws on,' Patsy declared. 'When the purchase orders start tricklin' in, they're the ones who'll make a killin'.'

'So long as they don't knock down the Palais,' Babs said, with a shrug.

'Aye, the Palais.' Jackie swung himself from the motorbike, executed a not inelegant glide and hopped up on to the bench by Polly's side. 'That's what I'd do if I had the real big money. I'd buy the Palais. I'd buy the Palais an' let you all in for free.'

'The Paragon, an' all?' said Babs.

'Yeah, why not?' said Jackie. 'Show any picture I liked, any time.' He spread his arms, balanced on one thin leg. 'How about you, Den? What'll you buy when we make our pile?'

'Brady's,' said Dennis, grinning. 'Brady's an' maybe the Parkhead brewery to make sure we never run out.' He gave a little rat-a-tat with the file on the top of the vice. 'An' a car, a big Italian car like Mr Manone's.'

'What sort is that, Tommy?' said Babs.

'Alfa.'

'Buy a bettah Alfa,' said Jackie. 'Yeah!'

With a surge, Patsy Walsh flung himself to his feet. 'You're all – all . . .'

Even articulate Patsy could find no words to express his disgust at their cheapness. He had attempted to open them to the future but they had refused to see anything except the gains it would bring them. It wasn't the first time their indifference had infuriated him, their inability to realise that decent housing and the right to work were far more important than what they could buy.

Polly sympathised with his frustration. She too was tempted to despise her peers more than she despised the red-necked hordes who fought each other with knives and bottles and razors: the Tongs and the Norman Conks, the San Toy, the

Redskins and the Bully Boys, the street gangsters with their comical names and childish pride. When she heard the yapping of the new breed, however, she doubted that no matter how the world changed there would never be equality.

She watched Patsy grab his cap and stalk out into the yard.

'Hoi, Patsy, don't take the huff,' Jackie called after him.

'Where you goin' then?' Dennis shouted.

'Work to do,' said Patsy, and kicked the door behind him with his heel.

Patsy let the night air soothe him. He loved the night. In the night you couldn't see the city's appalling squalor. He had no illusions. He knew what was out there. He had lived all his life in the sink-holes of despair that hid behind the old Victorian façades. He had visited the new suburban villas too, however, and had flitted stealthily through the drawing-rooms of the well-to-do, had peeped into bedrooms at clean, sleeping heads and had suffered not only anger but shame, shame that the city he loved was content to remain divided.

He had no job lined up for tonight. He'd wanted to stay inside, to talk to them, to try to make them see sense, but they had offended him and insulted his intelligence. What did Jackie Hallop and Dennis and the Conway girls really know about pride? They were hopeless cases, hopeless.

Hands shaking slightly, Patsy lit a cigarette and climbed the ash ramp towards the tunnel mouth.

The sky was coated with cloud, like a huge dirty blanket. Away below was the silver of the river, like a polished piece of metal, a spanner or chisel, say, or the blade of a cut-throat razor. Hands in pockets, he hunched his shoulders against the snivelling little wind that escaped from the empty tunnel and let his anger drift away.

'Penny for them, Patsy Walsh,' Polly said.

He started.

She had come upon him as lightly as a wisp of smoke, as silently as a shadow. He couldn't have done better himself.

'What do *you* want?' he said.

'My sister just doesn't understand what politics means to you.'

'She isn't the only one.'

Polly had put the Scotch tammy back on her head, had buttoned her overcoat to the very top button. She was slim and tall, almost military-looking in the high-buttoned coat. To Patsy the reeking haze that lay above the Gorbals seemed suddenly brighter.

'I shouldn't take things so seriously, should I?' he said.

'Oh, yes, you should,' Polly told him. 'Somebody's got to.'

He paused. 'Aren't you cold?'

'No.'

'You want a puff?'

'Please.'

He took the cigarette from his mouth and gave it to her.

He watched her take the Woodbine between finger and thumb and place it lightly against her lips. He knew that when she gave it back to him it would taste of lipstick. He waited patiently, happily, while she inhaled.

She gave him back the cigarette and blew out smoke.

She looked away across the rooftops to the silver river while he, watching her, tasted her lipstick on his lips.

'Nice,' Polly said. 'Isn't it?'

'Hmm,' he said.

'Would you care to walk me home?'

'Okay,' said Patsy Walsh and, just as he had seen the lovers do on the quays of Paris, took her hand in his.

'Oh, so it's yourself, is it?' Janet McKerlie stepped back into the hall. 'What time o' the night do you call this?'

'Sorry I'm late,' said Lizzie, humbly. 'Somethin' happened to the dash wheel an' we all had to wait while they drained the tank.'

'We didn't expect you anyway.'

'I always come on Tuesdays.'

'When you can spare the time, aye,' said Janet.

She went into the kitchen.

Lizzie followed.

There was no place else to go.

For over forty years the McKerlies had lived in this same one-room flat – a single-end – in the backlands behind Ballingall Street.

If Gran McKerlie and Janet had been less obsessed with their own little fifth-floor island, they might have noticed that the tenement had gone sliding downhill and was now shored up by four massive oak beams that braced the bulbous gable against the back of a sandstone tenement. They might also have noticed that the comparatively spacious and respectable little room in the comparatively spacious and respectable old building that Charlie and Helen McKerlie had moved into directly after marriage had deteriorated to the point where not even the grisly statistics of the Office of Health took account of it.

When the long-promised regeneration of southside slums finally came to pass, the first sunless tower with its sweating damp-courses, turnpike stairs and iron ventilation grids to fall to the ball-crane and sledge hammers would be this one and *Laurieston, Ballingall Street, Number 21, Backland, Stairs, 1st left, 5 up, right lobby, 7th door, facing* would be reduced to nothing but rubble and an uncherished memory.

Lizzie knew it, and worried about it.

Janet knew it, but chose not to acknowledge it.

Gran McKerlie didn't know much about anything. She seemed oblivious to the stench on the stairs, the influx of fleas in warm weather, the gargle of water from broken eaves or the noisy squabbles that took place in the dark passageways that folk still called 'the greens'.

Gran had a lot more to interest her than a Labour council's stuttering plans for a glorious Utopian future.

High in her eyrie – which she never left – Gran dwelled with her pains.

Everything else, except the power she wielded over Janet, was subsumed by her pains. Her pains were terrible. Her pains were constant. Her pains had more shades and hues than sunset over Arran and Gran had more words in her vocabulary to report the weathers of her pains than she had for anything else, except possibly the daily deviations of her bladder and bowels.

'And how are you tonight, Mother?' Lizzie said.

'Terrible, just terrible.'

Lizzie removed her coat, unpinned her scarf and hung them on the solitary hook behind the kitchen door.

'Is that a fact?' Lizzie said.

'It is, it is – a sad fact, but a true one,' said Gran McKerlie who, though she'd never heard of Socrates let alone Zeno, had grasped the principles of Stoicism by brute instinct. 'It's been a terrible day, terrible.'

'Is it your legs,' said Lizzie, washing her hands at the sink by the window, 'or is it your you-know-what again?'

'It's my you-know-what.'

'Since it rained she's had a lot of trouble with her you-know-what,' Janet explained.

Lizzie raised her head and stared – puzzled – into the window glass.

To the best of her recollection there had been no rain to speak of for the past ten days, an occurrence so rare in the west of Scotland in November that even the *Glasgow Herald* had been moved to remark upon it. But then her mother didn't read the *Glasgow Herald*, or the *Bulletin*, or the *Evening Times* or anything, not even the disingenuous little booklets about true love and matrimony that Janet sneaked in from the shop from time to time.

All day long her mother did nothing but ruminate in the broad, wooden-armed chair by the fire that Janet lighted first thing or, if the sun shone, by the sink at the window.

Lizzie could not have endured such inactivity and couldn't enter her mother's head and share the scant thoughts that occupied the old woman hour after empty hour, day after empty day.

There had never been much there to begin with, Lizzie suspected, but after twenty years of widowhood, crippled by peevishness and illness, there was nothing left to muse upon and nothing, of course, to plan for except another day, another year exactly the same as all those that had gone before. Her mother's mind now was as spartan as the kitchen.

The kitchen was furnished with three wooden chairs, a small table, a bed, a stove, a sink, a few pieces of crockery and a cupboard in which clothes were kept. There were four solitary ornaments upon the high mantelshelf above the range: a moon-faced clock, a pair of tiny boots fashioned out of polished brass, an empty letter rack and a pewter pot with two charred clay pipes in it – her father's pipes, the only mementoes of the time they'd shared with him.

No tinted photographs, no sentimental cards, no corks or ribbons or flowers, not even – as Babs had once remarked – the pickled egg that Grandpa had been about to bite into when the reaper cut him down.

Lizzie could no longer engage with her mother.

There was nothing left to engage *with*, nothing save a self that revelled in suffering and, Lizzie supposed, constantly pondered the mysteries of its own, quite bearable existence.

She dried her hands briskly, folded the towel and draped it on the wooden rack by the side of the sink. She was always tidy in Mam's kitchen, excessively tidy, otherwise Janet would berate her with pernickety little gestures and patient little sighs that screamed disapproval of her, Lizzie's, sluttish ways.

'Have you been takin' the bottle the doctor gave you?'
Lizzie asked.

'No use,' Gran said.

'No use,' said Janet.

'Bound me up.'

'Bound her up.'

'Did you tell him that?' said Lizzie, rolling up her sleeves.

'He's not interested.'

'Not in the slightest interested,' said Janet.

'Takes his money. Does me no good,' Gran said.

'Doesn't know what it is to suffer,' said Janet.

'Be old himself some day,' Gran said.

'Then he'll know all about it,' said Janet.

Lizzie advanced upon her mother. Without apprehension,
the old woman watched her daughter's approach. Inactivity had
laid great slabs of fat upon Helen McKerlie, ballooning out her
face and swelling her hands and feet, so that whatever minor
disorder had once affected her had blown up into genuine
ill-health. Her flesh was tender and bruised easily. Her joints
were locked, her organs swollen and sore.

None of this did Lizzie doubt or mock. She knew that
her mother was an invalid but, like the town in which she
lived, like the Scottish nation itself, Lizzie reckoned that the
woman had brought the condition upon herself by indolent
self-pity and a sense of persecution that had no basis in
fact.

'I'll lift,' said Lizzie, patiently, 'an' you take off her clothes.'

The ritual was as familiar as breathing. Janet did not even
need to nod.

'Ready?' Lizzie asked.

Gran answered, 'Aye.'

She grimaced as Lizzie slid her arms under her armpits and
– face to face, cheek against cheek – with a powerful heave
detached her from the wafer-thin cushions upon which she had
been seated since Janet had got her up that morning. Gran came

away reluctantly, like something large and recalcitrant – a mule, say – being dragged out of mud.

Though she was used to the stinks and stenches of the laundry, Lizzie pressed her tongue to the roof of her mouth to shut out the smell that rose from her mother's chair, an odour of decay, of unpardonable neglect which, if it had not been self-inflicted, would have been quite shocking and quite heart-breaking.

'Okay?' Lizzie asked.

'If he hadn't of bound me with his new medicine, I'd be all right.'

'He's a good doctor, but,' said Janet, as she worked on ties and buttons behind her mother's back. 'It's just his manner. He only charges ten shillin's if we let him come in the daytime. He's a good doctor, Mam, say what you like.'

'He's got me bound.'

'I thought,' Lizzie grunted, 'it was your bladder, not your bowels.'

'It's everythin',' the old woman answered.

'Everything, aye,' said Janet and, with a motion so swift that it might have been part of a conjuring trick, peeled off her mother's skirt, underskirt and big, back-tying drawers and swept them away, leaving the old woman clad only in a lambswool bodice, wrinkled lisle stockings and a pair of flannel shoes.

'Mam,' said Lizzie, 'lift your arms.'

'*Oooooh!*'

'Please. Try an' lift your arms.'

Janet approached. She held out a baking bowl filled with warm soapy water and a big perforated sponge, while Lizzie, one-handed, wrestled to remove her mother's winter vest.

The garments were clean, for Janet would not allow them to be otherwise, but the veined and bloated flesh beneath was not, or did not seem so. Though she had seen it so often before, Lizzie tried to look elsewhere.

At this moment she was grateful to her sister Janet; she

66

couldn't possibly have borne the sight of that body two or three times a day or, worst of all, to have slept with it, smelling it, feeling it against her flesh, its odours and essences, the contamination of age, seeping into her day after day, night after night. Now, with her fortieth year in sight, it was all Lizzie could do not to fling her mother from her and bolt from the stagnation that Gran and Janet represented, that effortless poverty of mind and body that once the girls were gone might grip and draw her down too.

She had to do something about it soon, very soon. She had to find five hundred pounds for a husband, any sort of a husband who would take her far away from this and give her, if not love, protection.

Mr Bernard Peabody? Perhaps.

'Mother, lift your arms again – *will you, please?*'

Lizzie felt the whorls and rolls of her mother's flesh stiffen against her palms, not with pain or indignation but in the unimpeachable knowledge that her daughter's indifference had been whittled away and that she, old and crippled though she might be, had gained the upper hand at last.

'Sorry,' Lizzie said. 'Sorry. I shouldn't have snapped at you. I'm tired, that's all. I've had a long day of it.'

'Haven't I?' said Gran McKerlie.

'Hasn't she?' said Janet. 'Haven't we all?'

'Your turn will come,' Gran prophesied.

'Your turn will come, Lizzie,' Janet added.

Staring bleakly over her mother's shoulder, Lizzie thought: Not if I can help it. Not if I can just lay hands on five hundred pounds and a husband to go with them.

'Janet,' she said.

'What?'

'Sponge.'

Bernard peered at the spot on the table where as a rule he placed his rent books.

'What's all this then, Mrs Conway?' he said.

'A bite to eat,' Lizzie said. 'Ham, egg, sausage. I'm sure you'll manage a mouthful before you scamper away. Haven't had your tea yet, have you?'

'As a matter of fact . . .'

Bernard checked himself. He recognised a bribe when he saw one. But this sort of bribe was hard to resist. In fact he might be doing Lizzie Conway an injustice. It might not be a bribe at all. It might be hospitality, good old Scottish hospitality which it would be churlish to refuse.

He swithered, wondering if she had spotted his weakness, if he was that transparent. He caught the aroma that drifted up from the plate. The eggs were fresh, sunny side up, the ham crisp, and the sausage had a plump bursting sheen to it that suggested it came from a tray in one of the better butcher's shops.

Saliva gathered in the corners of Bernard's mouth. He swallowed, hastily.

'No, I – I'd better not stop.'

'Nonsense,' said Lizzie Conway. 'Miserable night like this, a man needs something hot to keep him going. Give me your coat. Come on, Mr Peabody, give me your coat. You're drookit.'

Drookit he was indeed, drenched by the rain that had brought the dry spell to an end. Although he had splurged on a tramcar fare instead of walking across the bridge from Shannon, Peters & Dean's, he'd hoofed it from Eglinton Street and his feet were wet, his shoulders damp and his bowler felt as if it were floating on his hair.

He took off the bowler, held it by his side, let it drip discreetly.

Stooping, Lizzie detached the hat from his chilled fingers and placed it on the metal shelf above the range where, not surprisingly, it immediately began to steam like a small black pudding.

Bernard was sunk, and knew it.

He gave her his scarf and overcoat, accepted a towel and

rubbed his face, hair and hands with it. He folded the towel meticulously and placed it across the little wooden rack.

'Fried tomato?' Lizzie said.

'If – if there's one going.'

'Toast?'

'Please.'

He felt as if he were embroiled in one of those pleasant dreams that you have on a Sunday morning when you're having a long lie in or, more often, when you drift off in an armchair in front of the fire after a hard day. It wasn't just the fry-up that he found impossible to resist but also the kitchen's comfortable atmosphere and, yes, the woman's companionship.

He was too wet, too chilled to be nervous tonight and it wasn't until he had taken his third or fourth mouthful that it occurred to him why that might be. He blinked, glanced round the room, then asked, 'Where are the girls?'

'Out somewhere,' said Lizzie.

She had served him, had even put slices of buttered toast into a nice wire rack, had poured his tea. Now she was seated at the table with him, her back to the rain-splattered window, a cup held in both hands as if she were about to read his fortune in the leaves.

She had shed her apron and wore a striped cotton blouse with a woolly jumper over it, a wide black skirt. She looked, he thought, like an expanded version of his mother who, though tiny, emanated the same sort of *joie-de-vivre*. His mother, though, was less passive, less comfortable to be with, and far too nippy for a sixty-five-year-old widow.

Mouth full of sausage and egg, Bernard studied Lizzie Conway with a shade more intensity than was strictly prudent. No, he decided, she wasn't really like his old mum after all. It was just something in the eyes, a sort of tenderness, that had given him a false impression.

'All of them?' he said.

'Aye.'

Bernard didn't know whether to be disappointed or relieved that he would not be treated to a leg show from Babs. Relieved, probably. He wondered vaguely if the Conways talked about him after he left and if so what they said.

He chewed, swallowed, helped himself to toast.

'I don't think I've met all your daughters?' he said.

'No, not yet,' said Lizzie.

'Three, isn't it?'

'Aye. Three.' She paused, reading the tea leaves. 'What about yourself, Mr Peabody, have you got sisters?'

''Fraid not,' Bernard said. 'I lost both my brothers in the war.'

'Both!' said Lizzie. 'God, that's awful.'

'Not much fun,' Bernard admitted. 'One was drowned when the *Hampshire* went down. Kitchener was on that ship − not that it did our Charlie a lot of good. Mines don't have much respect for anybody's reputation.'

'My father's name was Charlie,' Lizzie put in, then, lowering her eyes, said, 'What about the other one, your other brother?'

'Nothing special,' Bernard said with a matter-of-fact lift of the left shoulder. 'The Somme.'

'An' you?'

'Nothing special,' said Bernard again.

'Heroes,' Lizzie said. 'Heroes all.'

'Did your husband . . . ?'

Lizzie nodded. 'March 1918. Near Baupaume.'

'Who was he with, what outfit?'

She raised herself a little, put down her cup, spread her skirt under her thighs, not meeting his eye.

Bernard had encountered far too much grief and embarrassment in the past dozen years not to recognise a warning signal. He was not in the least surprised when she changed the subject abruptly.

'Is it true you live in Knightswood?' Lizzie asked.

'Yes.'

'It's a long way from the Gorbals.'

'We used to live in Finnieston until we wangled a transfer.'

'Being in the trade, I suppose ...'

'Oh, no. It wasn't because I worked in a factor's office that we got a new house,' Bernard said, with just a touch of indignation. 'It's a council property.'

'Really!'

'Terraced cottage. Garden, and everything.'

'That must be nice.'

'It is. Very nice,' Bernard agreed.

'I'd like to see it.'

'Well ...'

'Some day,' said Lizzie, smiling.

'It's just me an' my mother, you see,' Bernard said.

'How many rooms?'

'Two bedrooms. Living room. Separate kitchen. Gas throughout. Outside appointments,' Bernard said. 'Not very large but quite, quite ...'

'Luxurious?'

'It suits us, Mrs Conway. It suits us just fine.'

'How did you – I mean, how does one get such a house?'

'The Housing Committee's very selective.'

He tried to keep his voice even, not to allow smugness to creep in.

The acquisition of a brand-new terraced cottage out in the suburbs had given a strange boost to his confidence. He was a council tenant now, a suburbanite, a citizen of good standing. In spite of his shyness, he had to admit that he did feel rather elevated, particularly when he made his calls in places like Lavender Court and saw how the other half lived.

He said, 'They won't take you if you have children.'

'Children of what age?' said Lizzie Conway.

'I really don't know. Any age, I suppose.'

She gave a wee grimace, as if the paucity of information disappointed her, then she grinned. 'I suppose you're a child.'

'Pardon.'

'Mother an' son.'

Bernard wiped a smear of egg yolk from the plate with a crust of toast and popped it in his mouth. He suspected that he was being quizzed about housing and that the free meal was her way of paying for his expertise. He was relieved that it didn't have to do with rent money, or the absence of it.

'I reckon that's true,' he said. 'The house is in my mother's name, though it's me that pays the rent.'

'So a widow *could* apply?'

'I don't see why not,' Bernard said. 'Though I've a feelin' all the cottages have already been allocated.'

'Here, you don't have to tell Shannon, Peters an' What-sit that I've been askin' questions about council properties, do you?'

Bernard laughed and shook his head. 'Of course not.'

'Thank God for that,' said Lizzie. 'It's just somethin' in the back of my mind. Nothin' fixed or definite. A daydream, you might say.'

'How would your daughters feel about bein' dragged away from here?' Bernard said. 'I mean, it's very pleasant in Knightswood but it isn't as – as lively, shall we say, as the Gorbals.'

'My girls will do as they're told,' said Lizzie, not sternly.

'At that age ...'

'What age?'

'Their age. Young. Youthful ...' Bernard didn't know what had prompted him to express such a patronising sentiment. 'Awkward,' he concluded, limply. 'Awkward's what I mean.'

'Don't you like them?'

'Well, yes, they seem like very nice, very well-brought-up young – I don't know them. I mean, I've only met them once or twice.'

'I've made you blush, Mr Peabody.'

'No. No. I'm just – just warm. It's the tea, I think.'

'More?'

He glanced ostentatiously at the metal clock that tick-ticked on the mantelshelf, then he fished a cheap Ingersoll from his breast pocket and checked the time on it too.

He got to his feet. 'No, really. I must be . . .'

'One more cup?' Lizzie tempted him.

'I'd love to, but I'll have to be on . . .' He fought to remember his manners. 'Thank you for the meal. I appreciate it.'

She fetched his coat and scarf and gave them to him, then she lifted down his bowler, still steaming, from the shelf above the range. But when he reached out for it, Lizzie smiled and refused to hand it over.

'I used to do this for my husband,' she said. 'Stand still, Mr Peabody.'

Short of rudeness, he had no option but to comply. He put his hand down between his legs, hoisted up the money pouch, buttoned his coat over it and then stood erect, a proper little trooper, while Mrs Lizzie Conway placed the hat upon his head and gave it a tiny wee squeeze to settle it over his hair.

She inspected him critically, adjusted his tie, picked a loose thread from the edge of a buttonhole and, with her forefinger, delicately wiped a little yellow smudge of egg yolk from his upper lip.

It was all Mr Peabody could do not to quiver.

He half expected Mrs Conway to round off the ritual with a little kiss.

'There,' Lizzie said. 'That's better. All smart. All ready for the fray.'

'Thank you,' Bernard said. 'Thank you very much.'

He stuck his case under his arm, patted the money pouch, turned towards the door, as dazed and detached as if this really were a fireside reverie.

'Mr Peabody,' Lizzie said. 'Bernard?'

'Yes.'

'Haven't you forgotten something?'

'What's that?'

'The rent money,' said Lizzie, laughing.

Chapter Five

In many companies the keeping of two sets of accounts was regarded as almost mandatory. The Manones, however, maintained not just two sets of accounts but several, for old Carlo and brother Guido knew that it was not the *polizia* who represented the biggest threat to the smooth running of a family business but court servants and inquisitive tax inspectors, and that Scots law, unlike the laws of Italy, was applied with Presbyterian rigour.

It was by no means impossible to bribe officials and make hand-outs to unscrupulous coppers but graft within the municipal administration was too expensive for even Guido and his nephew, Dominic, to invest in.

The Manones were not bookmakers; they merely financed bookmakers. The Manones were not house-breakers or bank robbers; they just happened to be able to make the loot from such enterprises vanish without trace. The Manones did not personally operate the loan sharking and protection rackets that flourished on the southside, though they were not opposed to arranging by proxy a little arson here or a beating-up there.

After all, in the wake of a stock-market crash, in the middle of a slump, who could blame you for protecting your interests.

Mr Shadwell, the Manones' chief accountant, was instructed to keep immaculate records but he was paid a substantial sum not only for on-page arithmetic but also to keep his mouth shut about all the off-page arithmetic that occurred upstairs in Central Warehouse Company's offices or on the deal table in the house in Manor Park Avenue.

The typewriter, adding machine and telephone – especially the telephone – were the tools with which Dominic controlled his urban empire and his time was taken up not with instilling fear or dispensing rough justice but with managing the men who managed the men who did.

Dominic was not discomfited by bloodshed but he was remote from it.

He spent much time lunching with bankers, lawyers and shipping agents and, in spite of his foreign origins, was accepted as part of the old boys' network that controlled much of the city's commerce: a caucus of well-heeled, well-educated Scotsmen whose greed far outstripped his own.

It was a man's world, of course, a world of private rooms, fine tweed and wool worsted, of beefsteaks, brandy and cigars, all salted with the faint, earthy streak of proletarianism that even the most exalted Scottish blue-blood, let alone a jumped-up member of the middle class, could not quite shake out of his system, not in dear, dark, dusty Glasgow at any rate.

Of late, though, Dominic had experienced a strange hankering to leave the grim Scottish city in which he'd been born, to mingle with people who knew him not, to stroll in the sunshine, perhaps, and dance with sweet *signorinas* under a hot Ligurian moon.

Dominic was not permitted to visit Italy or travel to America to visit his mama, sisters and his father, who was no longer young. Old Carlo was for ever reminding him by letter that some things are stronger than blood ties and that he was a Scotsman born and bred and had no right to desire more than had already been given him.

Uncle Guido was sympathetic, Aunt Teresa too. They were of the old school, however, steeped in traditions that seemed vain to Dominic. No matter how much they loved him, they could not understand him.

Aunt Teresa did all the cooking and bossed the local girls who came to the mansion every day to dust and polish and assist with the laundry. She was not by nature a compliant woman but she had learned to pretend to be obedient.

To her shame she had never given Guido a child, not even a daughter, and Uncle Guido still sought consolation in the arms of lively young things whom he encountered in the cafés and factories over which he, through Dominic, held sway. He would take off for two or three days at a stretch to tour the Manones' properties in the Alfa Romeo or, if discretion was called for, in a more modest Singer Senior Six. He would return from these trips sleepy-eyed and smug but with the work always done, the money collected and accounted for. Dominic didn't know precisely what his uncle got up to with the girls in the resort towns but he heard rumours now and then and he wasn't naïve enough to suppose that the friendships were innocent.

Given his position as head of the family he might have challenged the old man and demanded to be told what was going on – but that he would not do. It was enough that Guido returned with two black leather portmanteaux stuffed with cash and that, late in the evening after the maids had gone home and Aunt Teresa had retired to bed, his uncle and he, and Mr Shadwell too, would pour coins and banknotes on to the table, spread out ledgers, stock-books and great bundles of receipts and invoices and begin work, real work, making tallies and deductions and filling the plain brown envelopes by way of which the runners and scouts of the Manones' dark little army were paid.

Once in a blue moon Dominic would slip off by himself. He'd drive unaccompanied down the coast to inspect the ice-cream factory or drop in unannounced at one of the cafés. He'd chat with managers and staff, would inspect the books, nod, and drive home again, just to keep Uncle Guido on his toes and prove that he trusted no one, not even his nearest and dearest. He didn't take up on Uncle Guido's advice, though, to find a nice piece of skirt who liked a good time and who would be amenable to spending the night in bed with a handsome Italian, if only as a favour to the family.

Dominic would have none of that. He might have been raised without any religious beliefs worth talking about but he couldn't discard the ethics that had been dinned into him at high school. That odd, inimically Scottish system of values that made a virtue out of self-denial, that emphasised the meaning of respect without servility and honour, even among thieves.

Dominic's life was constrained by duty to his family. He quietly paid his dues to the *comunardo*, made sure he never short-changed his employees, transferred his father's slice of the profits to a bank in Philadelphia, USA, and, out of necessity, put in an occasional appearance at some of the Italian community's less public events. He refused to stoop to exploiting the position of power that had been thrust upon him, however; a position that, as he had grown from boyhood into manhood, had become such a millstone round his neck that he felt bowed down by it, reduced, as Uncle Carlo had been, to someone who existed only to serve the family and whose worth beyond that was questionable.

In the winter of 1930, a bleak season of strikes, riots and rising unemployment, Dominic Manone reached the ripe old age of twenty-eight.

Apart from attending another testimonial dinner hosted for him by members of the Rowing Club, he refused to celebrate the occasion, for he felt that he was going nowhere, that his life, like the nation's order books, was empty.

'What is wrong with that boy?' Aunt Teresa asked in the thudding dialect of the Genoese docklands by which she and her husband communicated when no one else was around. 'He eats nothing I cook for him. All he does is read the newspapers, drink coffee and smoke his little cigars. He is becoming more like you every day, Guido. He should go out more.'

'He has his businesses to attend to,' Guido answered. 'He has no time to be frivolous.'

'Frivolous,' Teresa Manone said. 'You are the frivolous one.'

'Shut your mouth,' said Guido, politely.

Reluctantly Aunt Teresa did as she was told.

She was three years younger than her husband and bore a distinct resemblance to a plump Atlantic seal. In a last defiant act of vanity, though, she still plucked her eyebrows, a habit that had reduced them to two thin startled crescents. When she scowled the fringe of soft grey down that adorned her upper lip darkened and she looked, so Guido thought, not just plain but ugly.

He often told her so.

She said nothing to contradict him.

She sat at the kitchen table – that long table where her husband, her nephew and the Jew counted out cash – and gave Guido a penetrating stare that amply substituted for criticism.

'What is it you would have me do?' Guido said. 'About Dominic, I mean.'

'Take him dancing?'

'*Dancing?*'

'Take him with you when you go away.'

'When I go – what? – when I go *dancing?*' Guido might have laughed off the woman's suggestion but he wasn't given to showing weakness of any kind. 'Do you want *me* to dance with him? Do you want *me* to teach him the steps?'

'You have taught him everything else,' Aunt Teresa said.

'Dominic does not want to dance.'

'He *should* want to dance. That's all I'm saying.'

'Where would I take him? To the Palais? How do you think that would look? A man of his stature turning up at the Calcutta?'

'There are other places.'

'What other places?'

'On the coast,' Teresa said.

'What do you know about the coast?'

'I've heard.'

Guido picked an olive from a bowl on the dresser, sucked on it thoughtfully, then spat the pit into his palm. He straightened the hump on his shoulders so that he towered over the tiny, seal-like woman. He didn't ask where she had heard, or what she had heard. He knew that she would not betray her confidantes. It would be the girls, the day-maids from Govan, who had brought her gossip. They were sharp creatures, shrewd enough to keep out of his way but he didn't doubt that they could be lippy when it suited them.

'Ballrooms,' Teresa said.

'I do not know what you're talking about,' Guido said.

'Girls,' Teresa said. 'Romance.'

'You think that's what your nephew needs — romance?'

'He is too much with old men, like you. Boy of his age needs sweethearts.'

'Is *this* your cure for a loss of appetite?' Guido said. 'Perhaps he's only constipated and could be cured by a dose of senna.'

'Why does he not like the girls?' Aunt Teresa persisted. 'Is there something wrong with him?'

'There is nothing wrong with him,' Guido said, bridling. 'If he wants girls he knows where to find them. He can pick a nice Italian girl from the Community if he really wants romance. If it's the other thing, the quick thing, he can find that too, without my encouragement or assistance.'

'He is not favoured in the Community.'

'No, he is too quiet for his own good.'

'It's because he is not a good Catholic, because he—'

Guido spat another olive pit into his palm and closed his fist. 'Be careful, old woman. It is not for you to criticise Dominic, even if he is your nephew.'

'I worry for him.'

'Worry for yourself,' Guido said. 'Dominic does what he was put here to do. Right now it's all as smooth as cream – but it may not always be so.'

'Is there trouble?' Teresa raised her brows. 'Trouble with the police?'

'Do not ask questions.' Guido paused. 'No, no trouble with the police.'

'Then he needs a sweetheart,' Teresa said.

'Jesus and Joseph!'

'He should not be so much alone.'

'So I should take him dancing, uh? To one of these ballrooms, uh?'

'Find him a sweetheart,' Teresa said, 'or better still, a bride.'

'Sure, sure,' said Uncle Guido. 'I will order him up a bride.'

'Why should you not?' Teresa said. 'It's time he married.'

She watched her husband, wondering if her advice would strike home.

'Yes,' Guido said, after a pause. 'Maybe, for once, you are right.'

And Teresa gave a little nod, and prudently said no more.

Stuart Royce and the Roysters had held on to the contract at the Calcutta Road Palais de Danse for going on a year and a half. That in itself was a feat that bordered on the miraculous, for the Brothers Grimm – actual name Grimsdyke – were notoriously slippery when it came to paying out wages. If it hadn't been for the intervention of certain individuals like Jackie and Dennis Hallop, and the transfer of modest sums in 'management' fees, then poor old Stuart would probably have had to beg for his bread, or leave.

The Manones knew nothing of the arrangement between

the Hallops, the bandleader and the Grimsdykes, although the Manones had put up big money to get the brothers started in the first place.

Rather to Dominic's surprise, the loan, with interest, had been paid off in full within two years of the Palais opening its doors to the public. Apparently it hadn't occurred to Dominic or Uncle Guido that it was almost impossible for a ballroom to fail even in the midst of a slump and that the Brothers Grimm, whatever their other faults, sure knew how to run a dance-hall.

The Calcutta was mobbed every night of the week.

It had a late-nite opening, with offical blessing, on Fridays, when trained dancers in swirling skirts and dinner suits competed ferociously for prizes. On Wednesdays pipers and accordionists played for devotees of *teuchter* – that is, Highland – music and you could work up a sweat flinging some old granny across the floor or be put out of the game for a week if some old granny decided to turn the tables on you. Monday was tango nite, all passion and pulled muscles. Tuesdays and Thursdays saw the advent of paid partners, young men and pretty girls who languished under a code of morals stricter than the Book of Leviticus. And Saturday? Saturday was 'crush' night when every Tom, Dick and Tabby who couldn't afford to go hunting up town packed the floor, toilets, corridors and staircases and, by half past ten o'clock, when the hall was filled to capacity, even spilled out into Calcutta Street to dance on the cobbles there.

As a dancer Jackie held himself in high esteem.

He had whiled away many a dreary afternoon cruising the floor of the Palais with a paid partner or receiving lessons in deportment from the more aloof young ladies who earned their sixpences at the Albert, the Imperial or the Locarno. He knew all the latest tunes and had perfected a series of ornate steps to enliven the standard walk-through of waltz, foxtrot and quickstep, and his tango was, well, just astonishing to behold, especially if you happened to be a specialist in spinal injuries.

Even bandleader Stuart Royce thought Jackie was the bee's knees and would snap his fingers and direct the overhead spot on to the couple who swept and swung and gyrated like true champions or who, when the lights were low, did a wonderful impersonation of mobile copulation hot enough to bring the house down, or the vice squad in.

It was all Babs Conway could do to keep up with him.

Sometimes she almost wished that she had taken up with Patsy Walsh instead of daft Jackie.

Patsy did not entirely approve of dancing. He regarded it as a bourgeois pastime and a distraction from life's grim realities. He would rail against it as a waste of time even as he held Polly in his arms and tried to stop her from leading. Patsy was awkward and unsure of himself. He wouldn't have been there at all if it hadn't been for Polly, who could charm the birds out of the trees when she set her mind to it and who still felt a need to keep a close eye on Babs who was becoming just too fond of Jackie Hallop, or so Polly thought.

Babs had told her that he was very manly, her Jackie, and not just on the dance floor. Three or four times now, filled with terpsichorean energy, he had almost had her knickers off in the lane behind the Palais. He also had a habit of clapping a hand to her bottom without warning which was not, emphatically not, Babs's idea of a romantic gesture. That said, she liked him, *really* liked him, and wouldn't *really* have exchanged him for a sobersides like Patsy Walsh.

Jackie had money, Jackie had juice and, even if he was a bit too grabby now and then, Babs knew that he liked her, *really* liked her.

She was flattered to be his girlfriend. The only thing that worried her was that the Hallops were such near neighbours that Mammy was bound to find out that her dear wee daughter wasn't popping out for an ice-cream or a bag of chips three or four nights in the week or that Saturday night wasn't reserved for going to the flicks with Polly and her pals.

It didn't take long for Babs to acquire a taste for deception. She soon discovered that 'secret lives' were rendered more satisfying simply because they were secret and even Polly had to admit that hanging out with the Hallops provided relief from predictable days in the office and tedious nights at home.

Anyway, Babs said, Mammy had no right to chide them for going out with boys, not when she was ploughing full steam ahead after Mr Peabody, who not only looked as if he didn't know how to dance but who looked as if he didn't know how to blow his nose without a woman to find his hanky.

So Babs danced with her carefree, blue-suited beau and Polly danced with staid Patsy Walsh, winter deepened, Christmas approached and, however you chose to interpret it, love of some sort was definitely in the air.

Sweating like a pig, Jackie had gone off to the toilet, not, as most young men did, to partake of a hasty swig of spirits or a pull at a smuggled beer bottle, but just to mop himself with a handkerchief and comb his hair.

The band were playing 'Make Believe', up-tempo.

Babs had glided out of the pack to find a seat by the long side wall.

She was dressed in a neat little frock of rather too heavy a material that Mammy had dug out of a second-hand store and had shortened for her. She was hot and sticky. She needed to cool down. She headed for a chair beside Polly but, just as the dancers closed around her, felt a tug on her arm and was pulled out on to the floor again, not by Jackie but by little Tommy Bonnar.

His suit was brown and shabby, the same suit he wore when he did business, and the hat was not jaunty. Half an inch of cigarette dangled from the corner of his mouth.

Babs said, 'If you're gonna dance wi' me, Tommy, at least take the damned Woodbine out your mouth.'

He opened his lips, let the cigarette fall to the floor and, with odd grace, extinguished it with his heel as he turned her and glided away towards the far wall. He was hardly much bigger than Babs who, even for a girl, was not considered tall. He held her at a decent distance and was respectful enough to keep her from being trodden on in the crush.

Even so, she did not like dancing with Tommy Bonnar, did not like the smell of him, an ineradicable smell of nicotine and grease, not sharp but musty.

Babs said, loudly, 'Jackie's in the—'

'I know where Jackie is.'

'Oh!'

'I want a word wi' you in private,' Tommy told her.

'Private? Is this your idea of private?' Babs had no respect for Tommy Bonnar, though Jackie had told her she should have. 'Anyway, I haven't seen you here before. Don't you like dancin'? You're not bad for a wee guy.'

He pulled her closer, the movement abrupt.

'How'd you like t' make a hundred quid?'

'Whaaa-at?'

'One hundred fins.'

'If you think I'm that kinda ...' Babs began, then said, '*How* much?'

'You heard.' Tommy had his stubby little arm firmly around her, her breast trapped between his shoulder and armpit. He angled his face so that he could talk, and she could hear, even above the blare of the band. 'Jeeze, you've a right high opinion o' yourself if you think you're worth that much.'

'Thanks a million,' Babs said. 'What *do* I have t' do for this mysterious hundred quid, then? Rob a bank?'

'Not exactly,' Tommy Bonnar said.

'What then?'

'Where you work.'

'Where I work?'

'Aye, Central Warehouse.'

Babs laughed nervously. 'I hope you're not suggestin' I rob the Central Warehouse Company?'

'Not you,' Tommy said. 'Not nobody.'

'What the hell *is* this?' Babs said.

She had become aware of the music, of the circulation of the spotlight, its slants and sly gleams across the heads of the dancers around her. She suddenly felt that they were all looking at her.

She tried to throw her head back and laugh again but Tommy had placed a hand on her shoulder. She could feel his fingers pressing the fringe of damp hair at the nape of her neck. She wanted to shout for Jackie to come and rescue her but she'd a feeling that Jackie would not be there, that Jackie knew all about Mr Bonnar's proposal, whatever it might be.

'We need a plan o' the buildin',' Tommy said.

'I'm not Polly. I can't get you plans.'

'We need to know certain things about the CWC.'

The band were lifting 'Make Believe' to a crescendo, dancers whirling and spinning. Tommy led her away, spinning too.

As a dancer he was lighter than Jackie, more in control. He slewed her round once, then again, fast enough to take her breath away. The music climaxed and stopped. Everyone clapped, whistled, cheered. Tommy put an arm about her waist and stroked her wrist just as if he had nothing on his mind but romance.

'If you're in,' he said, 'I'll tell y' what to do when the time's right.'

'Does Jackie know? Is he – in?'

'With or without you, honey, he's in it up to his neck.'

'What if I *don't* want in?' Babs said.

'Walk away an' keep your trap shut.' Tommy lifted his hand from her wrist to her throat and traced a fine, tender, tickling little line with the ball of his thumb from her earlobe to the point of her chin. 'Because if you don't . . .'

'I get it,' Babs said. 'Okay, okay. I get it.'

'You wanna think about it?'

She glanced across the dance floor.

Jackie was back.

Daft, carefree, dance-crazy Jackie was staring at her as if he'd never seen her before. She was not inclined to wave.

She was calculating faster than she had ever done before.

She earned forty-eight bob a week. Mammy earned forty-two. Polly's wage was fixed by burgh rates at forty-six shillings. What did all that that come to? Seven quid a week, give or take, for the labour of three working women, three *honest* working women. No wonder Patsy ranted on about injustice.

'I don't have to think about it, Mr Bonnar,' Babs said.

'Meanin'?'

'Count me in.'

It grew cold in the Conways' front room in the wee small hours. The glass in the window frame creaked with frost and, come morning, would be caked with white rime inside as well as out.

There would be no long lie-in either, even though it was Sunday. There was a tub wash waiting to be done and a fortnight's ironing piled up in the basket. Before noon the kitchen would be filled with steam, the ceiling pulleys dripping with wet clothes and there would be nothing much for midday dinner except soup and bread. Later in the afternoon one of the girls would have to go and visit Gran because Mammy would be too busy, and too tired.

Babs and Polly lay side by side in bed.

Snuggled against Polly's back, Rosie snored softly.

'Did Tommy say what you'd have to do?' Polly whispered. 'I mean, they're not going to give you a hundred quid for nothing.'

'Didn't Patsy say anythin' to you about it?' Babs asked.

'Not a flamin' word,' said Polly. 'Maybe he doesn't know.'

'Oh, he knows,' said Babs. 'I could tell by the look on his face.'

Polly said nothing for a while, thinking.

It had come upon them much quicker than she had supposed, yet at the back of her mind had always been the notion that sooner or later she or her sister would be drawn back into the fold, into that circle of criminal activity from which her father had escaped only by going off to die in the war. There was something fitting – no, not fitting, inevitable – something inevitable about the Conway girls being persuaded to follow in Daddy's footsteps. In an odd way Polly was surprised that it had not happened before now.

Perhaps that was the reason she had drifted into a friendship with the Hallops and with Patsy Walsh. Perhaps that was the reason she could not dislike Patsy and that, even now, she was not repelled by the idea of being involved in what amounted to a crime.

'A hundred pounds is a great deal of money,' Polly heard herself say.

'Yeah, I know.'

Babs pressed her forearms to her breasts.

She remembered how Jackie had touched her tonight, out in the lane behind the Palais. If they hadn't been surrounded by other couples necking away like nuts then he might have gone the whole way, whether she liked it or not. She'd been so taken aback by his ardour that she hadn't had any opportunity to interrogate him about Tommy Bonnar's plan. She'd been too excited to settle for conversation. She'd wanted his mouth on hers, his tongue in her mouth. She said nothing about any of that to Polly, who would certainly disapprove.

Polly said, 'Obviously they're planning a break-in.'

'I guessed that much,' Babs said. 'If they want me to get them a plan of the Central Warehouse you don't have to be a genius to work out where.'

'Tommy Bonnar's no burglar.'

'Patsy is.'

'What's in the warehouse that's worth stealing?'

'Plenty,' said Babs. 'Wireless sets, clothing, statues, cutlery. You name it, we got it.'

'Cash?' said Polly.

'I never see the cash,' Babs said. 'I'm just an invoice clerk. But there's a whoppin' big safe in Mr MacDermott's office on the second floor. You have to ask Mrs Anderson's permission before you're allowed in there. Her desk's right outside. I've only been in once. I was scared.'

'Scared? Why?'

'Because he's the big boss.'

'No,' Polly said. 'He's not the big boss. That's what puzzles me.'

'Eh?'

'Mr Manone's the big boss. Dominic Manone owns the warehouse.'

Babs sat up. A stream of cold air infiltrated the bed. Polly grabbed at the blankets and pulled them to her, sealing in warmth.

Babs said, 'I didn't know that. How did you find out?'

'Looked it up in the company register.'

'What's that?'

'In the Burgh Hall we keep a register of company holdings, not just for the burgh, for the whole southside,' Polly said. 'When you got the job with CWC I looked it up. I mean, how do you think you got the job in the first place? There must have been fifty girls up for it, right? Dominic Manone probably used his influence. Lifted the telephone – and Bob's your uncle.'

'Why would he do that for me?'

'Because Mammy asked him to.'

'Jeeze!' said Babs. 'I really didn't know that.'

Polly drew her sister down again. Heads together on the long pillow, noses almost touching, Polly said, 'If Tommy Bonnar is setting up a break-in, what's he doing robbing the CWC? He *works* for Dominic Manone, for God's sake.

Surely he's not gonna steal from his own boss.' Polly paused. 'Is he?'

'How would I know?' Babs said. 'Maybe we should tell the boys. Maybe *they* don't know Mr Manone owns the warehouse.'

'Don't be so flamin' daft, Babs,' Polly said. 'Of course they know.'

'I suppose they must,' Babs said. 'Oh, hell! I told Tommy Bonnar to count me in. I wisht I'd known. I wisht I'd known.' She kicked her feet, making the bed shake. 'That bastard Jackie. I could cut his bloody throat, stringin' me along. I thought all he wanted was – I mean, I thought he *liked* me.'

'He does, Babs. I'm sure he does.'

'It's all right for you.'

'It isn't all right for me.' Polly sighed.

'Patsy Walsh?'

'Yes, Patsy Walsh.'

'Oooooh,' Babs said. 'Like that, is it? Serious?'

'It's not like anything yet,' said Polly. 'And I'm not sure it's ever going to become serious.'

'Because of what I just told you?'

'Because of a lot of things,' said Polly. 'I'll tell you this, Babs: if Tommy Bonnar had asked you to help him rob anywhere other than the Manones' warehouse I would have been turning him over to the police.'

'Squeal? You wouldn't do that to Jackie, would you?'

'I might. I probably would,' said Polly. 'But if they are just going to take money from a robber like Dominic Manone – well, I can't see that it's such a wicked thing to do. I imagine Patsy will consider it a justified redistribution of wealth. It's dangerous, though, very dangerous.'

Babs rolled on to her back and crossed her arms over her chest. She stared up at the ceiling, at the wedge of frosty light that cleft a gap in the curtains. 'Maybe we should tell Mammy what's goin' on.'

'We can't,' Polly said. 'She'd go crazy if she thought we

were chummy with guys like Jackie and Patsy. She'd never let us out of her sight again.'

'Yeah, yeah, you're right,' Babs said. 'So — what do we do?'

'Just hang on,' said Polly.

'To what, but?' said Babs.

'To what we've got.'

'An' what's that?'

'Not much,' Polly said. 'Look, leave it to me. I'll talk to Patsy. I'll try to find out exactly what they have in mind.'

'When?'

'Tomorrow, if I can,' said Polly.

After nightfall the couple from the Calcutta Road wouldn't have dared saunter along the old bridle path that hung above the river. It was well outside Patsy's territory and he, and Polly too, knew only too well what would happen if they were spotted by one of the kids who patrolled the borders of the beat.

Gang members would gather like jackals out of the frosty haze that hung over the Clyde; eight, ten or a dozen ill-clad, ill-kempt lads who gave themselves status by protecting their nondescript patch from intruders, as if something valuable were to be found in the dank closes and rubbish-littered streets, something worth fighting for.

On Sunday afternoons, though, on the waste ground among the canting basins and graving docks there was activity of another sort. Here gamblers met to play pitch-and-toss or cards or once in a while pit two mastiffs one against the other, to wager on which dog, weltered in blood, would survive. Gamblers had their own look-outs, their own rationale, which was more than could be said for the strutting little tyrants whose pitiless lack of motive was legendary.

Even Polly knew they'd nothing to fear from the gamblers, provided they kept their distance.

She had located Patsy without much difficulty. He had been hanging around the Black Cat Café waiting for it to open at noon.

It was his habit to pretend that he was a Frenchman, to infiltrate the churchy crowd and drink black coffee and read the Sunday newspapers, not, unfortunately, at a table on the pavement but tucked away in one of the booths at the back where he could find some peace and quiet. Why he went there every Sunday noon was a little mystery, one of many that surrounded Patsy Walsh, but Polly had the feeling that it had to do with 'business' and did not ask him to explain himself.

That particular Sunday morning, however, there was no evidence to suggest that Patsy was waiting for a tick-tack man.

He seemed pleased enough to see her.

They drank coffee and smoked cigarettes in the chilly back booth until Polly had worked up enough nerve to raise the subject of the robbery.

'Babs told you?'

'Of course she told me,' Polly said. 'She's my sister, after all.'

'What do you think?' Patsy said. 'Will she co-operate?'

'For a hundred quid,' Polly said, 'my sister will do almost anything.'

'She won't come to any harm,' Patsy promised.

'No,' Polly said. 'I imagine all you need from her is inside information. What's Tommy Bonnar got to do with it, though?'

'It's his tickle.'

'Robbing the Manones is Tommy's idea of a tickle?'

Patsy shrugged. 'It's there for the takin',' he said. 'I've got no scruples about robbin' the Manones. They're just capitalists, black-hearted capitalists like everybody else in this lousy world.'

'Except the workers,' Polly said.

'Yeah.' Patsy had the decency to grin. 'Except the workers. You wanna take a walk, Polly?'

'What? Now?'

'No time like the present.'

'I should be at home helping out with the washing.'

'How excitin'!' Patsy said. 'I repeat, you wanna take a walk?'

'Where?'

'Down by the river.'

When she looked at him she felt a strange guilty thrill transmit itself through her. He wasn't handsome, not conventionally handsome, but he was rugged in his own individual way. More important, he was intelligent, well educated and well travelled. He cared about things that mattered, things other than money and motorcycles, betting and booze. He was so different from most of the other men she had met that she felt oddly privileged to be his companion.

'How long will it take?' she asked.

'Couple of hours.'

'All right,' Polly said. 'Let's go.'

She was hardly dressed for hiking and felt conspicuous in the empty wasteland behind the graving docks, even more so on the stretch of bridle path that perched over the river.

Unselfconsciously, she held on to Patsy's hand.

Patsy was dressed in a tweed jacket, collared shirt and chewed-up tie that gave him an air of near respectability. He carried no weapons. He knew that if they were caught on the bridle path by one of the young gangs there would be no way to avoid trouble except by plunging into the Clyde.

He didn't anticipate trouble this early in the afternoon. While respectable members of society trailed off to Sunday School or Bible Class or assembled for one sort of parade or another, most hooligans would be sleeping off hangovers or mooching about in front of the shuttered pubs or, if boredom had really taken hold, padding over to the park to kick a ball about or, better still, one of the drunken old down-and-outs who hadn't had the sense to scarper.

It wasn't where he'd have chosen to bring Polly Conway. It wasn't the Tuileries or the Tiergarten or any of the places that he dreamed of taking her and might take her one day, one day soon. But there were compensations: the vague, slightly uncomfortable excitement of sharing his work with her, knowing that beneath her almost middle-class restraint she was still enough of her father's daughter to understand, if not condone, what he was doing here and why he had brought her along.

'Is that it?' Polly said.

'That's it,' Patsy answered.

'Have you ever been inside?'

'Nope.'

'Thought you had been, dumping off stuff?'

'*Non permesso*,' Patsy said. '*Impedire.*'

'What does that mean?'

'Not allowed. Taboo. Entry forbidden to guys like me.' Patsy shrugged. 'I don't blame the Eye-tie, actually. The warehouse is part of a strictly legitimate business. Wouldn't look right for somebody with my reputation to go lollopin' in the front door with an armful of stolen goods, now would it?'

'How does Mr Manone shift the hot stuff?'

'No idea,' Patsy said. 'I collect my rake, that's all that concerns me.'

'You could collect more than your rake from this one,' Polly said. 'You all could, if you steal money from the Manones.'

'That's for Tommy to worry about.'

'That's what bothers me,' Polly said. 'Why is Tommy Bonnar setting up his boss's warehouse?'

'He needs fast cash,' Patsy told her. 'Tommy's up to his neck in debt to Chick McGuire, a guy who won't take no for an answer. McGuire's not one of Manone's bookies so Tommy can't go cryin' to Dominic to get him off the hook.'

'Couldn't he take out a loan?' Polly suggested.

'Maybe he has,' Patsy said. 'I don't reckon he'd have the gall to ask Manone, though. Old Guido would be furious if

94

he thought Tommy'd been placin' bets with the opposition. I mean, hell, we all know what Chick thinks of the Manones. There's been trouble before.'

'Even so,' Polly said. 'Surely Tommy's taking a big risk. How can he be sure that you won't tell Manone?'

'If anyone does, Tommy'll just deny it,' Patsy said.

'How about after the event?' Polly said.

'After?' said Patsy, as if he preferred not to dwell on consequences. 'Well, I mean, afterwards we'll have so much dough it isn't gonna matter.'

'What will you do with the money?' Polly said.

'Stash it away for a while, a long while,' Patsy said.

'And then?'

'Travel.'

'I'd love to travel,' Polly said. 'I'd love to see Paris.'

Patsy did not rise to the bait. She had lost his attention. He was focused now on other things, had, Polly realised, already begun work.

They had reached an elbow where the narrow path angled sharply away from the river and became a lane between the walls of Gerber's clothing factory and the Manones' warehouse. The warehouse stuck out ahead, a windowless gable blocked to a frontage that plunged straight down to the river.

The building had been erected on the site of a derelict cotton warehouse only twenty years ago. It had none of the quasi-Georgian or Gothic pretensions of other constructions that had been built before the Great War but was fashioned from plain-cut stone and red brick, more of the latter than the former. Delivery yard and reception area, tucked securely away behind black iron railings, faced out on to Jackson Street.

Patsy told her that he'd already reconnoitred the back of the building and had decided that while he might be man enough he certainly wasn't mad enough to try to effect an entry in sight of a busy public road.

As yet he had no idea what Bonnar wanted him to steal.

He just hoped it wasn't half a dozen pianos or a selection of three-piece suites. He figured it would be money, though, cash out of a safe, the exact location of which Polly's sister would be able to pinpoint without too much trouble.

'I didn't realise the building was so big.' Polly tilted her head. 'It makes you dizzy just looking up at it.' She glanced at him. 'What about the front?'

'This is the front,' said Patsy. 'I could probably get inside from Jackson Street but I'd be lucky to get out again. The night-watchmen are stationed there. An' if I can't pull the tickle without stovin' some poor bastard's head in then I'm not pullin' the tickle at all.'

'What if it's the only way?' Polly enquired.

'It's never the only way,' Patsy told her.

They walked back towards the river, to the point where the dirt path broke from the long blank windowless wall.

There was just enough clearance for Patsy to step out on to the wall and hold himself against it, straddling the corner of the building. He looked at the brickwork above, and down at the river that lapped and gurgled below his heels.

Then he laughed.

He stepped back and lowered himself to the pathway again.

'Drainpipes, ventilation cowls, open windows. Dear God, I could lead an army battalion in there an' out again.' He shook his head in amusement. 'If the safe's where I think it is, upstairs, then there shouldn't be any problem. Once your sister tells us exactly what office the safe's in and what kind of safe it is then we can push ahead as soon as Tommy gives us the tick-tack.'

'You're kidding,' Polly said. 'Is it going to be that easy?'

'Nope,' Patsy said. 'It's gonna be damned difficult. But basically all I need to do the job is some inside information – an' a boat.'

'A boat? What sort of a boat?' said Polly.

'Any sort of a boat,' said Patsy, 'just so long as it floats.'

'And presumably has sufficient capacity to hold a safe?'

'You've got it in one, Polly.'

'In and out by the river. Perfect!' Polly said.

In spite of her apprehension at the idea of being involved – however indirectly – in the commission of a crime, the daring and ingenuity of it appealed to her and washed away her immediate doubts.

She leaned against him and kissed him on the mouth. 'What a clever lad you are, Patrick Walsh.'

'Ain't I, though?' said Patsy and, taking her hand again, led her hastily along the bridle path, back the way they had come.

Chapter Six

There had never been any love lost been Thomas Bonnar and Alexander O'Hara. As young men they had fought on the midden-heads of Cumberland Street and across the high backs of the Calcutta Road.

The scar on Alex's cheekbone had been implanted by Tommy's knuckle-ring during a vicious bout of fisticuffs outside Brady's pub. Tommy, in turn, bore on his left buttock the purple wound of a knife attack that had been intended to emasculate him, which may have been no bad thing, given the shady state of his relations with his sister. The pair had only agreed to bury the hatchet when Guido Manone had offered them a financial inducement to do so.

God knows, Tommy had needed income so badly at the time that he would have licked O'Hara's boots if it had been required of him. He'd had an evil run with the bookies and owed money all over town. He was also supporting his sister, with whom he resided, and six of her eight living children, the other two having been farmed out. How many, if any, of the children were actually Tommy's was a moot point. Maggie Bonnar had never picked up a proper husband and had been so careless with her favours over the years that half the men on the Calcutta Road might have fathered them.

The view of most members of the Rowing Club was that

Maggie was lucky to have Tommy to depend on now that her looks had gone. She'd never been much of a looker in the first place and if Tommy had taken a small share of what was so freely offered then who the heck could blame him, since that sort of thing went on willy-nilly behind closed doors all the time. Besides, Maggie's poor wee ragamuffins were confused enough without being told that Uncle might be Daddy and their sisters also their cousins.

If Maggie had been a mare and her offspring colts, no doubt Tommy would have taken a keener interest in their lineage.

As it was he made no distinction between the children. He treated them all with a vague, distracted affection that bordered on indifference and, when flush, would give each of them a tanner to spend on sweets, pat each of them on the head, and go back to studying his *Sporting Pink* as if the children who crawled about his chair had no more individuality than kittens or pups. He treated Maggie much the same way, as if she were a skivvy or a landlady, not a sister or a lover or a wife.

Mostly, Tommy was not at home. He spent more time on the streets than the average pigeon. He was constantly on the trot, darting about the back courts and closes in search of runners to carry his bets or, after a good pay-day, taking himself off to a race meeting at Ayr or Lanark or into the stand at Ibrox Park to watch Glasgow Rangers win – or sometimes lose – his money for him. Then he would be off again, strutting the streets with that odd, pouter-pigeon gait of his, chest leading and feet following on, in search of drink or company in one of the pubs on the Copland Road or down at the Rowing Club in Molliston Street.

The Rowing Club was gloomy but comfortable, offering warm fires on cold days and cold beer when it was hot outside. It had a billiards table, a wireless set and a 'tap' wire, whose mechanism Tommy didn't quite understand, that brought news of results from all over the country in spite of the Manones' edicts, which Tony Lombard enforced, that no gambling took place on the premises and that no known bookmaker or bookmaker's runner be granted a membership. Gambling did go on, of course, but a modest flutter on a billiards match now and then wasn't going to have the coppers kicking down the door.

If it hadn't been for Alex O'Hara, Tommy would have spent more time at the Rowing Club. O'Hara practically lived in Molliston Street.

No matter what time of day or night Tommy slipped into the club O'Hara would be propped against the bar or lounging in the so-called coffee shop or stretched across the baize with cue in hand and a pint pot never very far away. He would smirk at Tommy and say something sarcastic, the sort of scathing remark that in the old days would have had Tommy reaching for his knife.

'Hey there, loser, still backin' three-legged cuddies?' was one of O'Hara's more imaginative greetings; or, 'See they lost again. Couldn't find a piss-pot if they was sittin' on it, Rangers.'

Tommy would bristle, would compress his lips on the wet inch of his cigarette, his jaw muscles aching with the effort of squeezing out a smile.

He would say, meekly, 'Aye, aye, Alex, they lost again,' while striving to bear in mind that if he stuck a blade in O'Hara at the bar of the Rowing Club he would be cutting off his one sure source of income, never mind what the coppers might have to say about it.

O'Hara was no less ruthless than Tommy when it came to extracting money, or blood, from petty creditors. But O'Hara had a better network of lookouts. He seemed to know everything that was going on south of the river, including how much he, Tommy, had lost that week and how much he was in hock to the three or four street bookies whom the Manones financed. So – simply to avoid being teased by Alex O'Hara – Tommy had fallen into the habit of backing his fancy with Chick McGuire instead.

McGuire was a rival of the Manones and Tommy doubted if O'Hara, for all his cunning, could possibly have an ear inside McGuire's office, so he was safe from insults, from injury to his pride, if not from the danger of piling up debt with someone whom the Manones did not, and could not, control.

It was unreasonable and illogical – nuts, in other words – for Tommy Bonnar to blame O'Hara, and via O'Hara the Manones, for the predicament in which he found himself at the beginning of the Christmas month. Tommy had never been over-endowed with brains, however, or with the insight required to acknowledge that most of the aggravation that had descended upon him in the course of his thirty-two years on earth had been of his own making.

How could he be blamed for the failure of three-legged cuddies to win races, for goalkeepers with soapy fingers, for the assaults that had landed him twice behind bars, for letting Maggie climb into bed with him when she was too drunk to know who he was? He wasn't to blame for *anything*; not even for running up a heap of debts with Chick McGuire before the roof fell in and Chick told him to cough up or prepare himself to greet the New Year from under a slab in the Southern Necropolis.

Therefore he could hardly be blamed for listening to the whisper, the tempting rumour, that the Manones would pay out their Christmas bonuses on Thursday December 20th; that on the afternoon of Wednesday 19th an unmarked van would be sent to the Paisley branch of the Bank of Scotland and be loaded with cash which – so Mr McGuire had heard – would be stored overnight in the safe in Central Warehouse in Jackson Street.

Now there was a thing, wasn't it? Mr McGuire had remarked quite casually. Rich pickings for anyone willing to set it up, for anyone so desperately strapped for cash that he didn't care if it *was* the Manones he was robbing.

How much would be in the safe was the question that

Tommy Bonnar had been about to ask but didn't have to, for it seemed that Mr McGuire had read his mind.

'Eight or ten grand, I reckon,' Mr McGuire had said, still very casually, 'given the number of staff the Manones employ. Just imagine, eight or ten grand lying there for the taking. Pity you work for the Eye-ties, Tom, isn't it?'

'Why don't you . . .'

'Not my scene, old son. Not my game, burglary.'

'Ten grand ain't just gonna be lyin' there waitin' for somebody to take it, though, say what you like.'

'Sure an' it is. Who'd dare knock off the Manones?'

'Somebody who's right off his head,' Tommy had said.

'Or someone,' Mr McGuire had reminded him, 'with nothing to lose.'

'I still think Tommy's off his bloody head,' Jackie said, with a grin. 'But if he's talkin' big money like that I don't care who we rob. Anyhow, the boat's a great idea. Nobody'll be bothered with the back o' the buildin' an' Patsy's sure he can get in up that back − front − wall.'

'Where do we get a boat, but?' said Dennis.

'We could build one.'

'Talk sense, Jackie. What do we know about buildin' boats?'

'Can't be that difficult.'

'Oh, but it can,' said Dennis. 'It's got to float for a start.'

'All boats float,' said Jackie.

'Only because they're buoyant.'

'Buoyant? What's that?'

'We'll steal one,' said Dennis.

'Where from?' said Jackie.

'There must be plenty o' them lyin' about the river.'

'Sure, tugs, yachts an' ocean liners,' said Jackie. 'We need one wi' oars.'

'Or a petrol engine,' said Dennis.

'Too noisy. We need a rowin' boat, a big one. Big enough for four.'

'Four?'

'You, me, Patsy an' Tommy.'

'Tommy? Is he comin'?'

'It's his show.'

'I thought he was just the brains.'

'If Tommy ain't there,' said Jackie, 'I'm not goin'. I want that wee squirt right where I can see him.'

'Tommy's all right.'

'Well, Tommy can be all right sittin' in the boat with us. If we get caught, he gets caught,' Jackie said. 'That simple.'

'We're not gonna get caught, but,' Dennis said. 'Are we?'

'Not if we get the right sorta boat. We'll need a lot of strong rope too, to tie the boat up while Patsy's inside. Rope or an anchor.'

'Anchors are heavy.'

'I know anchors are heavy, that's why I'm sayin' rope,' said Jackie. 'I'll take a walk round tomorrow an' see what I can see. I mean, if there's anythin' in the way of a rowin' boat that we can pinch.'

'How are we gonna get it from where it's at to the warehouse?'

'Dennis, Dennis, Dennis.' Jackie gave the side of his brother's head a gentle slap. 'Use your loaf.'

'How?'

'On the back of a lorry, of course.'

'Then what are you gonna do with it, for Christ's sake?' said Patsy Walsh. 'Park it in the close? Hide it under the bed?'

'I thought we could stash it in the yard,' said Jackie.

'How do you propose gettin' it to the yard,' said Patsy, 'an' from the yard to the river again?'

'On a lorry.'

'On a lorry? Right. Where do we get a lorry?'

'Borrow one from Georgie, like we usually do when we need a lorry.'

'Georgie Newton?'

'That's the man,' said Jackie.

'The same Georgie Newton who operates the Belville Garage an' services the Manones' motorcars?'

'Yeah. He's ... Oh, aye, I see what you mean,' said Jackie.

Patsy sighed. 'Look, I know where there's a boat. It's tied up by the steps at the back end of Hunter's Dock. Been there for years. Nobody ever uses it, far as I can make out. It's kept in case somebody falls into the dock, or somethin'. Regulations, I expect. I've been down, had a squint at it. It's big enough. What we do is, on the night in question, we climb into the dock, untie the boat an' take it downriver. I don't suppose you thought to check the tide tables?'

'What tide tables?'

'God, you must be the only guy on the Clyde who doesn't know what a tide table is.' Patsy's patience was wearing thin. Gritting his teeth, he went on, 'We need to catch the ebb, Jackie, otherwise it'll take us half the night to haul the boat downriver. High tide's at ten twenty-two. If we leave the dock at eleven that'll be about right. Close as I can calculate, it'll take us about a quarter of an hour to get down to the warehouse. We'll need rope, lots of it ...'

'Thought o' that,' said Jackie. 'Rope.'

'How about a grappling hook?' Patsy said. 'You think of that too?'

'A what?'

'A grappling hook,' said Patsy, 'for holdin' the boat steady while we're inside the warehouse.'

'No, I ...'

'There's one on the dockside, racked next to the boat.'

'Oh,' said Jackie, 'good.'

'There's a wee bit of bank just under the warehouse wall. It's steep and narrow but there should be just enough room to put one of you ashore to hold the bow rope.'

'Dennis can do that.'

'Fine,' said Patsy. 'Thank God, Tommy knows how to row.'

'So Tommy will be there, will he?'

'Sure an' he will,' said Patsy. 'It's his show.'

'What else do you need?'

'A lot,' said Patsy. 'I need the girl . . .'

'Babs?'

'Yeah, Polly's sister. I need her to find out exactly where the safe is an' what kind of safe it is.'

'The name of the safe,' said Jackie. 'Right.'

'We also need to be sure, absolutely, definitely sure that the big money's gonna be in the safe that night.'

'Tommy says—'

'Tommy says a lot o' things,' said Patsy. 'I don't want to get inside that warehouse, then inside that safe an' discover there's nothin' there but two mutton pies an' a tin o' condensed milk.'

'Okay, okay. We'll get Babs to keep her eyes peeled an' tell us when the money's arrived safe an' sound in the warehouse.'

'I'll talk to her,' Patsy said.

'I'll do it,' said Jackie. 'She's my doll. She'll do what I tell her.'

'Talk to her soon,' said Patsy. 'We've only got six days.'

'Definitely gonna be Wednesday then?' said Jackie.

'Yeah,' Patsy said.

'I'll talk to her tonight.'

'Oh, it's you, is it?' Babs said. 'What're you doin' here? You can't come in.'

'Your mammy's out. I saw her leavin'.'

'Yeah, but my sisters are still here.'

'Come out for a minute, just a minute then.'

'It's freezin' out there.'

'Gotta talk to you, Babs. It's important.'

'All right then – but just for a minute.'

She stepped quickly out of the house and followed Jackie down three flights of stairs into the back close.

She shivered in the night air. Her breath hung cloudy in the freezing dankness. She hated the courts at the back of the tenement at the best of times. Only when absolutely unavoidable would she take her turn at carrying ashes out to the midden or blankets to the wash-house. There were rats lurking out there amid the litter, cats that would claw your leg off if you so much as looked at them, and furtive little gangs of boys and young girls playing the sort of games that even she'd never been tempted to play when she was that age.

'I'm freezin',' she said again.

'Here, I'll warm you up.'

Jackie reached for her but she sidled away.

'What's eatin' you, sweetheart?' Jackie said.

'I'm not in the mood, that's all.'

'I've been waitin' for you to show up at the yard,' Jackie said. 'I thought you'd have been up to see us before now.'

'For what?'

'For – you know.'

Babs wrapped her arms over her breasts and squeezed with her elbows, not out of fear – not really – but to hold in what little warmth remained in her body. She wore only a skirt, blouse and cardigan, and couldn't understand why Jackie, in shirt-sleeves, showed no sign of feeling the cold. She half wished that he would insist on putting his arms about her, on kissing her against her will, would give her a sign that she meant more to him than a mere helper in whatever game he and Patsy and Tommy Bonnar were playing.

She said, 'I'm not sure I want to get involved after all.'

'*What*?' Jackie snapped and pinned her to the cold, sweating wall, fists against her shoulders. 'Jee-zus, Babs, you can't back out now. We're dependin' on you. I mean, you gave Tommy your word, you promised.'

'I did nothin' of the kind.'

'What's *wrong* with you? All you've gotta do—'

'I know what I've gotta do,' said Babs.

She pushed against him, thought of raising her knee and letting him have it where it would hurt most. But she wouldn't do that, not to Jackie. She knew that he was right and she was wrong. If she hadn't become so excited by the hundred pounds that Tommy Bonnar had offered, if she'd been thinking more clearly . . . it was too late to back out now. She *had* given her word, sort of, and had been avoiding Jackie only to make him come to her.

'Yeah, an' you know what Tommy Bonnar'll do if you let us down.'

'Carve me,' Babs said.

'Or Polly,' Jackie said. 'Or the other one, the deaf one.'

He let her go, put his hands in his pockets, hunched his shoulders and executed a few – not jolly – little steps before he spoke again.

'You didn't *have* to say yes, you know,' he reminded her.

'Well, with you in, an' Patsy – I didn't wanna let you all down.'

'So you'll do it?' Jackie said.

She could see his face in the flicker of the gas lamp that shed a broken and reluctant light into the recesses of the close. He stepped nervously in and out of the shadows, not dancing now but shuffling. He was as cold as she was, she realised, and just as apprehensive. She had expected him to do exactly what he had done, watch for Mammy leaving for Gran McKerlie's then come creeping upstairs. He hadn't been able to leave her alone after all.

She smiled, showing her teeth.

'Stop wettin' yourself, Jackie,' she said. 'I've done it.'

'Done what?'

'What you wanted me to do. Got all the stuff Patsy needs.'

He stopped moving, stared at her. 'You're kiddin'.'

'I'm not,' she said.

He leaned into the light, staring at her, still too uncertain to show relief.

'The safe's on the second floor, right at the back. It's in the fifth office along from the end of the corridor. Five windows along from the end of the buildin'. You listenin', Jackie?'

'I'm listenin'.'

'It wasn't easy gettin' myself in there.'

'How'd you do it?'

'Pretended I'd lost an invoice,' Babs said. 'I got Mrs Anderson to take me into Mr MacDermott's office to look for it. I knew we wouldn't find it 'cause I'd torn it up already an' flushed it down the toilet.'

'Clever girl,' said Jackie.

'The safe's against the left wall, lookin' in from the door to the window. The window's hardly ever open 'cause of the cold weather.'

'Can you open the window from the inside next Wednesday afternoon?'

'No. No chance. Just can't be done.'

'Okay. What about the safe?'

'Looks new. It's big, up to my chest. It's got a sort of medallion thing, like a shield, where the keys go on.'

'Who keeps the keys?'

'Don't know. Probably Mr MacDermott.'

'Maker's name?' said Jackie. 'For the safe, I mean.'

'Hobbs an' Company.'

'You sure?'

'I *can* read, Jackie.'

'This woman didn't see you examinin' the safe, did she?'

'Nope. She didn't much like me bein' there at all, though. Doesn't like the girls from the first-floor countin' office. Thinks we're all tarts. She had me in an' out of her precious Mr MacDermott's office in no time flat. Snotty bitch.'

'There's one more thing we need,' said Jackie.

'I thought I'd done my bit.'

'On Wednesday afternoon,' said Jackie, 'somebody'll be sent to the bank to collect the packet of money.'

'Mr MacDermott and Mr Grant usually do that. I mean, collect the wages. Mr Manone, the old one, takes them in his car sometimes.'

'How do they get to the bank if old Guido ain't around?'

'I'm not sure,' said Babs. 'Maybe they go in one o' the vans.'

'On Wednesday can you find out if the bonus money has arrived?'

Babs shook her head. 'I can't guarantee to be at the window or anythin'. I've got work to do, Jackie. I mean, I'm kept hard at it, at the desk.'

'Aye, right,' said Jackie, without scepticism. 'If you do, though ...'

'I'll get word to you.'

'Right.'

He kissed her, rather perfunctorily, and hurried back into his house, leaving Babs to find her own way upstairs.

Rosie knelt by the niche bed as if saying prayers. She had a book open before her and a paper bag filled with broken toffee. She read, chewed, and hummed a tuneless tune to herself, quite oblivious to what was going on in the room behind her. Polly sat in the armchair, her feet on the fender, toasting her calves and thighs. She was smoking a cigarette with considerable concentration. She blew a plume of smoke, made a little signal to Babs and got up and trailed her into the bedroom, leaving Rosie alone in the kitchen.

'What did *he* want?' Polly whispered, urgently.

'It's Wednesday. They're goin' after the bonus money.'

'Did you tell him what he needed to know?'

'Yeah. You don't mind, do you?'

'Mind? Of course, I mind. I don't approve of theft,' Polly said. 'On the other hand they're going to do it anyway so I suppose there's no harm in helping them do it properly. Especially if it's the Manones who'll suffer. To tell you the truth I wouldn't mind being there myself.'

'What'll I do with all that lovely dough, Polly?'

'Put it away for a long, long time,' Polly said. 'That's what Patsy and the boys intend to do with it.'

'Ah, come on. I wanna spend it.'

'Hide it,' said Polly again. 'Because if the Manones ever find out . . .'

'How can they possibly find out? I mean, what did I do anyway? I won't be robbin' their bloody safe, will I?'

'No,' Polly said. 'But you'll know who did.'

'So will you.'

'That's true,' Polly conceded.

'They'll be insured, the Manones,' said Babs.

'I wouldn't count on it,' said Polly.

'You mean they'll come huntin' for their money?'

'For sure,' Polly said. 'Oh, yes, for absolutely sure.'

'In that case, I'll hide it. I'll hide it under our bed.'

'Are you nuts?' said Polly. 'What if Mammy finds it? You can't hide it anywhere in our house.'

'We could bury it in the back green.'

'Don't be ridiculous, Babs.'

'Where then?' said Babs.

Polly seated herself on the end of the bed. She put the last inch of the Woodbine to her lips and sipped smoke, then, leaning away from her sister, stabbed the remains of the cigarette into a tin ashtray on the bedside table.

She rested on her elbows for a moment, staring thoughtfully

at the wall, then, rolling over, said, 'We could hide it in Gran McKerlie's. Nobody will ever go poking about in that dump.'

'What if Gran finds it,' said Babs, 'or Auntie Janet?'

'Don't think there's much chance,' Polly said, 'not if we hide it properly.'

'Like where?'

'Under the floorboards would probably be the best place.'

'In the kitchen?'

'In the hall cupboard,' said Polly. 'I'll make a point of checking it out on Sunday mornin' when Aunt Janet's at church.'

'Yeah,' Babs said. 'Not a bad idea, not bad at all.'

'Another sausage, Mr Peabody?' Lizzie was already standing at his elbow with the pan in her hand. 'It'll only go to waste.'

'What about yourself, Mrs Conway?'

'Oh, I've had all I require, thank you.'

'Well then, I don't mind if I do.'

He watched her plump hand exercise the fork. A sizzling pork sausage slipped neatly on to his plate. The supper invitation had not only been welcome but expected. In fact, he'd have been disappointed if Mrs Conway hadn't had the table set and the pan on the stove.

He was also pleased that Lizzie was wearing the same frock she'd worn last Friday. Somehow he'd already grown used to it. He'd thought about her in it many times in the course of the week, of Lizzie Conway's cosy kitchen, her kindness, her warmth, a warmth that had become part of a more generalised warmth that had affected him too. The office juniors had remarked upon the change in him, albeit sarcastically. Even his mother had noticed it and, as she'd put on her hat to trot out to the Women's Guild, had told him that he'd better mend his ways or face up to the consequences – whatever *that* meant.

Bernard had been smiling all week; he was smiling now.

He felt at ease, more so as the girls weren't around.

Obviously Lizzie had snaffled him for herself. He was not displeased by the development. Indeed, he had come prepared for it.

Nestling in his jacket pocket was a little box of sweets, six dark chocolates whorled into crests, each crest topped by a tiny red rosebud. The box itself looked as if it were made of real gold leaf and was tied with a piece of silk ribbon. The gift was small enough to indicate gratitude without being effusive, and expensive enough to please a woman who did not appear to enjoy too many of life's little luxuries.

He was eager to present it to her; or, he wondered, might it be better to lay it discreetly by the side of the plate for her to find when she cleared the table after he'd gone? He pondered his tactics while he chewed the sausage and mopped up egg yolk with a square of toast.

'How's your mother these days?'

The question caught Bernard off guard.

'My mother? Oh, she's – she keeps herself busy.'

'Lookin' after you?' Lizzie said.

'Well – well, yes.' He hesitated. 'She does other things too, of course.'

'Such as?' said Lizzie.

'Women's Guild.' He shrugged. 'Eastern Star, that sort of thing.'

Bernard was tempted to expound on the theme, to list all the groups and organisations to which his mother belonged and to explain that in fact he saw very little of her and suspected that her devotion to her friends and colleagues far outstripped her devotion to him. To be fair the council cottage in Knightswood was never anything but spotless and there were always clean shirts and whole socks in his drawer. Even so, he could not help but feel that he was allocated quite a lowly place in his mother's schedule of priorities.

Most nights he would find his dinner in the oven and a note in his mother's beautiful copperplate handwriting propped against the vase on the mantelpiece telling him how to turn up the gas and where she had gone and when he might expect her back. Indeed, at times it was like sharing the cottage with a ghost, the sort of restless entity that you only really saw out of the corner of your eye as it whisked away.

He bit back criticism, however, stifled his resentment and managed a loyal smile by way of defence.

Lizzie said, 'She must enjoy the company.'

'Yes, I expect she does,' said Bernard.

'It'll keep her from thinkin' about the boys.'

'Boys?' said Bernard.

'Your brothers, from broodin' about your brothers.'

'Oh!' Bernard said. 'I hadn't thought of that.'

It was true. Until that moment it just hadn't occurred to him that his mother's brisk and bustling behaviour had anything to do with Peter and Charlie or that she might be motivated by the inexpressible pain of having lost her favourite sons. He'd always imagined that he was the only one who still missed them. Mum never talked about them. She kept no photographs, no letters or postcards, nothing on display to remind her of them, or of the war.

Even his, Bernard's, medal had been hidden away in a drawer.

He squinted across the table at Lizzie Conway.

Her perspicacity made him uncomfortable. What she'd just said might very well be the truth, though; or was it just a charitable excuse for his mother's egotistical need to be the centre of attention? He'd have to think about that one.

Meanwhile, Lizzie emanated gentle and soothing sympathy.

Bernard cleared his throat. 'How did – I mean, how did *you* cope?'

'As best I could,' Lizzie answered. 'I'd three bairns to look after so I never had much time for grievin'. Anyway, there's a fair old difference between losin' two sons an' losin' one husband, especially a husband like mine.'

'He wasn't . . .' Bernard didn't know how to put it.

'No,' Lizzie said. 'No, he wasn't.'

'Is that why you were never tempted to – eh – to try again?'

'Marry again?'

'Aye. Yes,' said Bernard.

'I never married again because nobody ever asked me.'

'What?' Bernard said. 'I find that hard to believe.'

'True, though,' said Lizzie.

'Amazin',' Bernard said. 'Just amazin'.'

'What is?' said Lizzie. 'That nobody ever considered I'd make a worthwhile wife? No, no, there are too many single girls floatin' about for anyone to fancy a dowdy old hen like me.'

'You do yourself an injustice, Mrs Conway.'

'I think,' said Lizzie, 'you'd better call me Lizzie – especially if you're goin' to keep butterin' me up.'

'I didn't mean to offend you.'

'You can offend me like that any time,' Lizzie said, smiling. 'I haven't been paid such a nice compliment in many a long day.'

'Well,' Bernard said; he paused. 'You deserve it.'

'You're only able to say that because you don't know me very well.'

'Well enough, Mrs Conway.'

'Lizzie.'

'Lizzie, I pride myself on my judgement of character. In my profession, you don't get far without bein' a good judge of character.'

'Stop, please.' She laughed. 'You're makin' me blush.'

'I'm sorry.'

'I'm no retirin' violet, Bernard. Don't think that,' Lizzie told him. 'I don't sit around feelin' sorry for myself. The plain fact o' the matter is, I've got three daughters. No man in his right senses would take on that burden.'

'A nice family,' Bernard said, without thinking.

'Pardon.'

'I mean – eh – you seem to have brought them up very well.'

'I've done about all I can for them, all except Rosie. No doubt, within the next year or two, they'll find husbands of their own, an' fly the nest.'

'Is that not as it should be?' Bernard ventured.

'Aye, it is,' Lizzie agreed. 'But . . .'

'What'll you do then?'

'Well, one thing's for sure,' said Lizzie, ruefully, 'no man's goin' to rush to take me on now, not as a wife – or anythin' else.'

Bernard chose to ignore the implications of the last part of her statement. 'Why not?' he said. 'I mean, what's wrong with you, Mrs Conway?'

'Lizzie.'

'Lizzie. I mean, what's to *stop* you gettin' married again?'

'Look at me. I'm old—'

'You're not much older than I am,' Bernard interrupted, 'an' I certainly don't think of myself as old.'

'Different for men,' said Lizzie. 'Anyway, you're not fat.'

'Neither are you,' Bernard blurted out. 'You're' – he spread his hands helplessly as it dawned upon him just how daring the conversation had become – 'very attractive.'

'Thank you, kind sir,' said Lizzie, with a little bow, then, as if realising that she had made enough headway for one evening, pushed herself to her feet. 'Come along, there's someone I'd like you to meet.'

'Who?' he said, slightly alarmed.

'My daughter, Rosie.'

'Where is she?'

'Ben the house.'

'Oh!' Bernard said, thinking, Bedroom, bedroom: 'Oh. Yes. Fine.'

✳   ✳   ✳

As a rent-collector Bernard had seen more than his fair share of folk in bed. Everything from skinny wee babies wriggling naked and mewling to able-bodied men lolling against the bolsters with a ham roll in one hand and a bottle of brown ale in the other while their wives tried to convince him, Bernard, that the breadwinner had been struck down by a mysterious malady and that she just couldn't seem to find the rent this week.

He had encountered young mothers with milky breasts suckling their infants, elderly women carelessly displaying acres of veined flesh as they scrambled in search of his payment. Lads in the last desperate throes of TB. Lassies flushed and rasping with scarlet fever or quinsy throat. Even a fair number of what Bernard could only describe as tarts, girls who hoped that he might be tempted by their grubby sheets and bring a little cut-price trade their way – which, of course, he never did.

As far as Bernard was concerned all of this and more – much more if you included lodgers – was simply part and parcel of life in an overcrowded Gorbals tenement. But it was different in Lizzie Conway's house.

Ever since the landing door had been changed from dun to chocolate brown, ever since he'd first been confronted by the lady-lamp in the lobby, treated to a leg show by her daughter, Babs, heard soft music and smelled the perfumes that drifted from the bedroom, he'd been charged with curiosity as to what lay in the room to the front of the house.

He squeezed after the woman, past a monumental wardrobe.

He saw a large neatly made bed in the alcove to his right, a small chest of drawers, a gas fire, a chair, a lamp, a wireless set on a stand by the window. And he almost tripped over a gramophone on the worn strip of rug that marked the centre of the room.

The girl was on all fours by the gas fire, the light ruddy on her cheek. She wore a pleated grey skirt and had a cardigan thrown over her blouse but, in spite of the chill atmosphere, she was barefoot and bare-legged. A book was open on the floor in front of her. Her hair spilled across her face and she played with it, twisting it in her fingers, quite oblivious to the intrusion.

Lizzie said, quietly, 'Our Rosie's deaf. She can hear a wee bit but not much. She can read your lips, though, if you face her square, an' she can speak nearly as well as you an' me.'

The faint tingle of expectation that had been in Bernard vanished instantly. Even bare legs, the glimpse of a thigh as the girl stirred, did nothing to restore it. He experienced a terrible wave of pity, not just for the poor, deaf lass crouched like an animal on the floor but for Lizzie Conway too, for this burden that he hadn't known about.

'Rosie,' Lizzie shouted loudly. 'Rosie, you've a visitor.'

The girl frowned. She moved one hand and then the other, turning the way a cat would turn, padding round. She was neither surprised nor alarmed, not even wary, and was smiling even before Bernard leaned forward and mouthed at her, 'Hello, and what is your name?'

He had an almost invincible urge to stroke her as if she were indeed a cat.

She stared into his face. The intensity of her gaze set him back on his heels. Lizzie was directly behind him, peeping over his shoulder. He staggered, felt the woman's bracing hand on his back, righted himself and bent down again.

'My name is Bernard Peabody. I am . . .'

The girl sprang to her feet with all the grace of an acrobat.

She held out her hand. 'I am very pleased to meet you, Mr Peabody,' she said, in a flat, distinct voice. 'You're our rent-collector?'

'Bernard's also our friend, Rosie,' Lizzie said. 'Isn't that right, Bernard?'

'Yes, that's right. I – I am your friend.'

'Mammy has told me all about you,' the girl said. 'She is always talking about you. I am glad to get to meet you at last.

Maybe now I will not have to stay in the back room when you come.'

'What?' Bernard said.

'Maybe now I will not have to—'

Lizzie tapped her daughter's arm and said, very loudly, 'Tell Bernard what you're readin', Rosie.'

'Oh, this.' She stooped, plucked the book from the carpet and handed it to him. '*Great Expectations*. Have you read it?'

'No, not – not that one.'

'You should,' Rosie said. 'You really, really should.'

That flat quacking voice, that eagerness and enthusiasm: he was back a dozen years and more in the field hospital near Beaumont Hamel, back with the little bandsman who should not have been fighting at all: a boy, hardly more than a child, who had been caught on the Somme like so many others. He had gone out to get him, gone out under the guns; they had attacked under the guns, not knowing why they were being asked to do it: heavy howitzers, pounding away long-range all night long, flash after flash, thud after thud: four hundred millimetres lobbing nine hundred kilogram shells from ten kilometres away. Walking the boy in, walking in, whole and intact, the grin on his face a mile wide, his voice – like her voice now – flat and quacking, blood running unnoticed from his ears, a thin sticky trickle, like red saliva, the boy yelling enthusiastically, 'See me. See me. I done it. I done it,' everyone knowing that he had no notion of what he had done or what the blast from the heavy shell had done to him, yelling, 'See me. I come back. I come back.' The boy at Beaumont Hamel, the little bandsman, was dead before the sun came up.

Bernard held the book open in both hands.

'Perhaps I will read it,' he said, knowing that he would, to please her.

'There now,' said Lizzie. 'Isn't that nice?'

'Very nice,' said Rosie.

✻   ✻   ✻

When it came to working on Sundays Janet McKerlie had been
forced to put her foot down. Mr Smart, who owned the shop in
which she assisted, was nothing if not persistent, however. Every
five or six months for going on thirty-five years Janet had been
obliged to read him the Christian version of the Riot Act and
explain that though she had been stuck behind his counter for
what seemed like eternity she wasn't actually his slave and still
had a soul to call her own.

Mr Smart offered her overtime to take a turn behind the
counter from seven o'clock on Sunday morning until half
past midday.

He pointed out that the shop was, and always had been, a
dairy and that the good Lord himself had seen nothing wrong
in buying bread on the Sabbath and if He had been around in
the Gorbals in the present time, He would probably have nipped
in for a pint of milk, a quarter-pound of ham and a copy of the
Sunday Post.

One might safely say that Mr Smart was not a religious
man.

The shop was his church, retailing his religion.

If that made him a heathen in Janet's book then, damn it,
she would just have to adjust to it. He had threatened her with
dismissal, threatening to bring in a new assistant, a young girl
who would do what she was told and, of course, would be only
too delighted to undertake an extra half-day's work on a Sunday
to save a poor old man having to run himself ragged just to keep
the business ticking over. None of these arguments cut any ice
with Janet.

Latterly, she hadn't been waiting for Mr Smart to start
wheedling and threatening but had gone on the attack, sniping
at his niggardliness, his bad manners, his falling hair, his
increasingly obvious limp and his general all-round godlessness
which, Janet indicated, would wind up with him frying in hell
like one of his own rashers.

'You've been here a wheen o' years, milady,' Mr Smart would tell her. 'But dinna you think that means you can gi'e me cheek an' get awa' wi' it.'

'Sack me then, sack me, see where that gets you.'

'I could employ a nice young girl for half whit I'm payin' you.'

'What sort o' girl would work in a dismal wee hole like this an' put up wi' your godless whinin' for seventy hours a week for what you pay me?'

'I pay ye well, milady.'

'Forty-five shillings for seventy hours?' Janet would screech, as any hapless customers who happened to be waiting for service sidled discreetly out of the door. 'That's a measly tanner an hour. A tanner an hour, I ask you!'

'More, it's more. Do your arithmee-trick.'

'I've done my arithmee-trick,' Janet would tell him, banging about with the potato scales and brass weights or rattling the long, lean knives with which meat and cheese were dissected. 'However you add it up, Mr Smarty, it comes to exploitation. I am *not* workin' this Sunday.'

'I never asked you to work this Sunday.'

'You were goin' to, weren't you, but?'

'Me? Never. I wouldn't give you the satisfaction o' earnin' some extra money, Janet McKerlie, if you were the last woman standin' upright this side o' Gorbals Cross.'

On Sundays, then, Janet McKerlie had a long lie-in.

She wouldn't rise from her mother's side in the niche bed until after eight o'clock, then she would spend a determined quarter of an hour crouched in the lavatory instead of her usual constipated three minutes.

She would also light the fire, make the breakfast, get her mother up and dressed – which was all part of the daily routine – then she would erect the sturdy head-high wooden clothes-horse, drape it with a grey sheet and, hidden from the world's view, disrobe down to the scud, and, shivering, sponge herself from head to toe, as if to wash away all trace of contact with that doyen of iniquity, Mr Smart, before she went to worship God.

Her nieces had no notion what Aunt Janet did on Sunday morning, and even less interest. As a rule one or other of them had to be dragged over to Laurieston to call on the aged relatives and a willingness to take on the awful chore had become a useful negotiating tool among Lizzie's daughters.

'If you let me borrow your pink dress on Saturday, Babs, I'll take your turn an' go an' see Gran on Sunday.'

'Done,' would be the immediate answer, with spit on the hands and a rubbing of palms to seal the agreement.

Going to see Gran was one thing that the Conway girls wished to avoid. Babs usually came off best in horse-trading, for Babs had the best wardrobe, the most desirable array of clothes, cheap jewellery, make-up and scent and so detested her female relatives that she would negotiate all sorts of extravagant deals with Polly to wriggle out of taking her turn on the rota.

On that Sunday, however, Polly did not have to negotiate.

She was out of bed, washed, dressed and duly passed as 'presentable' by twenty minutes to eleven o'clock in the morning and was on her way through the cold, almost empty streets a few minutes later.

'What's wrong with her?' Lizzie mumbled, lifting her head from the pillow as the front door closed.

'Nothin',' Babs answered. 'I guess she just wants t' get it over with.'

'Don't blame her,' said Lizzie, and promptly went back to sleep.

'Who is it?'

'It's me – Polly.'

Flustered and blue-lipped, her Aunt Janet opened the door.

'What're you doin' here at this hour?'

'Thought I'd come early,' Polly said. 'Keep Gran company while you're at the church.'

'Oh?' said Janet, suspiciously. 'That means we won't be seein' your mammy tonight, I suppose.'

'Couldn't say,' said Polly. 'I expect you will, though.'

'Did she send you?'

'Nope.' Polly was crisp to the point of curtness with Janet. Positive assertions and a show of self-confidence always disconcerted the middle-aged spinster who had forgotten, or had never known, what it was to be young. 'Babs sent me. It was Babs's turn to visit but she isn't feeling well, so here I am.'

'What wrong wi' her?' said Janet, putting on her pudding-basin hat. 'I hope it isn't contagious?'

'Well, you never know with Babs,' Polly said. 'How's Gran?'

'Poorly.' Janet squared the hat, slipped on a pair of blue woollen gloves and stared straight into her niece's eyes. 'I have t' go.'

'Go on then.'

'Will you be here when I get back?'

'I expect so.'

'Don't leave her alone.'

'Nope,' said Polly. 'Go on. *Shoo.*'

Janet gave her a glare then left, closing the door behind her.

Polly hesitated.

She hadn't entered the kitchen yet. She could hear her Gran breathing, that odd, angry rasping and knew that at any second there would be a cry of 'Who is it? Who's there?' She stole a moment, though, to unlatch the door of the hall cupboard and open it.

Unlike most hall cupboards, the McKerlies' was neater than a foot-soldier's haversack: a broom, a brush, a canvas apron, a small shovel, a large shovel, two galvanised pails — both spotless — and a little wicker cradle in which reposed a collection of chopped kindling, a jar of paraffin and a small, wicked-looking axe with a hammer head. Not only was the floor of the cupboard neatly lined with linoleum, the walls had been papered with floral oilcloth of such quality that the mice hadn't been able to gnaw through it yet.

There was no dust, no droppings, no beetles, dead or alive, not even the withered remnant of a moth within the McKerlies' glory hole, a situation that seemed so unnatural that it gave Polly the creeps.

'Who is it? Who's there?'

Polly closed the cupboard door gently but didn't latch it. She went into the kitchen.

'Only me, Gran,' she said and, after sucking in a breath, lowered herself into the awful aura around her grandmother's chair and kissed the dear old lady lightly on the cheek.

'You're an early bird.'

'Couldn't *wait* to see you, Gran.'

'Huh! You'll be up to somethin'.'

'Pardon?'

'Up to somethin', if I know you. Where's Babs?'

'She's got a cold.'

'Aye, well, tell her to keep it,' Gran said. 'I'm no' wantin' her germs.'

'That's exactly what Babs said,' said Polly.

'What're you up to?' Gran McKerlie said, turning her head as Polly moved behind her to the sink. 'There's somethin' shifty about you today. Is it some man, some feller?'

'I really don't know what you're talking about.'

'Comin' early. Upsettin' everybody.'

'Well, sorry about that,' Polly said. 'How about a cup of tea, Gran? Reputed to soothe the most savage breast.'

'Is that impudence?'

'Nope,' said Polly. 'Advertising,' and, deliberately making the water roar, turned on the tap at the sink.

*　　　*　　　*

What had seemed like a marvellous idea back in Lavender Court was beginning to look pretty daft now that she was here in her grandmother's house.

It occurred to Polly that her master plan for hiding Babs's profits from the robbery under the floorboards was ridiculous, that it would be far simpler to plant the hundred pounds in a Post Office savings account and just hide the payment book. Something about the prospect of hard cash, though, generated tension in the region of the heart to the detriment of the brain. Babs might be willing to hide the cash for a while but Polly knew that her sister would never allow it to be salted away in something as vague as an account.

Polly had inherited her mother's stubborn streak. She told herself that as she'd made the effort to turn up in the backlands of Laurieston early on a Sunday morning then she might as well go through with it and see what sort of a hidey-hole Gran's hall cupboard would make.

She was still thinking in the abstract. She could not quite link what she was doing to what Patsy and the boys would attempt to do on Wednesday night. She, like them, dwelled only on results not consequences.

She had glimpsed Guido Manone through the window of the Alfa Romeo, and had spotted him now and then in the corridors of the burgh chambers. But she had seen the other one, Dominic, only once. She'd gone to a restaurant in Glasgow with three other girls from the office one night last spring and had bumped into Dominic Manone there just by chance.

He'd emerged from the restaurant in the company of another Italian. He'd had such an individual air about him, not at all cocky or swaggering, not assertive, that Polly had recognised him at once. He was also very handsome and when he'd glanced at her with his solemn gaze she'd found herself smiling as if she knew him. He, fleetingly, had smiled back. Then he'd gone off along the pavement with a neat, poised sort of gait, like a boxer, a bantam-weight.

Polly could not imagine Dominic Manone doing anyone any harm. He seemed no more threatening than any of the well-groomed men who came into the burgh offices day and daily, architects and engineers, builders and material suppliers, solicitors, and yet she hated him, had always hated him.

Polly didn't bother to listen to her grandmother grizzling on about her waterworks and the ignorance of the new young doctor who did not understand her suffering. Planted in the big, wooden-armed chair directly in front of the grate with everything close to hand – coal bucket and tongs, her sticks, the commode and the brass-tongued handbell with which she could summon assistance in case of emergency – there seemed to be precious little wrong with Grandma McKerlie that a modicum of exercise and effort would not put right.

She ate the toast that Polly made for her, drank several cups of strong tea and then, at last, informed the girl that she would 'have to see what she could do this morning'. She reached out for the commode with her crook-handled stick, heaved herself upright and began to fumble, thick-fingered, with her skirts.

Polly said, 'I'll leave you to it, Gran. I'll just be outside.'

'What if I fall?'

'I'll hear you.'

'What if I fall in the fire?'

'I'll only be in the hall.'

'Janet always stays.'

'Ah, well,' said Polly, heading for the door, 'I'm not Janet.'

Once in the hall, Polly knelt on the floor and placed the sole of one shoe against the kitchen door and gently eased open the cupboard door.

The linoleum was lilac-coloured, printed with a cubic design that, if you stared at it long enough, began to waver and accumulate into towers and tenements and tall chimney-stacks.

Polly blinked and, shifting the broom and one of the shovels, explored the edges of the lino with her fingernails.

On all fours with her backside in the air, she felt like the heroine in a Keystone Cops picture, or one of the goblins in the Princess's annual pantomime. She picked at the edge of the linoleum, lifted a corner and curled it carefully back upon itself, so that it wouldn't crack. In spite of the age of the building and seasonal infestations of bugs and vermin, the floorboards under the lino were remarkably clean.

They were also, Polly discovered, surprisingly loose.

Using the edge of the little shovel she eased one board from its place. Four small blunt nails, quite clean and polished, four little nail holes; the board, no wider than a hand, no longer than a forearm, seemed to rest lightly on top of the cross joists.

Polly drew the board away.

She could hear her grandmother's theatrical little groans that would, no doubt, be explained in graphic detail as soon as the show was over and Polly returned to the kitchen. She placed the board against the side wall.

The smell of dank plaster and dust tickled her nostrils.

She had no idea how deep the hole under the floorboards might be or, for that matter, what might be lurking there. She bit her lip, scrunched herself into the cupboard and, before she lost her nerve, plunged her hand into the hole.

It didn't go very far before her knuckles struck brick.

Gouts of dust, like fur, brushed her fingers and wrist.

She shrieked silently, forced herself to grope about.

The hole was shallow but wide. Very suitable. She would wrap Babs's money in greaseproof paper, put the package in a pickle jar and stow it here in the McKerlies' cupboard without fear of discovery.

And then, flinching, Polly felt it.

She drew her hand back sharply, sucking in breath.

It had shape, hard shape. Metal, not round like a gas or water pipe, but small and individual, like a bomb. Polly steeled herself, dipped a hand into the aperture once more, fished about, found the object and brought it out.

She sat back on her heels and, holding her find up to the light from the fanlight above the door, inspected it closely.

No bomb: no gun: no box: a cocoa tin, a Fry's cocoa tin, with the label still pasted on the side, a little faded but intact. The lid was tightly sealed.

Polly experienced a queer fluttering sensation in the pit of her stomach, a compound of fear and excitement and a faint premonition that she'd found something that should have been left alone. She picked at the lid with her fingernails until it flew off and skittered out of the cupboard into the hall.

'Polly? Polly?'

She sat back, furtive and guilty, no longer patient.

She held the tin in her lap, both hands closed over it as if to trap whatever it might contain.

She made herself call out, 'Are you finished, Gran?'

'What're you doin'? Are you in my cupboard?'

'No, I'm — I'm smoking a cigarette. Are you finished?'

'Nearly, nearly.'

Polly waited. Listening. Trembling.

She lifted her hands up and turned the cocoa tin upside down.

What fell out was a fat wad of banknotes fastened with a rubber band.

Polly stared down at it then, without rhyme or reason, without knowing quite why, murmured, 'Oh, my God! It's Daddy,' and suddenly began to cry.

Chapter Seven

Polly was shaken by the discovery of her father's hoard and the bizarre impulse that had driven her to choose exactly the same hiding place as he had done all those years ago. Her father had never had much more substance for her than a character in a fairytale and she resented the fact that he had died somewhere among the poppy fields, not heroically or definitively but in the same shifty and uncertain manner in which he'd lived.

Now, abruptly, he had been restored to her and as she had sat cross-legged in Gran McKerlie's tiny lobby holding the cocoa tin and the roll of banknotes she had felt his presence so strongly that she had begun to wonder if she'd been drawn there by a supernatural force to remind her whose daughter she really was. It had taken an effort of will on her part to hide her distress from her grandmother, to cook up a plausible excuse and, minutes after Aunt Janet had returned, take her leave, run down the slimy stairs and out of the backlands and away across Eglinton Street as if to outstrip him and leave the spectre of his influence lagging far behind.

She had run home to Lavender Court, to a houseful of steaming washtubs and laden pulleys because she had nowhere else to go and desperately needed to talk to Babs just as soon as the coast was clear.

'*How* much?' Babs cried.

'Three hundred and twenty-four pounds.'

'My God!' Babs exclaimed. 'Think of all that money lyin' there, just lyin' there for all those years. Did you count it?'

'Yes.'

'An' there was only three hundred?'

'And twenty-four pounds, yes,' Polly said.

'I thought he'd got away with eight hundred. That's the story, anyway.'

'Perhaps it was exaggerated,' Polly said.

Babs nodded. 'Yeah, or he spent the rest before he joined up.'

'How long did he have?' Polly asked. 'I mean, between the money being stolen and him joining up?'

'Dunno,' Babs said. 'Days, weeks – not very long.'

'*Could* he have spent five hundred pounds in such a short time?'

'Maybe he had debts – like Tommy Bonnar?'

'Don't say that,' Polly snapped.

'Say what?'

'Don't compare Dad to Tommy. He wasn't at all like Tommy Bonnar.'

'How do you know?'

'Mammy told us what he was like.'

'Yeah, but we only have her word for it.'

'I remember him,' Polly said. 'I remember what he looked like, how he used to take me on his knee and read to me, and how he would come into the room and tuck us into bed.'

'Yeah, but we've no idea what he was really like, have we?' Babs said, impatiently. 'Anyway, who cares now? Where is it?'

'Where's what?'

'The money, the loot.'

'Oh, that,' said Polly. 'I put it back.'

'You did *what?*'

'What else was I going to do with it?'

'Bring it back, bring it here. It's our money, ain't it?'

'I'm not so sure it is,' said Polly.

'Come off it, Poll,' Babs said. 'If it ain't ours, whose—'

'Dad stole it from the Manones. It's the Manones' money.'

'Oh, sure!' said Babs, squirming on the bed. 'Are you just gonna waltz up to Mr Manone an' say, "See what I found, sir. Sorry it's five hundred light." Are you gonna hand it over to a guy who's soaked Mammy for a fortune over the years? Nah, nah. It's ours, Polly, our legacy. We're entitled to it.'

'We'll have to give it to Mammy.'

Babs stopped squirming. They were alone in the bedroom, seated together on the bed. It was late in the afternoon. A drizzling, depressing dusk had crept down over the backs and enveloped the city. With nightfall the rain had increased in density and pattered on the front window and trickled audibly in the guttering. Outside, gas-lamps hissed inside soft angelic halos and the cobbles gleamed, all clean for once, and picturesque.

In the kitchen Rosie was wringing out sheets. Mammy was taking down clothes that were dry and piling them in the basket to be ironed. It struck Polly that there was something unfair about Sunday chores so close in kind to those that occupied her mother during the week; Sunday gone, used up, and nothing for Mammy to look forward to but a trek through the rain to Laurieston to help put Gran to bed. She felt a sudden deep, deep sadness within her, a sense of just how much Mammy had lost, how much she had sacrificed to bring them up.

She thought of the money in the cocoa tin, a daft wee tin in a daft hiding place, so ordinary, so unimaginative that it didn't seem worthy of a man who'd had the gall to steal from the Italians.

'If we hand it over to Mammy,' Polly said, 'we'll have to tell her what I was doing rooting under the floorboards in Gran's house. And you know what that'll mean.'

'The ball,' said Babs, nodding, 'on the slates, yeah.'

'Look,' Polly said, 'the money's been hidden for – what? – thirteen years and nobody's stumbled on it. They're not going to find it now, are they? I mean, the chances of that happening are astronomical.'

'The chances of you findin' it were astronomical,' Babs reminded her.

'That's true.' Polly gave a little shiver. 'But I had a valid reason for looking there. I'm beginning to wonder if I wasn't drawn to it.'

'Drawn to it?' said Babs. 'God, you don't mean . . .'

'I don't know what I mean.' Polly got up. 'All I know is, we can't do anything about it, not right now, not this week.'

'Because of the boys?'

'Yes,' said Polly, decisively. 'After Wednesday we'll be able to add another hundred pounds to it and then we can decide what we're going to do.'

'Spend it,' said Babs, gleefully.

'Or give it to Mammy.'

'All of it?'

'All of it,' Polly said.

'For what, but?'

'To pay off Dominic Manone.'

'God, but you're jumpy tonight.' Patsy reached over the marble-topped table and covered her hand with his. 'You're shakin' like a leaf, Polly. What's wrong? You worried about tomorrow night?'

'Yes.'

He drew his chair closer to the table, leaning so close that his brow brushed her hair. 'That's nice.'

'Not for me it's not,' said Polly.

'I've never had anyone worry about me before.'

'Well,' said Polly, 'don't get too used to it.'

'What does that mean?'

'If you think I'm going to hang around and be sick in the toilet every time you go out on a job, think again.'

He pulled back a little but continued to cover her hand with his. He looked away, at the deserted tables, the counter, the window, at rain beating down, rain streaked by the lights of the pub across the empty street and harried by the big wind that rampaged among the tenements.

'Do you want it to last, Polly? This thing between us, I mean.'

'How can I answer that?' Polly said.

'You said—'

'I know. I know. I'm talkin' through my hat. Don't pay any attention,' Polly advised. 'I'm all upset. I think it's the weather.'

'It isn't the weather,' said Patsy. 'You're really worried about me.'

'Haven't you had a sweetheart before?' Polly said.

'I've had girls, if that's what you mean.'

'I mean somebody you cared about?'

'In my line of work—'

'Would you give it up?' Polly interrupted.

'For you?'

'For me or for somebody else. For the right girl.'

'Can't say.' Patsy thought about it. 'Probably not.'

'How much profit will you make from the warehouse job?'

'Accordin' to Tommy, a lot.'

'Enough to retire?' said Polly.

'Retire from what?' said Patsy. 'In my line o' work you don't retire.'

'You just go on doing it until you're caught?'

'I've never done time,' Patsy stated. 'I've no intention of doin' time.'

'You're too smart ever to get caught, is that it?'

'You said it, I didn't.'

'But not smart enough to quit?'

'You're determined to reform me, Polly, aren't you?' Patsy

said. 'Put it this way, I'm not gonna quit before Wednesday night, not even for you.'

'What'll you do with the money?'

'Travel.' He rested his elbows on the table, his back to the window. 'I like to see how folk live in different places. You'd like it too.'

'I'm sure I would,' said Polly, stiffly.

'Come with me.'

'How can I?'

'Easy,' Patsy told her. 'Pack your smalls in a bag an' leave.'

'My mother would just love that.'

'She'd understand.'

'I doubt it,' Polly said.

'If I made an offer like that . . .'

'Oh, it's an offer, is it?' Polly said.

'If I made an offer like that to your sister, she'd jump at it.'

'In that case why don't you ask Babs to go with you?'

'I don't want Babs,' he said. 'I want you.'

'What, to keep your bed warm?' Polly was beginning to feel slightly nauseous again. She lifted her coffee cup and sipped the lukewarm liquid cautiously. 'I'm not like Babs. Babs never thinks ahead. She'd go off with you because it wouldn't occur to her what would happen when she came back.'

'Who said anythin' about comin' back? What's so bloody wonderful about Glasgow?' Patsy said. 'There are a thousand, a million other places to live, all better than this dreary old town.'

'Why do *you* keep coming back then?'

'I really don't know,' said Patsy. 'Because it's home, I suppose.'

'Why don't you go to Russia and become a total Bolshevik?'

'No – thank – you.'

'I thought you supported the Communists?'

'I do, but not enough to want to live in Russia.'

'You don't do anything right, do you, Patsy?'

He gave a little *tut* followed by a sigh, both soft. 'Stop naggin' me, Polly. I've enough on my plate without you goin' on about commitment.'

'That's it. That's the word I couldn't think of.'

He glanced again at the rain teeming over the tenements. He could hear the hum of the ice-cream cooler behind the counter, the muted sound of a wireless in the back of the shop, the muffled roaring of the wind.

Apparently it hadn't occurred to Polly that heavy rain would raise the level of the river and that a strong wind would make handling the boat difficult. He wished now that he'd chosen another plan, one that didn't involve boats. He could have taken care of the watchmen, as Jackie had suggested, have lugged the safe off on the back of a van or lorry. He'd never been that kind of thief, though, had never gone out on a job with the intention of hurting anyone. He was a cat-burglar not an armed robber. Stealth not violence was his stock-in-trade.

Polly said, 'I'm sorry, Patsy.'

He said, 'Sorry for what?'

'Nagging. I just don't want anything to happen to you.'

'Like bein' pinched, you mean?'

'Anything bad.'

'Have no fear, sweetheart,' he said. 'Nothin' will happen to me.'

She got up, came around the little table and eased herself on to his knee. He leaned his shoulder against the wall and put an arm around her. Mr Fascetti, old Joe, would be watching them in the long mirror but Patsy didn't care.

He laid his brow against her hair, smelled the odd, rather aromatic odour of it, like marzipan, like nutmeg. Her skin was warm, smooth and unblemished. He felt old beside her, holding her against him, old and rather weary. He thought of Paris, of Florence, of that tiny town in the Swiss Alps whose name he could never remember where he'd drunk frothy hot chocolate at a table outside in the snow under a brilliant blue sky, and how dull and lonely it had been.

He placed his hand on her breast outside her coat.

He could feel the swelling but not the shape. He kept his hand still, a tender gesture, not intrinsically sexual, no more so than the weight of her thighs on his lap. He had never held her like this before and when he kissed her it seemed different, inexplicably different from kissing at the close-mouth or in the lane behind the Calcutta. It was like kissing after making love, after passion had been expended and only love remained.

'When will I see you again?' Polly whispered.

'On Saturday,' he told her. 'On Saturday, at the dance.'

'And it'll all be over?'

'Bar the shoutin',' Patsy said.

Wee Billy Hallop eventually opened the door in response to her tentative knocking. He wore a ragged blue jumper over school shorts and his feet and legs were bare and dirty. He looked, Babs thought, like a ragamuffin but this, she knew, was due more to carelessness than neglect. He glowered at her, his flat, spoon-shaped face buckling in on itself until it seemed to be nothing but a brow and an underlip, both bulging with indignation.

'Is your brother in?' Babs said. 'Your brother Jackie.'

'Gimme a ciggie then.'

'I haven't got a ciggie.'

'G'an, gimme a ciggie.'

'I'll give you a cuff on the flamin' ear in a minute,' Babs said, then, raising her voice, called out, '*Jackie, are y' there?*'

He appeared out of the bedroom, lifted his brother in a casual bear-hug and slung him away out of sight into the kitchen.

'Come in,' Jackie said.

'Nah, I gotta get upstairs. I've a message.'

'What message?'

'The money arrived.'

'You saw it?'

'Aye. It was just luck. I was in the lav – the toilet about half past three o'clock an' I thought I'd open the window on the off-chance. I saw them bringin' it into the warehouse from a van.'

'Who?'

'Three o' them. Mr MacDermott, Andy Ross an' Mr Manone.'

'Which Mr Manone?'

'The old one, the uncle.'

'Right,' said Jackie. 'You're sure it was the cash?'

'Five canvas bags. Mr MacDermott an' Andy Ross carried two each an' the old man carried one.'

'Definitely the money?'

'Five bags. Definitely.'

'They didn't see you, did they?'

'How could they? I was inside the lav – the toilet on the first floor.'

'Good girl.'

He peered at her for a moment and she could tell that he was tempted to kiss her but that his nerves wouldn't let him.

'Good girl,' he said again, then, empty of conversation, closed the door.

Polly was already at home. Tucked back into the alcove, she was seated on top of the bed, cross-legged. She had removed her coat, hat and shoes but still wore the prim jade green twin-set and black pleated skirt that her position as a clerk in the burgh office demanded. An ashtray was balanced in her lap and she was smoking, not languidly but in a manner suggestive of last meals and firing squads. When Babs came into the room she looked up, frowning.

Rosie occupied the bedroom's only easy chair. She was reading a newspaper by the light of the lamp. She appeared quite unconcerned about anything and oblivious to her sisters' conversation.

Babs said, very quietly, 'It came, the money.'

'You saw it?' said Polly, sitting forward.

'Saw them bringin' in the bags.'

'Did you tell Jackie?'

'Yep.'

'So it's on,' said Polly.

'Yep.'

'Oh, God!'

'What's on?' said Rosie, lowering the newspaper.

'None o' your business,' said Babs.

Rosie smiled over the top edge of the *Citizen* and proceeded to observe her sisters with unabashed interest. 'Is something interesting happening?'

Babs removed her coat and cap and placed herself directly before the armchair, blocking off Rosie's view.

Speaking quietly, Polly said, 'Is it still raining?'

'Nope,' Babs said. 'It's stopped.'

'That's always something, I suppose,' Polly said.

'You worried?' Babs said.

'Worried sick,' Polly admitted. 'Aren't you?'

'Nah. They know what they're doin', the boys,' Babs said.

'Do they?' said Polly. 'I wonder.'

'If they do what?' said Rosie, who had slipped out of the easy chair to lip-read her sisters' conversation from a more convenient angle. 'If who do what?'

'Damn it, Rosie!' Babs shouted. 'I thought I told you to mind your own bloody business.'

Rosie pursed her lips and widened her eyes into the expression of mock innocence that Mr Feldman so detested.

'Oooooow!' She tapped her forefinger to her mouth. 'It is all right, ladies,' she said. 'My lips are sealed.'

'They'd better be,' said Polly.

'Here, this ain't gonna be so easy, is it?' Dennis Hallop said.

'I never said it would be easy,' Patsy told him. 'If you'd been listenin' in the first place, you'd have sussed that out for yourself.'

'Where's Tommy? Isn't Tommy supposed to be here?'

'Tommy's gone to the dock to check on the boat. We'll meet him there.'

'What's all that stuff you got there, Patsy?' Dennis asked.

A battered canvas-sided suitcase fastened with rope stood on the floor of the shed. Draped across the long bench were four lengths of manila rope which Patsy had checked inch by inch to make sure they were sound. He put his hand on top of the case.

'Bolt cutters,' he said. 'The safe's on the second floor so it isn't likely to be cemented but it might be bolted down. Also, some solid iron bars and a jack.'

'A jack?' said Dennis.

'How else do you think I'm gonna get the safe up to window height? I'm gonna slide it across the floor, jack it on to a desk, slide the desk to the window an' lower the safe down to the boat in a cargo net.'

'Where's the cargo net?'

'Tommy has it.'

'Where'd he get a cargo net?' said Jackie.

'I gave it to him,' Patsy went on. 'Will you stop askin' so many idiotic questions, please? I know what I'm doin'. I've done it before.'

'Talk us through it one more time, but,' said Jackie.

'Right, one more time. I climb up with the ropes. I remove the right window an' gain access to the office where the safe is. I fix a rope. Jackie climbs up it to join me, leavin' you, Dennis, an' Tommy in the boat. Assumin' I can't open the safe where it stands, which isn't very probable, then we'll load the safe into the net an' lower it through the window down into the boat.'

'What do one o' them Hobbs' safes weigh?' said Jackie.

'A hell of a lot,' said Patsy.

'I hope we can shift it,' said Jackie.

'If Babs has the model right,' Patsy said, 'we should be able to manage.'

'Once you're clear o' the buildin' an' back in the boat, we row downriver to the swing park at the end of Shotten Street,' Dennis said. 'I remember that bit.'

'I'm glad you remember somethin',' Jackie said.

'We manhandle the safe on to the stone ramp under the railin's,' Patsy went on, 'where I blow it open with a strong charge o' powder.'

'You done that before too?' said Dennis.

'Often,' said Patsy. 'Often enough anyway. It's deserted down at the end of Shotten Street that time of night so nobody's gonna bother us. We take the bags out an' sling them over the railin' into the play park. We push the empty safe down into the deep water an' we let the boat float off on the tide. God knows where it'll be washed up. It doesn't matter. We climb over the railin's, empty the bags into four tool-bags that Tommy's also got stowed in the boat. Then we split, one at a time, an' catch separate late-night trams back into the Gorbals. If things go right, we should all be back here by one. Jackie'll leave the gate unlocked. No lights, remember. Got that, Dennis?'

'Got it,' said Dennis.

'We'll count an' divvy up the cash an' be on our merry way,' Patsy said. 'Unless we make a hash of it the Manones won't even know they've been robbed until the cleaners arrive in the mornin', by which time we'll have the dibbens hid away safe an' be tucked up in our little beds, sleepin' like babies.'

'Who pays Babs?' said Jackie.

'It comes out of the first cut.'

'I'll give it to her,' said Jackie.

'I'll bet you will,' said Dennis.

'Now,' Patsy said, 'any questions?'

'Nah,' said Dennis, airily. 'I reckon it's gonna be easy meat.'

'You think so?' Patsy said.

'Sure,' said Dennis. 'Piece o' cake.'

'What happens afterwards, Patsy?' Jackie asked.

'I'll tell you what happens afterwards,' Patsy said. 'Afterwards the Manones go ravin' mad.'

'An' what do we do?'

'Lie low, wee man, lie low.'

In spite of the soft hat and a trench coat that made him look more like an American G-man than a matelot, Tommy Bonnar turned out to be handy with a pair of oars. In fact, if the Ferryhead Rowing Club had not merely been a front for less athletic endeavours Tommy would surely have been its champion, for, many years ago, he had worked for the Harbour office and had learned how to navigate small craft in and out of the docks that lined the upper Clyde.

It had been a happy time for young Tommy; all too brief. Eventually he had fought with his immediate superior, a dour, tattooed, hard-drinking devil by the name of Slezack, and had carved him up one night on the wharf outside the Harbour offices. Charged and found guilty of assault, Tommy had lost his job, had served a spell in a borstal and had never looked back, at least not openly.

Jackie and Dennis had never been on the river before except on ferries. They were almost overwhelmed by the number of bulky cargo vessels and ocean liners that flanked the shores. Blunt, crouching tugs and fireboats, crenellated dredgers, the great, grey naked hulls of sloops and cruisers all seemed to be part of the fabric of the city, lying cheek by jowl with the tenements. As the longboat glided past docks and wharves and dead-end streets, the Hallops sat motionless, cowed not by what they were about to do but by the fact that they were out on the broad, dark river in a boat that seemed no bigger than a matchbox, a boat so small and puny that it was practically invisible.

Fortunately Tommy Bonnar knew where he was going. He sucked on the cigarette that clung to his lip and tried not to show how much he was enjoying himself. He hadn't expected to experience the arrogance of boyhood ever again, to feel the muscle of the river through the oars, to see the night sky snaking ahead and taste the strong brown metallic wind that slapped the waves against the bow. The river ran high with winter rain, though, and an ebbing tide drew the boat along faster than even Tommy had anticipated.

They reached the bridle path, the warehouse in a quarter of an hour. Feathering one oar Tommy steered the longboat into the steep banking. Patsy, poised and ready, scrambled ashore. Flinging himself down, he hauled on the bow rope so that the boat swung on her length, then, with Jackie grappling with the boat-hook, came into position under the warehouse wall and clung there, tenuously moored.

'You got her, Tommy?'

'I got her.'

'Can you hold her?'

'Aye, no bother.'

'Jackie, gimme the case.'

However cool and rational Patsy might appear, however professional his approach to burglary, what drew him back wasn't just the promise of easy money but those moments of heightened awareness when every fibre of his being seemed to buzz with life and all the petty concerns that plagued him were burned away, reduced to a hot, hard little spot of concentration which was more intense, more satisfying than anything else in life, even the sexual act itself.

He had chosen this approach in the full knowledge of its hazards and difficulties. If he was going to shaft the Manones then he had to shaft them properly. Of course, he could have stormed in the front door of the warehouse with a gun in each hand and a mask over his face like a bloody cowboy. But he wanted to do it the hard way. He *needed* to do it the hard way, to make it too daring for an inside job.

He fished a pair of black rubber-soled pumps from the case, put them on, laced them tight. He slung one of the rope coils over his head and around his back then gripped the drainpipe that ascended the line of the wall. He tested it, leaning back, then glanced down.

Tommy and Dennis were bobbing up and down in the longboat. He paid them no heed whatsoever. The boat was Tommy's business. His business was to get up to and into the office forty feet or so above his head.

'Okay?' he said.

Jackie nodded. 'Okay.'

Patsy began the climb.

Chapter Eight

Soon after he stepped through the window into the manager's office, Patsy knew he was in trouble.

The climb itself had not been particularly strenuous. Heights didn't bother him and the drainpipe had provided secure holds for his hands and feet.

Straddling the narrow window sill forty feet above the river, he had used the coconut mat and bolt cutters as confidently as if he'd been standing on the ground. He had pressed the mat against the glass with his knees and, using the cutters one-handed, had tapped away until the glass beneath it cracked. Lifting the mat away, he'd tapped again. A crescent of glass had fallen inwards with an almost inaudible tinkle. He had listened intently for half a minute or so and then, with no clang of alarms inside the building, had reached down his gloved right hand, had found the aperture and the brass handle and had opened the window outward, letting it swing away.

He slung his bag of tricks in first, then, dipping his body, had nimbly followed, stepping silently on to the carpeted floor of the manager's office. He had fished his torch from his pocket and had switched it on.

The office was just as he had imagined it, broader than it was long; an imposing teak-wood desk faced away from the window, a swivel chair behind it, two wooden chairs in front of it, metal filing cabinet to the left; a cheese-plant in an enamel pot cast sinister shadows in the far corner. The door to the outer office was panelled with ribbed glass, a name stippled across it at chest height. Patsy paused again, listening again. He could hear no sounds from inside the building, only the sloughing of the wind through the open window. He went to the glass-panelled door, opened it and looked out into the secretary's office.

It was large, with a double desk, typewriters, telephones and a whole wall of wooden filing cabinets. There was one entrance door, no windows. Patsy walked down the aisle between the desk and the cabinets and tried the door handle. Locked. He returned to the manager's office, closed the glass door and focused the torch beam on the safe that stood against the right-hand wall.

That was when he knew he was going to have trouble.

Babs Conway hadn't lied. It was a Hobbs, a big spanking-new Hobbs, a model he'd never seen before, one that hadn't even shown up in the catalogues. It had a bland look to it, smooth and implacable, without so much as a hinge showing. The shield that Babs had mentioned was a sliding cover behind which lay a combination lock, sunk an inch into solid steel.

Patsy hunkered before the safe and studied it.

There was nothing much to study. He stuck the end of the torch in his mouth and leaned forward. He wrapped both arms around the safe in a bear-hug and tried to move it. It rocked a little, just a little – just enough to indicate that it wasn't bolted to the floor. Its bulk was enough to protect it. He felt down the back of the brute with his fingertips and found nothing except two slight ridges where the welding had been finished off. He had a feeling that what he was dealing with here was a double-lined safe, a steel box set inside a steel box with some sort of fireproof lining between the layers.

He sat back on his heels and twiddled the lock's rotating dial. It made no discernible noise, not even a faint click.

Leaning closer, torch at eye-level, Patsy examined the housing of the lock and found it to be as tight as a bloody drum. Even if he had been inclined to rouse the neighbourhood by firing a black powder charge there was no means of setting one. The only feasible way into this brute, Patsy decided, was to attack it with sledgehammers or cut it open down the back seams with an oxy-acetylene torch; not the sort of thing you could feasibly hope to do in ten minutes in the playground at the bottom of Shotten Street.

He should have quit there and then. He should have packed up his gear, climbed out of the window, shinned down the rope, got back into the boat and said, 'Okay, lads, let's forget it.' But there was a recalcitrant streak in Patsy Walsh, an angry little core of Scottishness that made him feel as if he'd been cheated out of what was rightfully his. He'd been born with it in him and it had been fed and nurtured by the culture in which he'd been raised. It was the gene, the mute, unmalleable gene that Patsy shared with the Hallops, with Bonnar and O'Hara and all the other fancy wee fly-men who struggled to earn a fast buck or a dishonest crust; even, for all he knew, with Guido and Dominic Manone, though they were Italians and probably more sensible.

Patsy put down the torch.

He crouched like a wrestler, wrapped both arms round the safe once more and gave it everything he'd got. He strained, he struggled, he lifted the brute a half-inch off the floor and, shuffling, moved it back four or five inches from its original position against the wall. Blood pounded in his head and chest. He felt dizzy, swollen with the excessive effort. He sipped air through clenched teeth, regripped the safe and then, defeated, lowered it to the floor again.

Sweating and shaky, he sat back on his heels.

At that moment Jackie clambered through the open window and dropped to the floor. He was draped like a gladiator in the cargo net, a coil of manila line looped over each shoulder. He was white-faced and trembling; heights were not to his liking. He was also considerably irked because Patsy hadn't been there to encourage him. 'Where the hell've you been?' he hissed.

'Where do you think I've been?' said Patsy.

'Jeeze! Is that it? Have you no' got it open yet?'

Impatiently, Jackie untangled himself from the net. He slung it and the ropes upon the desk and, to hide his anxiety, seated himself upon one of the wooden chairs. Panting, he rested his elbows on his knees and glowered at the Hobbs, stark and stubborn in the pool of torchlight.

'Can y' not open it, Patsy?'

'Nope.'

'You'll just have t' blow it then?'

'Nope,' Patsy said, still squatting before the Hobbs. 'We're gonna have to take it with us an' open it somewhere else.'

'Look at the size o' it, for God's sake.'

'Yeah, I know.'

Jackie sighed. 'Is this Plan B?'

'Nope, this is Plan Zero.' Patsy got up. 'A new plan entirely.'

'A what?'

'Somehow or other,' Patsy said, softly, 'we're gonna have to get this brute back to your yard an' open it there.'

'Our yard?' Jackie shot to his feet. 'Here, haud on a minute ...'

'Or leave it where it is,' said Patsy.

'Give up?' said Jackie. 'After climbin' all the way up that bloody wall? I'm not leavin' here without that safe.'

'Fine,' said Patsy. 'In that case, we'll have to get it into the cargo net and up on to the window ledge so we can lower it down into the boat.'

'Can we do that?' said Jackie.

'We won't know till we try,' Patsy said.

Hands on hips, Jackie did a nervous little war-dance before the Hobbs.

'What if someone hears us?' he said.

'They won't,' Patsy said. 'We're on the second floor, remember. There's an empty office between us an' the corridor.'

'What about the night-watchmen?'

'Forget the soddin' watchmen,' Patsy said. 'Gimme that coil of rope. The quicker we're out of here the less chance . . .'

'Yeah, yeah, yeah,' said Jackie.

'Jackie?'

'What?'

'The rope.'

The *Seneca* was one of a fleet of twenty-eight steamers and sixteen motor-ships owned by the Danish line of Moller & Kramp. She was 450 feet in length between the perpendiculars, with a dead-weight tonnage of 8,225. She drew twenty-six feet and five inches of water when loaded. She was propelled by a Burmeister & Wain diesel motor operating on the two-cycle, double-acting principle and had an average service speed of fifteen knots. When she eased down past the coal conveyors below the Kingston Dock she was doing nothing like that, of course.

To Dennis Hallop, however, she seemed to be moving at the speed of light, a gigantic block of greeny-grey metal bearing down upon him out of the semi-darkness. He shouted aloud, flung himself into the bows of the longboat and covered his head with his forearms while the *Seneca*, remote and disinterested, rolled past, and the longboat bobbed wildly up and down on the wash that slapped and slopped against the banking.

Dennis, cowering, heard the creak of mooring ropes, the groan of the little boat's timbers, the thrash of the cargo liner's single prop and the gabble of waves all tumbling in upon him. He had never been so scared in his life. He lay in a foetal position for several minutes after the medley had diminished and the vessel had gone on downriver. When he finally looked up the first thing he saw was Tommy Bonnar seated calmly in the stern, oars tucked under his armpits, hat tipped back, cigarette still dangling from his lip.

'What – what the hell was that?' Dennis asked.

'Boat,' said Tommy.

'Jesus, I thought . . .'

Tommy Bonnar laughed, a little croak of laughter, and shook his head.

Ashamed and embarrassed, Dennis elbowed himself into a sitting position. The boat was still rocking and bobbing but the ropes that held her close to the bank under the warehouse wall seemed to have held.

'It's all very well for you, Tommy,' Dennis groused.

'What is?'

'I never learned how t' swim.'

'Swim,' said Tommy. 'Who's talkin' about swimmin'?'

'I thought we were gonna be sunk.'

Shaking his head once more, Tommy nudged the oars and brought the longboat back up into position directly beneath the wall. He glanced up at the second-floor window, at the faint smear of light that showed in the opening, light that moved and darted about but did not appear to become any stronger. Something was wrong. Walsh and Jackie had been inside for the best part of twenty minutes. They had given him no sign, no signal, and he hadn't heard anything that sounded like a charge going off.

Tommy was a lot less calm than he appeared to be. He was also chilled to the bone; he wore only his old brown suit and trench coat, no jumper or pullover. He wasn't going to show weakness, though. One jabbering idiot on board was enough to be going on with. He stared sullenly at the stern of the *Seneca* receding into the distance, at the lights of the ferry scribbled on the rough surface of the Clyde, at the cranes and the lamps that lit the quays on the north shore. At the lights of the city streets pricked out of the night sky beyond. The wind brought the sound of a train, or a tram, rattling faintly across the river, and he shivered at that wan and lonely sound.

'Where are they? What're they *doin'* up there?' Dennis said.

'Search me,' said Tommy.

He spat the butt of the cigarette over the side and watched the black water swallow up the coal. He crossed the oars over his chest and fumbled in his trench-coat pocket for his packet, his matches. He lit a fresh Woodbine, coughed, flicked the match into the dark water, coughed again.

Tommy knew what it was like to have to wait.

He had been waiting all his life, living with a vague, twisted anxiety coiled inside him, a nameless fear that everything was about to change, threaded with the worse fear that nothing would ever change. Drink didn't eliminate this feeling of hopelessness. Backing winners didn't take it away for more than an hour or two, and women – women were too stupid to understand anything. Here, riding on the river as he'd done when he was a boy, he felt despair come in upon him like the wash from something huge and powerful and mysterious, something too big for him to cling to.

Even so he waited with uncanny patience for Walsh to drop a great big bag of money into his lap, for everything to come out right for once.

'Look,' Dennis said; without haste, Tommy turned his gaze to the wall just as a rope came skittering down. 'They've got it. By God, they've got it.'

Without the crank-jack – and Patsy's ingenuity – the job would have proved impossible. Even with the crank-jack the safe was almost intractable. The ten or twelve feet between its station against the wall and the edge of the manager's desk might have been miles for all the headway that Patsy and Jackie were able to make using brute strength alone. Even with the safe roped, they had been unable to shift it more than a quarter of an inch at a time, to grind it over the carpeted floor with the manila stretching and yielding with every concerted tug.

At first they had been stealthy in their movements, then desperation had set in, disregard for the noise they were making. Only Patsy's experience and self-control had brought him back to reality and, resting, he had applied his brain to a situation that was in danger of becoming a farce.

He sat cross-legged before the safe and glowered at it.

Jackie, still panting, said, 'We could send for Dennis. He's strong.'

'He'd never make it up the pipe.'

'We could tie a rope ...'

'Forget it.'

'If we do it this way we'll be here all bloody night.'

'I know,' Patsy said.

'I mean, even if we get it to the bloody desk, we'll never be able to lift it.'

'I know,' said Patsy again.

'If only that cow Babs had thought t' tell us ...'

'Jackie, shut up.'

Jackie was silent for thirty seconds.

Then he said, 'It's comin' up for half eleven, Pat. We've missed—'

Patsy uttered a little snarl and leaped to his feet.

Jackie quailed, forearm flying to his face to protect himself. Patsy went straight past him, though, walking fast, hardly seeming to walk at all but floating then flying out of the glass-panelled door into the outer office, torch cupped in one pink fist. Jackie didn't have the temerity to follow. He waited, leaning against the top of the safe, his fingers curled around its edges as if by some simple act of levitation he might render it weightless.

He was still in the same position when, only seconds later, Patsy returned.

'We're in luck,' he said, and opened his hand.

'What's that?'

'Soap,' Patsy said. 'Just one bar but it might be enough.'

'Where'd you find it?'

'In the secretary's drawer. Polly told me that Babs told her that the manager's secretary was a mean old bitch. So I reckoned she might keep the soap and towels under lock an' key. An' I was right.'

His enthusiasm was back, the despair gone out of him. While Jackie watched, puzzled, Patsy cut the bar of soap in half using a penknife from his pocket. He laid the two halves on the desk and, stooping, rolled back the carpet as far as the safe, drawing it to one side and exposing the wooden floorboards.

'Oh, yeah!' said Jackie, quietly.

Patsy was already assembling the crank-jack that he had taken from the bag by the desk. He knelt and inserted one of the steel rods into the jaws of the jack and then, with Jackie's aid, lifted the front edge of the safe just enough to slip the trailing edges of the carpet out. He kicked them away, grunting, and manoeuvred the rod of the jack into place. He locked the lever on to the jack and began to crank on it and watched the front of the safe lift and the angle of balance change.

'Jackie, the soap.'

'What?'

'Put the soap under the front of the safe.'

'Oh, right.'

Jackie did as he was told to do, nervously slipping the small bars into place under the rim. Hardly had he jerked his fingers away before Patsy reversed the action of the lever and cranked the front of the Hobbs down again.

'Won't it crush ...' Jackie began.

'Won't matter.'

Patsy darted around to the side of the safe and, with an effort, inserted the steel extension rod beneath it. He cranked, lifted the safe up at the back so that its weight was resting on the forward rim, on the crushed bars of soap.

'Hold this,' he told Jackie and carefully transferred the crank handle into Jackie's fists. 'For Christ's sake don't let it go.'

'This is very — very technical,' Jackie said. 'You sure it's gonna work?'

'It had better.'

Patsy doubled a length of the manila rope around his forearm and looped it under the back of the safe, knotted it firmly, then, working fast now, ran the line back over the top of the safe. He pulled on it, taking in all the slack and all the yield. The safe budged not one inch.

'Not gonna work,' said Jackie. 'I could've told you so.'

'Wanna bet?'

Patsy unbuttoned his trousers and made water.

'Aw, naw!' said Jackie. 'That's disgustin'.'

'Any better ideas?'

He buttoned his fly, grasped the rope in both hands and drew upon it steadily. After a moment he felt the Hobbs yield and move reluctantly towards him, then, squeaking, begin to slide by little fits and starts across the wet floorboards.

'Jeeze, I don't believe it,' Jackie said. 'You want me to pee too?'

'No, thank you,' Patsy said.

There was no final act, no last bit of manoeuvring that made the rest easy. Even so, as each muscle-racking action was successfully accomplished, the safe jacked up and tilted against the edge of the desk — crushing it horribly — and lifted clear of the floor, Patsy really began to believe that he was going to pull off the coup of a lifetime.

The struggle with dead-weight metal had dulled his caution and his only concern as he fought to fit the Hobbs into the cargo net was that the safe would not go through the window space. He kept his doubts to himself, however, and enjoyed, moment by moment, the succession of tiny achievements. What they would do with the Hobbs once it was in the boat, how it would be conveyed from the riverside at Shotten Street to the Hallops' repair shed in the heart of the Gorbals was too much for his imagination to cope with. First things first; one step at a time, he told himself, while Jackie, knackered by his efforts, groaned and grunted and complained.

More rolling back of carpet, more laying down of crumbs of soap, more heaving and sweating to shift the desk with the safe on top from its original position and ram it hard against the outer wall, level — dead level — with the window frame. By now the Hobbs was webbed in rope of various textures — hairy hemp and smooth manila — and looked less like a safe than a captured animal, some swart, stocky beast, exhausted by the chase, not dead but resting, gathering its strength for one last effort of resistance.

'Now what?' said Jackie, thickly.

Patsy was half out of the window, looking down. He could see the longboat directly below and thanked his stars that Tommy Bonnar was sailor enough to have kept it there for the best part of an hour. He signalled with the torch, a meaningless flash, and received by way of acknowledgement a wave from Dennis Hallop. He wriggled back inside the office and climbed on to the top of the safe, on top of the desk. He had Jackie hold the torch while he separated out one rope from another and ran two double lines of the manila down to the floor. He leaped down, went on all fours and drew the loose ropes under the desk and out again, weaving them — one each — against the desk's stout little wooden legs.

It was engineering, crude but necessary. He had no intention of losing the lot now, of letting the safe plunge out and down without something solid to brake and check it. The next part, though, would be dangerous and probably noisy, for he suspected that the Hobbs was heavy enough to wreck the framework of the desk. He gathered all the tools and stuffed them into the bag, picked up his cap and stuck it firmly on his head, put on the heavy leather gloves.

It was now exactly a minute after midnight.

If the Manones' night-watchmen were worth anything at all they would be starting out on their rounds about now, checking the warehouse bay by bay, corridor by corridor, office by office. Rough estimate, Patsy reckoned that they had about fifteen minutes to get the safe off the premises and the longboat downriver. He still nurtured a faint hope that the night-watchmen would be typically lazy sods and that the disappearance of the safe would not be discovered until morning. But things had not been running in his favour so far and he was no longer inclined to optimism.

'Gimme the jack,' he said.

Jackie gave him the jack.

Patsy fitted the steel rods back into the crank-jack's jaws and slid them under the cargo net in which the safe was wrapped. He clambered on to the desk again and pumped the lever, lifting the safe up and forward until it was poised, teetering, on the edge of the window.

'Jackie, take hold on that rope. That one, yeah. Hang on tight.'

'Is this it?'

'This is it.'

'Okay,' said Jackie, grim and manly now. 'Go.'

Balanced balletically on one foot, Patsy gave the safe a single swift kick. As it swayed and began to topple outward, he leaped to the floor and grabbed his share of the rope. He felt vibrations shudder through the framework of the desk, heard the teak crinkle and creak. He saw the desk heel upward and jam itself against the window. For an instant the safe was clearly visible, a great dark hairy bundle clinging ape-like to the sill – and then, unbalanced, it was gone.

Patsy had looped the manila line around his waist and ran it through his hands the way rock climbers did. Even that wasn't enough. From the corner of his eye he saw Jackie skitter and sidle forward on tiptoe. The desk hopped into the air, its stout little wooden legs breaking off as if made of balsa. Then he was dragged forward too, snatched almost off his feet. He dug in his heels, felt them slither, felt the motion of the Hobbs as it swung in space somewhere outside and heard Jackie screaming as the rope sizzled through his hands.

'*Hold on. For Christ's sake, hold on,*' Patsy shouted, even as Jackie's rope snapped and slithered away and, with a flick of its tail, disappeared.

Jackie sprawled across the desk, still shrieking.

For one glassy, isolated moment Patsy supported the full weight of the Hobbs, the ropes angled diagonally away from him, shifting, shifting, shifting with tiny clockwork-like movements, an inch at a time.

It was not that he could not hold it, rather that it would not be held.

He felt as if his spine were being wrenched through the front of his body and his arms torn from his shoulders, then there was nothing – air, emptiness, an absence of resistance – and Patsy, craning backward, fell down upon the floor.

'It's comin', it's comin',' Dennis chanted. 'They got it. They got it. Here it comes. Here it comes. Hold her steady now, Tommy. Hold . . .'

It looked almost weightless, like a huge bundle of straw bouncing softly against the wall. It looked as if the wind had charge of it, toying with it and that if it was released it would float away like a balloon, bobbing and billowing to alight intact somewhere about Oatlands. Even when it scraped the wall and flirted away, the cargo net robbed it of density and for two or three seconds Dennis Hallop's joy seemed justified.

Tommy Bonnar, looking up too, paddled the oars, edging the longboat into position. He was irked at Dennis for shouting but he was also relieved to see the safe, for however dark his pessimism, however deep his melancholy, he had no particular wish to have his throat cut by one of McGuire's hirelings.

'*Hold her steady now, Tommy. Hold . . .*'

Then it wasn't floating any more.

It was falling, leaping out and falling, plummeting straight down upon them like a fragment of the dark and starless sky.

'Oh, Jesus!' Tommy sighed, a split second before the safe struck the boat and plunged straight through it into the river. 'Here we go again.'

Dominic had been dreaming of how he imagined Italy to be and, like embroidery around the edges, of being feted by a host of pretty, young *signorinas* in a sunlit village square. It had not been a sensuous dream, however, for in his subconscious mind he was just a wee bit afraid of the girls, all of whom seemed to have their hands stretched out in gestures more begging than beckoning.

Where the dream would have taken him and how it would have ended, Dominic never did find out.

Stooped over the bed like a stork, Uncle Guido shook him gently.

Dominic snuffled and opened his eyes.

'Did you not hear the telephone ringing in the hall?' Guido said.

'No.'

'Our warehouse has been broken into.'

Dominic sat up. 'What did they steal?'

'The safe.'

'The safe from MacDermott's office?'

'Yes.'

'Is that all?'

'That appears to be all.'

'Idiots!' Dominic said. 'Do we know who did it?'

'Apparently they got away.'

'How?'

'In a boat,' said Uncle Guido. 'What do you want me to do? Do you want that I should telephone the police?'

'No, we will deal with the matter ourselves,' Dominic said. 'Call Tony and tell him to bring round the car.'

'What, now?' said Uncle Guido.

'Yes, now,' said Dominic Manone.

Chapter Nine

Babs hardly slept at all on Wednesday night. It hadn't dawned on her until then that because of her association with Jackie she too would be forced to face the music. It was all very well for Polly. She would be tucked away in the Burgh Hall offices. But she, Babs, would have to walk into the lion's den, into the warehouse, and pretend to know nothing about the break-in.

Worry wakened her and drove her from bed.

Although it was barely daylight, she stationed herself at the window in the hope that she might catch sight of Jackie or Dennis passing into the close below, but the only person she did see was Mr Hallop toddling off on early shift.

'Go downstairs,' Polly urged. 'Go and knock on the Hallops' door and ask to talk to Jackie. See how things went.'

'Go yourself.'

'He's not *my* boyfriend.'

'He's not mine either.'

'Oh, come off it, Babs.'

'Well, all right. Maybe he is – but I'm not gonna knock on his door,' Babs said. 'What if the coppers are already watchin' the house?'

'That's ridiculous,' Polly said.

'It's all very well for you, you haven't done anythin'.'

'No, but I'm worried about Patsy.'

'We'll see if there's anythin' in the newspapers.'

There was nothing in the newspapers, however, no banner headline, no item tucked away on page four, no mention of a robbery in the Stop Press.

By that time – on the tram on her way to work – Babs regretted her refusal to knock upon the Hallops' door. Now she would be obliged to walk into the red-brick building on Jackson Street not knowing what had happened or what she would find there.

The building looked exactly the same as it did every morning, except that there were a few more vans in the yard.

Babs slunk into the foyer and climbed the stairs to the first-floor cloakroom. She listened to the rattle and *ting* of typewriters in the pool. Everything seemed normal so far. She went into the ladies' cloakroom and found Miss Crawford, the office manageress, powdering her nose in front of the mirror above the wash-basin.

Miss Crawford wore her customary hard-bitten expression but Babs thought that her cheeks were red and her eyes pink, as if she'd been crying. There was no tremble, no trace of tears in her voice, though.

'Ah, Miss Conway!' she said. 'You're an early bird.'

'I – ah – I just . . .'

'It's just as well.' Miss Crawford snapped shut her powder compact. 'There's been some trouble upstairs.'

'Trouble? Wha' – what sort of trouble?'

'An attempted break-in, I gather.'

'Attempted?'

'Some fool tried to rob Mr MacDermott's office during the night.'

'Got – got caught?'

'What? No, no. In any case' – Miss Crawford stood directly in front of her; Babs had nowhere to focus but on the woman's face – 'you're wanted upstairs.'

'Me? Who wants me? The police?'

Miss Crawford tutted. 'What would the police want with the likes of you? Mr Manone wants a word with you, that's all.'

'What could Mr Manone possibly want with me?'

'I haven't the foggiest idea,' Miss Crawford said. 'But I suggest that you smarten yourself up, girl, and don't keep him waiting.'

Babs had never encountered Dominic Manone face to face. Her first sight of him was from the end of the aisle that ran through Mrs Anderson's office into Mr MacDermott's office. Mrs Anderson wasn't seated at her own desk but at another smaller desk. The woman who was usually at the small desk wasn't there at all. The overhead lights were on. Both doors were open.

Babs noticed at once that the window glass in Mr MacDermott's office had been replaced by a board, a neat, raw board of pine planks that blotted out most of the daylight. Two panes of glass partly wrapped in cardboard and with globs of putty stuck on the corners leaned against Mrs Anderson's desk and a man – a glazier? – in a boiler suit was talking to someone on the telephone.

'What do you want?' Mrs Anderson said.

Babs could hardly move her lips. She loitered at the end of the aisle, not daring to move. 'Miss – Miss Crawford said – Miss Crawford sent me.'

She couldn't take her eyes off the man in the distant office: a young man, not tall but strong-looking and very handsome. He wore a dark blue lounge suit with narrow lapels, a white shirt and a pale blue silk tie that seemed too dressy for that hour of the morning. He had a canteen coffee cup in one hand and a tiny cigar in the other and smoke drifted all about him.

As soon as he noticed Babs he put down the cup and beckoned.

Babs was anything but reassured.

Mrs Anderson watched her as she projected herself up

the aisle between the desk and the cabinets and entered the manager's office.

Mr MacDermott was not in the office, only Mr Manone and another Italian-looking man who sat on one of the wooden chairs with his arms folded. Mr MacDermott's desk had been moved to one side of the room, near the plant pots. It, the desk, looked as if it had been chewed by a pack of wild dogs. There was a doggy smell in the air too, faint but acrid. The carpet had been rolled up and propped against the wall by the open door.

There was no sign of the safe.

Mr Manone smiled at Babs, a gentle smile, almost shy.

'You're Lizzie Conway's daughter, aren't you?'

'Aye — yes, sir.'

'Barbara, if I recall.'

'Babs, sir, that's right.'

'How long have you worked for us, Babs?'

'Nearly three years.'

He lifted the coffee cup and sipped from it.

The man on the wooden chair just on the edge of Babs's vision stirred slightly. Babs darted a glance at him. He too was handsome, but he was older than Dominic Manone; not as old as her father would have been if he'd survived the war but certainly as old as her mother. He had a thin, sharp-featured sort of face and dark, watchful eyes.

Dominic nodded.

'I take it you know who I am, Barbara?'

'Aye — yes, sir.'

'No doubt you're wondering why I asked to speak with you?'

'I've no idea about that, Mr Manone.'

'Didn't you hear that we were broken into during the night?'

'Miss Crawford mentioned it, I think.'

'You have only just arrived?'

'I'm not due to start till nine.'

He stood before her at a polite distance, rocking a little on the balls of his feet while he observed her reactions.

Babs wondered if he was impressed or if he could see right through her and already knew that she had sold out the Central Warehouse Company. She also wondered where Jackie was, where the safe was, if the boys had got clean away and when she would receive her hundred quid; a little dab of mendacity was almost enough to calm her down.

'Don't you know why I've asked to speak with you?'

'No, Mr Manone.'

'I've been acquainted with your mother for many years,' he said. 'I've the greatest of respect for her. She's an honest woman. Are you honest, Babs?'

'I try to be, Mr Manone.'

'Someone broke into Mr MacDermott's office,' Dominic went on. 'As you can see they've made rather a nasty mess of the place.'

Babs opened her mouth, then closed it again.

'It seems to me,' Dominic Manone said, 'that it's the work of hooligans.'

'I – I suppose it could be,' Babs agreed.

'On the other hand it may have been what is called "an inside job". Do you know what that means?'

'Yes,' said Babs, nodding.

He placed a hand on her shoulder; nothing friendly about the gesture, Babs sensed, nothing flirty.

'What I wish you to do for me is keep your ears open, so that if you hear anything that might give us a clue who thought they could break into Manones' warehouse and get away with it ... Well' – he smiled, released her, shrugged – 'it would be nice if we could remind these guys that crime does not pay.'

Babs tried to appear solemn and responsible. She managed something between a scowl and a pout. 'If they didn't get away with anythin', though ...'

'They did damage,' Dominic said. 'They were stupid to break in to my property. They must be taught a lesson.'

'I don't know who could've done—'

'Sure you don't. But a smart girl might hear things that we won't.'

'I'll – I'll see what I can find out.'

'Good.' His eyes had gone to sleep. 'Perhaps you'll hear something here in the warehouse or possibly in the streets. You'll do this for me?'

'I will, Mr Manone.'

Babs felt a strange smug glow light up within her. If Dominic Manone had known who was behind the break-in then he wouldn't have sent for her. He was fishing, just fishing. She reckoned that Jackie and the boys *had* got away with the safe, that this guy, this big-shot, hadn't a clue who'd taken it or where it was now. He didn't want the police involved. She couldn't blame him for that. But he did want his money back. He must be a whole lot less smart than she'd given him credit for, though, if he thought an office clerk – even if she were Lizzie Conway's daughter – would hear anything that would finger the culprits.

'Maybe you will hear some talk when you go dancing,' Dominic said.

'Dancin'?'

'At the Calcutta.'

'I don't go ... Well, aye, sometimes I do go there.'

'Perhaps somebody will mention a name, drop a name.'

'They might, aye,' said Babs.

'And you will pass that name on to me.'

'Tell Mr MacDermott, you mean?'

'No, you will tell me. Your mama knows where to find me.'

The man on the wooden chair unfolded his arms and placed both hands on his knees. He wore a heavy woollen overcoat, a homburg hat and black shoes. He looked, she thought, like a polished version of Tommy Bonnar, an Italian version. He stared at her and then, even as she watched, gave her an insolent little wink.

'I'll do what I can, Mr Manone,' Babs promised, then, unaware that she had just been threatened, let him guide her to the open door and see her off down the long aisle back to the safety of the counting house.

Dominic watched the girl depart. She had broad hips and a confident little bottom that in eight years or ten would become fat. She was an archetypal Scot of Irish descent who, like her father before her, was fuelled by a mixture of low cunning and crass stupidity. If she had been male instead of female she would have been one of his street runners instead of a clerkess.

He put the cigar to his lips and tried to coax it back into life.

Tony Lombard struck a match and held it out to him.

Dominic fired the tobacco leaf, blew smoke. 'What do you think, Tony?'

'She's the one,' Tony Lombard answered. 'She's in it up to her neck.'

'Unfortunately,' said Dominic, 'I think you may be right.'

'You want I should do something to her?'

'No,' Dominic said, 'not yet, Tony, not just yet.'

They were hidden in the back booth of a café halfway along Paisley Road West. It was the last place that anyone who knew the Manones would expect to find them. The café owner — not Italian — had no more than a notion that the gentlemen were important. They ordered and ate sausage sandwiches and asked for coffee to be served in a pot. The café owner was both attentive and discreet. He had noticed the expensive motorcar parked outside at the pavement's edge, had respect for anyone who owned such a vehicle.

Uncle Guido wiped grease from his chin with a handkerchief and took a sip of the appalling coffee. 'You looked tired, Dominic,' he said, in Italian.

Dominic answered in the same language. 'No more tired than you.'

'What do you think they intended to do with it?'

'The money? Pay off debts, I expect,' said Dominic. 'At least one of our boys is mixed up in it, of that I'm sure.'

'I hope you are not going to let them get off with it?'

Dominic did not deign to answer his uncle's question.

He broke the sandwich with his fingers and put a piece into his mouth. He was no less fastidious than the old man but he had more relish for the flavoursome meat and was, in fact, rather enjoying himself.

He had a certain grudging sympathy for the nitwits who had stolen the safe, a certain admiration for the ingenuity with which they had effected its removal. He gave no sign to Guido that this was the case, for he did not want to be thought to be anything less than serious about the insult to the family. These days, it seemed, you couldn't trust anybody. He would see to it that the night-watchmen were reprimanded for slackness, that metal grilles were put up on the waterside windows.

What really amused him and took the edge off his anger, though, was the thought of the burglars hauling the safe into a shed or a quiet back court and going to all the bother of breaking it open only to discover that it was entirely empty, that all their struggles with soap and jacking devices and ropes had been so much wasted effort.

Guido said, 'Are you thinking that they did not get away with it at all?'

'It could be at the bottom of the river, I suppose,' said Dominic.

'We could always hire a diver to . . .'

'Let it go. We lost nothing but the safe itself.'

'And face,' Uncle Guido reminded him.

'I am not forgetting about the loss of face,' said Dominic.

They had just visited the Paisley branch of the Bank of Scotland and had withdrawn from a contingency account exactly the sum that the stolen safe had purportedly contained. The banknotes had been packed into a briefcase which now reposed under the café table, protected by Uncle Guido's size tens.

The contingency account had barely withstood the mauling and had only a pound or two left in it. But, in Dominic's view, it had been necessary to act in a clear, above-board manner, to withdraw the staff's Christmas money from a legitimate source. Only five people knew that the sum that had allegedly been stolen was three and a half thousand pounds, not eight thousand. Only four people, including Brian MacDermott, knew that the money had not been housed in the Hobbs at all but was locked in an innocent-looking locker in the warehouse boiler-room from which place, later that afternoon, Guido and Tony Lombard would redeem it and transport it back to Mansion Park Avenue.

'Nobody knows that the money was not in the safe. Why do you not report the theft?' Guido said. 'If it is reported then we can claim the sum from our insurance and make three and a half thousand pounds profit.'

'I considered it,' said Dominic. 'I also considered how the coppers would love to get into our warehouse and what sort of disruption they would cause over the busy Christmas week. Besides, it was not a robbery. It was hooliganism. A window was smashed, a desk broken. Some pig pissed on our carpet. Nothing was stolen.'

'The insurance people do not know that.'

'Sure, sure,' said Dominic. 'But there is a time to make profit – and this is not it. There is also a time to keep quiet – and this *is* it.'

'The cost of the safe?'

'Minimal.'

'Will you purchase another Hobbs?'

'Immediately.'

Guido hesitated. 'I hope, Dominic, that you are not pedalling soft on this business because of the woman.'

'Woman? What woman?'

'Frank Conway's wife.'

'She is not involved.'

'No,' Guido said, 'but her daughter might be. Tony says—'

'Tony is only guessing,' said Dominic. 'I am not soft pedalling on anyone, Uncle. Maybe Tony's right and Barbara Conway *is* the inside contact, but I'm not going to go out there and start swinging until I know who did this thing and who is really behind it. Our boys are good boys, if stupid sometimes. I do not want to put one against the other if I can avoid it. First I will find out who did this thing and then I will make them pay for it.'

'Take them out, do you mean?'

'Maybe. Yes, maybe even that.'

'Anything less will not be acceptable,' Guido said.

'Acceptable to whom? My father?' Dominic said. 'My father is in Philly where things are done a little differently. If the idiots *had* got away with three and a half thousand pounds then I would be dealing with the situation differently. Everything is going good right now, Uncle, and I do not want to give the coppers an opening, not even a little one.'

'That is only horse-sense,' Guido admitted.

'MacDermott will do what he is told to do. If anyone asks him, he will tell them that nothing was stolen.'

'Nothing *was* stolen,' said Guido. 'Only an empty safe.'

'Exactly.' Dominic grinned. 'Do you not see how much of a circus this is? It is better than a pantomime. Whoever took our money — one of our boys or somebody else — they will know now that we are not so casual as we appear to be. Come on, Uncle, was it not clever of me to use the safe as a dummy?'

'That is true. But you *are* clever, Dominic,' the old man said. 'I have never thought otherwise. It is not your clever head but your less-than-clever heart that sometimes bothers me.'

'What do you want?' said Dominic. 'Do you want me to invite all our boys to Bernie's garage and mow them down with machine-guns? We are not in a war with anyone. Let the razor-kings do their crazy war dances and the Workers' Movement organise its riots. It keeps the police occupied, keeps them from breathing on our necks. We are businessmen, nice Scots-Italian businessmen. We do not shed blood.'

'Unless it becomes necessary,' Uncle Guido said.

'We are a long way from it becoming necessary.'

'I hope you are right.'

'I *am* right. I am *always* right, Uncle, and don't you forget it.' Dominic pushed away his plate and cup and got abruptly to his feet. 'Come on, pick up the briefcase, settle the bill and let us get back to the warehouse and pay our employees what they are due.'

'What will we do then — about the thieves, I mean?'

'Let them sweat for a day or two.'

'Or run away?'

'That intelligent they're not,' said Dominic and, with Guido tailing behind, strode quickly out to the car.

It had never occurred to Polly that Patsy would live in a run-down tenement and have relatives of his own to look after. Logically she realised he must reside somewhere but she had been disinclined to separate Patsy from the image he presented of himself, to sully her belief that he was a lonely rogue, free of the sort of ties and commitments that affected the rest of the community.

She had already begun to suspect that as far as Communism went Patsy was more Pale Pink than Turkey Red and that his enthusiasm for the rights of the working man was an intellectual pursuit not unconnected to snobbery. He was self-educated, well read, articulate, periodically well off, and had travelled further afield than any fifty Clydeside citizens chosen at random. That he also made his bread by robbing the better-off seemed glamorous now or, if not glamorous, certainly different, certainly stimulating.

Unlike Babs, Polly was not immediately depressed by the circumstances of the warehouse robbery. She disliked the Manones. In fact, she detested the Manones. Though she'd had no clear idea what Dominic Manone had looked like or what it was that still linked him to her family, over the years he had become Polly's bogey-man, her *bête noire*, a scapegoat for all the unpleasantness that the Conways had endured.

Even in Wellshott Primary School she had equated Dominic Manone with the bullies who tormented the weaker boys or pulled the girls' pigtails; also with those domineering teachers – female as well as male – who made life miserable for everyone. When, around fourteen or fifteen, she had reached the age of reason, she had become aware that her hatred of Dominic Manone might be a substitute for hatred of the father who had abandoned her but whom she could not quite find it in her heart to blame.

Seldom, if ever, did she think of her daddy, whereas she thought of Dominic Manone quite a lot. But the discovery of the hidden hoard under Gran McKerlie's floorboards had affected her more than she cared to admit.

It had brought her father into the foreground again and pushed the Italian bogey-man, the blameful stranger, into the background. Indeed, if it hadn't been for Patsy's plan to relieve the Manones of a small fortune within the week she might have completed the transference and have acknowledged that she owed her job in the burgh offices to a man she had always despised and that good things as well as bad were mysteriously connected to the Italian.

When Polly arrived in the burgh offices there was no talk of a break-in at the Manones' warehouse, no circulating rumours. Throughout the morning she kept her head down and her ears open but heard not a chirp about happenings at the CWC. It wasn't until one of the burgh architects brought in an early edition of the *Evening Citizen*, however, and it too was devoid of news that Polly began to fret.

As soon as she was released from her desk at half past five o'clock she made a beeline round to Brock Street, at the back end of the Gorbals, where, in a flat over the Washington Bar, Patsy resided.

It wasn't Patsy who opened the door to Polly's urgent knock but a small, bald-headed, bad-tempered man of about fifty clad in a snow-white undervest and a pair of patched moleskin trousers held up by a canvas belt. He had no hair at all. His scalp shone as if it had been greased with whale-oil and Polly could see upon it, raised like a relief map, a series of prominent ridges. His face too was scarred, the cheekbone under his left eye concave, the brow above hairless.

'I'm looking for Patsy,' Polly said.

One eye pinched and closed – the good eye, the real eye; the other was of glass. It stared out at her, not blankly but with a weird glittering ferocity as if it were not artificial and opaque but a mirror to magnify the anger that simmered in his soul. He answered Polly with a word, the harsh, punched-out, Anglo-Saxon word that for some men defined all women. Polly had heard the word often before; it still made her wince.

Before she could complain, the man turned and yelled over his shoulder, telling someone inside the flat that a so-and-so had called for him and that he had better get his arse out of the chair and see what the so-and-so wanted.

Polly regarded the man as contemptuously as he regarded her.

He still had his arm up, holding the door.

She could make out a tussock of grey-white hair under his

armpit and running out of it like a pale vein or a worm-cast another of those long-healed but still livid scars.

'What caused that?' she said. 'Shrapnel?'

When he widened his eyes she saw that the glass eye had no life in it after all, that it was dead to every reflection.

She waited for rage, for another eruption of obscenity.

He grunted, amused – possibly – by her audacity.

'Wire,' he told her. Then turning again, he shouted again, 'Patrick, get out here,' and stepped back and limped away.

Patsy took his father's place in the narrow doorway.

And Polly knew at once that it had all gone wrong.

Those 'ordinary' members who came clumping down Molliston Street that cold Thursday night in search of warmth and shelter and an inexpensive pint were doomed to disappointment, for the doors of the Rowing Club were well and truly locked against them. A hand-printed notice – *Committee Meeting In Progress* – tacked to the paintwork provided sufficient information to prevent even the most irascible dimwit clamouring for admission and, if the notice wasn't enough to deter them, then a glimpse of the sleek, dark shape of an Alfa Romeo motorcar parked a little way down the street most certainly was.

Inside the Rowing Club there was no sign of the management committee as such and a meeting of quite a different order was in session.

The bar had been open for half an hour, with drinks on the house. But Mr Manone's boys had been uncommonly abstemious and had drifted into the windowless room at the rear of the building nursing nothing more intoxicating than a half-pint of beer or a glass of well-watered whisky. They had been summoned from various corners of the territory during the course of the afternoon by word of mouth, and all Mr Manone's top aides were present, including Tony Lombard, Alex O'Hara and – a head cold notwithstanding – sniffy little Tommy Bonnar.

In spite of all that Guido and Tony had done to prevent it, rumours of what had taken place in the warehouse had sifted on to the streets and with all the enthusiasm of washerwives gathered round a pump the lads had exaggerated the few scant facts in their possession until the tale had become one of blazing revolvers, slaughtered night-watchmen and the sort of zigzag pursuit down the Clyde in speedboats that would have had a Saturday matinée audience roaring its appreciation.

Dominic did not remove his overcoat. He laid his hat and gloves on one of the dining tables that had been pushed against the wall. The long room smelled of coal smoke, fish fries and beer and, on that damp December night, held tobacco smoke in thin blue-grey bands. Chairs were ranked before the open fireplace as if for a prayer meeting but not even Tommy Bonnar was disrespectful enough to sit down.

Poor sniffing Tommy coughed into a crumpled handkerchief.

'You should be in your bed,' Alex O'Hara told him in a stage whisper.

'I was in ma bed,' said Tommy.

'You shoulda stayed there.'

'Aye, an' how would that've looked?' Tommy croaked.

Alex O'Hara chuckled and shook his head at Bonnar's discomfort.

Whatever had happened at the warehouse a summons from Dominic Manone was not something you dared ignore. Besides, there was always a possibility that Guido would be on hand with his scuffed leather grip filled with brown envelopes and you would go home with a pocketful of the crinkly. Guido was on hand but there was no sign of the scuffed leather grip. The grim old Italian looked even grimmer than usual. The boys stirred nervously, sipped from their flat half-pints, puffed their cigarettes, and waited to be told what would be expected of them.

There were no preliminaries, no clearing of the throat, no

polite little rappings on the table or calls for order. Dominic leaned against the table and started talking. He informed them that the Central Warehouse had been broken into, a safe removed from the manager's office and taken off downriver in a small boat, and that the job had probably been pulled by locals.

Tommy Bonnar had the temerity to ask why Mr Manone thought the job might have been done by someone local.

Mr Manone explained his reasoning.

Irish Paddy asked if the boat had been found.

Mr Manone said that the boat had not been found.

Irish Paddy asked if the matter had been reported to the police.

Alex O'Hara guffawed audibly while Mr Manone, with more patience than the question deserved, explained his reasons for not summoning the police. Alex O'Hara asked if Mr Manone wanted them to conduct the investigation.

Mr Manone said yes, that was what he required of them and indicated that there would be a finder's fee for anyone who turned up the money or a portion thereof.

'An' what d' you want us t' do when we catch the bastards?'

'Tell Tony,' said Dominic Manone.

There was little or no discussion.

The meeting closed at nine minutes to seven.

Dominic, his uncle and little Tony Lombard left immediately.

Soon after that Alex O'Hara left too, heading for Brock Street and Patsy Walsh's flat above the Washington Bar.

Patsy invited her in. There was nowhere else for them to talk. Polly wouldn't be welcome in any of the bars that flanked Brock Street and the Black Cat Café was just too far away to make the hike worth while.

To Polly's surprise the single-room apartment was sparsely furnished. She had somehow expected it to be more cluttered. There was no linoleum upon the floor and only a single thin rug before the grate. There were two hard little armchairs by the fireplace, two wooden ones at the narrow table and the room had a scrubbed, almost sterile air.

The old man, Patsy's father, paid her no attention. He did not even seem interested in learning her name.

He opened a drawer beneath the niche bed, took out a clean blue shirt and a necktie. Back to her, he put on the shirt and knotted the necktie. Then he pulled a jacket and a cloth cap from a hook in the alcove and put them on too. He seated himself on one of the armchairs and drew a pair of boots from under it, tugged the boots on and laced them up.

Patsy said, 'Listen, Paw, you don't have to go out.'

'I'm goin' anyway.'

'You're not workin' tonight, are you?'

'Naw.'

'Then you stay here an' we'll—'

The old man called Patsy a dirty name, stamped his feet firmly into the boots and headed, limping, for the door.

Standing awkwardly by the narrow table, Polly heard the landing door slam and only then did she ask, 'What happened?'

Patsy moved towards her. He put his arms around her and would have drawn her to him if she hadn't held back.

'You look terrible,' Polly said. 'What happened last night?'

'A cock-up,' he said, 'a right royal cock-up from start to finish.'

'Didn't you get the money?'

'Nope, we didn't get the money.' He seated himself on a kitchen chair. 'The money's still inside the bloody safe an' the safe's at the bottom of the Clyde. We lost it. We nearly lost Dennis an' all.'

'Couldn't you open it?'

'Open it? We could hardly even move the bloody thing.'

'Did Babs ...'

'It wasn't her fault. If it was anybody's fault it was mine. I shouldn't have listened to Tommy Bonnar. The whole thing was nuts from the start. The ropes snapped while we were lowerin' the safe out the window,' Patsy said. 'The safe fell straight down into the boat. Smashed it to pulp. We were lucky it didn't hit Tommy or Dennis. They were flung into the water. Guess what? Dennis can't swim. He was halfway to bloody Greenock before Tommy managed to fish him out. I'll say that for the wee bugger, he really kept his head — Tommy, I mean.'

'What about the boat?'

'It sank without trace, what was left of it.'

'And the safe?' said Polly.

'It's still down there — with the money inside.'

'Won't it show up at low tide?'

'Tommy says not. Tommy says it'll be lost in the silt.'

'Do you believe him?' Polly asked.

'I don't have much option,' said Patsy. 'Tell you what I'm not doin' — I'm not goin' fishin' for the bloody thing. If Tommy wants it, he can get it himself.'

'Are you hurt?' Polly asked.

'Bruised, that's all.'

'What about the others?'

'Dennis is okay. Jackie's got burned hands.'

'Are they bandaged?'

'I dunno. As soon as we were all safe we scarpered in different directions. Tommy an' Dennis were soaked to the skin. They walked home, I expect.'

'So you don't know whether or not Jackie's hands are bandaged?'

'He's a big boy. He'll be all right.'

'Oh, yes,' Polly said. 'Unless Dominic Manone finds him.'

Patsy glowered up at her. She wasn't offering sympathy.

'If the safe's under water and the boat sank then the Manones won't know that you didn't get away with the money,' Polly said. 'They'll be on the look-out for the money and for anything that might give them a clue who did the job.'

'Like bandaged hands?' said Patsy. 'Yeah. Unless they decided to report the break-in to the cops an' let the law deal with it.'

'Haven't you been out today?'

'I've been in bed.'

'There's nothing about the break-in the newspapers,' Polly said. 'If it had been reported then surely the press would have got wind of it.'

'I see what you mean,' said Patsy. 'The Manones would rather write off eight thousand quid than have the cops askin' awkward questions. That's all to the good as far as we're concerned.'

He reached in his trouser pocket, brought out a packet of Woodbines and offered one to Polly.

She shook her head. 'I have to push off now.'

'Why? My old man won't be back for hours.'

'Is that it, your family? Just you and your father?'

'Yeah, just us.'

'Where's your mother?'

'She an' my two sisters died of influenza five months after my old man was released from the military hospital. He survived the war – at least some of him survived the war – then the bloody Spanish influenza wipes us out. Maw was sick for half a day, that's all. Couldn't even get her to a hospital she went so quick. My sisters were taken in but it was too late. Pneumonia got both of them. Eleven an' nine. Evelyn an' Margaret. Boom – gone.' He lit a cigarette and tossed the burned match into the fireplace. 'Makes you think, eh, Polly? Made *me* think anyway. Put everythin' into perspective.'

'I have to go,' said Polly. 'I really must. Mammy will fret if I'm not home soon. Anyway, I need to warn Babs to be careful.'

'You be careful too, Polly.'

'Me? I'm not involved.'

'Maybe not.' Patsy got up. 'But be careful anyhow.'

He held the cigarette at arm's length and pulled her close.

She sensed his weakness, a lost quality, as if all assertiveness had been sucked away by the events of the night. She hugged him, kissed his mouth. Part of her wanted to stay, to let him make love to her, to merge his worries with her own, but another part of her desperately wanted to escape.

She touched her lips regretfully to his.

And someone hammered loudly on the landing door.

Chapter Ten

The motorbike, a Norton overhead valver, was seven or eight years old and had seen service on several mountain circuit TT races. According to the guy from whom Dennis had bought the machine it was in perfect working order and only needed a light overhaul to restore it to its former glory. Neither Dennis nor Jackie were taken in by the patter. They knew very well that the bike had been stolen and was, anyway, a knocker. They had several cannibalised parts for other old Nortons stashed away in the shed, though, and Dennis had offered thirty bob for the bike which the guy had eagerly accepted, thus confirming the Hallops' opinion that the bike had been stolen.

It lay now in pieces on an oily old tarpaulin on the ground, plugs and valves floating in jars on the bench above and its frame propped up on two little piles of bricks ready to be rubbed down and repainted. Dennis had somehow lost his enthusiasm for continuing with the job, however, and Jackie, with his torn hands gloved, could barely hold a cigarette let alone a spanner or a brush. He had spent the afternoon huddled in front of the stove, feeding it from time to time with lumps of coke that he hoisted up between his palms as clumsily as a bear trying to lift a ball.

Dennis was none the worse for his ducking in the Clyde but he still smarted from the humiliation of having had to be rescued by Tommy Bonnar and the even greater humiliation of having had to slosh through the streets dripping wet. Fortunately there had been few folk about at that hour to point and jeer and, even more fortunately, no coppers to ask awkward questions.

There was no guilt in either of the young men and very little apprehension. To their way of thinking the only thing they'd done wrong was to bungle the break-in — and for that they blamed Patsy Walsh. Since they hadn't got off with the safe and had reaped not a penny from their enterprise they considered themselves not just hard done by but also virtually blameless; so blameless, in fact, that they hadn't even bothered to lock the gate of the yard or bolt the door of the shed.

When, about half past six, an out-of-breath Babs burst in upon them they didn't leap up or even start but turned gloomily from contemplation of the stove and growled in unison, 'What the bloody hell d' you want?' a greeting that pleased Babs not at all.

'I want my hundred quid for a start.'

'Hah!' said Jackie, turning back to the fire.

'What d' you mean "hah"? Do you know what I've been through today because of you, Jackie Hallop?'

He held up his gloved hands. 'Worse than this, dear?'

'I was questioned — I was *grilled* by Mr Manone himself.'

'So what?' said Dennis.

'So I want my share.'

'Share of what, sweetheart?' said Jackie.

'The money.'

'There is no money,' said Dennis. 'We never got nothin'.'

'Liar!'

'It's true, but,' said Jackie. 'Patsy dropped the safe in the river before he could blow the bloody thing open.'

'That's not what Mr Manone told *me*.'

Dennis got up slowly, frowning. 'What's this about Manone?'

'Mr Manone told *me* you got away wi' the lot,' Babs fibbed.

'Then he's a liar,' said Jackie. 'Ask Patsy Walsh if you don't believe me.'

'How do I know Patsy's not in on it too?' said Babs.

Jackie held up his gloved hands placatingly. She was mad all right, scared too. 'Why was Manone askin' *you* questions?'

'He wants me to ...' Babs flushed.

'Squeal?' said Dennis.

'Naw, not squeal exactly. What happened t' your hands, Jackie?'

'Don't change the subject.' Dennis came forward, bulking over her. 'How come Manone picked you to question?'

'He knows my mammy.'

Jackie said, 'Look, Babs, you didn't tell Manone about us, did you?'

'What d'you take me for?' Babs said. 'Where's my money, Jackie? You're not talkin' me out o' my hundred quid.'

'One more time, Barbara,' Dennis said. 'There is no money. Manone wants everyone to think he wasn't robbed so he won't have to call in the cops.'

'He didn't tell me that,' said Babs.

'Bloody hell!' Dennis exclaimed.

'Listen, sweetheart,' Jackie said, 'Manone's a crafty bugger but maybe he does *think* we got away wi' the money. That could be it, couldn't it, Dennis? Maybe nobody's looked for the safe yet.'

'Where is it?' Babs said.

'I told you, at the bottom o' the Clyde.'

'What's it doin' there?'

'It's a long story,' said Jackie.

'Is that what happened t' your hands?'

'Yeah.'

'What about Patsy?'

'Patsy!' said Dennis, spitting on the ground. 'Sod Patsy.'

'He's all right,' said Jackie. 'We're all okay.'

'You won't be if Mr Manone catches you,' Babs said. 'Are you tellin' me the truth about all this?'

'Cross ma heart.' Jackie fashioned an appropriate gesture. 'Dominic Manone ain't gonna find out it was us.'

'Unless somebody tells him,' said Dennis.

'No hundred quid,' Babs said. 'God! After all I've been through.'

'I'll make it up t' you, Babs,' Jackie promised.

'How?'

'I'll take y' dancin' on Saturday.'

'With those mitts? No thanks.'

'Next week then. Christmas.'

'Forget it, Jackie.'

'Uh-huh!' Dennis murmured. 'Are you on the turn, dear?'

'On the turn, nothin',' said Babs. 'I'm just – just annoyed.'

'Annoyed enough to suck up to Dominic Manone?'

'Don't be so bloody daft, Dennis.' Babs pursed her lips. 'I just don't think I should be seen with either of you for a while.'

'She is,' Dennis said. 'She's on the turn.'

'Why, but?' said Jackie. 'Why won't you go out wi' me?'

'Use your loaf, Jackie,' Babs told him. 'Mr Manone's out for blood an' if he spots me wi' you he might start to put two an' two together.'

'Can't see that,' said Jackie. 'We'll be safe enough at the Calcutta.'

'You're not safe anywhere,' Babs screeched. 'Can't you get that into your thick skull, Jackie Hallop? Right now you're poison.'

'That's not a very nice thing t' say, Babs.' Jackie sulked. 'After all we've meant t' each other. I thought we had somethin' nice goin' on?'

'Nice? If this is your idea o' nice . . .'

'She's suckin' up to Manone,' Dennis stated.

'*I am not suckin' up to anybody*,' Babs shouted. 'I just don't think

I owe you anythin', Jackie, not after what you've done to me. Promisin' me money an' then lyin' about it.'

'I'm not lyin',' Jackie declared.

'He's not lyin',' said Dennis.

'Anyway, I've had enough o' you lot,' Babs said.

'Is this goodbye then?' said Jackie.

'Yes, this is goodbye,' said Babs.

'Don't count on it,' said Dennis.

'Oh, it's yourself, Alex,' Patsy Walsh said, casually. 'Come on in.' He stepped back and allowed O'Hara to enter the kitchen.

Polly was seated in a chair by the fire still wearing her overcoat and hat.

O'Hara glanced at her, looked round at Patsy and grinned. 'I didn't know you had company.'

'She's a friend,' said Patsy. 'Polly, this is Alex O'Hara.'

'Polly, pleased t' meetcha.'

'If you've business to discuss,' Polly said, 'perhaps I should leave.'

'Yeah, that might be a good idea,' Patsy said.

O'Hara would have none of it. 'You in residence here, Polly?'

'God, no.'

'You got a man somewhere else?'

'No.'

'Where you from?'

'Gorbals.'

O'Hara paused, then said, 'Lavender Court, right?'

'How did you ...'

'You're Rosie Conway's sister.'

'Yes, I am, as a matter of fact.'

'I see,' O'Hara said. 'Yeah!'

'I don't know what you think you see, Mr O'Hara,' Polly said, 'but Patsy's just a friend of mine, no more an' no less.'

'Good friend, but?'

'Alex ...' Patsy began.

O'Hara held up a blunt finger to silence him, then asked Polly, 'You sleep wi' this guy?'

'Of course I don't sleep with him,' Polly said. 'What do you take me for?'

'So you weren't here last night?'

'As it so happens,' Polly said, 'I was.'

'All night?'

'Nope, not all night.'

'Till when?'

'Half past eleven. Maybe nearer midnight.'

'Is that a fact?' said O'Hara.

'Yes,' Polly said, 'that is a fact.'

'Alex, what the hell's goin' on here?' said Patsy. 'What you askin' her all these questions for? What's it to you who I – who I'm friendly with?'

O'Hara ignored Patsy's protest.

He continued to focus his attention on the girl. She was cool, he had to give her that. Her cockiness reminded him of Rosie's only it was more mature, more superior. She didn't like him – he didn't expect her to – but she wasn't afraid of him either and that worried him. He felt himself shrink from her unyielding gaze. Give him ten minutes alone with her and he'd make her change her bloody tune. He'd teach her a bit of respect.

'What'd your mam have t' say about you gettin' home so late?'

'She was asleep,' Polly said.

She sensed a subtle shift from aggression to wariness, from wariness to sexual speculation. She had a vague understanding that O'Hara was afraid of her and wouldn't know what to do with her except cause her pain. She could see in his eyes, in the sour little wrinkling of the lids, a longing to hurt.

'Who else was here last night?' O'Hara glanced round. 'Your old man?'

'He was on shift,' Patsy answered.

'So it was just you an' the lady here, gettin' up to mischief?'

'Look, I've had about enough o' this,' Patsy said. 'Either you tell me what's goin' on or you get the hell outta my house.'

Polly said, 'He thinks you stole Mr Manone's safe.'

'What?' said Patsy, feigning astonishment. 'What safe?'

Polly said, 'I was just about to tell you when Mr O'Hara came in and interrupted me. Somebody stole a safe from the Central Warehouse last night.'

'How d' you know that?' O'Hara said.

'My sister told me.'

'Rosie, how did—'

'Not Rosie. My other sister – Babs.'

Patsy managed a bark of laughter. 'Jeeze, is that what all the fuss is about, Alex? You thought it was me done the warehouse? I might be a daft bastard at times but I'm not that daft. How much did they get off with?'

'Four or five thousand,' O'Hara said. 'Manone wants it back.'

'I'll bet he does,' said Patsy.

Polly studied Alex O'Hara carefully. She had taken a risk in admitting that she already knew about the robbery. It was logical that she would know, however, that Babs would have told her. Just how much logic a thug like O'Hara would apply to any given situation Polly had no idea; less, she suspected, rather than more. She was tempted to spell it out for him, to amplify her lie, but decided to let him make the running.

O'Hara said, 'How come your sister knows so much about it?'

Polly answered without hesitation. 'She works for the CWC.'

O'Hara sat back. 'Uh!'

Polly didn't dare lift her gaze to look at Patsy who stood by the table, hands bunched loosely into fists.

Polly said, 'Mr Manone – Dominic – spoke to her about it this morning.'

'An' you came right up here to tell your boyfriend?' O'Hara said.

'Of course I did,' said Polly. 'I know what Patsy does for a livin'.'

'You thought it might be him, right?'

'Nope,' Polly said. 'I knew it couldn't be Patsy 'cause I was with him.'

'Aye, but not all night,' said O'Hara.

'Long enough,' said Polly. 'I came to tell him because I thought he might know who'd be smart enough to row off downriver with a safe full of money.'

'Down the river?' said Patsy; another bark of laughter. 'Clever, clever.'

The chair creaked as O'Hara eased his weight back.

He was still squinting, though, still with that wrinkle of doubt about the eyes. Short of drawing out a knife or a razor he could do no more to threaten them, however, and he was too cautious to resort to physical violence just yet, particularly now she'd mentioned Manone's name.

'You don't know who might've done it then?' O'Hara said.

'No idea,' said Patsy. 'Down the river? Jeeze, that's rich.'

'Mr Manone ain't laughin',' Alex O'Hara said.

'I'll bet he isn't,' said Polly.

Five minutes later, seconds after O'Hara had left the flat, Polly was sprawled diagonally across the top of the alcove bed. She was still fully dressed but her coat was unbuttoned and her skirt hitched up. Patsy's hands caressed her thighs above her stockings and cupped the moist warm pocket of her knickers. He did not enter her but lay heavily upon her, rubbing urgently against her, making her gasp and thrash and lift herself up in aching little spasms that were partly pleasure, partly pain.

At that moment she couldn't separate sense from horse-sense. She realised that he might take her and that she wouldn't resist. That she wouldn't be a girl, a virgin any longer and would have to carry a secret of her own and the worry that went with that secret. That she would have no one to trust with that secret other than Patsy himself and she wasn't at all sure that she wanted to give him that much power over her. After a while, though, she stopped thinking altogether and surrendered helplessly to the strange, untrained rhythms that moved through her body.

Patsy did not attempt to undress her. His love-making was forceful but not insistent. It was accomplished without penetration. Polly still wore the silly cup-shaped hat that Aunt Janet had given her at New Year a year ago. She stared up into Patsy's face, urging him to take her but even in the throes of a loving act he remained controlled. She wanted to shout that she was ready, that she wanted him inside her but the spasms were becoming more frequent, more and more demanding and when he came against her thighs she responded with a single, profound spasm of fulfilment that left her dazed by its intensity.

Patsy pulled back from her at once, his eyes wide with horror.

'God, Polly. I'm sorry. I'm sorry.'

She eased herself up, holding her skirts away from her sticky thighs.

'For what?' she heard herself say.

'I didn't mean it to be like that, the first time.'

'It's all right.' Polly leaned forward and kissed him, first on the brow then on the lips. 'I wanted you to do it.'

'But it wasn't right,' Patsy said. 'I don't know what came over me.'

'I do,' said Polly and, flustered at last, asked him if he would be good enough to fetch her a handkerchief.

*　　*　　*

'I don't know why you're so pleased with yourself,' Babs said.

'I'm not pleased with myself,' said Polly, 'not particularly.'

'You're lyin' there grinnin' like the cat that ate the canary.'

'Am I?' said Polly, sleepily. 'Well, maybe I am. I'm just glad it's all over and that none of the boys got caught.'

'Do you really think it's all over?'

'Babs, I'm too tired to worry about it any more tonight.'

'Jackie's hands . . .'

'Patsy says they'll heal up in a day or two.'

'Patsy, Patsy! He's no better than the rest o' them.'

'Leave Patsy out of it,' said Polly 'It's not his fault you squabbled with Jackie. You should have been more sympathetic.'

'Aye, an' I should've been paid.'

'They didn't get away with anything. They didn't make any money.'

'Mr Manone said—'

'Don't tell me you're going to take Dominic Manone's word for it,' Polly said, 'instead of believing the boys.'

'I don't know who to believe. After all I done for—'

'Babs.'

'What?'

'Shut up an' let me sleep.'

'Okay, okay,' said Babs.

Chapter Eleven

The theory was that the Pope himself would not know what to make of St Margaret's Institute for the Education of the Deaf and Dumb. Few people did: it was neither clearly Catholic nor Protestant in a town where your identity was defined by the colour of shirt you wore and which football team you supported, but the Institute's history ran counter to such simple-minded definitions.

It had been founded by a Baptist who had made a fortune trading in tobacco and who, as a late convert to God and a hearing trumpet, had struck a bargain with the trustees of the Gorbals parish poorhouse to administer a fund in his name; a promise that had gone the way of all parish promises as the years had rolled by and the Baptist's family had died out one by one.

Next a convocation of nuns from the silent order of St Irene had tried to muscle in on the act by buying up the land on which the crumbling little building stood; a manoeuvre that had led to the infamous Deaf and Dumb riots of 1871 and one of those bits of administrative carpentry that had resulted in what some folk regarded as an ecumenical disaster and others had lauded as an ingenious example of civic compromise involving not only Catholics and Protestants but the odd Jew as well.

As odd Jews went Mr Feldman was odder than most. In

appearance he was something of a stereotype, a great brown bear of a man with a curly beard greying at the edges, and huge hairy-knuckled hands that could sign in the language of the deaf with a dexterity that seemed at odds not merely with his size but with his enormous booming voice. He emanated not severity but authority and his presence in the Institute's boardroom would set the hearts of wispy little nuns to beating faster and terrify those governors who opposed him.

Nothing that Mr Feldman did was for his own aggrandisement, however. He had one interest in life, one dedicated purpose: to coax words from the mouths of deaf-mutes and restore in them the memory of forgotten sounds. He was an expert teacher – tender, patient and firm; an expert fund-raiser too when some gadget or device that would assist the work of the Institute came to his attention and the wind had to be raised to purchase a new micro-telephone or valve-amplifier or one of the latest 'teletactor' vibrating plates that had just come upon the market from America.

To his little charges Mr Feldman was a prophetic figure who seemed to be everywhere and know everything. While they held him in reverence they were never afraid of him, for he was, above all, the essence of fairness and even the youngest sensed that he always had their best interests at heart.

He would be there to welcome them when they trooped in of a morning and would be there at the gate when they trooped out again at four o'clock, arms folded, beard bristling, quick to spot a drayman who was driving too fast or a careless carter or a coalman who had failed to respect the fact that the children on the pavement could hear nothing, or nothing much, and that shouting at them to clear off and leave the cuddy alone was not only pointless but insulting.

'YOU,' Mr Feldman would roar. 'HOLD THAT ANIMAL STILL, PLEASE.' Even those children who could hear nothing at all – true congenitals – would feel the vibration of the master's voice and, with a confidence that he had instilled in them, would pull gargoyle faces at the coalman or carter and, with Mr Feldman egging them on, would scamper across the thoroughfare, safe to the other side. Then they would turn and wave and the master would wave to them and they would go off around silent street corners into silent closes warmed by the feeling that Mr Feldman would be standing behind them, not just tomorrow but throughout the whole of the rest of their lives.

Rosie feared the loss of Mr Feldman's approval more than anything.

She might defy Polly and chafe against the maternal bit on occasion but she obeyed Mr Feldman without question. When he told her to do something she did it. When he told her not to do something she did not do it. She obeyed him because discipline had been dinned into her as part of the process of learning not just how to speak coherently but also how to make a world that perceived her as deficient understand that she was anything but.

'Talk to me, Rosie,' Mr Feldman would say, his red lips animate within the curly brown curtain of his beard. 'Come along, girl, imbue me with the pearls of your wisdom. Talk. T-aw-k. Tongue. Mouth open. Back of the throat.'

'I can talk,' Rosie would utter, indignantly.

'What are you going to say?'

'What do you wish me to say?'

'That is up to you. En-gay-dje me in con-ver-say-shon, please.'

She was quick to pick up half-heard sounds, to interpret the unfamiliar words that the master pronounced.

After several years of training she no longer knew whether she heard words or saw or felt them or which particular set of receptors was involved in the act of comprehension, only that she could understand and communicate and that she had Mr Feldman to thank for it.

She still cared enough about the master's opinion to be

embarrassed when at a quarter past four o'clock on a Friday afternoon Alex O'Hara showed up at the gate of the Institute and, leaning against the stone post with his hat tipped back and his hands in his pockets, gave her one of those sly little smiles that, taken out of the context of Molliston Street, seemed even to Rosie to be lecherous rather than affectionate.

For one awful moment she saw Alex O'Hara as he really was, stripped of the glamour that she had imposed upon him, the little-girl silliness that she had confused with a romance.

They were not a suitable couple. Never had been. Never would be. He was not her sweetheart. He was not *fit* to be her sweetheart. When she saw him there at the Institute gate she experienced no lift of the heart, no raising of the spirits, but rather a leaden realisation that she had made a monkey of herself and that Mr Feldman would be bound to think so too.

'YOU, SIR, WHY ARE YOU LOITERING THERE, PLEASE?'

Alex O'Hara rolled his shoulders from the gate-post, glanced insolently up and down the street, then, as if he had just noticed Mr Feldman, touched a finger to his breastbone and mouthed the word, '*Me?*'

'YES, YOU, SIR.'

Mr Feldman was right behind her.

He stood on the step at the door of the main entrance, his hands on Rosie's shoulders, while two girls and three boys from the advanced class piled up behind them, goggle-eyed with curiosity.

'Ah'm waitin' for her.'

'ARE YOU, INDEED?'

'Aye, ah'm are indeed.'

Mr Feldman stooped. Rosie felt his beard press against her cheek.

'Rosie, is this true? *Do* you know this man?'

'Yes, Mr Feldman.'

Alex O'Hara sauntered a few steps into the narrow schoolyard. The children behind Mr Feldman swayed.

'She knows me,' O'Hara said. 'I've been sent t' take her home.'

'Who sent you?' Mr Feldman said.

'Her mammy.'

'Really?' Mr Feldman said. 'Are you a friend of Mrs Conway?'

'I'm everybody's friend,' Alex O'Hara replied. 'Right, Rosie?'

'Rosie, is it safe for you to go with this man?'

'Yes, Mr Feldman.'

'What is his name?'

Slurring the words nervously, Rosie said, 'His name's Alex O'Hara.'

'Come on, man,' O'Hara said. 'I ain't gonna eat her.' He held out his hand. 'Come on, Rosie, your mammy's waitin'.'

Mr Feldman knew perfectly well how O'Hara made his bread and whose interests he represented. He even had an inkling of the sort of relationship that Lizzie Conway might have with this man and while he did not approve he was enough of a realist to acknowledge that the Conway woman was doing her best for her children in the only way open to her. He had been resident in the Gorbals long enough to remember Frank Conway's mysterious disappearance a dozen or so years ago at a time when so many young men were being sucked into oblivion, yet it jarred him to think that Rosie might be dragged into that society, that all his teaching, all his moral instruction, would be wasted if she became a criminal's sweetheart or, worse, a criminal's wife.

Reluctantly he removed his hands from Rosie's shoulders and let her walk down the steps to the playground.

She did not take O'Hara's hand, thank God, but simply fell in beside him, tailoring her long-legged, loping step to the man's indolent shuffle as if he, O'Hara, were the child and she the adult.

Mr Feldman sighed.

One of the girls tapped his elbow and, when she had his attention, mouthed an eager question: 'Is he her boyfriend, Mr Feldman?'

'CERTAINLY NOT,' the master roared. 'SHE IS FAR TOO YOUNG FOR BOYFRIENDS,' then, taken aback by his own vehemence, hurried his not-so-little charges out of the playground and into the silent street.

O'Hara tried to hold on to her hand but she was too conscious of the Institute, at least its roof, peering from above the row of little shops at the end of Brooke Street and had the idiotic feeling that Mr Feldman might be straddling the tiles or clinging to a chimney-pot and that at any moment she would hear his massive voice ringing in her ears, warning her not to be a fool.

She did feel foolish and – for the first time – scared of Alex.

If he had been tactful and had waited for her at the corner of Keane Street then she might have kidded herself that he cared for her and that the meeting represented a step forward in their limp relationship. But to have him just appear at the Institute gate like that, to embarrass her before Mr Feldman and her classmates – no, that was too thoughtless, too blatant, too crass to leave much room for self-delusion.

She walked fast, faster than Alex. He skipped to keep up with her and then, as they came around the corner into the bottom end of the Calcutta Road, grabbed her arm and pulled her in against the wall of Brady's pub which, at that hour of the afternoon, wasn't open for business.

The short end of the Calcutta Road was awash with mothers and small children, solitary shoppers, old men hanging about waiting for the pubs to reopen. Lorries from the back gate of the Kingston Iron works ground over the cobbles and from Latimer Road came the sparky blue flashes of tramcars turning sharply to head out past the new synagogue on to the Rutherglen Road.

There were more horses than motorcars, more carts than vans, and the smell of horse manure mingled with the ever-present odours of coke smoke, coal smoke and the albuminous vapours of the Russia Road Chemical & Dyeworks.

Four thirty and already dark; the shortest day was less than a week away and the cold grey cloud that had lidded the Clyde valley for the past few days had thickened with impending rain. Streetlamps were already lighted and shop windows glimmered, not cheerily, in the pungent dusk.

He grabbed her arm not to slow her pace but to draw her off the pavement and steer her into one of the gloomy close-mouths that opened between the shopfronts.

The gas had not yet been turned up on the common stair and the darkness was pricked only by the windows of the tenements across the backs, crushed down into scribbled reflections on the long, litter-filled puddles that turned the backs into unwholesome ponds.

Rosie did not know where she was. She yielded not to Alex O'Hara's will but only to his strength. He dragged her with him forcibly then, drawing her past him, drove her out into the back court like a lamb to the slaughter. There was no sign of a weapon, of a knife blade in his hand but Rosie had the impression that he had one in his pocket and that if she resisted him he would not hesitate to use it.

She gasped with fear. She couldn't form words, couldn't make her throat work or her tongue curl. She uttered no coherent protests at his treatment, nothing except a plaintive 'auk, auk, auk', then when he flung her against the tenement wall, 'Ma-Ma-Maaa', like the cardboard squeaker in a cheap doll.

He thrust a hand behind her head, clasped her neck and brought his mouth to hers. He nuzzled his frozen lips against her mouth, sliding his nose this way and that across her face as if they were Eskimos. There was no love in him, only a vinegary sort of lust that circumstances had given him an opportunity to exploit. He jerked his hand from behind her head and placed it, fingers spread, in the middle of her chest. He pressed her back against the sandstone wall which was slicked with black soot and dusted with ash.

There was a window to Rosie's right, lighted, and a window above to her left, windows above that, windows all around. She could see the shapes of women floating like fish inside their kitchens, the shapes of clothes hanging on loose ropes across the high backs. She could see the crenellated edge of the sky whorled with the sifting grey smoke that made up the air that Glaswegians breathed and upon which they thrived. In the half-light from windows and sky she could see spittle on Alex O'Hara's upper lip – spit or perspiration, she did not know which.

She made no attempt to escape.

'Can you hear what I'm sayin' to you, Rosie?'

'*Auk.*'

'Can you hear what I'm sayin'?'

She managed to nod, to utter a word that was not a word, '*Uh-huh.*'

His face was an inch from hers. He held his body back, bent from the waist as if he were reading her the riot act. He was calm, though, icy calm. Even inside her envelope of fear she sensed that this was business for Mr O'Hara, business not pleasure.

'Mun-nay,' she said. 'Tam-marra.'

'Forget the money.' O'Hara spoke distinctly, making his lips move and tongue show. 'I want to know where you were on Wednesday night.'

'La' nigh'?'

'No, Wednesday night. At home? In your own house, right?'

'Uh-huh.'

'With your mammy?'

'Uh-huh.'

'With your sister, with Polly, right?'

'Uh-huh.'

'What time was that about?'

'Aw – aw nigh.'

'All night?'

'Uh-huh.'

'You'd better get this right, Rosie,' he told her, pressing his hand flat against her chest again. 'I'm not playin' the game wi' you now, honey.'

'Yes,' Rosie managed to utter.

'Your sisters were in the house wi' you all o' Wednesday night, right? They didn't go out, right? Not even Polly?'

She would have lied to him if she had understood what sort of truth he wanted from her. How Polly and Babs had become involved in her non-existent affair with Alex O'Hara was beyond her comprehension.

He pressed hard, the heel of his hand just above her breasts.

She squeaked.

'*Right?*' he said, savagely.

'Yes, aw – all night.'

'They never went out at all on Wednesday night?'

'Nam ... No. Neffer.' She shook her head. 'Never.'

He drew back, fumbled in his pocket and produced a crumpled packet of cigarettes. He lit one and offered it to her. She took it, her hands trembling, her cheeks wet with tears.

'That's all I needed t' know,' Alex O'Hara told her.

He smoked too, blowing the smoke away from her. He glanced at her and for an instant Rosie thought that he might be going to start on her again. She was more afraid of his mouth, of his kisses, than she was of his hands. She held the lighted cigarette between her finger and thumb, ready to stab into his face, but he did nothing now and seemed idle, almost easy in her company.

'Come on then, Rosie,' he said. 'I'll walk you home.'

'No,' Rosie said, distinctly. 'I will manage myself.'

'Suit yourself.'

She put the cigarette to her lips and drew in smoke. The

act of inhaling soothed her, made her feel adult and gave her breathing space. She took two puffs, dropped the cigarette and ground it flat with the heel of her shoe. O'Hara watched. He was grinning sheepishly now as if embarrassed by what he had done or had discovered a spark in her that he hadn't suspected was there.

Rosie said, 'Are you finished with me?'

'Aye. Go on.'

She walked away from him into the dark tunnel of the close.

'Rosie?' he said.

She did not turn round.

'See you later, Rosie,' Alex O'Hara called.

Rosie did not hear him.

She was running pell-mell for the street.

Polly did not even have an opportunity to fit her key into the lock, for no sooner had she arrived at the door than it flew open and her mother grabbed her by the arm and yanked her into the hall.

'What the devil have you been up to?' Mammy demanded.

'Me? Nothing,' said Polly, quailing before the onslaught.

She caught a glimpse of Babs in the doorway of the bedroom and Rosie, wrapped in an old shawl and looking like a tinker's lass, in the kitchen.

She had been thinking of Patsy and what he had done to her on the bed. Unfamiliar sensations had teased her throughout the day. Friday bustle in the burgh offices had not dispersed them. She had been glad when it turned half past five and she had been released. She had walked home slowly through the first chill sift of rain, trying to sort out her responses to her first sexual encounter and wondering why she did not feel more ashamed.

When Mammy pulled her into the house, therefore, Polly's

first thought was that Mammy had somehow learned what had taken place on top of Patsy's bed. But even as she ducked to protect herself from punishment, Polly realised that something else had riled her mother, for her temper contained more panic than true rage.

'What?' Polly said. 'What have I done now?'

'She knows,' Babs called out. 'Mammy knows about us an' the boys.'

Polly dived into the bedroom and managed to close the door.

Backing towards the window, Babs called out, 'She knows about everythin'. Rosie told her.'

Babs had not even had time to take off her coat and hat. How farcical, Polly thought, how unladylike; yet she experienced a wave of relief that she wouldn't have to explain what Patsy had done to her and why she hadn't resisted. She flung her handbag on to the bed just as Mammy burst in, her cheeks hot with temper, eyes bulging. It took all Polly's courage to face up to her.

'What has Rosie been telling you?' Polly said.

'About them boys.' Lizzie corrected herself. 'Those boys downstairs, and the one you've been hangin' about with. It's all your fault what happened to Rosie tonight.'

Polly felt a dart of panic. 'Rosie? What did happen to Rosie?'

'O'Hara got to her,' Babs said. 'He knows you lied about stayin' with Patsy on Wednesday night. The alibi's blown.'

Polly felt weak at the knees. She groped for the bed, seated herself on it.

'Did he actually hurt Rosie?' she asked.

'No,' said Lizzie. 'But he scared the wits out of the wee soul.'

'That's my fault,' said Polly. 'I should never have encouraged her to deliver Manone's payments. I should have done it myself.'

Lizzie squatted by the bedside. She still reeked of disinfectant and her hands were raw. She'd had no opportunity to rub
them with the lanolin ointment that kept her knuckles from
cracking and her fingertips from peeling. There had been a
time before they could afford soothing creams and lotions when
Mammy's hands had been so rough that she had had to wear
thin crepitous leather gloves all the time. Polly felt a pang of
conscience at the memory. She reached up, took her mother's
hands and closed her smooth, smudgy fingers over them.

'Listen,' she said, 'if you want to know what's happening, I'll—'

'I told her already,' Babs said. 'I didn't have much option,
Poll, sorry.'

'What have you to be sorry for?' Mammy said. 'The only
thing you should be sorry for is gettin' mixed up with that crowd
downstairs.'

'They work for Dominic Manone,' Polly said.

She felt a certain stiffening within her, a grievance that her
mother would accuse them of consorting with Gorbals wild men
when she herself had been married to one and still saw fit to
visit the Italian now and then and accept his favours. There
were certain debts in the Conway account that could never be
paid off, not debts of honour but obligations to a past from
which none of them could ever quite break free.

Suddenly Polly saw the reasons for Mammy's anger and
panic. She had sustained her debt to Dominic Manone to keep
her daughters, her prized possessions, free of their father's
influence, to raise them inch by inch out of pervasive poverty.

They had lived in slums but they were not of the slums.
The brown-painted door, the rugs, the cushions, the floral-print
curtains, the wireless set and gramophone were not frivolous
luxuries: they were statements of identity. It was not about
money, had never been about money. It was about self-respect
and responsibility, about discipline and conscience. Mammy
wouldn't rest until they – her girls – were married to men

who did not thieve and threaten for a living. Now that plan had been imperilled by their stupidity and recalcitrance. Small wonder that her mother was angry.

Polly said, tearfully, 'Mammy, I'm sorry. So sorry.'

'Me too,' said Babs, hastily.

Lizzie crouched by the side of the bed. Her cheeks were stained with tears but all trace of temper had gone. She was breathless, trembling and hurting but when Rosie appeared in the doorway, shawl about her shoulders, Polly felt a touch of hardness, of the unremitting Conway selfishness that had been her birthright. Even Rosie's flat, quacking voice irritated her for a moment.

'I did not tell O'Hara anything,' Rosie said.

Polly knew that this was not the truth, that this little scene of family unity and forgiveness was not a solution, not an end but a beginning.

Twenty minutes later Mr Peabody turned up to collect the rent.

And five minutes after that – O'Hara.

Chapter Twelve

Polly did not know why she was so relieved to see the rent collector that Friday evening. She had harboured feelings of resentment against him ever since she'd learned that Mammy was eyeing him up as a potential husband. She didn't jump to conclusions, like Babs, or dismiss him as a fool but none the less she considered him too weak to be worthy of a woman like her mother.

When she thought about Mr Peabody – which wasn't often – Polly thought of a man who had never been young, who, stuffy and prissy and lacking conviction, was already trapped in perpetual middle age. She had lied only to flatter him and to please Mammy, had stated 'absolutely' that she thought that rent-collecting was a manly occupation. She did not really consider it so, any more than she considered clerking a manly occupation or set any store by the neat brown suits and trilby hats of the young surveyors who frequented the Burgh Hall offices or by the navy blue three-pieces of pompous burgh councillors who confused their petty power with masculine appeal.

When she tried to tally up the qualities that made a man what a man should be, Polly inclined towards the boys who lived close to the edge; not the dumb or lazy but those hearty young males who flooded out of shipyard gates or poured, running, from under the steelworks' towering gantries, their faces grimed but not grim and who, if unemployment caught up with them, joined the back of the dole queue with the same gruff optimism with which they had squared up to wage-slavery. She liked the look of them, liked the dirt on their cheeks, the sweat on their brows, their callused hands, their vigour; the fact that they would never willingly trade independence for security and that, in them, the muscles of revolt were still firm enough to slither and tighten.

In some – Patsy Walsh for one – she detected an astonishing absence of meekness and a willingness to risk freedom for the *right* to be free. Some, like Patsy, would die before they would settle for servitude and that, for Polly, made them seem daring and, in a curiously disembodied way, desirable. But on that Friday evening less than a week before Christmas, less than a fortnight before the old year ticked into the new, Polly was relieved when Mr Bernard Peabody entered the kitchen and in his usual fumbling, self-conscious manner removed his hat and scarf and spread his books upon the table.

'I'm sorry, Bernard,' Mammy apologised, 'but we've had a wee bit of an upset an' I haven't had time to start your supper.'

'That's quite all right, Mrs Con – Lizzie.' The agent cleared his throat and, twisting stiffly from the waist, looked round at Polly's mother with genuine concern. 'Is there – is there anything I can do to help?'

'No,' Lizzie said. 'No, thank you. It's a family matter.'

'If it's a question of not having the rent ...'

'It isn't that. Even if it was I wouldn't expect you ...'

'I know,' Bernard Peabody said. 'I know you wouldn't but ...'

The conversation was halting, not lame. Behind each inconclusive phrase Polly detected intimacy. Her mother often referred to Bernard Peabody, had even waxed humorous about him but Polly hadn't suspected that there was also a warmth in the relationship now that superseded the small favours for which her mother might have once been angling.

'I could poach you an egg,' Lizzie suggested.

'No, really . . .'

'Babs could go out for a fish supper if you . . .'

'No. Honestly!' Bernard Peabody said.

Polly noticed how her mother's eagerness embarrassed him, as if the rapport between them was a mutual secret that they did not wish to share. If he had witnessed Mammy's tantrum twenty minutes ago, Polly thought, he might not have been so enamoured. She watched him fuss with his pencil and notebook. Mammy put the coins on the table and stood close to him while he counted them into his purse. He made out a receipt and stuck a gummed label into the Conways' rent book. Given the circumstances, he didn't seem inclined to linger and Polly guessed that the 'romance' between the factor's agent and her mother would progress no further tonight.

He rose, closed his books and put them in his case, buttoned his overcoat. 'No collection next Friday but I'll be here the day before Hogmanay. Tuesday. You'll be due two weeks then, I'm afraid.'

He reached for his hat and scarf and, for the first time, looked directly at the girls. To Rosie, he said, 'I'm reading that book you recommended. *Great Expectations*. It's very interesting.'

Rosie smiled, and nodded bleakly.

'You don't look very well, lass,' Bernard said. 'Is it the flu?'

Rosie, reading his lips, shook her head.

A knock upon the landing door caused all of them, even Bernard, to look up. It was not a heavy sound, not urgent, not threatening. Even so, Polly felt her stomach contract with apprehension.

'Who can that be?' Lizzie said.

'Aren't you expectin' anyone?' said Bernard.

'No one I can think of,' said Lizzie.

'Aren't you going to answer it?' Bernard said.

'I suppose I'd better,' Lizzie said.

Bernard did not follow her into the hall. He put on his hat and wound his scarf loosely about his neck then waited, watching the door until Alex O'Hara eased himself into the kitchen.

'Hello, Rosie,' O'Hara said. 'Did you forget t' tell them I was comin' round tonight?'

'Leave me alone.' Rosie stood up. The shawl slipped from her shoulders, revealing a school blouse, a pleated skirt, bare legs. 'Just leave me alone.'

'Ain't you I've come for, sweetheart,' O'Hara said. 'It's her.'

'Polly?' Lizzie said. 'What do you want wi' our Polly?'

O'Hara was not a large man but his presence seemed to fill the kitchen. His movements were cat-like, not clumsy. He ignored Bernard completely.

'You lied to me, Polly.'

'I did not,' said Polly.

It had come in at last, come in from the streets.

Polly stared in horror at the flat sweating face, the frozen mouth and icy eyes. This was the myth, the legendary beast that they had always been taught to fear. They had known of its existence, of course. They had dwelled within its shadow, had heard it screaming in the night in the dark alleyways behind the tenements. They had read of its violent excursions in newspapers and heard the mean tales that gave Glasgow its evil reputation. But they had never been forced to look it dead in the eye before, to confront it face to face and acknowledge that they were part of it.

Polly had never seen a cut-throat razor laid open. She had seen how men used them; tiny blood-flecked tabs of paper stanching shaving cuts first thing in the morning, a steel blade whisking blithely on a strop viewed through the window of a barber's shop, the glimpse of a bone handle peeking from a waistcoat pocket – and scars, many scars, the unmistakable badges of assaults too cold-blooded to contemplate or fights so fierce, vicious and prolonged that no decent person could imagine them. It was from this that they had been taught to run and hide. Now it was here, O'Hara was here in their kitchen and they, in a sense, had invited him in.

The razor didn't look like a weapon. In spite of its ground blade and the black handle snuggled into O'Hara's palm it seemed old-fashioned, almost quaint, and too delicate to be harmful.

Polly stretched out an arm and elbowed Rosie deeper into the corner by the side of the range. She pressed her knees together, made ready to leap away. Out of the corner of her eye she saw Babs hunched against the niche bed.

'You shouldn't have lied to me, Polly,' O'Hara said. 'Me an' mah wee friend here have a way o' gettin' at the truth.'

'I told you,' Polly said. 'I told you the truth.'

He was resting now, or seemed to be. He leaned an elbow upon the table and held up his right hand, wrist laid back as if balancing a glass on his palm. She could see the razor clearly, the knuckle of steel where it joined the handle, the concave shape of the blade, even the Royal Crown and patent number engraved along its length. He allowed her to contemplate it for several seconds until she could almost feel its scald upon her cheek, its cold kiss upon her lips.

'You weren't wi' Patsy Walsh on Wednesday, were you?'

'Yes, I was.'

He inched forward, came within striking distance. Polly fixed her gaze upon the blade, watching it twist so that the edge was towards her. He fashioned a little strike, a slithering dart like a snake's tongue. Polly flinched but made no attempt to defend herself.

'Walsh done the warehouse, didn't he?' Alex O'Hara said. 'Him, Jackie Hallop – an' who else? Bonnar, Tommy Bonnar?'

'Why don't you ask them that question?' said Bernard Peabody.

'Who the hell're you?' O'Hara, distracted, enquired.

'A friend of the family,' Bernard said. Lizzie touched his arm, plump fingers spread. Neither he nor she knew what the signal meant. He took a wild guess. 'Why are you botherin' these young ladies? Shouldn't you be out askin' Walsh and the Hallops? Or are they a bit too much for you. Are you the sort that prefers bullying girls to squaring up to men?'

O'Hara was still bewildered. Polly could see the grinding of his sluggish intellect.

'Who sent you here?' Bernard said. 'Not Mr Manone, surely?'

'Aye, Mr Manone.'

'What – to carve up Mrs Conway's girls?'

O'Hara swore. He had been rendered indecisive, his threat made impotent. Polly noticed that her mother continued to rest her hand on Mr Peabody's arm as if it were he not Alex O'Hara who needed to be restrained.

'What the bloody hell d'you know about it?' O'Hara demanded.

'More than you might think,' Bernard said. 'Maybe I did the warehouse job and these ladies know nothin' about it. Pause an' think about that.'

Polly watched the flat face writhe with concentration, twist into folds like the skin of some rare breed of dog. She felt a little gulp of premature relief but when O'Hara lunged at her, arm raised, she flung herself backwards, taking Rosie and the armchair with her out of range of the razor's arc. He swiped again, grunting in frustration. She heard Babs scream, Mammy shout. Crouched behind the armchair Rosie uttered little squeaks and chitterings, more like laughter than fear. The next thing Polly knew O'Hara's left arm was bent up behind his back, his cheek was squashed flat upon the table and the hand that held the razor was ensnared in Bernard Peabody's fist.

Bernard had gone for the wrist but had found the hand instead. He had closed his fist over the razor, gripping the blade instead of flesh. She watched O'Hara's smothered, ineffectual struggle as Bernard leaned over him, levering his arm up until it seemed that it would snap. Saw too how Bernard clung to the razor, encompassing it as firmly as if it were made of rubber, not steel. Saw blood well up like jam between his fingers.

'I think,' Bernard said, 'that's enough of that, Mr O'Hara, unless you fancy havin' your arm broken.'

It came away not abruptly but stickily, both fists so weltered with blood that Polly could not tell who had released it. Then she saw that Bernard had gained full possession of the razor. He held the razor high, the black handle waxy with blood, then he tossed the weapon at the window. It struck the glass and fell, tinkling, into the sink.

Bernard stepped back from the table and allowed O'Hara to crank himself to his feet. The bent arm remained bent, slung across his belly. He hugged it, nursing it, his face not just bloodless but spongy with pain.

'I want mah razor back,' he said.

'You're not gettin' your razor back,' Bernard told him. 'If you're thinkin' about trying to fish it out of there, I'd advise you to think again.'

'Who the hell are you?'

Bernard lifted his damaged hand to his mouth, put the wound between his teeth and bit down on it. Nothing showed in his face, nothing except a trace of arrogance, not even arrogance, Polly thought, but an odd sort of satisfaction as if dealing with Alex O'Hara had taken him back to another time when he had also been obliged to deal with the realities of life. When he took his hand away from his mouth his chin was streaked with blood. 'I told you,' he said, 'I'm a friend of the family.'

'Mr Manone' – O'Hara crabbed towards the door – 'Mr Manone's gonna hear about this.'

'Too damned right he is,' Lizzie declared. 'I'm goin' to tell him. I'm goin' to tell him what you did,' and then, because she had every excuse for forgetting herself, aimed a kick at Alex O'Hara's rump to speed him on his way downstairs.

Under the flow of tap water the wound became visible. It was clean-lipped but deep, so deep that Polly thought she could see bone at the bottom of it. She stood by him and did exactly what he told her to do while her mother poured him a glass of whisky from the bottle she kept for emergencies.

Bernard drank it in a single swallow.

'Another?'

'No thanks, Lizzie. I still have my rounds to do.'

'Your rounds?' Lizzie said. 'With that hand you should be going to the hospital not out on the streets.'

He extended his hand into the running water again and examined it with astonishing objectivity. He flexed his fingers, making blood well from the wound.

'I don't think any tendons are severed. Lucky really.'

'You call that lucky?' said Babs.

Polly said, 'It looks to me like it needs stitches, Mr Peabody.'

'If I go for stitches then I'll have to report it.'

'Tell them you were attacked on the stairs,' said Babs.

'I think,' Bernard said, 'that a lint pad an' a tight bandage will do the trick until I get home.'

'What's your mother gonna say?'

'I won't tell her,' Bernard said. 'Well, not until tomorrow.'

Polly said, 'How many more calls do you have to make?'

'Five.'

'How long will that take?'

'Couple of hours.'

'If I might ask' – Lizzie unearthed the biscuit tin that served as a medicine chest – 'what do you do with the money, the money you collect?'

'Put it in a night safe in the bank next door to our office.

I make out a deposit slip, put it in a bag with the money and slide the lot into the chute.'

'Can you write with your left hand?' Polly asked.

'I can manage a legible signature,' Bernard answered.

He had taken off his overcoat and bloodstained jacket and instructed Polly to cut away the sleeve of his shirt at a point above the elbow. It was an old shirt anyway, so he said. He told Polly to take off his tie and showed her how to fashion a temporary tourniquet. She noticed that when she touched him Mr Peabody did not display any of the shyness that had been, until then, his hallmark. He didn't preen either, though, didn't seem particularly proud of what he'd done or aware of how brave he'd been. He was quietly matter-of-fact about the whole thing, Polly thought, and gave no hint of the pain he must be suffering.

At length the flow of bright red blood eased and began to coagulate. With a towel under his forearm Bernard transferred himself from the sink to the table where Lizzie had laid out lint, bandages and an iodine bottle and where she dressed the gaping wound exactly as Bernard told her to do.

Babs lit a cigarette and gave it to him.

He took it, smiled his thanks, and drew in smoke.

'Is that chap liable to come back?' he said. 'If you'd like me to stay . . .'

'Oh, Bernard, Bernard.' Lizzie laid down her sewing scissors, wrapped an arm about his neck and kissed him on the ear, on the cheek, on the side of the mouth. 'I don't know what we'd have done if you hadn't been here.'

Bernard took another draw on the cigarette and blew smoke away from Lizzie's tear-stained face. 'I'm just glad I could be of help.'

Polly sluiced away the blood in the sink. She washed her hands, plucked a towel from the hook, turned, and said, 'I think we owe you an explanation.'

'Not necessary,' Bernard said.

He glanced at Rosie who had come to the end of the table and was staring at him as if he'd suddenly acquired a halo and wings. The shawl was draped about her shoulders and, in the aftermath of her terror, she seemed to have shed four or five years from her age, to have become a child again, round-eyed and uncomprehending. Bernard winked at her. She smiled wanly.

Polly came to the table and seated herself on one of the chairs. Bernard was seated too, his bare arm laid upon newspapers while Lizzie worked upon the bandage, cutting two long tails and wrapping them firmly around his wrist.

'Too tight?' she asked.

'A wee bit tighter, please.'

She applied pressure, tied a knot and then another.

Polly said, 'I think you're entitled to be told what all that was about.'

'It's none of my business,' Bernard said.

'Don't you even want to know who that guy was?' said Babs.

Bernard hesitated. The Conway girls were all around him. He was the centre of attention, no longer an object of teasing scorn and mockery. He had no difficulty in hiding his pain. He had endured much worse than this. They claimed you couldn't remember pain but he certainly did and how good it had made him feel when it finally subsided.

In a field hospital at Hazebrouck they had given him morphine and had sent him back to recuperate at a place near Cassel. They hadn't sent him home. He had got himself off the morphine p.d.q. because he had seen what it did to others, worse than the drink. He was back at the Front in a fortnight because they thought he might be malingering and, anyway, they were down to stemming the Boche advance with cooks and storemen, anyone who could carry a rifle.

'He's one of Dominic Manone's boys, isn't he?' Bernard said.

'His name's O'Hara,' Polly told him.

'Oh!' Bernard said.

There had been enough nameless enemies in his life; he didn't need another to add to the list. When he looked at the girls around the table and at Lizzie Conway he felt a curious sense of separation from the grey-clad figure that had walked behind him all these years, tugging at his greatcoat tails and urging him to keep down, keep low, and take no chances.

'O'Hara is a bad one,' Rosie said.

'I rather gathered that,' said Bernard.

The iodine was biting. Cold sweat started on the back of his neck and down his breastbone. Polly Conway was right: the gash probably did need a stitch or two. He certainly wouldn't be doing much work with a pen for the next few days. He wondered what sort of tale he could tell Mr Shannon that would absolve him from culpability and keep his wage coming. Perhaps Mr Shannon would find something else for him to do; unless he managed to make his left hand work as well as his right? He thought about that, vaguely, while – less vaguely – he became conscious that Polly Conway was holding his arm and that Lizzie was hugging him about the neck.

He searched his soul for the primness that had always protected him, discovered that it had evaporated. He could smell whisky, iodine, even blood but also the comforting aroma of Lizzie Conway's kitchen, distinct and womanly. He leaned his head against Lizzie's hip for an instant then righted himself and said, 'Are you in debt to O'Hara?'

''Course we're not,' Lizzie replied.

'Come on, Mammy, no use trying to hide it,' Polly said. 'We're in debt to Dominic Manone and probably always will be. My daddy ran off with hundreds of pounds of the Manones' money and got lost in the war. Since then we've been paying it back in monthly instalments.'

'That's terrible,' Bernard said. 'What a burden!'

'A debt of honour,' Polly said, 'that's what the Manones call it.'

'Rubbish!' Bernard said. 'It's plain extortion.'

'That's why O'Hara turned up here tonight,' Polly said.

Bernard had been tramping the streets of the Gorbals for years and had heard lots of rumours about Guido Manone's nephew. He knew just how much power the Manones held not only in criminal circles but in the community at large.

'I can lend you something if you really need it.'

'Oh, Bernard, no,' said Lizzie. 'You've done enough for us.'

'Would you really give us dough if we were stuck?' Babs said.

'Yes. I don't like bullies, you see,' Bernard explained.

Mammy was brusque suddenly. 'We couldn't possibly accept your money, Bernard.'

'Well, if you do need it you know where to come.' Bernard pushed himself to his feet, looked round for his jacket. 'You know what they say: It's no loss what a friend gets.'

Polly and Babs helped him struggle into his jacket and overcoat. He wound the scarf around his neck and put on his hat. He looked shaky but claimed that he was strong enough to do his rounds, deposit the takings and survive the long rattling tram ride out to Knightswood.

They all accompanied him into the hall and out on to the landing.

'I hope he's not waitin' down there,' Babs said. 'Bloody O'Hara, I mean.'

'He won't be,' Bernard said. 'He'll have had enough for one night,' and then, quite boldly, stepped across the landing to the Gowers.

Dominic had dined in Goodman's Restaurant near St Enoch's Square with four old school chums. Three were practising solicitors, the other a dental surgeon. A convivial bunch, they set more store by the fact that they had shared an alma mater than by anything that had happened since. They were well aware how Dominic earned his living but, being men of the world, did not hold it against him and carefully steered the conversation away from topics that he might find embarrassing.

It was after eleven o'clock before Dominic decanted himself from a taxi-cab in Manor Park Avenue and after drawing in a few lungfuls of damp night air walked to the front door of the mansion and rang the bell.

Uncle Guido opened it.

'Tony is here. He is waiting to speak with you.'

'What about?' Dominic asked.

'The robbery.'

'How long has he been waiting?'

'Half an hour, maybe less.'

Sobriety came upon him quickly. He felt a twinge of annoyance that an enjoyable evening would end with family business but the feeling soon passed and by the time he entered the living-room he had all his wits about him.

Tony was seated on the sofa, a plate balanced awkwardly on his lap and a coffee cup and saucer held in his hands. Aunt Teresa was urging him to eat the last of the smoked ham and pickled cucumber sandwiches that she had prepared for him, an effusive display of hospitality that even Uncle Guido had been unable to prevent. Aunt Teresa had also been quizzing Tony about his girlfriends and fishing to find out if her nephew had his eye on anyone in the Community. Even Tony had a hard time dodging the woman's questions without seeming rude and his relief at seeing Dominic was palpable.

Aunt Teresa might take a chance with Tony Lombard but she was far too shrewd to risk offending her nephew and, within seconds, had cleared the cups, saucers, plates on to a tray and had vanished from the room, leaving the men alone.

Tony wiped crumbs from his chin with a handkerchief and lighted a cigarette. He spoke Italian, a blurred, drawling version of the language that he had picked up from the Sicilian

grandmother who had been responsible for bringing him to
Scotland and who had raised him to be a helper to the Manones.
She had been Guido's mistress a long time ago and might even
have wound up as Guido's wife if she had been younger and
better looking. She lived with a granddaughter and her Scottish
son-in-law downriver in Skelmorlie now and rarely came up
to town.

Tony said, 'It seems that Walsh might have pulled the
job.'

'Go on,' said Dominic.

'That is O'Hara's opinion,' Tony continued. 'He tele-
phoned me from Brady's public house and asked me to meet
him there.'

'Did you go?'

'Certainly, I went.'

'Was Alex sober?' said Dominic.

'No, he had been drinking for some time before I got there.'

'What did he tell you?' said Guido. 'Tell Dominic what he
told you.'

'He told me Walsh pulled the job but that Tommy Bonnar
organised it.'

'Tommy?' said Dominic, surprised. 'Does O'Hara have
proof?'

'None to speak of,' said Tony.

'Then he is whistling in the darkness,' Dominic said.

'Tell him the rest of it,' Guido said.

'According to O'Hara,' Tony went on, 'one of Lizzie
Conway's daughters knows all about it and can put the finger
on those involved.'

'The blonde daughter who works at the warehouse?'

'I think it is another one, the older one.'

'Is this O'Hara's proof?' said Dominic. 'Gossip from some
girl?'

'You should listen,' Guido said. 'You know how these things
happen.'

'Her name is Polly,' Tony said. 'You obtained work for her three or four years ago, I think.'

'So?'

'She is Patsy Walsh's girlfriend,' Tony Lombard said.

'Do you see?' said Uncle Guido. 'You should be listening.'

'I am listening,' Dominic said. 'I am just not sure who I am listening to.'

'I am only telling you what O'Hara told me,' Tony Lombard said. 'You want that I should do something about it? Go see Walsh, maybe?'

'Or the girl, go see the girl,' said Uncle Guido.

'Did she also put the finger on Tommy Bonnar?' Dominic asked.

Tony shook his head.

'Obviously the girl knows something,' Uncle Guido said. 'Someone will have to go talk to the girl.'

'You want me to do that?' Tony Lombard said.

'No,' said Dominic, after a pause. 'I will talk with her myself.'

'When?' Guido asked.

'Tomorrow,' Dominic replied.

His mother's Co-op calendar was tacked up behind the door of the kitchenette. This late in the year steam from wash-tub and cooking pots had done its worst and the cheap paper was wrinkled like old parchment. Bernard could barely make out the illustration – a kitten playing with a ball of wool – let alone his mother's pencilled script and it took him several seconds to decipher the code that told him she had gone to a Guild carol concert in Partick.

Bernard had no idea who she had gone with. Few of the names that his mother scattered in his direction ever stuck and he had no wish to become embroiled with her chattering acquaintances. Over the years his mother had often tried to match him up with a long-toothed spinster or a comparatively youthful widow, daughters of Guild friends who were on the look-out for husbands. Bernard would have none of it and switched his primness up to full volume whenever one of the poor, desperate creatures was thrown in his path.

Partick Halls? A late night, probably. Chips afterwards, or tea in a Merkland Street café. The last tram out to the suburbs.

Bernard had eaten nothing since lunch. Although he had no appetite to speak of, he poached a couple of eggs and brewed a pot of tea. He ate at the table in the living-room and felt better afterwards. He had about half an hour, he reckoned, to do what he had to do.

First he sponged the blood from his jacket and applied a little of the stain-remover that his mother favoured. He put the jacket on a wire hanger and hung it to air on the wardrobe door in his bedroom. It was cold in the living-room. He would have re-lighted the fire in the grate but he did not think that he could manage to lug coal from the shed in the back garden. From the chest of drawers in his bedroom he extracted a metal box and carried it to the table in the living-room. Scissors, a fresh pad of cotton wool, a long bandage. Seated at the table, he cut off the dressing that Lizzie had put on.

The wound had bled considerably and the lint pad was soaked. He carried the pad into the kitchen along with the remains of the bandage and stuffed them into the pail that his mum used as a dustbin. He worked left-handed, found it less difficult than he had anticipated. He bathed the wound with warm water from the kettle then examined it again. It hadn't occurred to him that a deep, clean, almost surgical incision could be so insulting to human flesh. He was concerned about infection, of course, and about damage to the median nerve which, if he remembered his first-aid training correctly, bridged the radial and ulnar bursa. He still hadn't lost sensation in his fingers and could wiggle his thumb effectively; good signs, he reckoned.

Tomorrow afternoon, however, he would take himself round to Dr Begg's new surgery and have it properly examined. Stoical he might be, but stupid he wasn't and he could ill afford to take time off work, not even a day or two, to let the damned thing heal. He worked quietly, awkwardly, cleansing and dressing the wound as best he could. He used his teeth to tug the bandage tight, to help him draw the knot. When that was done he put everything away again, removed his torn and bloodstained shirt and hid it in a newspaper parcel under his bed. He would get rid of it tomorrow, like evidence.

When Mrs Violet Peabody, reeking of chips and vinegar, came breezing into the living-room at twenty minutes past eleven o'clock, she found her son seated at the living-room table clad in pyjamas and an old donkey-brown dressing-gown that had once belonged to his father. He had a mug of strong tea by him and a big lined jotter open before him and was diligently scripting numbers and names in pencil across it, his brow furrowed in concentration, the tip of his tongue protruding between his lips.

'What are you doin', Bernard?'

'Nothing. Just some work. How was the concert?'

'I've heard better. The baritones were off key all night long,' his mother said. 'What happened to your arm?'

'Hand,' Bernard said, not looking up. 'Caught it in the paper cutter at the office. It's not serious.'

'Does it hurt?'

'No, hardly at all.'

He waited for her to come to him, to display a little concern, a little peek of interest, to take his hand and lift it, roll back his sleeve, see what sort of a job he'd made of the dressing. He waited vainly for sympathy, her touch, a quick fond peck upon the cheek to comfort him and help with healing. He knew, of course, that it wouldn't come, that she would do as she always did — nothing; that she would scurry off into the kitchen to make herself cocoa and toast a bread roll, or prance off into her bedroom to the left of the narrow wood-panelled hall to take off and brush her best tweed coat or ease off her shoes, that her routine comforts would take precedence over his.

He did not hate her, did not resent her, did not even dislike her. He was just disappointed in her, tinged by the feeling that somehow she had let him down. The feeling was far from novel. It had lain stale within him since the war; until he had met Lizzie Conway, in fact, Lizzie and her pretty daughters, until he had touched and been touched by a loving woman, and the heavens hadn't opened and judgement hadn't come zigzagging down from the clouds.

He listened to his mother singing in the kitchenette, energetic, bustling, utterly self-absorbed. He knew that she would not ask about his wound again.

He went on writing left-handed, practising left-hand disciplines.

'I don't know what's wrong with young men these days,' he heard her call out. 'It's the same all over. Mrs Tennyson's daughter nearly got married to a baritone. Did I tell you that?'

'No.'

'Clydebank male-voice choir. Big chap. Plater in Brown's.'

'No!' Bernard murmured, as his mother's cheerful little voice continued to echo from the kitchenette, brittle and shallow as the tiles themselves.

'No!' he said. 'No, no, no!'

'Bernard? Are you listening to me?'

'Yes, Mother,' Bernard said, and went on writing quietly, quietly dreaming of Lizzie Conway and what life might be like for him in Lavender Court, taking care of Lizzie and her pretty, wayward girls.

Chapter Thirteen

Three Saturdays in four Polly was obliged to work until one o'clock. She did not complain about the schedule. Being well indoctrinated in the conditions of public service she tended to regard a Saturday off not as an entitlement but as a favour conferred upon the clerking staff out of the goodness of the councillors' hearts. Besides, Saturday was a busy day for local councillors. They were mostly ordinary working men, and a couple of women, who had been elected to protect the interests of what had been – but was no longer – a small independent unit within the dominion of the City of Glasgow.

Passing of the Local Government (Scotland) Act eighteen months ago had thrown things into a state of confusion. Even Mr Laughton, the Clerk Principal, was no longer absolutely clear how power devolved downward through the reconstituted county councils or who was expected to do what for whom. The ten good men and true – plus two women – who had been elected to serve the community for a three-year term carried on much as before, for policy in the higher realms of administration seemed to be directed not at preserving the *status quo* but mainly at appointing convenient scapegoats to take the blame for financial mismanagement further up the monkey-puzzle tree.

By the end of 1930, therefore, there was no such thing as a burgh council operating in the Gorbals. Officially it had become a nominated local council working within the remit of a county council who – this being Glasgow – had been brought within or were certainly answerable to the City Corporation.

Polly, then, was an agent employed by the Corporation to carry out functions excisable within a district and, as far as she could make out, to do more or less what she had been doing before. This, alas, still involved working three Saturdays in any given month, not galloping out of the archway at the side door of the old Burgh Hall building until five minutes after the hour of one o'clock, and not displaying too much youthful elation that might indicate that she was damned glad to quit the place and that if it burned to the ground before Monday she would shed not one solitary tear.

Polly was a model of decorum, of course, brisk but lady-like. At twenty she was no silly wee lassie. She no longer consorted with riffraff from the dole queues or those girls who, like her sister Babs, had escaped the factory floor more by good fortune than merit. Accountants from the Assessor's Office or the Department of Finance, not to mention visiting architects and engineers from Transport or Road Works, thought her very superior and would have been surprised to learn that her mother worked in the slops of a laundry and that Polly skiddled home not to a nice little villa in Giffnock or Cathcart but to a tenement flat in the sump of the Calcutta Road.

They would also have been surprised to learn that the haughty object of their desire was halfway to falling in love with a professional thief and that the man behind the wheel of the sleek black motorcar that was moored almost out of sight behind the iron railings of Morton Street United Free Church was none other than Dominic Manone.

Polly did not notice the Alfa Romeo at first.

She was in a hurry, eager to be home, to fry up a mutton chop and a few potatoes for a hasty dinner, to change out of her dark jacket and skirt into something less business-like and be off round to Patsy Walsh's house in the hope of catching him at home.

She had news to impart, bad news.

She was desperate to learn how Patsy would react to this latest development and to assure him that *she* hadn't betrayed him to O'Hara. She didn't really understand why she was so anxious to keep Patsy sweet, not to have him think ill of her. Was it only because of what had happened between them on the bed or was there more to it? Was she more like Patsy Walsh, beneath the skin, than she cared to admit?

She crossed the corner of Morton Street, walking fast.

Behind her the other girls from the burgh offices dispersed, heading towards Eglinton Street or around the broad corner into the bottom of the Pollokshaws Road. The morning drizzle had eased into one of those damp nondescript December afternoons when tenements and sky seemed to merge into each other and even the passers-by had a blurry look as if they had been cut from coarse brown cardboard.

Polly was far too impatient to hang about for a tramcar.

She darted across the roadway between cars, carts and buses and turned into Farmhead Loan, a narrow pub-less street of quiet tenements that would bring her out into the nether end of the Calcutta Road. She did not even see the Alfa until it was almost upon her.

It came prowling up behind her on the wrong side of the loan. It slid to a halt ten yards or so in front of her, tyres bumping over the kerb and on to the pavement. Before it had come to a proper halt the passenger door opened wide enough to block Polly's progress. She stopped. She hesitated, turned and might even have run back the way she had come if the man – Dominic Manone – had not told her to get in.

She went forward, stooping, handbag held tightly against her breasts as if she suspected that he might try to do what his lackey, O'Hara, had failed to do and wound her with a blade.

'Do you know who I am, Miss Conway?'

225

'You're Mr Manone – Dominic Manone.'

He was alone in the car, at the wheel. He wore a soft, dark blue wool overcoat and a turkey-red scarf. No hat or cap. His hair was jet black, wavy but not sleek. If he had worn a hat then he would have looked older, she thought, older and more sinister. The absence of a hat lent him a certain candour, a frankness that took the edge off her apprehension.

'Now you know who I am, will you get into the motor-car, please.'

'What for?'

'I have something to say to you.'

He was still leaning to the side, holding the door open.

She could smell leather upholstery, a faint whiff of cigar smoke, not too heavy, not overpowering. His eyes were dark brown, not teasing, not mocking but with a trace of anxiety in them, or possibly polite concern.

'Get in, Miss Conway.'

'If you've something to say to me, just say it.'

'I don't think it is right for you to be seen talking to me on the street.'

He did not grab, did not beckon. If he had done, Polly told herself later, she would have turned on her heel and left.

'Please,' he said.

Polly got into the Alfa, and Dominic closed the door.

In the course of Saturday morning Dennis put the Norton together again.

Jackie and he had been up early and had startled their father by passing him in the close as he had come in from night shift. He had peered at them and had tentatively repeated their names – 'Dennis? Jackie?' – as if they were half-forgotten acquaintances. Then, shaking his head in disbelief, he had gone on into the house to roll into bed, and the boys had gone trudging off downhill.

It was not the urge to earn an honest crust that had driven Sandy Hallop's lads out into the drizzle at the ungodly hour of half past seven o'clock but a peculiar restlessness whose source neither Dennis nor Jackie could identify. *Guilty consciences? Us? Never! Jeeze, man, what do you take us for?* Nevertheless, the cluttered apartment at No. 10 had somehow lost the sense of inviolable security that even occasional late-night visits from coppers had failed to dent and without which both the Hallop boys felt decidedly shaky.

As soon as they had reached the repair shop, however, they had felt just a little less vulnerable. Dennis had started work on the Norton while Jackie, carefully picking kindling from the bucket with his gloved paws, had lighted a fire in the stove. He needed cheering up. Thinking of Babs Conway made him depressed. Thinking how gay and glittery the Calcutta ballroom would be in Christmas week depressed him further, for, although he couldn't dance, he'd still have to pay a call on the Grimsdykes just to make sure they paid Stuart Royce his dues. Such matters lurked in the back of his mind. What he really craved was comfort, comfort and warmth and a sense of being somewhere that lay beyond every threat that had ever crept into his consciousness – a collection of fears that did not include appearances in court, short spells in jail or purling over the handlebars of a motorcycle travelling at high speed.

In fact, if his hands hadn't been so tender he might have fed petrol into the tank of the big Ariel Hunter that was racked under canvas at the rear of the shed, have pointed the wheel at Eaglesham and have ridden out into the rain. Crouched on the saddle in padded oilskins he would have tackled the twisting moorland tracks that snaked across Corse Hill to Darvel, Drumclog and Caldermill and have blown all his fears away. But he couldn't ride yet, couldn't dance yet, couldn't do a soddin' thing yet except sulk and hurt and worry.

He squandered the morning seated in front of the stove

drinking mug after mug of Camp coffee and smoking cigarettes while his brother checked the Norton's crank bearings and rockers, steering head and fork links, and generally made sure that the machine was fit to advertise in the *Motor Cycle* and worth twenty-five quid of some sucker's money.

It was going to be one of those days, Jackie decided, one of those dead, nothing-to-look-forward-to days that had marred his childhood and lured him into the streets at an early age in search not of pleasure but simply relief from the monotony of being a small, powerless boy in the dreary acres of the Gorbals in the gloom of mid-winter afternoons.

Shortly after noon young Billy turned up. Jackie sent him down to the Co-op to buy a tin of bully beef and half a dozen bread rolls, and the brothers, Billy included, lunched *al fresco* on the bench before the stove.

Halfway through the meal Billy lifted his head.

Corned beef and bread roll dripped raggedly from his mouth. For an instant, he had the furtive mien of a small animal caught tearing at a lion's kill.

'Somebody's comin',' he said as the door of the shed creaked open.

'Only me,' Tommy Bonnar announced.

'What d' you want?' said Dennis.

'Lookin' for Patsy. Thought he might be here.'

'Well, he ain't,' said Jackie. 'Haven't seen him since you know when an' I don't care if I never see the bugger again.'

'O'Hara's on to him.' Tommy wiped his nose on his coat sleeve and coughed. 'The word is we got away wi' five or six thousand quid.'

'Well, we bloody didn't,' Dennis said, as if that were an end of the matter.

'Manone's offerin' blood money,' Tommy said.

Billy chewed with a grinding motion of the jaws, the meat in his mouth already reduced to pap. Tommy glanced at the boy and frowned.

'Brother,' Jackie explained. 'What d' you mean – O'Hara's on to him?'

'Sniffed him out straight off,' said Tommy. 'Was round there last night.'

'Who told you?' said Dennis.

'Patsy's old man.'

'How much is Manone offerin'?' Dennis said.

'A lot,' said Tommy. 'Enough t' get O'Hara's interest.'

'Think he knows about us?' said Jackie.

'Naw, only Patsy. Only suspicions.'

'What d'you do, Jackie?' Billy said. 'What d'you get off wi'?'

'Shut your mouth, kid,' Dennis told him.

'Patsy won't crack,' said Jackie.

'But *she* might,' said Dennis.

'Babs?' Jackie said. 'Nah, nah.'

'I mean the other one – Polly.'

Jackie set down the enamel coffee mug and rubbed a hand over his jaw, the grubby fabric grating on two-day stubble. He pondered for a second, then said, 'She's Patsy's problem.'

'She's *our* problem, for Chrissake,' said Dennis.

'Aye, maybe Dennis is right,' said Tommy.

'What's that supposed t' mean?' said Jackie.

'She knows Dominic Manone, doesn't she, but,' Tommy stated.

'Her mam does, aye,' Jackie admitted, grudgingly. 'Everybody knows Lizzie's payin' off interest to Manone. She as good as told me that Dominic Manone was her protector the very first time we met.'

'Who takes the dough to O'Hara every month?' Dennis said.

'The kid sister,' said Tommy. 'Rosie, the dummy.'

'Jeeze!' said Jackie. 'Don't tell me you think the girls would sell us out?'

'How do I bloody know?' said Tommy, coughing again. 'I ain't screwin' one o' them.'

'Well, I ain't either.' Jackie grinned in spite of himself. 'Not yet.'

'Women!' Dennis snarled. 'Soddin' bloody women!'

'Patsy's the one,' said Jackie. 'If it's Patsy they're on to then he's the one we gotta worry about. Where is the bugger anyhow?'

'I wisht I knew,' said Tommy.

'Maybe he's done a bunk,' said Jackie. 'Gone off t' France or somewhere. I mean, you know what Patsy's like.'

'He's broke,' said Tommy. 'Broke an' in hock.'

'You sure?'

'I'm sure,' said Tommy. 'Told me himself last week.'

'Hey!' Jackie sat up straight. 'You don't think he could be dead already?'

'Naw,' said Dennis. 'Patsy? Naw, not Patsy Walsh.'

'Jeeze!' said Jackie. 'I mean if they've already got to Patsy, what hope is there for the rest o' us?'

'Bugger all,' said Tommy.

He drove out through Hutchesontown into Oatlands, swung down McNeil Street into Adelphi Street and brought the Alfa prowling to a halt on the river road.

Polly had never been inside a private motorcar before. Padded leather deadened the clatter of trams, the thunder of trains, the crying of the gulls that hovered above the brown waters of the Clyde. A few football supporters were already trickling towards the stadium via the bridges but the chalky outlines of the People's Palace across the river on Glasgow Green seemed misty and remote. She felt pleasantly cut off from the bustle of the city.

If anyone but Dominic Manone had been at the wheel she might have enjoyed the experience. As it was, she was reluctant to betray herself, to appear less than sophisticated. She had not asked where he was taking her or why they had stopped at this particular spot.

She looked from the side window, thinking how odd it was that the boundary line that separated the parliamentary divisions ran straight up the middle of the river. She wondered if the rowing teams that sculled their graceful shells above the tidal weir realised that they were dipping in and out of royal history. When she turned from the window she found that he was staring at her.

'What?' she said. 'What is it?'

'You do not look at all like your mother,' Dominic said.

'I should hope not,' said Polly.

'Why do you say that?'

'Would *you* like to be told that you looked like your father?'

'I can hardly remember what my father looks like.'

'Your uncle then,' said Polly. 'You know what I mean.'

'Yes, I do know what you mean.'

Dominic conceded the point without relaxing his grave, unobtrusive scrutiny. She wondered if he hid his feelings deliberately or if this was how all Italian men behaved. She could not read him as easily as she read Patsy. There seemed to be nothing on the surface and, for all she knew, nothing much beneath as if he were too handsome to have any character at all.

He said, 'I am trying to find out who robbed my warehouse.'

'I have no idea what you're talking about,' Polly said.

'I think that you do.'

'Is that why you sent Alex O'Hara round to our house last night?'

'To your house?' Dominic said. 'I did not know of this.'

Polly wondered if his surprise could possibly be genuine.

She said, 'Well, you'll know about it when my mammy comes to see you.'

'Did he – did O'Hara hurt you?'

'Hah!' said Polly. 'What do you think?'

'I really knew nothing of this,' Dominic said.

He adjusted his position, hand on the back of the seat an inch from her shoulder. If he touches me, if he brushes me with his fingertips or gives me a pat to reassure me then I'll know he's lying, Polly told herself.

To her relief he sat back, leaned his arms on top of the steering wheel and stared through the windshield at the empty street and the traffic that flowed, foreshortened, over the Albert Bridge.

'Did he hurt you or frighten you?' Dominic said.

'Both,' said Polly. 'He frightened all of us, especially my sister Rosie. And he cut the hand of a – a friend of ours who happened to be visiting at the time.'

'A female friend?'

'No, a man,' said Polly.

'Did your friend report the assault to the police?'

'My mother persuaded him not to.'

'Am I to take it,' Dominic said, 'that you told O'Hara nothing?'

'What was there to tell?' Polly allowed exasperation to show. 'We know nothing about what happened at the warehouse, nothing except what my sister Babs told us. How could we? I can't imagine what O'Hara thought a bunch of women might be able to tell him.'

'Something that your friend Walsh might have let slip.'

Polly had expected to be challenged about her friendship with Patsy. O'Hara had caught her out in a lie and, being as shrewd about some things as he was ignorant of others, had come rushing in like a blind bull. The fact that she *was* protecting someone made it difficult to feign innocence. If Mr Manone had picked on Babs for this little 'chat' Babs would immediately have negotiated terms – which, perhaps, was what Dominic Manone expected her to do.

'I was with him that evening,' Polly said. 'With Patsy Walsh, I mean.' She hesitated, calculating how much of the truth would seem like the whole truth. 'I wasn't – I wasn't in bed with him, if that's what you might be thinking.'

'You did not spend the night?'

'No, I left quite early.'

'How early?'

'Nine or half past.'

She waited for his next question, sure that it would concern Patsy.

He glanced at her, arms still folded on top of the wheel. She could smell a spicy sort of odour, very faint and pleasant. She was dying for a cigarette but did not have the gall to ask for one or take one out and light it.

'Is your sister okay?' Dominic said.

'O'Hara shouldn't have scared Rosie, particularly as she doesn't hear very well.'

'No,' Dominic agreed.

'My mother is furious.'

'I will talk with her,' Dominic said.

Polly said, 'I thought you protected people.' He glanced at her, an eyebrow raised. This time she was sure that his surprise was genuine. She went on, 'Isn't that how you make your money? Don't people pay you to protect them from the likes of O'Hara? Don't we pay you enough?'

'You pay me all I ask for,' Dominic said. 'But that is a debt – the interest on a debt, I should say. I have done things for your mama . . .'

'Now you want us to do something for you,' Polly said.

Her hands were cold. With the engine not running the interior of the car had rapidly become chilly. She kept still, though. An instinct told her that she had nothing to fear from this man.

'You want us to tell you who broke into your warehouse in Jackson Street and stole your money,' Polly said. 'That's a bit ironic, don't you think?'

'Ironic?'

'Implausible.'

'What is implausible?' Dominic said.

He no longer pretended to stare down the empty street. He stared at her instead. A speculative little glint in his dark eyes added dimension to his character. Polly found it difficult to despise him. He was as unlike Patsy Walsh as it was possible to be and yet behind his smoothness he too seemed self-contained and just a little desolate.

'That you should have to come to folk like us to get what you want.'

'You know nothing about me, Polly.'

'No,' Polly agreed. 'But you think you've been betrayed.'

Again the glint in the eye, the compression of the dark brows. She had surprised him again, by her perspicacity this time rather than her boldness.

'It's *that* you can't put up with, Mr Manone, isn't it?'

He paused, considering. 'I am not so sure I have been betrayed.'

'What will you do if it turns out you have been?' Polly said. 'Assert your authority. Take revenge?'

'Perhaps.'

'What if you make a mistake?'

'Pardon?'

'What if it was all a mistake?'

'Was it?' he said. 'If you tell me it was a mistake I will believe you.'

She smiled, not smugly. 'I don't know whether it was a mistake or not. I don't know who betrayed you, if anyone did. But if I did . . .'

'You would not tell me?'

'Why should I?' Polly said. 'Out of gratitude for what you've done for my mother and my sisters?'

'O'Hara should not have threatened you.'

'It makes no difference,' Polly said.

'To me it does.'

'Really? Why's that?' said Polly.

'Because I have respect for you, for your mama.'

'Because she pays you ...' Polly began.

'For other reasons too.'

'To do with my father?'

'I did not know your father, not well at any rate.'

'You were only a boy when he went away, weren't you?'

'Not much more than a boy,' Dominic agreed. 'Not quite old enough to fight in the war.'

'Do you regret that?'

'Do I regret what?'

'Not having had a real war to fight in?' Polly said.

'Of course not. I am glad of it.'

'So, instead, you've got this war of your own going on.'

'No,' he said. 'No, you do not understand how it is with us.'

'Business?' Polly said. 'Business and respect and honour? Right?'

He seemed about to answer her, to put something into words that might excuse or at least reveal what he wanted with her, why he had brought her here and what the conversation signified. He said nothing, though. He lifted a leather-gloved hand and tapped it on the top of the steering wheel, then reached for the ignition key and started the engine.

'Where are you taking me now?' Polly said.

'Home. To your home.'

'I thought you didn't want us to be seen together?'

'If you know nothing and have nothing to hide what does it matter?'

'I didn't say I'd nothing to hide. I've plenty to hide,' Polly said.

'Not concerning who robbed my warehouse, however,' Dominic said.

'Not about that, no.'

'In that case you can have no objections if I drop you at your close.'

'None at all,' said Polly.

'And if I wait for you outside?'

'Wait for me? For what?'

'Does your mother not have a payment to make this afternoon?'

'Dear God!' Polly exclaimed. 'Is that what all this is about? Are you fretting in case my mother won't shell out your miserable fiver?'

'I take it you will not be sending the girl, the little one?'

'Rosie? Sending her where?' Polly said. 'To meet with O'Hara? Don't be ridiculous. Of course we won't.'

'So you will be the one to make the payment?' Dominic said.

'I suppose I will be, yes.'

'I will drive you,' Dominic said. 'I'll wait in the motorcar while you tell your mother where you are going and until you pick up the money then I will personally drive you to the Rowing Club.'

'To meet with Alex O'Hara?'

'Yes.'

'Why don't I just give you the fiver?' Polly said. 'I assume it finds its way into your pocket eventually.'

'The money is not the point,' Dominic said.

Polly frowned. 'You want O'Hara to see us together, is that it?'

'Yes.'

'What a jolly good idea,' said Polly.

He had been drinking by fits and starts since the pubs opened at eleven. Only habit had steered him towards Molliston Street about half past two o'clock. He was sufficiently sober to realise that the odds against Rosie showing up were impossibly long but just sufficiently tipsy to imagine that she might actually have enjoyed the rough stuff and come looking for a bit more of the same.

He had done nothing about Walsh and Bonnar. Serious thinking would be necessary before he made his next move. He had a hunch that Bonnar and Walsh might be waiting for him. After what had happened last night he didn't want to charge into anything. Anyhow, he'd still had his regular collections to make and more than a few fivers were tucked into his pocket before he succumbed to the temptation to nip into Brady's for a quick one.

Brady's wasn't his only stop as he meandered across Bridge Street, down Nelson Street into the Paisley Road, and after the pubs closed down to the Rowing Club where the bar remained open all afternoon. There he handed his collections to Tony Lombard who counted the cash and put it into an envelope marked with his name. Then he ate a couple of mutton pies and a pickled egg, washed down with a pint of heavy.

By that time it was almost half past three and dusk was settling in, streetlamps were being lighted and an inexplicable melancholy entered O'Hara's soul. He wandered into the billiard room in search of Tommy Bonnar before he remembered that Tommy was high on his list of suspects and, being a wise wee man, wouldn't be hanging around looking for trouble. Then he tried to talk to Tony, but Tony would have none of his blathers. Eventually, more sober now than not, he wandered out into the street and, hands in pockets, shoulders slumped, peered towards the corner in the hope that he would see Rosie skipping towards him just as if nothing had happened.

He was still standing there, a Gold Flake dangling from his nether lip, when the Alfa prowled into view.

At first he thought Guido was at the wheel, Dominic in the passenger seat but as soon as the motorcar stopped he saw that Dominic was driving and that the person beside him was a girl.

He did not recognise her at first.

It wasn't Rosie, though. He knew it wasn't Rosie.

He removed the cigarette from his mouth, dropped it to the pavement and watched the girl climb out of the Manones' motorcar.

She had long legs inside a pleated black skirt, a haughty look that suggested she might be a toff. It wasn't until she moved into the circle of light that fell from the Rowing Club's doorway that he recognised Polly Conway.

He felt a stab of anger. This was the bitch who had humiliated him. He hated her for not cracking, for letting Walsh do things to her, for looking the way she did, for being so far above him that he could never hope to do anything to her except pull her down. Pull her down is what he would have done if it hadn't been for the motorcar and the man inside the motorcar.

Dominic Manone got out of the driver's door. He folded his arms and leaned on the Alfa's sloping roof.

Mr Manone said nothing.

Mr Manone did not interfere.

Mr Manone watched the girl come up to him and offer him the note. She held it cocked between finger and thumb. She wore skin-tight kidskin gloves that made her hands look slender and ladylike. She dabbed the fiver towards him.

'Take it,' she said.

He glanced at Mr Manone, who gave no signal to tell him what to do.

'Come on, you bastard, take it,' the girl said.

He uncoupled his hand from his overcoat pocket and reached out for the banknote. She swallowed it up in her hand, not teasing the way Rosie did but with an arrogance that he found almost vicious.

He blinked. He could see her sneer, and within the same corona, the same field of view, the Italian behind her.

He blinked again, rage numbed by bewilderment.

'Do you want this too?' the girl said.

When he saw what she had in her other hand he stepped back.

It was an involuntary motion like a spasm in a nerve, a tic over which he had no control. He stepped back, arm raised to protect his face.

She held the razor – his razor – in her gloved hand.

'Come on,' she said, 'take it. It's yours, isn't it? Take it.'

He wanted to look at Mr Manone but he couldn't take his eyes off the girl, off that vixen face, off the coil of brown hair that bobbed across her cheek, off the open razor in her fist. He had never seen a woman brandishing an open razor before and the spectacle made him queasy.

She came forward again. He backed away, heels knocking on the steps of the Rowing Club. He thought some of the boys might be behind him – Tony Lombard, Irish Paddy – but they were not his boys, not when Mr Manone was there; you owed loyalty only to the man who paid you.

He covered his face with his forearms.

'Know what you are, O'Hara?' the girl said. 'You're a born coward.'

She tossed the razor – his razor – on to the pavement, the banknote after it. She pivoted on her heel and walked away, turning her back on him as if he posed no threat at all. She leaned on the slope of the roof of the Alfa.

'Now, Mr Manone,' Polly said, 'now that's done I would be grateful if you would drive me home.'

'By all means,' Dominic said politely, and stepped around the bonnet of the motorcar to open the passenger door.

Babs said, 'So what did he do then?'

'I dunno,' Polly said. 'Just stood there, looking sick.'

'I don't mean him,' Babs said, 'I mean *him*.'

'Dominic?' Polly said. 'He brought me back here.'

Lizzie glanced over her shoulder. 'Did he tell you to call him Dominic?'

'No,' Polly admitted. 'But – well . . .'

'Don't you go gettin' ideas above your station, my girl,' Lizzie said. 'It's Mr Manone to the likes of us.'

'Yes, yes,' Polly said.

'What did it feel like,' Babs said, 'squaring up to O'Hara?'

'Terrific! Absolutely terrific!' Polly said. 'Never felt so – so . . .'

'Powerful,' Rosie suggested.

She leaned across the table, watching and listening intently.

'Not exactly powerful,' Polly said. 'That's not the word. Excited, maybe. So much in – in control.'

'Because *he* was with you, of course,' Babs said, nodding.

Lizzie transferred two plates of minced beef pie hot from the oven. A bowl of mashed potatoes and a dish of green peas already graced the table. When the oven door opened the heat in the kitchen became almost stifling. She carried two more plates to the table, seated herself and began to eat.

'I'd love to have been there,' Babs said, 'just to see that bugger's face.'

Lizzie, saying nothing, ate.

She looked weary and was more reticent than usual while her daughters chattered around her. She spooned potato on to Rosie's plate and with a wag of the forefinger indicated that she, Rosie, should begin to eat. She knew that the sprightly little winds of youth had blown many of the clouds of doubt away. They carried nothing for long at that age, Lizzie reminded herself, and were perhaps the better for it.

'Are you going to Manor Park tomorrow?' Polly said.

Lizzie shook her head.

'Why not? I told Dominic to expect you.'

'I'm sure he'll be holdin' his breath,' Lizzie said.

'I thought, if you're going – I thought I might come with you,' Polly said.

'Oh, aye! Aye-aye!' said Babs. 'What about poor old Patsy then?'

'I may go round there later tonight,' Polly said.

'Dancing?' Rosie said, loudly.

'Not dancin',' said Babs.

'I don't want you goin' anywhere by yourselves,' Lizzie said quietly.

'Why not?' Babs cried.

'Because I say so.'

'Mammy, I've got to see Patsy some time,' Polly said.

'I'm goin' to Grandma's. You can come with me if you like.'

'What's the alternative?' Babs said.

'Stay here, stay in the house. All of you.'

Babs sighed and shovelled a forkful of minced beef pie into her mouth. In fact, she hadn't intended going out. She'd broken with Jackie and wouldn't go chasing after him. If he was as keen on her as he said he was then he'd come panting after her in his own good time.

Meanwhile, she'd lie low for a week or two. Christmas was coming up and she could do with a few long lies, a few days just lounging about the house taking it easy. By the look of the weather it wouldn't be a white Christmas or even a grey New Year, just another of those dreary seasons when all it did was drizzle. If the worst came to the worst she would persuade Polly to go along to the Hogmanay dance at the Socialist Sunday School, though that was hardly going to seem like a *Wow!* after dancing with Jackie at the Calcutta.

Alex O'Hara's visit was still fresh in her memory and she didn't have to be told how edgy things were on the street or why Mammy didn't want them going out alone. While she resented the trouble that Jackie Hallop had got her into she didn't anticipate that it would last long, not now that Polly had Dominic Manone on her side; not even madman O'Hara would dare defy Mr Manone.

'Nice, ain't he?' Babs said. 'Mr Manone, I mean.'

'Very nice,' said Polly. 'Not what I expected. Very pleasant and polite.'

'Handsome too.'

'Yeah.'

'Did he say anything about our daddy?' Rosie asked.

Her sisters stared at her.

Lizzie went on eating, eyes down.

'Why would he do that?' said Polly.

'I thought you might have asked him,' Rosie said.

'Well, I didn't,' Polly said. 'We had more important things to discuss.'

'Like what?' said Rosie.

'Like . . .' Polly shrugged.

Her face was flushed with the heat of the kitchen but excitement had given her an appetite that not even Rosie's stupid questions could blunt. She covered her moment of uncertainty by filling her mouth full.

She wondered what Dominic Manone would have for his supper, what succulent Italian delicacy would be on his plate. Memories of the afternoon remained astonishingly vivid. Being in the motorcar, being alone with Dominic, the intense satisfaction beating bully-boy O'Hara at his own game had given her a tangy taste of power – yes, power *was* the word for it – that made everything seem bland by comparison.

'He didn't know your father,' Lizzie said.

'He's says he did,' said Polly. 'Slightly.'

'Oh, you did talk about Daddy then?' said Rosie.

'Just a mention in passing.'

Lizzie laid down her knife and fork, squaring them on her plate. She looked up. 'Who's comin' to help me with Grandma?'

'Tonight?' said Babs. 'Why tonight? What's wrong with tomorrow?'

'I've got somethin' else to do tomorrow.'

'Like what?' said Babs.

'Like none of your business,' Lizzie said.

'To do with Dominic?' said Polly.

'To do with me.' Lizzie hesitated. 'Might as well tell you, I suppose. I'm goin' to visit Mr Peabody.'

'At home?' said Rosie.

'Aye. It's long way across town to Knightswood,' Lizzie said, 'so I don't know when I'll be back. That's why I'm goin' to Grandma's tonight.'

'Why are you visiting old Peabody?' Babs said.

'To see how his hand is,' Polly suggested, 'and to give him our thanks?'

'It's the very least I can do, don't you think?' said Lizzie.

And Polly answered, 'Oh, yes.'

Chapter Fourteen

Walking through the streets of the Gorbals on a dank Sunday morning on the shortest day of the year did not bear comparison with being driven around in an Italian motorcar but it was only as she approached the café that Polly realised that she didn't want to be there for other reasons too. She found herself hoping that Patsy would not turn up but he was already installed at a table in the rear, shabby and unshaven and to judge by his expression no more pleased to see her than she was to see him.

He watched her work her way between the tables, nudging past two elderly women whose weekend treat was to share a dish of raspberry ice-cream after mid-morning mass at St Ninian's. She looked exceedingly smart, her hair shiny, her black overcoat clinging to her hips. She wore a hat that he hadn't seen before, close fitting with a shallow crown, the brim pulled down so that it almost covered her eyes. She came up to him, head tilted back, fretful and – so Patsy thought – supercilious. 'I didn't think you'd be here,' she said.

'Then why did you bother to come?'

'On the off-chance.'

'Do you want a coffee?'

'I can't stay long.'

'Aren't you gonna sit down?'

She scraped out a wooden chair and perched on it, legs

stretched into the narrow passageway. Patsy signalled, ordered two coffees.

'I thought you might have gone,' she said.

'Gone where?' he said.

'Paris. Berlin. Somewhere abroad.'

'Usin' what for money?' Patsy said.

'I don't think you should stay in Glasgow.'

'Is that what your friend told you to tell me?'

'My friend?'

'Manone.'

'He isn't my friend.'

'You ride around in his fancy motorcar, don't you?'

She gave a curt nod to affirm that she had expected him to know that. She had been well aware that Dominic Manone was showing her off around the neighbourhood, deliberately flaunting their connection in the hope that it would stir resentment and that resentment might lead to a squeal. She had been dazzled by the ride in the Alfa, disarmed by Dominic Manone's courteous charm but she had not been blind to the fact that he was using her in much the same way as Patsy had done.

It wasn't that she had grown weary of Patsy – she hadn't known him long enough for that – or that she despised him for what he had done. There had been no defining moment when her attitude had changed, no *volte face*. Through no fault of his own Patsy seemed to have become part of a more complex equation. For some reason – or no reason, perhaps – she preferred to blame Patsy for her present emotional muddle.

She said, 'He wanted information – which he didn't get, of course.'

'Why do you say "Of course"?'

'I wouldn't let you down.'

'How do I know that?' Patsy said.

'You'll just have to trust me.'

'I see.'

'You don't see anything,' Polly said. 'Dominic Manone's far too subtle to be caught out that way. Don't you know what subtle means?'

'Yeah,' Patsy said. 'As it happens I do know what subtle means.'

'I'm sorry,' Polly said. 'I shouldn't have said that.'

'Say what you like,' Patsy told her. 'I ain't gonna believe you anyway.'

'Thanks,' Polly said. 'Thanks a million.'

'I know more about Dominic Manone an' how he works than you do, Polly,' Patsy informed her. 'You think O'Hara's dangerous? He's a babe-in-bloody-arms compared with Manone; and I don't just mean because Manone's an Italian.'

'I don't know what you're talking about,' said Polly. 'Who spotted us?'

'Wee Billy Hallop. God, he could hardly not spot you when Manone's black Alfa was planted outside your close for half the afternoon.'

'Where were you?'

'What's that got to do with it?'

'Didn't you go to the Calcutta last night?'

'No,' Patsy said, impatiently. 'No, of course I didn't go to the Calcutta.'

'Neither did I,' Polly told him.

She shifted her legs as the coffees were brought to the table.

She reached for the cup and sipped, felt the liquid scald her tongue. She was annoyed that the conversation with Patsy seemed to be increasing her confusion. He stubbed out one cigarette and lit another. He looked drawn, his quick suave energy blunted. She recalled the weight of him upon her on the bed, his masculine energy; then his tact, his apology, his failure to *insist*, a consideration that she was now inclined to dismiss as timidity.

She took a deep breath and told him about O'Hara's visit.

'Did he hurt anyone?' Patsy asked.

'Only Mr Peabody.'

'Who's he?'

'The rent-collector.'

'Did O'Hara carve him?'

'Cut his hand.'

'Police involved?' Patsy asked, frowning.

'No, no police. Mr Peabody's a friend of my mother's.'

'God, it's no wonder you're upset, Polly.'

'I'm not upset. I am perfectly calm.'

'So that's why you went to see Manone, to get O'Hara off your back?'

'Yes.'

'Crafty old Dominic would want somethin' in exchange.'

'He wanted information,' Polly said. 'I didn't tell him anything.'

'Did he ask about me?'

'He thinks we're sweethearts.'

'Sweethearts?' said Patsy.

'We aren't, of course.'

'There you go with that "of course" again,' Patsy said. 'It doesn't matter what Manone thinks. He can't prove a bloody thing. He's got his outfit runnin' far too smoothly to want to rock the boat without good reason. I'm sorry you got dragged into all this, Polly.'

'Not half as sorry as I am.' She sipped at the coffee again, cooler now. 'My mammy would say it's all my own fault for falling into bad company. What would've happened if you had got away with Manone's money?'

'Tommy would have squared himself with the bookies. Jackie and Dennis would have blown the lot on fancy new motorcycles.'

'And you?'

'I'd have been outta here.'

'Leaving everything behind?' Polly said.

'Not everythin',' Patsy said. 'Maybe I'd have taken you with me.'

'Maybe I wouldn't have wanted to go.'

He shifted position. He looked wistful, Polly thought, but not contrite or regretful. He said, 'Moot point, anyhow.'

'Unless you pull another one.'

'Another what?'

'Robbery, burglary – whatever you call it.'

'Jobs like that don't grow on trees, Polly.'

'Is that why you went in on it?'

'Yeah.'

'Greed?' Polly said.

'Yeah. Probably.'

'How much would you need to take you to France for a while?'

'Paris? Oh, a hundred, hundred an' fifty quid would see me right for the best part of a year. I'd find a nice little *pension* – know what that is?'

'A boarding-house,' said Polly.

'A nice cheap little *pension* somewhere in the Quarter.'

'What would you do with yourself all day?'

'In Paris,' Patsy said, 'there's always plenty to do.'

'Find a job?'

'Maybe, once I'd learned the lingo properly.'

'You really should go, Patsy,' Polly said.

'You tryin' to get rid of me?'

'For your own sake, you should go.'

'If I had the money, an' if you'd come with me . . .'

'What?'

'I'd be off like a shot,' Patsy said.

'I couldn't – I can't leave right now.'

'Why not? What's holdin' you?'

'My mother needs me.'

'Apron strings?' Patsy said.

'Not apron strings – consideration,' Polly said. 'Responsibility.'

'Implyin' that I don't have any? My old man can take care of himself. He's always been able to take care of himself.'

'I wasn't talking about you, or your father,' Polly said. 'All I'm saying, Patsy, is that you'd be safer out of this place right now. I just don't want to see you come to grief.'

'So you think I'll come to grief, right?' Patsy said. 'Is that why you won't come away with me?'

'For God's sake, I'm only trying to warn you.'

'Are you scared of me, Polly?'

The question caught her off guard. She could not give an answer without thought. The fact of the matter was that she was scared of Patsy Walsh, that what she had felt for him, however fleeting, had been frightening. She had also been afraid *for* him and some trace of that fear remained within her now, more than a trace if she was truthful with herself. She had Dominic Manone behind her but Patsy did not. Patsy's enemy was her protector. That paradox, that anomaly made her apprehensive.

'Come on back to my place,' he said.

'What?'

'Now. Right now. Come on back to my place.'

'I – I can't.'

'You won't, you mean.'

'I can't. I can't. I have to get back home. My mammy's . . .'

He grinned. 'I know what you're scared of, Polly.'

'God, you really are a bastard, Patsy.' She got to her feet. 'I only came here to warn you . . .'

'Yeah, I thought as much.'

'If you need money . . .'

He looked up at her, rueful and amused. 'You can get it for me? Is that the deal? Is that what your friend Manone told you to tell me? He'll save face by payin' me to scarper? If I run now then I'll take the blame. Maybe all Manone wants is a scapegoat.' He paused. 'Maybe that's what happened to your old man. Maybe he was lucky that the Germans finished him off.'

'I'm going home now,' Polly said.

She felt near to tears. The good feelings, the safe feelings that Dominic Manone had engendered had been thoroughly dissipated, scattered to the four winds. Patsy wasn't proud or stubborn; he was stupid. She should have recognised that right from the first, before she became involved with him. Stupid: not much better than Jackie or Dennis Hallop, perhaps even doomed to wind up like wee Tommy Bonnar.

Her tears were for herself, not for stupid Patsy Walsh.

'I'm stayin' put,' Patsy told her. 'I ain't runnin' away. I've nothin' to run away from. Manone's not gonna do anythin' bad to me.'

'How can you be so sure?'

'Because you won't let him,' Patsy said.

'I'm going,' said Polly.

'*Arrivederci* then,' said Patsy.

Lizzie had seen fields and hills before but what she could not recall having seen before were fields and hills lying right on folks' front doorsteps.

Fields and hills, trees and sky; a wide expanse of pure slate-blue sky unsmudged by the brimstone breath of furnaces and foundries and the heavy cloying brown haze of a million reeking chimneys. Even on that mid-winter day the Knightswood sky formed a clear, uplifting presence over the tail of the Great Western Road and the wide, tree-lined boulevard to the north-west.

The door of Mr Peabody's terraced cottage opened directly on to a broad pavement. Its windows looked out not on a medley of traffic or towering tenements but on fields, parklands and a coppice of mature trees that, even in the gloom of a December afternoon, seemed to swim in a clear pastoral light. Lizzie could just imagine the place in summer, all green and leafy and, as she stepped from the deck of the tramcar, she inhaled a breath of cold, rich, loamy air that cut into her dusty tubes like balm. Bliss, manna, heaven, a practical and attainable paradise where she and her daughters would flourish, where nothing awful ever happened and the neighbours would all be as open and gentle as the landscape.

'Yiss,' said the widow Peabody. 'If you're selling pegs, I'm not buying.'

'I'm not sellin' pegs,' said Lizzie. 'I'm not sellin' anythin'. Is this where Bernard Peabody lives?'

The woman in the doorway was small but robust. She had red cheeks and reddish hair – dyed, for sure – and the sort of pinkish complexion that no amount of pancake make-up could ever disguise. She was not like Lizzie, however, not swaggering and threatening, not bulky. She had a nippy sort of temperament that evinced itself in nippy little movements, like a clockwork mouse that would whirr round and round in noisy circles until its spring gave out.

'It might be,' the widow Peabody said. 'I'm going out in a minute.'

'Good for you,' said Lizzie. 'Is Bernard at home?'

The woman glared, eyes pink with hostility.

'Who is it, Mum?'

Bernard came to the door, a trim wooden door with dark brown varnish and a crescent of thick green glass set at eye-level.

He wore a dressing-gown over a collarless shirt, and flannel trousers. He had a pair of old sandshoes on his bare feet. He looked a little tousled as if he'd been napping by the fire. The bandage on his hand was ghostly pale in the gloom of the alcove that led, doorless, to the living-room.

Bernard was taller than his mother. He crouched behind her in a manner protective and comical, as if he were about to leap-frog over her straight into Lizzie's arms.

'I came to see how you were,' Lizzie said.

'Come in, Lizzie, come away in,' said Bernard.

'She can't come in,' Mrs Peabody stated, 'because I'm going out.'

'Mother . . .'

'I'm not leavin' you alone in the house with a strange woman.'

'Mother, this is Lizzie Conway. She's an old friend.'

'I'll say she is – she's twice your age.'

'Mother, please,' said Bernard, squirming a little.

'Very well, Bernard, if you must have this person in the house then I won't go to my Bible group. I'll forgo my pleasure for yours.'

Mrs Peabody snatched off her hat. Her reddish hair was probably natural. It had no trace of frizz and clung like a knitted cap to her skull. Just before the bell for round one, as it were, Lizzie tried to estimate her opponent's age. Sixty-two or -three, she reckoned.

'That's up to you, Mum,' he said. 'But Lizzie's come a long way to call on me an' I'm dam – blessed if I'll be sending her away without refreshment.'

Mrs Peabody glanced up at her son then back at Lizzie who, without a blush, said, 'Didn't Bernard tell you about us?'

'Us?' Violet Peabody piped.

'Aye,' said Lizzie sweetly, 'old friends, we are, old, old friends.' Then, to get the bout properly started, kissed Bernard smack-dab on the lips.

Polly said, 'I don't think Mammy will be coming tonight, Gran, so if there's anything we can do to make you comfortable just say the word.'

The old woman shifted her weight ponderously in the wooden armchair, skipped a glance from Polly to Babs to

Rosie and, with a prescience that surprised them all, said, 'Has she got herself a man?'

Babs said, 'Are you nuts? I mean . . .'

Polly hastily intervened. 'She's visiting a friend, a female friend.'

'More important than comin' to see her poor mother.' Janet was making tea, a gesture that owed more to habit than hospitality. 'Friends before family, friends before family, I suppose.'

Grandma McKerlie grunted, whether in agreement or disapproval her granddaughters hadn't the faintest idea. Polly reckoned that her gran found the presence of three young Conways gathered all together just a wee bit daunting. Perhaps, Polly thought, we bring a whiff of fresh air into her stagnant life and she glimpses what she's been missing all these years. Then she decided that such a thought was patronising, even heretical and that she should have more respect for the poor old dear and not be so ready to condemn a generation who had had things much tougher than she could possibly imagine.

Observing her grandmother and aunt, Polly tried to picture what it would be like to have most of your life behind you, all mistakes made and accounted for, all passion spent, all promises fulfilled, almost the whole story written and nothing left to do but wait for the end. Instead she found herself wondering how the couple would cope if they happened to stumble on the fortune that was hidden under the floorboards in the hall cupboard.

How would they spend it? What would they buy? A Merlin motorised invalid chair so that Gran could get out and about again? Dresses from Daly's, furs from Karter's, furniture from Bow's? Fresh meat, best cuts, every day? China tea, Kenyan coffee, canned fruits? Cream cakes from Fergusson's, chocolates from Birrell's? Would they go on holiday to gay Paree or down the water for a week in Largs? Would they give some of it away to the church or the Institute? Would they share their good fortune with the family?

Probably not, Polly told herself: she simply couldn't imagine what Janet and Gran would do with money and suspected that it would bring them only confusion and bewilderment, not happiness.

Aunt Janet emerged from the cupboard carrying a teapot and a plate of home-baked almond cakes, curious bullet-shaped objects that none of the Conways would touch with a bargepole.

'So it isn't a man then?' Janet said. 'I heard it was a man.'

Babs glanced at Polly who managed to remain inscrutable.

'Don't know what she'd do with a man at her age,' Gran said.

'Aye, at her age,' said Janet, 'she wouldn't know what to do with a man.'

'Mammy is younger than you,' Rosie pointed out.

Babs told her, '*Wheesht.*'

'I heard there was trouble at your house on Friday night wi' two men fightin' on the doorstep,' Janet said. 'I heard it had to do wi' what happened at the Central Warehouse last Wednesday.'

'Where did you hear that?' Babs asked.

'At the dairy,' Janet answered. 'I hear a lot o' things at the dairy.'

Now she thought of it Polly realised that Mr Smart's corner shop, like all corner shops, was bound to be an oasis of gossip. The dairy might be a quarter of a mile from Lavender Court and a lot further than that from the warehouse but the southside was the southside and rumours travelled from one end to the other faster than a flock of sparrows.

'At the dairy, aye,' Grandma McKerlie said. 'Is it true, but?'

'No, Gran,' said Polly. 'It isn't true.'

'It's true about the warehouse,' Babs said, shrewdly. 'But the rest of it's rubbish. I mean, we'd know if there'd been a fight on our landin'.'

'Who is he then, this man?' Gran said.

'Nobody,' Babs said, impatiently. 'There's no man.'

'Only Mr Peabody,' Rosie put in.

'Who's Mr Peabody?' said Janet.

'Our rent-collector,' said Polly.

Grandma McKerlie said, 'Is he the one that was fightin' wi' her?'

'Dear God!' Babs put a hand to her brow. 'Mr Peabody only comes to collect the rent, Gran. He's not got his leg ove—' She shrugged.

'A rent-collector, huh!' Janet poured streams of pale yellow tea into the cups on the table. 'I thought she could do better for hersel' than a rent-collector.'

'Mr Peabody is a nice chap,' said Rosie.

'Gives her tick, I suppose,' said Janet.

'Nothing of the sort,' said Rosie who, for some reason that Polly could not fathom, seemed to be uncharacteristically argumentative today. 'Mr Peabody would not give tick to anyone. He lives in Knightswood.'

Janet had heard of the garden suburb but the name meant nothing to Gran McKerlie and Knightswood might as well have lain west of the Limpopo as west of the Clyde. In fact, now that she considered it, Polly realised that none of them had ever been out to the end of the tramlines and that Gran McKerlie wasn't the only one to whom the West End was unknown territory.

In the same moment – her concentration sliding away from the spartan kitchen and her droning aunt – she wondered where Dominic was right now and what aspect of business occupied him on a Sunday afternoon, or if he joined the rest of the Italian community in what seemed to her like one long act of worship at one or other of the chapels that dotted the city. She could almost imagine him kneeling before a crucifix, crossing himself devoutly, for his soft-spoken, gentle manner seemed quite close to piety. When he lit a candle or said a prayer today, she wondered if he would spare a passing thought for her.

'Polly?' Babs said.

'What?'

'I think Gran needs the you-know-what.'

The girls went out into the narrow hall while, within the kitchen, amid the teacups and bullet-shaped cakes, their grandmother struggled from the chair to the chamberpot and, by the sound of it, strained to make water.

'How long do we have to stay here?' Rosie asked in a stage whisper.

'Another half-hour at least,' said Polly.

Babs was kneeling before the cupboard door. She hunkered on her heels, knees spread, one hand upon the woodwork.

'Is that where the money is?' she said.

'Yes,' Polly answered.

'Can we look? Can we take a peek?'

'What is going on?' said Rosie, frowning.

'No, we can't take a peek,' said Polly. 'Don't be ridiculous.'

'What are you two talking about?'

'Nothin',' said Babs. 'None of your business.' She pressed her forehead against the cupboard door, and sniffed. 'God, I can just about smell it.'

'What? Gran?' said Rosie.

'Plu-ease!' Babs exclaimed; then to Polly, 'I think we *should* take a peek just to make sure it's still there.'

'It's still there,' said Polly. 'Where else would it be?'

'Go on.'

'*No.*'

Aunt Janet jerked open the door from the kitchen and peered at her nieces gathered guiltily in the gloom of the hall. 'What're you whisperin' about?' she said. 'An' what are you doin' down there, Babs?'

'Cramp,' said Babs, lifting herself and grimacing. 'You know – cramp.'

'Oh!' said Janet; and because this was a misfortune that she

wouldn't acknowledge let alone discuss, ushered the girls back
into the kitchen without another word.

The sky had changed from slate to navy blue and contained
more stars than Lizzie had ever seen before, all glittering with
a brilliance that seemed almost artifical. A new moon had risen
over the trees at the top of the parkland. It too looked too
perfect to be real, like a prop from a Princess pantomime or
an illustration from one of Rosie's books of fairytales.

The night wind brushed light and cold against Lizzie's lips,
a keen, clear little wind that came off the hills and brought a
sense of the countryside that lay beyond the mountains that
stretched away into a grand and innocent infinity.

Along the line of the Boulevard – in the middle distance –
a tramcar raced, its lights bobbing. The lights of the suburbs
were not dense but individualised, streetlamps and house lights
and the lights that lit the steeples of the newly built churches
that had been given pride of place amid the dwellings. Lizzie
had expected Knightswood to be different – and it *was* different
– but she hadn't expected it to make her feel different too.

'Pretty, isn't it?' Bernard said.

'Aye,' said Lizzie. 'Oh, aye, it is.'

She hugged his arm so that they walked along the pavement
not just in step but in cosy harmony, a one-ness that Lizzie
hadn't experienced for years.

The afternoon had not been a total disaster after all.
Whatever her other failings – and they were many – Mrs
Peabody could not be faulted as a hostess. Once it had become
apparent that Bernard would not be denied 'his visitor', Mrs
Peabody had set about impressing her guest. She had lavished
upon Lizzie such heaps of freshly cut gammon sandwiches and
buttered fruit loaf, such piles of scones and pancakes and
dainty little sponge cakes that Lizzie had made quite a pig
of herself, a demonstration of appreciation that had softened

Violet Peabody's attitude to the big woman from the Gorbals and had led if not to friendship at least to temporary rapport.

Lizzie had been sensible enough not to divulge the cause of Bernard's wound and had supported the lie that he had told his mother. She had admitted, however, that she'd been concerned about the injury and that she and her daughters – she was careful to mention her daughters – had given the wound attention when Bernard had turned up to collect the rent.

All these little half-truths Mrs Peabody had appeared to swallow without paying much attention. She had been as quick as a hawk to swoop on any titbits of personal information that Lizzie dropped, however, and had demonstrated an immoderate interest in Lizzie's age, Lizzie circumstances, Lizzie's family and, most especially, in Lizzie's intentions towards her son.

'She isn't so bad, you know,' Bernard said as he walked Lizzie along the road towards the tram stop. 'Once you get to know her.'

'She's devoted to you, that's for sure.'

'No, she's devoted to herself,' said Bernard, with a little chuckle. 'I'm just part of her life, not the centre of it.'

'She *should* be devoted to you,' Lizzie said.

'Oh, now ...'

'You're a good man, Bernard, a brave man.'

'Oh, really, Lizzie, I only did what anyone would have done.'

'You faced up to O'Hara like a hero.'

'I couldn't stand by an' see him bully a young girl.'

She patted his bandaged hand gently. 'Will it cost you time off work?'

'I doubt it,' Bernard said. 'I never take long to heal. Meanwhile I'm doin' quite well writing with my left hand. It only takes a bit of practice.'

They walked on, saying nothing for a while.

Cottage rows had given way to gardens and neat semi-detached villas. Lizzie suspected that Bernard had steered her away from the nearest tram stop. Up ahead she could see the high-hung lights of a crossroads and, by following the contours of the parkland and distant hills, had a notion that he might be leading her towards the Boulevard.

She said, 'My husband wasn't like him, you know.'

'He was a soldier, wasn't he?'

'No, he was a crook,' said Lizzie. 'No good beatin' about the bush. He was a crook, but he wasn't a bully.'

'Did he work for the older Manone, the one who went off to America?'

'Aye,' Lizzie admitted. 'They say he stole a large sum o' money from the Manones before he joined the army. If he did, though, I never saw a penny of it. An' I never got a pension either, since there was some mix-up about whether Frank was dead or not.'

'Missing in action,' Bernard said, nodding.

'I never understood what that meant,' said Lizzie.

'Buried under tons o' earth,' Bernard told her. 'Blown to pieces. Drowned in the mud. Burned beyond recognition. Nothin' left to identify. That's what it meant.'

'You saw all that?'

'Yes,' Bernard said. 'Most of it.'

She did not ask him to explain or expand. She sensed his reticence and the reasons for it. She gripped his arm a little more securely, lifted her chin and tasted the clean wintry wind once more. The war was in the past. What she'd had today was a glimpse of the future, a future free of tenements and dank closes and the stink of disinfectant, of being in debt to Dominic Manone and the whole sinister circle of crooks and cowards that had been Frank's legacy.

Even if the Corporation Housing Department would agree to allocate her a house in Knightswood she wouldn't be able to afford it. Only when the girls were married and off her hands and Manone paid off in full would she be free to cross the river and put the Gorbals and all it stood for behind her.

Would she be free to marry again.

And by that time it might be too late; she might be too old.

She felt within her, in the very rhythm of her step, a sudden desperate quickening, an urgency the like of which she had never known before.

They were close to the cross now, to the confluence of several roads and avenues, the great broad river of the Boulevard with its new tramlines and tree-plantings, its shoals of soft grass, running forth before her. She could see three churches and a school from the dip of the corner and the sky, an amazing breadth of sky, stretching away in all directions, far above the rooftops.

She drew Bernard to a halt.

'What's wrong, Lizzie? Are you out of breath?'

'Just a bit,' she said.

He took her in his arms.

Sunday night in the suburbs; they were long past the age when such exhibitions were excusable. Bernard didn't seem to care. He pressed her against him in a bear-hug and although they were swaddled in winter coats and scarves and kept apart by layers of wool and flannel, Lizzie could feel the ardour in him, not lust or even longing but a strangely uninhibited surge of affection that somehow transcended need.

He kissed her mouth.

His lips and her lips were cold but that did not seem to matter.

'Lizzie?'

'Hmm?'

'Sorry, but I think I love you. Sorry, but I think I do.'

She leaned against him, breast against his chest, hat brushing his chin.

'What're you sorry for, Bernard?' she asked. 'It's me should be sorry.'

'You? For what?'

'For not bein' young, for not bein' beautiful enough for you.'

'God, Lizzie!' he told her. 'You are. *You are.*'

'Nah.' She shook her head joyfully. 'Nah, nah, I'm not.'

'Why won't you believe me?' Bernard said.

'Because I know better?'

'Lizzie.' He took her face between his hands and said, 'Lizzie, I mightn't be much of a gentleman but I'd never lie to you. I love you. I mean it.'

He kissed her again, lingeringly, and pressed against her and under the wrappings, under the wool and flannel, she felt the years melt away, felt slender and supple again, so youthful and alive that just for one brief brilliant moment she was almost tempted to believe that what he said was true.

Chapter Fifteen

Christmas for Dominic had never been a merry time, nor did he much care for the Scottish tradition of celebrating New Year with a welter of glad-handing, back-slapping sentiment and excessive amounts of whisky. Perhaps because he was himself a cold fish he tended to dismiss his neighbours' warm-heartedness as affectation. In the dog days of December, however, he was obliged to hide his prejudices and to perform the role that fate and his family had allotted him, to pretend that he really was a jolly fellow who wished only goodwill to all men and – with discretion – one or two women as well.

Dominic kept abreast of what was happening in the world at large. He was well aware that in many towns and cities throughout Britain the Italian colonies were being brought together and given dignity by the organising powers of the *fascisti*. In spite of leanings towards 'the other side', he was just deceitful enough to keep his nose clean with the Glasgow *fascio* while still paying his dues to the Union of Italian Traders.

Influence and power were elements that Dominic well understood. He watched with interest as the Communities began to organise themselves. He was not dismayed by the composition of steering committees made up of honest, upstanding citizens, activists who had at last found focus for their drive and energy. He did not consider them misguided. He was, after all, primarily a businessman. The fact that he invested his money in ventures that were at best shady and at worst criminal did not seem to count against him, for unlike the Sabini or Cortesi families in London a thoroughly respectable front screened his more colourful activities.

Dominic did not think of himself as a gangster. He thought of himself as an employer, a benefactor, a responsible citizen. Consequently he did not scorn the appeal of the social clubs' dinner dances and summer outings.

After all his papa, way back, had been a founder member of Glasgow's *Società di Mutuo Soccorso*, a piece of local history that hadn't been forgotten by older members of the Community and that added a certain piquancy to capturing the bashful young Manone for an appearance at a wedding party or a dance or an all-male smoker or in persuading him to address one or other of the *associazioni* in his capacity as a successful businessman.

How could he do else but pay lip-service to the principle of fascism, *Onore, Famiglia e Patria* – Honour, Family and Fatherland – that had always had such a grip on the southside *paesani* and one by which most of them had lived their lives? He was less sure about 'Fatherland' than most of his countrymen, though, for his dealings were with Scotsmen and Irishmen and Jews rather than upright Italians, and his loyalties were often divided.

Never more so than that evening just before Christmas when he returned from the Rowing Club with Uncle Guido to find his Aunt Teresa entertaining guests in the big front parlour.

He was cold, hungry and preoccupied. A meeting with Tony Lombard had thrown up information that he would have preferred to ignore. In fact, if Uncle Guido hadn't been leaning over his shoulder he might have dismissed Tony's news as unreliable and swept it under the carpet. As the Alfa drew up in the drive of the house, therefore, Dominic's mind was on other things, churning over a situation that he hadn't encountered before, a matter that would require from him the sort of decisions for which Uncle Guido's training, and Uncle Guido's advice, had left him unprepared.

Guido rang the bell. Receiving no answer, he opened the front door with his latch-key. He called out his wife's name, upstairs and down, while Dominic took off his hat, scarf and overcoat and, still possessed by chilly thoughts, moved directly into the parlour to pour himself a brandy.

The women, all three, were sipping mulled wine.

The silver bowl that the Società had presented to Dominic's father before his departure for America – and which his father had negligently left behind – stood on a linen cloth on a mahogany side table, steaming quietly. Hand-cut crystal glasses and filigree silver holders were lined up by it, together with a plate of slices from the rich, brown, nut-filled *torta* that his aunt had baked some weeks ago and which, it seemed, had at last reached maturity.

The older woman he recognised at once: a tiny, wrinkled, whey-faced *nonna* to whom Teresa gave an inordinate amount of respect. Her name was Columbina Trevanti. She hailed originally from Tuscany and was one of the great clan of Lucchesi that made up a large part of Glasgow's Italian community. She was severe, hawk-eyed, deeply religious and, although her husband had been dead for forty years, still draped herself in widow's weeds and proudly claimed not to understand a word of English – which was not, Dominic thought, much of an advertisement for her intelligence.

He put his annoyance to one side, however, and because Teresa expected it of him, bowed and kissed the back of the grandmother's papery hand as reverently as if she were some sort of Papal nuncio.

'Madam,' he said, mischievously neglecting to speak Italian. 'What a pleasure it is to welcome you into my house.'

By way of acknowledgement she gave him a hawk-like stare and a dip of the head. He continued to hold her hand just a moment longer than deference dictated. The little black lace mitten hung loose about her wrist and thumb and he was tempted to adjust it, a gesture that would have affronted his aunt and damned him for ever in la Signora Trevanti's eyes. He put the hand down and turned his head.

The other, much younger woman was a stranger. He had never met her before; if he had he would surely have remembered it. She was the most beautiful creature that Dominic had ever seen, raven-haired, dark-eyed, with one of those noses that may have been straight or may have had about the bridge a trace of the patrician, that slight outward curve so beloved of the Venetian masters. Her lips were moist, red and unanointed. Her lashes were long, and modesty, not coyness, prevented her from lifting her gaze from her lap. She was too lush ever to model for the Virgin, though, and, now that he looked at her closely, seemed more Rubens than Titian.

In Italian, Aunt Teresa said, 'I wish to present to you la Signora Trevani's granddaughter. She is from Barga and has recently arrived in this country.'

Dominic bowed but did not kiss her hand.

He knew what this was, what was intended. He was grateful to his aunt for bringing such a beauty to him and, in response to the sentimental notion that some day, in forty or fifty years' time, it might be a meeting that he – that they – would wish to recall in every detail, strove to engrave the moment in his memory.

Speaking Italian, he said, 'What is your name, Signorina?'

She moved the hands heavily, folding one over the other, and still did not look up at him. She said, 'Anna. I am called Anna.'

Aunt Teresa said, 'She is Anna Casciani. She is the daughter of Nonna Trevanti's daughter, Augusta, who is married to Gio Casciani.'

Dominic said, 'I do not think I have met them.'

'They do not live in this country,' the old woman said; then added, 'If ever you have a need to meet them you will have to travel to Barga.'

'I see,' said Dominic. 'I understand.'

He was still smiling his solemn smile, mixing welcome and gravity.

The redness of the young woman's lips had been caused by the wine and her hair, now that he considered it, was coarse.

When she finally glanced up he realised that there was no moment here, nothing that he would ever be called upon to cherish. She was lush and beautiful, yes, but he felt not one tweak of desire for her, only sadness that he must disappoint her – and himself – by reneging on the half promise that had been made on his behalf. She looked at him soulfully, heavy-lashed, jet black eyes moist. For an instant he thought he detected pleading there, a numb pleading that, at another time, on another day, might have touched his heart.

'Do you have work, Anna?' he asked, brusquely.

'No, sir. I do not have work yet.'

'I am sure that my uncle will be able to find you a suitable employment, if that is what you wish?'

'Yes, sir, that is what I wish for.'

'Good.' Dominic bowed to his aunt, to the old woman, to the helpless girl from Barga. 'I will talk to Guido about it. He will be in touch with la Signora Trevanti in due course. Now, ladies, if you will pardon me, I have a great deal of work to do this evening, so I will leave you to your conversation and your wine. It is a pleasure to have met you, Signorina Casciani. I hope that your stay in our country will be a happy one.'

Dominic turned and left the parlour, closing the door behind him.

He lingered by the parlour door for a moment but heard nothing, no mutterings, no sobs. In three or four minutes, as soon as politeness allowed, the old woman would lead her granddaughter away and he would probably not encounter the girl again; or if he did she would be keeping company with some dapper young man from the Lucchesi, son of a pasta baker or oil importer who would make her a better husband than he ever could.

With a rueful shake of the head Dominic put the beautiful girl from the old country out of his thoughts and moved softly across the panelled hall towards the stairs, thinking now of Polly Conway and how soon he might contrive to meet up with her again.

It was only recently that city offices and the Corporation's sundry departments had seen fit to close on Christmas Day. Shipyard and steel workers and all those who laboured in service trades and industries were still obliged to celebrate the Christian festival as best they could, without benefit of holiday.

In the tally of hours worked and rates paid, of profit and loss, no account was taken of Christmas and Scotland did not close its doors, as it were, until noon on New Year's Eve; at which hour the workforce streamed from yards and factories straight into bars and public houses to inaugurate two days and nights of patriotic toasts, ancestor worship and general claims of universal brotherhood that got more raucous and less convincing as the Old Year trickled away.

Lizzie and the girls had spent Christmas Day quietly at home, exchanging small gifts in a sort of embarrassed fashion, putting up a paper-chain or two and devouring a large steak pie and an even larger Scotch trifle.

Lizzie had been obliged to pay a dutiful call on Grandma McKerlie. She had taken Rosie with her while Polly and Babs used their free time to catch up on household chores, and on sleep. There had been a dreary, rather dormant feeling to it all, not just in the Conway household but elsewhere in Lavender Court, for the Hallops too were lying low, though Dennis had sold the Norton and a nice little 250cc Matchless to a dealer from Hamilton for thirty-eight pounds the pair and there was no shortage of ready cash.

On Monday evening, to Lizzie's surprise, Bernard had appeared at the door with a box of chocolates and a half-bottle of port but he'd stayed only long enough to swallow a cup of tea before he'd hastened off again to make, so he'd claimed, a few late calls in the neighbourhood.

Of Patsy there had been no sign at all and Polly hadn't the gall – or, indeed, the inclination – to seek him out.

Though Babs had sighed and dithered, eventually neither she nor Polly had deemed it wise to turn up at the Calcutta for any of the festive dances, and so had missed out on a gang fight that had taken place just outside the hall on Saturday the 28th, a real ding-dong affair by all accounts with blades flashing, lassies screaming and blood staining the cobbles. It was a mercy, so folk said, that nobody had got killed.

The week, the month, the year limped to a conclusion and the Gorbals, like all wards and towns in Scotland, braced itself to bid farewell to one grim year and, with a bewildering optimism, to welcome in another.

Mr Manone's collectors were out early on Hogmanay.

It was one of the tangled rituals of the season that debtors be given ample opportunity to start the New Year with clear consciences and clean slates and, by the same token, that creditors were paid whatever trifling sums might be owed them. Thus, later, Janet McKerlie would be able to claim that she had been the last person to see Tommy Bonnar alive.

This claim, of course, was patent nonsense. Tommy had made his rounds in early afternoon, had called in at the Rowing Club well before four o'clock and was holed up in the Washington Bar shortly after five. Dozens – nay, hundreds – of men had eyeballed him and more than a few had conversed with him in the period between one and midnight. Such evidence didn't deter Janet McKerlie, though. Showing a flair for fiction that Edgar Wallace might have envied, she stuck to her guns and announced that she had sensed that wee Tommy Bonnar was not himself and that she, and she alone, had seen the shadow of death hovering over him.

Whatever Janet had seen – tobacco smoke being the obvious answer – it certainly wasn't her boss, Mr Smart. He had gone off for a 'wee refreshment' with a potato merchant from Lanark and hadn't returned until after two.

Tommy, on the other hand, had shuffled into the shop about a quarter past one; nothing unusual in that. Sometimes it was Tommy, sometimes Irish Paddy who dropped by the dairy but one or other of Mr Manone's insurance collectors would turn up without fail every Friday or, in holiday weeks, a day or two early to pick up the envelope that Mr Smart left under the tray in the till.

Mr Smart had been shelling out ten shillings a week for as long as Janet could recall. No, not quite. Before the war it had been five shillings and long, long ago – when she'd been hardly more than a girl and her brother-in-law had been the collector – it had been just half-a-crown. Come to think of it, Mr Smart was probably the Manones' oldest customer and the appearance of one of Manone's lads was a regular part of the week, like the arrival of a milk cart from Loft's farm or egg crates from Chisholm's.

Ten shillings was a not inconsiderable sum for a small shopkeeper to muster from takings that accumulated in pennies not pounds. Mr Smart didn't grudge it, however, and Janet had long since stopped wondering what benefits it brought, for whenever there had been a spot of bother with local hooligans – a window broken, a barrel of English apples stolen, a daylight theft from the unlocked till – matters had been settled without summoning a constable and the inevitable appearance of Health Inspectors and busybodies from the Department of Weights and Measures.

Mr Smart had been 'compensated' by way of a brown envelope containing money and once by the appearance on the doorstep of a heavily bandaged young fellow lugging a sack of English apples which, out of the goodness of his heart, he'd decided to return, along with two home-cooked hams and four unplucked chickens to make up for any inconvenience his 'mistake' might have caused.

Small wonder that Mr Smart didn't grudge ten shillings a week. In a neighbourhood where your laces could vanish out of your boots without you knowing it, three or four minor 'inconveniences' in a dozen years spoke of a protective power – slightly less than divine – that was certainly worth appeasing.

Janet McKerlie wasn't the last person to talk with wee Tommy Bonnar before his tragic demise then, not by a long chalk. But talk with him she undoubtedly did. And if the shadow of the Grim Reaper was lurking in the doorway behind him she was just the lady to recognise it, given that she and her old mother talked of little else but death and dying.

'Mornin', Jinty,' Tommy Bonnar coughed into his hand. 'All set for the big night then, are ye?'

'Aye, all set, Tommy.'

'Got the gin bottles on ice?'

'We'll no' be needin' ice in this weather, I'm thinkin'.'

'You're right. It'll be hot toddy for t' toast the Auld Year awa'?'

'Maybe just a drop,' Janet conceded. In fact two bottles of Standfast were already reposing in the pot cupboard where her mother couldn't reach them and two lemons were hidden in the pocket of her overcoat in the back shop. 'We're not much for celebratin' in our house, though.'

'Much like m'self,' Tommy said, with a wry smile. 'A quiet Hogmanay at home'll suit me just fine this year.'

Janet handed over the envelope and watched it vanish into Tommy's breast pocket. She said, sceptically, 'That'll be right.'

'True, but,' Tommy said. 'Been a bad year for me. Nothin' seemed t' go right at all. I doubt if next year'll be much better. In fact, it'll probably be a damned sight worse.' He gave a cough, a sigh. 'Anyway, I'll be wishin' you an' yours a good New Year, Jinty.'

'An' to yourself, Tommy, an' to yourself,' said Janet.

Then he'd pushed himself away from the counter and, shoulders sagging under his stained trench coat, battered little hat pulled down on his brow, the last half-inch of a cigarette hanging from his lip, he had slouched out into the street to face his final destiny.

Bells rang, factory hooters sounded, ships on the river whooped their whistles and the gang of Goodtime Charleys, girls as well as boys, that had gathered at Gorbals Cross let out an uproarious cheer to greet the New Year, their ardour undampened by the thin drizzle that tumbled down out of the sky.

Beer bottles, whisky bottles and glasses of various shapes and sizes went the rounds. There was much back-slapping and hand-shaking and a bit of passionate kissing around the Parisian-style monument. Impromptu choruses of 'Auld Lang Syne' led to a conga line that went round and round and in and out for a while. Then one serious young man leaped on to the monument and, hands clasped at his breast, sang 'A Guid New Year to One and All' in a rich tenor voice that brought tears to the eyes and a lump to the throat and might even have mellowed the rougher element in the crowd if the songbird hadn't then slipped into 'The Old Rugged Cross', a liberty that brought glassware smashing about him and, for some if not others, robbed the celebration of much of its fun.

In No. 10 Lavender Court, Lizzie Conway's girls leaned from the front-room window. They were excited, though for no particular reason since none of them planned on going out on the tiles; stimulated by the promise of the untarnished year ahead, a year in which they might continue to make their marks on life and receive in return – as Lizzie could have told them – such marks as life might chose to lay upon them.

Lizzie did not join her girls in the front room or share their eagerness to lay another year to rest. As always at this time she was possessed of strange wistful longings and a feeling that time, like a Highland river, had begun its tumbling plunge down off the heights. She did not toll off the years, though, did not make nostalgic tally of losses and gains, did not seek to separate good times from bad. She just preferred to be alone, all alone during the two or three unmagical minutes when the clock on the mantelpiece ticked up to midnight.

This year, though, it wasn't so bad, not so bad at all.

When the clock chimed and the racket outside started and the first bloodcurdling yells came from the tenements and some idiot blared away on a bugle as if 1931 was thundering in upon them like a cavalry charge, Lizzie turned her head and glanced towards the kitchen door. Any second now her daughters would rush from the bedroom into the lobby and fling open the front door and the Gowers, the surly, sullen brother and sister who lived across the landing, would make the supreme sacrifice and actually exchange a few words of greeting without, of course, setting foot across the step, an act that would have been considered not just bad luck but almost treasonable to any true-born Scot.

Although she knew it would not happen, that it was asking too much of him, too soon, Lizzie toyed with the notion that Bernard might come leaping up the stairs with a bottle in one hand and a ring in the other and, throwing himself down upon his knees, demand that she become his bride.

In the two or three seconds that it took the clock to count to twelve, the thought, the wish became so strong that it seemed like its own fulfilment and left her not disappointed but rueful when instead of Bernard her girls, her three darling daughters, flung themselves upon her, crying and laughing, and demanding that she pour them a drink.

She had purchased a bottle of sweet fizzy wine to go with the bottle of whisky that tradition demanded she have on hand.

She had put out plates of sausage rolls, sultana cake and crusty black bun and, with the fire blazing bright in the range, the kitchen shining like a new pin and her daughters romping about her, she was content to let the dream of becoming Bernard Peabody's wife remain a dream, a little mirage that bobbed and floated hazily along the horizon, and to be that which she had always been, Lizzie McKerlie Conway, no wife but a widow, and mother to three growing girls. Except that they were growing girls no longer. They were women, young women. Their need of her and her influence over them would inevitably dwindle and this year or next year she would surely waken up to discover that she had lost them – even Rosie – that they had gone out to face the world on their own which was, she realised, just as it should be.

'Mammy, are you crying?' Rosie asked.

'Nah, nah.'

'She always cries at the New Year,' said Babs. 'Everybody her age does.'

'Well ...' Lizzie said, helplessly. 'Well ...'

She felt Polly's arms around her waist, Polly's brow rubbing against her shoulder and, glancing down, saw that her oldest had a little rim of tears, clear and shimmery, in her eyes too.

'I know, Mammy. I know,' Polly said, very quietly.

And Babs, expertly plying a corkscrew, said, 'Right. Who wants what?'

The Conways barely had time to drink one anothers' health, to beseech the two-faced god to bestow wealth and happiness upon the family and bring abundance in the shape of full employment back to Clydeside, before a cry went up on the landing and a booming fist beat upon the landing door.

Polly and Babs glanced at each other nervously but Rosie, picking up the vibrations, grinned and said, 'First-foots, I do believe. Will I open the door?'

'No,' said Polly, hastily. 'That's Mammy's job.'

She looked at her mother, frowning. She had no need to put into words what was on her mind: that this was no cheerful guest bearing traditional symbols of plenty but some merchant of violence who had come to spill blood not bounty all over the kitchen floor.

'*Ahap – ahap – ahapp-ppy New Year,*' a voice yelled.

And Babs said, sighing, 'It's only Jackie Hallop.'

'I'll let him in,' said Lizzie. 'If you want me to, that is.'

'I thought you couldn't stand him?' Polly said.

'I can't,' said Lizzie. 'But it isn't up to me. Babs, will I let him in?'

'Sure,' Babs said, more pleased than not. 'It's New Year's, after all.'

Jackie did not come alone. He brought his brother Dennis with him and one of the sisters, Louise, who was just about old enough to tag along. They rushed into Lizzie's house on a wave of jubilation as if all the problems that had accumulated in the closing weeks of 1930 had vanished at the stroke of midnight and forgiveness as well as forgetfulness had descended upon all and sundry.

There was indiscriminate kissing and hugging, a sharing of drink, a mildly manic quality in Jackie that manifested itself in a need to prance about. He wasn't drunk, not even tipsy, just filled with relief that Mrs Conway had seen fit to open the door to him and that Babs had apparently decided to forgive him his past transgressions and had even let him kiss her without protest. For Jackie this was a good start, the best sort of start to the year and his high spirits soon infected the Conway girls and even swept away some of solemn Polly's reserve.

Rosie brought in the gramophone, wound it up, and coaxed it to play a scratchy old record of 'Everybody's Doin' It', to which Jackie and Babs danced in the space between the table and the sink and Louise, who'd been at the whisky as well as the sweet white wine, sang a version of the chorus that would have brought a blush to Lizzie's cheek on any other occasion.

It was about a quarter to one when Jackie merrily suggested that they all go out and Babs shouted, merrily, 'Yeah, yeah. *Everybody's* doin' it,' and Lizzie said, 'Where? Who?' and Jackie said, 'Down the Cross, Mrs Conway, just down the Cross for half an hour.'

And, after a pause, Lizzie said, 'All right then. Polly, go too.'

And they went, all of them except Rosie who in that fickle way of hers elected to stay at home and keep Mammy company, mainly because crowds made her uncomfortable and she, of them all, retained a fear that Alex O'Hara might be out there, lurking, and that it would be better not to run the risk of meeting up with him again, face to face, no matter what Polly said about Mr Manone being on their side now.

They were gone in minutes, coated, hatted and chattering, storming off down the dank stairs out into the noisy streets while Rosie, not at all depressed at being left behind, wound up the gramophone and put her good ear to the metal sound box and listened, smiling, to the other side of the scratchy black record, and Lizzie loitered all alone on the landing, smoking a cigarette, listening to another song entirely, one that nobody else could hear.

For some reason best known to himself Tommy Bonnar did indeed return to the top-floor flat in Lilyburn Street at the back end of the Calcutta Road to bring in the New Year in the bosom of his family.

The fact that he was half seas over and barely able to find the close let alone the stairs might have had something to do with his decision not to loiter in the streets, but there may have been other reasons too. He was certainly in a bad way when he reached the fourth-floor landing and it was all his little nephews and nieces could do to guide him into the single-end and steer him to a chair by the fire where, still clad in trench coat and hat, still with a cigarette hanging from his lip, Tommy flopped down and instantly fell asleep.

It was then about twenty minutes to midnight and the size of Tommy's family had been considerably reduced by Maggie's defection several hours beforehand and by the departure of three of her offspring, led by nine-year-old Colin, on a begging spree. After all it was Hogmanay, a time when the generosity of Glaswegian drunks knew no bounds where kiddies and small animals were concerned, a fact of which Maggie's brood were very well aware.

For this reason the little tearaways – two boys and a six-year-old girl – picked up a stray dog, a ragged mongrel too weak to escape pursuit. They carried it turn about in their arms and trailed from public house to public house, asking for pennies with a pathos that was all the more poignant for being calculated. Even after the pubs closed at ten, fish-and-chip shops and coffee stalls stayed open and there were plenty of folk about. Tommy's nephews and niece, to be polite about it, bought chips and hot pies and ginger beer with the pennies they had wrung from passers-by. They fed the dog and stored some chips in greasy paper to take back to Lilyburn Street for the babies, the three- and four-and five-year-olds who had rescued Uncle Tommy from a night on the stairs.

Wet through, big-eyed and shaky with the need for sleep, they might even have trailed home before midnight if the lure of the gathering at Gorbals Cross had not proved too strong. Hidden in the midst of the crowd, they counted out the minutes to midnight, cheered in the New Year, listened to the singing, watched the fights and petted the dog they carried in their weary arms, turn and turn about.

Meanwhile, Maggie was sprawled on the bed of a man she had met in the back bar of Brady's, an amiable and persuasive stranger who lodged not with a family but in a room of his own in a boarding-house near Eglinton Toll. Maggie had no idea who the chap was and by the time she staggered back to the boarding-house with him she was so topped up with gin and brandy that she might have been going off with the Man in the Moon for all she cared.

Whether the stranger had intercourse with her or whether he did not Maggie Bonnar had no clue.

Shortly before midnight she passed into a state of insensibility that was her idea of bliss, a sleep so deep and sound that nothing could waken her from it, not bells or whistles or hooters or, about ten minutes past the hour of one, the clang-clang-clang of the Southern Division fire brigade hastening to answer its first call-out of the year, a summons to a tenement fire in Lilyburn Street in the backlands of the Calcutta Road.

Chapter Sixteen

The silence in the streets was uncanny. It was already after eleven o'clock in the morning but there was hardly a soul about and all the shops, even wee corner dairies and newsagents, were shuttered and barred. Along the length of the Calcutta Road not a bus or tramcar was visible. Even at the road's end the thoroughfares lay empty as far as the eye could see.

Night rain had washed the smoke away and over Glasgow as well as the Gorbals the sky was a clear liquid blue. But the gutters still ran with mud, back courts contained great dark spreading lakes and the eaves of old buildings dripped and dribbled, their sandstone walls puckered with moisture.

At the top of the tenement in Lilyburn Street there were no signs of the fire that had claimed three lives.

Polly had to push herself to enter the close and walk through to the backs to detect evidence of it. Even that was little enough, hardly more than another stain on the stained building, a sooty thumbprint high on the wall close to the roof. The kitchen window was not broken, merely cracked, and beneath the ledge, above the common lines of wash, was a salty sort of splash-mark left, perhaps, by the firemen's hose.

Polly returned through the close, turned right and set out for Brock Street, her heels clicking on the rain-washed pavement, a little rat-a-tat echoing from each deserted close.

She felt tight and tense yet very clear-headed, unlike the majority of citizens who were sleeping off hangovers behind closed curtains and would not surface until dusk signalled the start of a second round of revelry, not in pubs and bars tonight but in the crowded, crumpled tenements where friends and families met to eat and drink, and drink some more.

She walked fast, very fast, breathlessly fast. She covered the mile between the Calcutta Road and Brock Street in less than a quarter of an hour.

So far she was the only one of the Conways who had heard about the fire.

When they had returned from the street party at Gorbals Cross, Polly had seen Babs and the Hallop boys safely into the Hallops' house before going upstairs to bed. It had been two or half past by then but she had risen early, remarkably early, to visit the closet on the half-landing. On the stairs she had encountered Mr Gower, the Conways' neighbour; surly Mr Gower, to whom ill-tidings were meat and drink. He had told her of the fire and that two wee weans and a man named Bonnar had been smothered to death by smoke. How he had come by this weight of information in the wee small hours of New Year's Day was a mystery that he did not see fit to explain.

Polly's first impulse had been to waken her mother. But Lizzie, with Rosie cuddled beside her, was fast asleep in the kitchen bed. And Babs, much the worse for having spent most of the night imbibing beer in the Hallops' kitchen, was so stupefied that Polly could not rouse her at all. So she'd made toast and tea and smoked a cigarette and then, driven by a need to escape from Lavender Court, had dressed herself in her Sunday best and had gone out in search of more information.

She had encountered the constable at the corner of Keane Street. He had been hanging about aimlessly, trying to appear alert in the dead hours of a New Year's morning. He had been surprised to see a pretty young woman out and about so early, had answered her questions willingly and told her all he knew concerning the incident; how emergency crews from the fire station and ambulance service had turned out, how policemen from Southern Division had cleared the tenement, and how, as soon as the bodies had been removed and the building had been declared safe, all the tenants had trooped back inside and resumed their celebrations as if nothing untoward had happened.

When the constable had asked if she had known the victims Polly had shaken her head. Managing a smile of sorts, she had wished him all the best and had gone on her way down Ferrier Street into the Calcutta Road, possessed by a need to see for herself where Tommy Bonnar had been murdered before she went to Brock Street to track down Patsy Walsh.

'Wait, Polly, just hold your horses,' Patsy said. 'Nothin' you've told me so far indicates that Tommy was murdered. Accidents do happen.'

'Where's the woman he lived with then?'

'Maggie, his sister,' Patsy said. 'God knows!'

'Perhaps she's dead too.'

'Nah, nah. She'll be on the randan somewhere. She'll turn up in her own good time.'

'To find her brother an' two of her children dead an' her house boarded up?' Polly paused, scowling. 'Perhaps it's no more than she deserves, leaving her bairns to fend for themselves on Hogmanay.'

'Tommy was with them, wasn't he?'

'Fat lot of good that did the poor wee mites.'

'Are you okay, Poll?'

'No, I am not okay. Where were you last night?'

'Right here.'

'With your father?'

'No, he went to bring in Ne'erday with his sister. Hasn't come back yet.'

'So you were on your own?'

'Wait a bloody minute, Polly. I hope you're not suggestin' that I had anythin' to do with this?'

'No, but I think somebody did,' said Polly.

They were alone in the Walshes' kitchen. A faded cotton curtain was still drawn over the window above the sink, though the sun had struggled out and there were planes of light on the wall above the grate and on the alcove bed which, Polly noted, was already made up. On a cork mat on the table were a single plate with egg stains upon it and a single teacup and saucer. It all looked normal, she had to admit.

Patsy was plainly not hung over. He had shaved and wore a clean turtleneck black wool sweater and black corduroy trousers. There was an air of 'French' about him, of apache, not ruffian but robber. He conversed without any of the didactic little flourishes that she had grown used to over the weeks.

'I've been in Tommy's place,' he said. 'It's a tip, a dump. Beddin' an' filthy old clothes strewn all over the floor and enough grease on the walls to start the fire o' London.'

'It didn't burn much,' Polly said. 'Smoke killed them, not flames.'

'I thought you said one of the wee ones was still alive.'

'That's what the policeman told me.' Polly nodded. 'The baby, the smallest – they put her on a breathing machine and rushed her off to the Victoria Infirmary in an ambulance.'

'She won't be able to tell them much.'

'Tell who?' said Polly. 'The police?'

'The Procurator Fiscal,' Patsy said. 'The coppers will lay their evidence before him an' he'll conduct a fatal accident enquiry.'

'Not a murder enquiry?' said Polly.

'If the Procurator finds enough proof, sure, it'll be murder.'

'Will he find proof?'

'How the hell would I know?' Patsy said. Then, 'Probably not.'

'Whoever did in Tommy Bonnar was clever enough to fake an accident,' Polly said. 'You and I both know why Tommy died last night.'

'Come off it, Polly!' Patsy said, patience wearing thin. 'Chances are Tommy wasn't murdered at all. He probably fell asleep with a ciggie in his mouth and set the bed on fire. Happens all the time. What with leaky gas pipes, blocked flues an' open grates those old tenements are notorious fire traps.'

'There wasn't a fire,' Polly said again. 'At least not much of one.'

'What happened to the other kiddies? Last I heard there were five or six stayin' in Tommy's house.'

'Three were found out in the street.'

Polly had been a citizen of Glasgow and a dweller in the Gorbals far too long to be surprised. It was one of the strangest of all anomalies in the working-class character that children could be so loved and so neglected.

'What'll happen to them?' Patsy said.

'What do you care?'

'For God's sake, Polly, stop gettin' at me,' Patsy snapped. 'I'd nothin' to do with Tommy's death.'

'You helped,' Polly said.

'Because of the thing at the warehouse, you mean?'

'You thought you'd got away with it, didn't you?'

'I thought nothin' of the kind,' said Patsy.

'If Dominic Manone had one man and two children murdered in cold blood what makes you think he'll balk at having you killed too?'

'That isn't the way the system works, Polly.'

'The system!' She got to her feet. 'What system, what bloody system?'

'At least *you're* not in any danger from Manone.'

'I'm not worried about me. I'm worried about you,' Polly said. 'As for your bloody system — that's nothing but a myth. You might kid yourself that there are rules, some sort of order to it all, but there isn't. The damned "system" didn't choke Tommy Bonnar and those poor wee kiddies. Some guy went in there and did it. I'd like to know who it was and why.'

'Easy, easy.' Patsy rose. 'No need to get so het up.'

He tried to put his arms about her. She would have none of it. She refused to have her rage demeaned, to be treated as if she were nothing but a ranting, hysterical female. If justice had been meted out to Tommy Bonnar then it was false justice, crude male justice, not a fact of nature or an act of God. Anger drained colour from her cheeks. She was as pale as milk, pursed lips pale too.

'You don't care, do you?' she said. 'You're just as hopeless as all the rest of them. Hopeless in every sense of the word.'

'Something went wrong, Polly, that's all.'

'Tell that to Tommy Bonnar's kiddies.'

'What can I do about it now?'

'Get yourself out of here.'

'With what? I haven't any—'

'Money?' Polly said. 'I told you, I can get you money. How much? Tell me again, how much?'

'I won't take Manone's money.'

'It isn't Manone's money. It's *my* money. How much, Patsy?' Polly said. 'What will it cost to get you out of here?'

'Like I said, a hundred and fifty would do nicely.'

'So,' Polly said, 'if I give you a hundred and fifty pounds you'll promise to clear out of Glasgow.'

'Are you doin' this because of Tommy, because of O'Hara, or because you want rid of me?' Patsy said.

'Because I want rid of you.'

'Yeah,' he said. 'Right.'

She had told him the truth — and he hadn't believed her. He could not imagine that she would pay him to leave, that she was capable of purchasing her freedom from him. For all his supposed depth of character and claims to understand the world, he was still too much the male to perceive that she meant exactly what she said, that kissing, cuddling and sexual rehearsal had not been enough to deceive her.

'Sunday night,' Polly said. 'I'll bring it to you on Sunday night.'

'Hey, you're serious, aren't you?'

'Perfectly serious,' Polly said. 'I'll give you the money if you promise to steer clear of Glasgow until it's safe to come back.'

'When will that be?' he said.

'I've no idea,' said Polly.

He stared at her, unsure just what she expected in return. He wondered if the Italian was behind her offer, if the Italian had been behind everything right from the start, the Italian or the Italian's money or the Italian's pride. He wondered if he should take Polly Conway instead of the money, or if there was some clever way to play it so that he might wind up with everything, Polly *and* the money *and* revenge, all wrapped up in one neat big ball.

Even if the Italian *was* paying, it was too good an opportunity to turn down. He'd been more spooked than he cared to admit by news of Tommy Bonnar's death. He doubted if Dominic Manone would endorse a plan that left the matter so unresolved, particularly if the point of killing Tommy had been to satisfy pride and reassert authority.

And the kiddies – he tried not to think about the kiddies.

'Okay,' he told her.

'You promise?'

'I promise.'

'Where will you go? Paris again?'

'Yeah, Paris,' Patsy said. 'Why don't you come with me?'

And Polly, shaking her head, said, 'No.'

'Why not?'

'Because my life's here.'

'An' mine isn't?'

'No,' Polly said. 'Yours isn't.'

*   *   *

At Guido's insistence the Manones had brought in the year some forty miles down the coast from Glasgow.

For three or four years now Alberto Pirollo had invited them to a party in the Promenade Café and each year Dominic had found a polite reason to refuse. This year, however, Uncle Guido had put pressure on him to show his face at Pirollo's New Year celebration, for the Manones were co-investors in the Promenade and, slump or not, the big new café-restaurant that overlooked the Firth of Clyde was proving to be a money-spinner.

In addition, Pirollo had his eye on two other sites in Ayrshire resorts where cafés on the grand scale might do well and he was keen to involve the Manones at an early stage in the planning. Dominic also knew that Guido had been sleeping on and off with Alberto's younger sister who was – theoretically – married to an accountant of the non-Italian variety, and that she, the sister, had been putting pressure on Guido too.

Dominic was surprised, therefore, when Aunt Teresa was loaded into the Alfa, along with travelling rugs, overnight bags and a selection of expensive New Year gifts for Alberto and his family and Guido drove all three of them down the coastal road into Ayrshire.

Dinner and the dance that followed it were very lavish. Pirollo and his family proved to be genial hosts. Sixty people, almost all Italians, welcomed in the New Year in the reception area that backed the restaurant and Dominic danced with seven or eight pretty girls, including one of Pirollo's daughters whom the indefatigable Aunt Teresa kept pushing in his direction. Dominic wasn't interested in Lina Pirollo, though she was modest and young, as Scottish as he was, and pretty too in a dainty sort of way. He was polite and friendly towards her, however, for he had received a cable from his father telling him to enquire further about Pirollo's expansion plans and not to antagonise the family, something that Dominic had no intention of doing anyway. About half past three o'clock Guido, Teresa and he retired to the rooms they had booked in the Isle of Arran Hotel, one of the best on the coast, and went to sleep.

Dominic was up and dressed by nine. He walked from the hotel to the Promenade via the back streets and enjoyed a private breakfast with Alberto and his eldest son – another Guido – at a table in the bay window. Wintry grey cloud covered the islands and the sea, alas, and the window was speckled with rain. Dominic concentrated on the plans that Pirollo had brought with him, together with a rough estimate of what Dominic's involvement might be and what it would yield in profit. It was not a morning for definite decisions, though, and Alberto and his son were content to put their propositions before Dominic and learn that he was interested in principle.

They drank strong coffee, smoked and talked until almost one when Uncle Guido brought the Alfa prowling along the Promenade Road from the back of the Isle of Arran. Dominic shook hands with the Pirollos, hugged them, thanked them and promised to be in touch. Then he went down the carpeted stairs and out of the big front door of the restaurant.

The promenade was empty as far as his eye could see, sweeping away round by the headland, past quaint little old buildings at the harbour and out again into swirls of pearly rain that cloaked the hills to the south. There was a brisk little swell on the sea, the touch of a breeze and Dominic could taste the cold salt in his mouth. He experienced a surge of energy, an inclination to start out along the empty promenade and walk and walk and walk in the hope that somewhere along there, waiting for him, he would come across a girl, not just any girl, one in particular, and that they might walk together the whole length of the promenade and back again.

'What is wrong with you?' Uncle Guido said. 'Did it not go well?'

'It went fine,' Dominic told him. 'Fine. Everything is okay.'

'You will make a deal with Pirollo?'

'I'm prepared to think about it,' Dominic said.

'Then think about it inside the motorcar,' Guido said. 'I want to get home before it becomes dark.'

Dominic climbed into the Alfa and Uncle Guido drove back to Glasgow, back to Manor Park Avenue where, pacing up and down outside the gate, Tony Lombard waited to tell them the sad news.

One glass of Co-op sherry consumed at a minute after midnight could hardly have caused Bernard's lethargy. Even so, he felt so lazy and relaxed next morning that he stayed in bed until midday and spent the early part of the afternoon dozing in an armchair by the living-room fire.

There had been a good deal of friendly traipsing between the cottages but at his mother's insistence Bernard had put out the lights at half past midnight to deter callers. Mrs Peabody might be gregarious but she was also a wee bit of a snob who preferred the company of specially selected friends to that of mere neighbours who, like her, had been culled out of the riverside slums of Finnieston, Anderston and Partick. She was also – here Bernard sympathised – affected by a time of year when she could not help but recall her deceased sons and husband and regret that the passage of years carried them ever further from her. All she had left was Bernard – and she didn't think much of him, even although he provided for her and never got into trouble.

On Friday the Women's Guild would hold a sandwich lunch in the church hall, a high point of the season for Violet Peabody. She spent much of Thursday afternoon in the kitchen baking scones and cakes for this treat. It was after four o'clock before she appeared, still aproned and rather floury, gave Bernard a little dig to rouse him and placed two bowls of oxtail soup on the table.

Bernard had been busy weaving a lovely daydream and felt

so benign that he ambled from the chair to the table and seated himself without a murmur of complaint at the lateness of the hour.

He regarded his mother fondly.

Less fondly, she looked up and said, 'What are you grinnin' at?'

Bernard said, 'I'm thinking of getting married.'

Brown soup dribbled back into the bowl and one little droplet clung to his mother's bottom lip. She stuck out her tongue, licked it away, then, after a two or three-second pause, said, 'Not today you're not.'

'No, not today.' Bernard laughed. 'Soon, though. Before the year's out.'

'You can't afford to get married.'

'Oh, I reckon I can – just about.'

'You can't stay here,' his mother told him. 'I'm not sharin' my kitchen.'

'In that case I'll apply for a house of my own.'

'They'll never give *you* a house, not at your age.'

'They might,' Bernard said. 'Failing which I can always go an' stay with my wife over in the Gorbals.'

Mrs Peabody put down her spoon, dabbed her lips with a napkin.

'It's her, isn't it? The one who came here the other day?'

'Lizzie, yes.'

'I didn't like her.'

'I didn't expect you would.'

'She's an old woman.'

'Of course she isn't an old woman,' said Bernard. 'She's only a year or two older than I am.'

'More like six or seven, I'd say.'

'That hardly makes her Miss Haversham, does it?'

'I thought her name was Conway.'

'It is,' said Bernard. 'I was just making an ... never mind.'

'Don't you take that tone with me, my lad.'

'What tone?' said Bernard.

'I've seen a lot more of life than you have.'

Still relaxed and determined not to squabble, Bernard wondered if that was strictly true. He knew what the ladies of the Guild thought, how they took unto themselves the whole burden of suffering that the war had engendered, how they mocked their brothers and husbands and genuinely believed that a life devoted to cooking, keeping house, raising children and making ends meet was far more arduous than the lives their menfolk led. Men, after all, only laboured fifty hours a week in the belly of a ship in Browns or Fairfields, in the nauseating heat of Dixon's Blazes or the Kingston Iron Works, underground in a coal pit or out on the North Sea in all weathers on the deck of a trawler.

There was also the matter of the Great War, a conflict that had – some said – given women a little taste of freedom, though the cost in grief and hardship had been far too high for women as well. Even so, Bernard wondered what the ladies of the Guild really knew about hardship, if they would have been so scathing about the male of the species if they had been obliged to scurry like rats along a stinking trench or endure night after night of bombardment or, in a windless dawn, to slither over the top and charge headlong on to the guns – all for King and Country, Hearth and Home, for the Girls that were left Behind.

Bernard said, 'I've no doubt you have, Mother, but it's not a question of who's suffered the most or who's seen most of life. It's really dead simple. I want to get married. I intend to get married.'

'To this Conway woman.'

'Yes.'

Nothing she could say or do would make his temper fray at the edges. He had never felt so thoroughly at ease before, as if he had been waiting out the time since the Armistice for just this moment, the moment when he could put all the emptiness, all the cowering, behind him by allowing himself to fall in love.

He had been conservative and abstemious and patient. He had been dutiful and industrious and uncomplaining. He had been the perfect citizen, the perfect son for far too long. But now he was in love and he would bring to bear all the discipline and fortitude that the army and society had inculcated in him, all the courage, to get the woman he wanted and make her his wife.

'She won't be able to give you children.'

'She might, if we decided . . .'

'She has children. She's got girls near your age.'

'Nice girls,' said Bernard. 'One of them's deaf.'

'They can't come here.'

'I know that,' Bernard said.

'Have you – has she . . . Is this why you . . .'

'No, Mother, no, no,' said Bernard. 'Nothing like that.'

'But she *has* set her cap at you, a woman of her age.'

'Aye, she's set her cap at me,' said Bernard. 'What's more, I like it.'

'Gorbals,' his mother said. 'Gorbals – I never thought I'd see the day.'

Bernard broke bread into his cooling soup and supped with his spoon.

'Anyway, I haven't asked Lizzie yet and there's a lot to be settled before I do,' he said, between mouthfuls. 'But I thought it only decent to let you know what's on my mind so you'd be prepared for it.'

'Decent isn't the world I'd use.'

'Mother, I'm in love with the woman.'

'That won't last.'

'It might,' said Bernard. 'In any case I'm willin' to take the chance.'

'What about me? What'll become of me?'

'I'll make sure you're looked after,' Bernard said. 'I'm not desertin' you. I'll carry on payin' your rent for one thing.'

'But you won't *be* here,' Mrs Peabody said. 'You'll be with her.'

'That's true,' said Bernard.

'You won't love *me* any more, Bernard, and – and you're all I've got left.'

'Of course I'll still love you.' Bernard put out his bandaged hand and patted the back of her wrist lightly, awkwardly. 'Think of it this way, Mum, you won't be losin' a son, you'll be gainin' a daughter.'

'An old woman, huh!'

'A good woman,' Bernard said.

'That,' said Mrs Peabody, grimly, 'remains to be seen.'

Dusk came late to the valley of the Clyde. The sky had cleared and, by half past four o'clock, a frosty sharpness in the air caused Polly's breath to cloud as she entered the avenue that bordered the park.

She had located Manor Park easily enough with the aid of a little brown-backed Glasgow atlas that she had filched from the Burgh Hall reference library several months ago but the trek from the Gorbals, added to the morning's excursions, had left her leg-weary. She paused at the gate for a moment to catch her breath and screw up her courage before she walked up the gravel drive and, heart pounding, approached the Manones' front door.

There were three men in the front parlour. Nobody had thought to close the curtains. From his position on the couch, Uncle Guido was first to spot the girl. He put down his coffee cup, craned his long neck and said, 'Someone is coming to our door. A young woman, I believe.'

Dominic shot out of his armchair and swung round to face the window.

'Well, well, well!' he said. 'It's Polly Conway.' All three men peered at the girl from the long window. Streetlamps bloomed yellow against the lavender sky and privet and laurel bushes loomed in the dark garden. 'I had better let her in,' said Dominic eagerly.

'Teresa will do it,' Guido said.

'What the hell does Frank Conway's daughter want with us?' Tony said.

'I think she might want to trade,' Dominic said, while, like an echo, the doorbell rang.

'Trade? What does *she* have to trade with?' said Tony.

'That's what we'll have to find out,' said Dominic and, ignoring his uncle's warning growl, hurried out into the hall to greet his new recruit.

She was impressed and rather intimidated by the scale of the house and the size of the dining-room into which Dominic led her. It was not that she found it comfortable – far from it. The black marble fireplace was empty and the electric bulbs in the ceiling pendant shed a wan, unconcentrated light. The bulky table and sideboard were in dark stained wood and the tall chairs' padded upholstery had a slightly musty smell that made Polly think of crypts and mausoleums.

The room was cold, though Dominic in his high-cut waistcoat and shirt-sleeves did not seem to notice. He wore sleeve garters like an Italian street trader and when he drew out a chair for her at the long polished table she noticed that his wrists were downed with dark hair, which somehow made him seem less boyish and more threatening.

She tried to recapture the anger that had brought her here, the hot, swelling temper that news of Tommy Bonnar's death, and Patsy's reaction to it, had roused in her. But it was gone, that rage; she was left with a fluttering sense of her own frailty and the knowledge that she had nothing with which to protect herself against this man except her ability to keeping him guessing.

Dominic seated himself at the head of the table, back to the uncurtained window. He leaned back, put his hand to his chin and studied her for a moment, then, without shifting position, said, 'I think I know why you're here. I assure you – I swear to you – I had nothing to do with what happened to your friend Bonnar.'

'Tommy Bonnar wasn't my friend,' Polly said. 'I hardly knew him.'

'It is because of what happened last night that you are here, though?'

'Yes,' Polly said. She had to start somewhere. 'What happened to Tommy Bonnar wasn't an accident, was it?'

'It may have been.'

'I find that hard to believe.' Polly's tone was as chilly as the air in the dining-room. 'I don't think coincidence stretches that far.'

'Coincidence?' said Dominic.

She chose her words with care. 'The last time we met, not that long ago, you asked me for information about the warehouse robbery.'

'So?'

'You were looking for the men responsible.'

'That is true.'

'When I asked you if you'd take revenge on them ...'

'You suggested that the robbery might have been a mistake.'

'Yes, but now there are two "mistakes" to take into account,' Polly said, 'and I don't believe in that much coincidence. You also assured me that you didn't know that Alex O'Hara had called at our house and intimidated us.'

'Which was the truth.'

'Could setting fire to Tommy Bonnar's house have been something else that O'Hara did without informing you first?'

'I doubt it.'

'Why do you doubt it, Mr Manone?'

'Alex would have used a blade.'

'Did you tell him to use a blade?' said Polly.

He looked at her, head to one side, still speculative but perhaps just a little amused, not by what she was saying but by her temerity in daring to say it at all. 'Am I right in thinking that your mother doesn't know you have come to see me today?' Dominic said.

'Our business has nothing to do with my mother; well, not much,' Polly told him. 'It's a matter between you and me, Mr Manone, which is the reason I took the liberty of intruding on your privacy on New Year's Day.' She was unaware that her speech had begun to match his rhythm, his correctness. 'You haven't answered my question.'

'I did not tell O'Hara to do anything to Tommy Bonnar. After all, I had no reason to want Tommy hurt.'

'Unless he was one of the men who tried to steal from you?'

'I have been out of Glasgow for two days,' Dominic said. 'I only found out about Tommy a couple of hours ago. I don't know what happened. I'll have to wait for the result of the Fiscal's report just like everyone else.' He slid his hand from chin to mouth, covered his lips with his forefinger. 'Did Tommy Bonnar steal from me?'

'How would I know?'

'I think you do,' Dominic said. 'I think that is why you are so upset about Tommy's death.'

'Doesn't it bother you at all that two wee kiddies are dead an' another one's in the hospital?' Polly said.

'It bothers me,' Dominic said. 'It also bothers me that the mother of the children couldn't be found at the time. That she left six small children to fend for themselves while she went out drinking and to pick up men.'

'Perhaps she had to.'

'She did not have to,' Dominic said.

'You know that for sure?'

'I know that for sure,' Dominic said. 'Incidentally, the sister turned up. She came back to Lilyburn of her own accord about one o'clock today. The police found her and took her into custody. She'll be charged with neglect or some such thing and imprisoned for a little while. He other children, the survivors, have been taken into the care of the local authority and are billeted at Randolph House Children's Home. The small child in hospital is not in danger.'

'How do you know these things?'

'I have a telephone.'

'And friends in high places?' said Polly.

'And friends in high places,' Dominic agreed. 'If it was only concern for the children that brought you to me you may rest assured that they will be taken care of, that we will look after them.'

'We?'

'Tommy worked for us. We have an obligation to his family.'

'Will you look after them the way you looked after us?'

'The situations are not at all the same,' Dominic said. 'Tell me what really brings you here today? You want to trade, do you not?'

'Trade?'

'I think you have information. I think you have decided on a price for it.'

She pushed her chair back a little and turned towards him, crossing her legs under the pleats of her skirt. The last of the light had drained from the sky and all she could see in the glass was a reflection of herself floating in a cube of half-light that seemed to come from no definable source. Dominic rested so far back in the dining-room chair that she could see nothing of him in the mirrored cube and for a split second had the impression that she was entirely alone. She inscribed a little circle with her shoe, looking down at it, while Dominic, finger still pressed to his lips, waited politely.

'I don't want your money,' Polly said.

'What do you want?'

'I want – I need a promise I can trust.'

'What sort of promise?'

'Not to – not to do anything else to anyone.'

He sat forward suddenly, a shrug of the shoulders, almost a lunge.

Polly started in spite of herself. He leaned his elbows on the table and thrust his face towards her; no boy now, no meek and uncertain adolescent. His expression altered when he smiled; it was not a smile of amusement but of anger, or near anger, as if she had tried his patience too far. Polly held herself still, the foot still, raised her shoulders and met his angry gaze without flinching.

'All right,' Dominic said. 'Let's stop beating around the bush, Miss Conway. I think that you have guessed that I have lost money. Do you know who stole from me?'

Polly nodded.

'Do you know where my money is?'

Polly nodded again.

'Did Walsh send you here to make a deal?'

'No,' Polly said. 'He'd kill me if he even suspected I was talking to you.' She gave a tiny sigh, blowing out her lips. 'Patsy's inclined to think I'm working for you as it is. If he knew I'd come here today . . .'

Dominic raised a hand, showed her the palm.

'I can flatten Patsy Walsh if I choose to do so,' he said. 'But I do not operate in that way. Whatever you may have heard, Polly, I do not resort to such methods if I can avoid it.' He placed his hand flat on the table, not violently, not slapping. 'You're about to tell me that the safe's at the bottom of the river, aren't you? You're about to tell me that Tommy Bonnar set up the job and that your boyfriend Patsy Walsh pulled it off, or should I say did not pull it off, not properly. How much information are you willing to give me? Will you tell me that the Hallops are also involved? I figured that out long ago.

'I also figured out that your sister Barbara told them where the safe was placed within the building. But' – he raised his hand again, showed her the palm again – 'I cannot prove any part of it. Sure, I could send O'Hara to scare the living daylights out of Jackie Hallop, and Jackie would probably blurt out the whole idiotic story. But then I would be forced to do something about it. I do not want that. I do not want to have to act upon a certainty. Do you understand?'

'Because of the police?'

'Because I'm in *business*, Polly.'

'Do you really believe that?' Polly said.

'I do, absolutely I do.'

'Taking money from innocent people is not business, it's extortion.'

'Innocent people?' Dominic said. 'I would be interested to hear how you define "innocent". Let me put it to you this way: if it's proved that Tommy Bonnar's house was deliberately set on fire then that would be an act of murder, would it not?'

'Of course.'

'If the guilty party is found what would you have done to him?'

'He should be hanged,' Polly said.

'Fine,' Dominic said. 'Let's suppose the guy who carried out the act, who set the fire that killed Tommy and the children, was obeying instructions from another party; would that other party be equally guilty?'

'More so,' Polly said.

'No matter what Tommy had done?'

'Nothing Tommy did could justify killing him, never mind two innocent children. Surely you aren't going to tell me that the kiddies were somehow to blame as well?'

'No, the children were entirely innocent.'

'You see,' said Polly. 'That's my point.'

'An eye for an eye?'

'In this sort of case, yes.'

'You would have the person, or persons, executed?'

'I would.'

'Even if the question weren't hypothetical? Do you know what—'

'Yes, I know what hypothetical means,' said Polly. 'I just don't see what any of this has to do with me?'

'It does have to do with you, Polly. It's the sole reason you're here. You believe in justice, in judicial revenge. You believe that a society should protect its own and seek retribution from those who offend against society,' Dominic told her, 'provided decisions are made and punishments meted out by someone else.'

'That's what courts are for, what judges are for?'

'Certainly,' Dominic said. 'But if you were the judge . . .'

'I'm not. I don't know anything about the law.'

'What law?'

'The law of the land, of Scotland.'

'Yet you would have this man, this murderer executed?'

'If he was found guilty, yes.'

'What if I told you that Patrick Walsh was responsible for Tommy Bonnar's death and the deaths of the children: would that make a difference?'

'I don't believe you. Patsy wouldn't . . .'

'I'm not saying he did,' Dominic told her. 'But if he had, what then?'

'He would have to be tried,' Polly said.

'And if he was guilty?'

'No,' she said. 'No, you're trying to make me say things I don't mean.'

'You would *not* have him executed? Because you know him, because you care for him, perhaps, you would bend the law just a little? You would plead extenuating circumstances, you would begin to dilute the notion of innocence, to water it down. No?'

There was more to it, Polly realised, than hypothesis, than mere debate. He was putting her on the spot and she felt again the precariousness of her position. These were matters that she hadn't considered, matters to which Dominic Manone had obviously devoted much thought. He sounded plausible in his argument but she could not be sure that he was not trying to trap her, to wring from her an admission that she might later regret. Was he trying to tell her in a round-about way that Patsy Walsh was Tommy's killer? Was he letting her down gently?

She said, 'If a man's guilty of murder he should be made to pay for it.'

'Unequivocally?'

'If he's guilty I'd give the same answer, whoever he happened to be.'

'It is, then, a principle with you?'

'I suppose it is,' said Polly.

'I see,' said Dominic. 'I see. Now, tell me, do you still wish to trade?'

'No,' Polly said. 'In any case, what do I have left to trade with? You already know all about it.'

'Sure, but I can't prove it,' Dominic said.

Polly looked down at her shoes. 'They didn't get away with it. They didn't get away with the safe or the money.'

'Is that what they told you?'

'Yes, and I believe them.'

Dominic gave a little *huh* of amusement. 'Then where's my cash?'

'As you surmised,' said Polly, 'at the bottom of the river.'

'I should probably go fishing for it then?'

'That's up to you.' Polly placed her feet upon the carpet, a thin, hard carpet with a russet design. She stood, not hurriedly. 'There would be no certainly that you would find it, of course.'

'Ah!'

'In fact,' Polly said, 'I doubt if you would find it.'

'Because it isn't there at all?'

'How do I know? They may be lying. I can't be certain.'

'So' – Dominic eased himself from the chair – 'after all

our talk no resolution is possible, at least in the matter of the warehouse robbery.'

'That's how it looks,' said Polly.

He stood close to her, not tall enough to be intimidating. He was, in fact, almost the same height as she was, no more than an inch taller. Nothing she had said seemed to have offended him. He was smiling, not broadly but with a little twist of the lip that lifted his sallow cheek into something like a dimple. That, she felt, was wrong, all wrong; a man like Dominic Manone should not have a dimple. But then a man like Dominic Manone should not engage in rational and logical discussion, should not concern himself with justice or even fair trade.

He laid his hand on her sleeve. She felt herself shiver. It was something she could not control. There were no words that could excuse what she felt at that moment.

'I regret what happened to the kiddies,' he said. 'I regret what happened to Tommy too, though he was not quite so innocent as you may imagine. There's usually a trace, a hint of collusion somewhere if you look hard enough for it.' He steered her towards the dining-room door. 'I think we all collude in shaping our own destinies, don't you?'

'I – I don't know.'

It was dark outside now, the last of the twilight gone.

He said, 'I will drive you home.'

'No, I can ...'

'It is the least I can do, Polly, after all you've done for me.'

'What do you mean?'

'In helping me make up my mind.'

'To do what?'

'To do nothing,' he said. 'Nothing, that is, that will concern you.'

'Or Patsy?' Polly said, quickly.

'Or Patsy,' said Dominic Manone.

Chapter Seventeen

It seemed to Polly that the pace of life quickened in the first days of 1931. She had been reassured by Dominic Manone but not entirely taken in by his left-handed promises, if, indeed, they were promises at all, and she returned to the routines of the Burgh Hall office nursing an odd sense of accomplishment.

She reported to Babs most of what had been said at Manor Park Avenue. Babs in turn passed on a garbled version to Jackie Hallop who was so relieved to be officially off the hook that he shelled out ten shillings to take his rediscovered sweetheart to the Locarno in Glasgow where the world's champion ball-room dancers were giving an exhibition. Dennis went out and got drunk.

What Patsy Walsh did with himself that first weekend of the year nobody knew and, it seemed, nobody cared. The consensus of opinion was that he was still sulking because he had bungled the warehouse robbery. It didn't occur to anyone, not even Polly, that Patsy might be suffering guilt at the deaths of Tommy Bonnar and poor, shabby Maggie's two wee bairns.

Maggie herself appeared before the Fiscal Depute, answered a multitude of searching questions, was released on bail – put up by Dominic – and charged to appear before the Sheriff on Monday week. She was then escorted to the Victoria Infirmary by Irish Paddy and wept inconsolable buckets over the wheezing two-year-old in the cot in the children's ward before going off to spend the night not in Irish Paddy's bed, God no!, but on a mattress on the floor of Irish Paddy's mother's house in Cranston Street, across the river.

Spurred on by Tony Lombard, there was also much activity down at the Rowing Club; a devising of little white lies necessary to satisfy the authorities and regain for Maggie whatever pitiful possessions had been rescued from the fire, to ensure that the surviving offspring were found a good home somewhere out of the city, if, that is, the Panel saw fit to hand them back into Maggie's care; and, when the bodies were finally released, how to give Tommy and his kiddies some sort of a send-off, i.e. a decent burial.

Arranging the affairs of the late Thomas Bonnar wasn't foremost in Dominic's mind, however. He indicated to Guido what he was prepared to do – quite a lot – in that direction and let his uncle sort out the details with Tony, Irish Paddy and another Manone employee named Breslin whose brother was, of all things, a priest.

Dominic had other things to think about, not least when he might see Polly Conway again and how he might set their relationship on a less edgy footing. He was shy about Polly, tentative, a mood that affected his judgement in another pressing matter. He took big stick from Guido, little stick from Tony for his indecisiveness. He was even tempted to cable his father in Philadelphia to request advice. But he knew only too well what his father would tell him to do and that his father would then write to Guido and ask what sort of man he had raised when he, Dominic, would not undertake to protect the family name and family honour without all this stupid flimflam and soul-searching.

If she had not been so entranced by Bernard Peabody – so entranced that she sang to herself while she worked the rakes through the troughs on her Saturday shift – then Lizzie might have realised what was going on behind the scenes and have tried to prevent it. She, however, had lost her heart completely and with it her reason, not her mental faculties so much as her *raison d'être*, that restless need to interfere in the lives of her daughters and other poor folk who might need a shoulder to cry on or the aid of a strong right arm.

Lizzie was a goner, radiant as a sunbeam, pinked out of existence for love of an estate agent's clerk. Her chum McIntosh spotted the change at once and, being a man of kind heart and romantic disposition, guessed the reason for it. He even teased her about it lightly until Lizzie blushed like a tea-rose and admitted in a hoarse but not coarse whisper that matrimony was quite definitely in her plans, if not this year, then next year, just as soon as she could get her daughters settled and pay off a few outstanding debts.

Meanwhile Scotland trudged back to work, back to the dole queue, back to the long drag of the winter's second half. The joy of New Year celebrations and all the false optimism that they had engendered vanished swiftly.

Within a year Labour would be routed at the polls and a National Government would take over. Within a couple of months King Alfonso would abdicate and Spain would declare itself a Republic. Within a week Pope Pius would announce the Church's opposition to communism, capitalism and all forms of sexual liberation. Within three days, late on Saturday night to be exact, Babs Conway would sacrifice her virginity to Jackie Hallop while standing upright in the back close of No. 10 Lavender Court, an experience that left her sore, unsatisfied and slightly bewildered.

Within fifty-six hours of calling upon Dominic Manone at Manor Park Avenue Polly would decide that she wouldn't really feel secure until Patsy Walsh left Glasgow and that the only way she could bring that about would be to reclaim her daddy's stash from under the floorboards in Gran McKerlie's cupboard and that the sooner she did it the better it would be for all concerned, especially – so she convinced herself – for Patsy.

Larceny came easy to Polly; Daddy's genes were working well. She performed her first act of pillage with all the aplomb of a seasoned professional and, to her surprise, with hardly so much as an increase in pulse rate. She climbed the backland stairs in Ballingall Street, Laurieston, at twenty minutes to eleven o'clock with pockets empty and skipped down again at five minutes to one with pockets full; with Daddy's assorted banknotes tucked about her person and the cocoa tin – empty save for coppers – left where it was, the boards, brooms, brushes and pails all neatly back in place.

'What have you been up to?' Aunt Janet enquired as she took off her Sunday-best hat and unwound her scarf.

Sweet-faced and blameless: 'Absolutely not a thing.'

'Did she go?'

'Yes,' said Polly.

'Number one or number two?'

'Both, I think,' said Polly.

'Don't you know?'

'No, I don't know,' Polly said and, feeling strangely justified, took her leave soon after.

'I thought you were kiddin',' Patsy said. 'I really thought you were kiddin'. A hundred an' fifty smackers. Where did you get them?'

'Not from Dominic Manone,' said Polly. 'That's all you need to know.'

'Come off it, Polly. I can't take your money.'

'Isn't it enough?'

'Oh, aye, it's more than enough.'

'Then accept it graciously and get out while you can,' Polly said.

'Easier said than done.'

'What? You promised you'd ...'

'I saw Jackie this afternoon,' Patsy said. 'He tells me we

don't have anythin' to worry about, the pressure's off. Is that true, Polly?'

'Perhaps it is for him, but not for you.'

The banknotes were arranged in neat bundles on the Walshes' kitchen table. Patsy had seen more cash than this plenty of times. Five years ago he had robbed a carpet manufacturer's house out in Lenzie and had come out with five hundred pounds in loose notes. The haul had taken him to Spain, Switzerland, eventually to Germany, yet he'd been back knocking on his father's door almost before the old man realised he'd gone.

'What did you have to do to get it?' he said.

'I didn't have to do anything to get it,' Polly said.

'Did you steal it?'

'What do you take me for, Patsy? Of course I didn't steal it.' She had the lie ready. She hoped it might impress him. 'It's savings. My personal savings. Money my daddy put into an account when I was born. Been earning interest ever since. I decided the time had come to make use of it.'

'Mighty generous of you, Polly,' Patsy said. 'Why are you so damned anxious to get rid of me?'

'We've been through all this before,' Polly said. 'I just don't want you to wind up dead, like Tommy Bonnar.'

'Jackie tells me it's all been settled, that Manone's satisfied.'

'Manone will never be satisfied.'

Polly was conscious of just how overblown the statement sounded, how theatrical, an utterance more suited to Dominic's long, gloomy dining-room than to an ordinary working-class kitchen. Sighing, she reached for the little bundles of cash. 'If you don't want it, I'll find another use for it.'

'No,' he said, quickly. 'I didn't say I didn't want it.'

'It's not as if you're tied to the Gorbals, like the Hallops. You've been to Europe before. You keep telling me how wonderful it is.'

'It would be even more wonderful if you were with me.'

'I'll be here when you get back.'

'If I come back, you mean.'

'Nothing's for ever, Patrick.'

'Patrick? Oh, very formal all of a sudden.'

'Stop it,' Polly said. 'Take it or don't take it.'

'I'll take it.'

'And go?'

'Aye, an' go.'

'When?'

'This week some time.'

Polly said, 'Where's your father?'

'At chapel.'

'I didn't know you were Catholic.'

'Methodist chapel,' Patsy said. 'Why are you askin'? Do you want to kiss an cuddle for a while? On the bed?'

'No,' Polly said. 'I don't think that would be a good idea under the circumstances.'

'What happened, Polly? It looked so promisin' for us,' Patsy said, 'then it just went to hell. Was it because of what I tried to do that night?'

'That isn't it.'

'Well, you're no fool.' Patsy began to sort out banknotes, not counting so much as arranging them. He was quick-fingered and dextrous but also casual, unexcited by handling so much cash. 'It doesn't take a genius to figure out that you don't want to get mixed up with a guy like me in case I run into trouble an' wind up in jail.'

Polly said, 'Yes, I suppose that's it.'

'Middle-class loyalty.' He shook his head. 'I don't blame you. It's not your fault. At least give me one kiss before I hit the trail.'

He opened his arms in an extravagant gesture and Polly walked around the table and into them. He pulled her close, tilted his hips, rocked against her. But he was not aroused and there was a mocking quality to the embrace. Polly put her hands behind his neck and kissed him lingeringly, without desire. She had exorcised him, got rid of him, saved herself for someone else, someone better. She couldn't have spent her father's legacy on anything more worth while.

'See you, Poll,' he said.

'Yes,' Polly said. 'See you, Patsy,' and went out and downstairs into Brock Street before he noticed the tears in her eyes.

Tony had accompanied his mother and father to evening mass. To please his mother he had even taken confession and eked out a few acceptable sins to keep the father happy. He wondered what the good father would have said if he'd known what mortal sins Tony had really committed since his last confession, or if the old holy man could possibly have guessed what a nice clean-cut Italian gentleman would be getting up to in the course of the next few days.

Tony hadn't quite reached the age when cynicism gives way to doubt or doubt bleeds into fear. He did his bit, he did his best. He kept his parents in style and visited them regularly. He did not worship false gods. He worshipped only one god and required no priestly rigmarole to communicate with that god.

'All right,' Tony said. 'We know who did for Tommy; what do you want me to do about it?'

'I'm not sure yet,' Dominic said.

'You have to be sure. You have to act. That Irish-born bastard will be sitting in his mouldy office laughing up his sleeve at us.'

'How much did Tommy owe him?' Dominic asked.

'Nobody knows for sure. Two, three hundred, maybe,' Tony said.

'In that case,' Dominic said, 'I think I should pay him off.'

'Jesus and Joseph!' Uncle Guido exclaimed.

'I think I should go call on him tomorrow,' Dominic said.

'Go call on him?' said Tony. 'You can't set up a meeting with a man who has just had one of our boys done in. McGuire doesn't give a toss about the money Tommy owed him. He did it to insult you. To test you. Next thing he'll be picking off our runners, then it will be our collectors.'

'I do not think so,' Dominic said.

'Paying him off will not keep the peace,' Uncle Guido said. 'Paying him off will be interpreted as a sign of weakness.'

Dominic said, 'You do not have to set up a meeting, Tony. I will go by myself, all by myself.'

'To pay him off?' said Guido.

'Yes, to pay whatever Tommy owed him,' Dominic said, 'then to kill him.'

'You?' Tony said. 'You will kill him?'

The parlour was so quiet that you could hear the wind ruffling the shrubs in the garden outside.

'No,' Dominic said. 'We will let O'Hara do it. Very quietly. With a knife.'

'Oh, yeah,' said Tony, grinning. 'Alex will just love that.'

It was always a puzzle to Patsy how his father managed to remain a member in good standing of the Methodist fellowship. He, Patsy, assumed that the old man must have some kind of split personality; either that or a guardian angel who sat upon the tip of his foul tongue to check the flow of casual obscenities that made up a good sixty per cent of his father's customary conversation.

What was undeniable was that twice-weekly attendance at Methodist meetings did the old buzzard a power of good and that he returned from the Elliston Street chapel minus much of his sustaining bitterness. It would be back next morning, of course, or might even return in the course of the evening, seeping into the operating eye then down into his mouth so that by bedtime, even without a drop of drink in him, Paw

Walsh would be braying curses with all the conviction of an apocalyptic prophet.

Patsy got to him early, while he was sober and comparatively sane. He did not need his father's approval for what he was about to do, merely his attention for a few brief minutes.

'I'm goin' off again for a while,' Patsy said, while his father was busy at the stove in the cupboard making himself a pot of tea. 'I don't know how long I'll be away.' The hunched, heavily muscled shoulders did not so much as stiffen. Patsy heard the click of the spoon on the caddy, the clack of the kettle going back on the gas ring. 'Are you okay for cash?'

'Aye,' his father said. 'I'm fine.'

'You want me to leave you somethin' to be goin' on with?'

'Naw.'

His father emerged from the cupboard with a china mug cupped in both hands. He dipped his mouth to the scalding liquid and supped noisily.

Patsy said, 'It'll probably be Tuesday, Wednesday at the latest.'

'Right.'

'If anybody comes lookin' for me you don't know where I am.'

'Right.'

Patsy watched his father sup again from the mug. The glitter was coming back, that ferocious little flicker in the pupil of the eye and, bizarrely, a matching glint in the glass. In a moment the glass eye would begin to water.

Patsy said, 'I don't know where I'm goin' exactly. Maybe Paris.'

'Yon so-and-so goin' wi' you?'

'Polly? Nah.'

'She know you're leavin'?'

'Yeah.'

'She knocked up?'

'Don't be daft,' said Patsy.

The old man sat down in a chair by the fire. He still wore boots, his Sabbath boots, polished to a high gloss. He looked down at them, the mug in both hands, scowled at his feet as if at an enemy. Patsy knew better than to offer to unlace them for him. Besides, the glass eye had begun to water.

The old man said, 'You pull a job?'

Keeping it simple, Patsy answered, 'Yeah.'

'Get much?'

'Enough,' Patsy said.

'You sure yon so-and-so's no' preg-enant?'

'Not by me she's not,' said Patsy.

'Right,' the old man said and, putting the tea mug to one side, bent to tackle his laces.

The question of what to do about Rosie Conway's future had been on Mr Feldman's agenda for some time. Rosie was by far the brightest and most promising of final-year pupils but come June she would be too old to remain at the Institute for even one more term.

The trustees and Mr Feldman between them usually managed to find work for 'graduates' of the Institute, no matter how severely impaired. Copy typists, storemen, cleaners, ground-level bricklayers, apprenticeships in skilled crafts like book-binding or French polishing, one bright boy in the chemical laboratory of the Russia Road Chemical & Dyeworks, one bright girl sewing costumes in the Princess Theatre, another learning hairdressing: wherever his students wound up they had to take their licks, alas, suffer taunts and abuse and be treated as if they were not just deaf but daft.

The master did his best to instil into them a realisation that the faults lay in the prejudice of their tormentors and whatever anyone said to or about them they must hold on to both pride and temper and prove themselves not just capable but superior to those around them.

Rosie needed no such inspiring talk to put the pepper into her. She had always been sure of herself, too sure perhaps. When he'd discussed the prospect of employment with her, for instance, she had been confident that the world would be waiting to welcome her talents with open arms.

Mr Feldman knew that Rosie's sisters were employed, one by the CWC, the other by the burgh council, but it was not until he saw Rosie being led away by one of Manone's henchmen that everything clicked into place and he realised to his horror that Elizabeth Conway's crooked connections had not been severed after all, that Manone or one of his ilk had been paid to obtain the sisters work and that Rosie might be destined to follow the same route and be drawn into marriage or worse with one of Manone's thugs.

The notion of Rosie, his star pupil, sliding into that murky region made Mr Feldman pretty mad. And Mr Feldman pretty mad was not a pretty sight. His poor wife and three grown children bore the brunt of it, for teaching at the Institute was suspended for the holidays and Mr Feldman had to bide his time before he could do what he did best: take remedial action.

Oswald Shelby, Sons & Partners, Books, Rare Books, Bindings & Manuscripts – which if you ever happened to get young Miss Florence Shelby, a reformed flapper, on the telephone emerged as one unintelligible word – had been at the centre of the book trade in Glasgow for the best part of seventy years. In that time their premises had shifted from a handcart at the top of old High Street to a shop at the bottom of Queen Street and, just before the war, to their present august location in Mandeville Square, a stone's throw from the Royal Exchange and no more than sniffing distance from their main rivals, John Smith's, just around the corner in St Vincent Street.

In terms of style and stock Shelby's had Smith's knocked into a cocked hat. There was an air of distinction about Shelby's that no other booksellers, not even Smith's, could match. And as far as pedigree went there were Oswald Shelbys going back and back; all of the old beggars, except the very first, still alive and kicking and dabbling about in the trade, so much so that it was not entirely unknown for Mr Shelby Very Senior to be bidding against Mr Shelby Slightly Junior for the same desirable lot in one of Edmiston's Wednesday morning auction sales.

'Mr Shelby, please.'

'Which Mr Shelby would that be, sir?'

'Mr Oswald Shelby.'

'Which Mr Oswald Shelby?'

'How many are there?'

'Four, sir. And Robert.'

'Robert? Who's Robert?'

'Oswald the sixth. We generally call him Robert.'

'Why do you call him Robert?'

'To avoid confusion, I think.'

Mr Feldman suffered no confusion as to who was who in the Shelby dynasty or who it was that managed the shop these days. He had been acquainted with Oswald Shelby Junior for the best part of thirty years and the boy, Robert, since he'd first appeared, seated like an ornament on the cataloguer's desk, sucking an ebony pen-holder.

On Saturday, the first full day of business after New Year, Mr Feldman tracked Oswald Shelby to his lair on the third floor of the elegant building. This was not the top of the house by any means; the art deco elevator ground up another three floors into teeming attics where binders and repairers laboured at long tables under the skylights and the odour of glue was heady, to say the least of it. Mr Feldman had already placed several boys with Shelby's, a couple in the packing and dispatch department and three in 'binding'.

After a preliminary handshake and a cordial exchange of Ne'erday greetings, therefore, Oswald Shelby was not entirely surprised when his old acquaintance eased into a familiar spiel.

'A girl, you want me to take on a girl?' Mr Shelby said.

'She's a perfectly respectable young lady,' Mr Feldman said.

'I have no doubt of that,' said Mr Shelby. 'But she is none the less ... a girl.'

'You have girls. You have daughters.'

'This is a recommendation?' said Mr Shelby.

'I would like you to train her.'

'As a binder?'

'As a cataloguer.'

'A cataloguer?'

'What's wrong with that?' said Mr Feldman. 'She may be hard of hearing but she isn't blind.'

'I do not need another cataloguer.'

'Is it because she's female?'

'I have no such prejudice.'

'Then you will take her?'

'I did not say that.'

'But if you have nothing against—'

'Whoa,' said Mr Shelby. 'I will not be bullied into anything.'

'She writes a fine clear hand and is certificated on the typewriting machine at forty words per minute. She is neat and personable.'

'All of this I do not doubt. But I have no opening for a gir— for a cataloguer at this time.' Mr Shelby was as small as Mr Feldman was tall. They were, however, of an age, and had played against each other so often at the Glasgow Chess Club that there was between them an intangible rapport that dispensed with the need for tact. 'I am not going to be flanked on this, Abe, you need not think it.'

'Her name is Rosalind Conway.'

Mr Shelby sighed. He was a neat little man with fine, silvery hair and trim, rather foxy features. He dressed as his father did, in high collars and prominent cuffs and a nice line in morning coats, not to mention a watch-chain and breast-pocket handkerchief. He had none of Mr Feldman's bear-like assertiveness, however; his manner was sharp, like peppermint.

'How old is she?'

'Sixteen.'

'Is she mute?'

'No, she has the sort of hearing loss that might one day be cured. There are interesting developments in surgery that might—'

'Is she intelligible?' Oswald Shelby interrupted.

'Perfectly. Given her handicap she is exceedingly articulate.'

'Hmmmmmm.'

'Does that mean you will take her on?' said Mr Feldman.

'We can always find room for another cleaner, I suppose.'

'NO,' Mr Feldman declared, far too loudly. 'I mean – no. She's far too intelligent to be stuck with a mop or feather duster. I'm offering you a good girl here, Oswald. Given the miserable wages you pay your staff I'd have thought you'd be glad to have another willing victim. Besides ...'

'Besides? I knew there would be a "besides",' said Mr Shelby.

'I'd like her to work here.'

'Why?'

'I'd prefer her to work for you, not – not someone else.'

Mr Shelby paused. 'Are you flattering me?'

'Certainly not,' said Mr Feldman. 'Better the devil you know, etcetera.'

'Who is this someone else you do not want the girl to work for?'

'Dominic Manone. Do you know who that is?'

'I know who that is.' Mr Shelby paused once more. 'I'm running a business here, Abe, not a mission for potentially wayward females.'

'When will you see her? Friday?'

'I have to be in London on Friday. It's viewing day at Christie's for an assortment of old Gaelic manuscripts in which we have an interest.'

'The Macpherson Collection?'

'Yes.'

'Do Shelby's have a client?'

'We do. Ten items in particular if, that is, they prove to be genuine.'

'Is there doubt?'

'There is always doubt,' said Oswald Shelby. 'The girl, send her in for interview at half past two o'clock one week on Thursday. I make you no promises, however. I give you no guarantees. Understood?'

'Understood,' said Mr Feldman, and smiled quietly into his beard.

There were two men at the top of the steep wooden staircase that led to Chick McGuire's office. Neither of them gave any sign that they were impressed by the unexpected visitor or that they were aware who he was.

They were runners, both of them. They would be out on the streets by half past eleven, taking up posts on corners near the gates of Harland & Wolff's shipyard and, a little later, at the doors of the Clyde Foundry. They were out of the same pack as Alex O'Hara but older, and taller. They would be paying out winnings on the results of Saturday's Churches League fixtures as well as the full Scottish card and receiving bets on the evening's programme of greyhound racing at Carntyne, the Albion and White City.

As he entered from the seedy back street Dominic experienced an unusual tightening in the muscles of his stomach. It was not the sight of the two heavyweights peering down the dimly lit staircase that brought it on but rather the thought of Tommy Bonnar and how often Tommy must have slipped secretly up these same stairs. He wondered just which dogs Tommy would have backed tonight: Mother's Double, Diamond Dick, Brickey's Boy? Sure losers, every one. He, Dominic Manone, had backed a loser in Tommy but he would never admit that to anyone, not now the poor wretch was dead.

He approached the top of the staircase. He looked up at the heavyweights. They were stationed directly at the top of the stairs. There was a landing of sorts, wooden-floored, a skylight, a lavatory with an open door and one door amidships, closed.

Dominic said, 'You know who I am. Tell him I'm here.'

'Whut fur ur ye here, but?' one of the men said.

'I don't talk business with runners,' Dominic said softly. 'Open the damned door. I assume he's in there?'

'Whut if he is, but?'

Dominic took his hands out of his overcoat pockets. He flaunted no weapon, none at all. He stood below the men, disadvantaged by his position. He let his hands hang loosely by his sides and contemplated the runners passively for a moment or two. Then he snapped out his hands, caught the larger of the men by the foot and with a swift savage little jerk twisted foot and ankle against the natural limit of the joint. Dominic heard the man scream. Ducking and stepping to one side, he pulled the man off balance and heaved him head first down the staircase. He looked up. 'Now will you open the door, please.'

A second later he stepped into Charles McGuire's cluttered little office and, turning, shot the bolt on the door behind him.

McGuire wore tweeds and a Fair Isle pullover in a fancy pattern. He had been sipping tea from a floral cup and barely had time to put down the cup and scramble from his chair behind the desk before Dominic was upon him.

'Now wait,' McGuire said. 'Just wait, just hold on.'

'No,' Dominic said. 'I prefer to pay you now.'

'Pay me? Pay me for what?' He had turned an odd colour, not white but pink; the shade, Dominic thought, of imported tinned salmon. 'You don't owe me anythin'.'

'I think I do,' said Dominic.

He stood at the edge of the desk. He could have touched

McGuire without stretching his arm out by more than six inches. Between them was a strew of race cards, newspapers and the beige-wrapped notebooks in which McGuire kept records of odds and form. Also two telephones and a stubby, powerful-looking wireless set with silver knobs and three convex glass dials.

Dominic didn't know much about the art and craft of making book. He had been to the track a few times with Guido and kept an eye on the form of horses, dogs and football teams but he had no taste for gambling and left the management of the five agencies in which he had a financial stake to Tony Lombard and Irish Paddy who kept peace between rival gangs of touts and paid a handful of police constables to look the other way from time to time. Even so, there had been trouble at the horse tracks last summer, blood shed at Ayr and a dozen arrests made after a fight at Lanark; nastiness on the streets too, involving bludgeons, knuckle-dusters and the ubiquitous razors. Dominic didn't doubt that Tony had it right when he said that McGuire was flexing his muscles.

McGuire had control of himself now. He sat down in the squeaky swivel chair and drank a little tea from the floral cup. He tried to smile his Irish smile, full of cocky charm and blarney but he was still too unsure of Dominic's intention to be at ease.

'What is it you think you're owin' me then, Dom?' he said. 'I'll be takin' anythin' that's offered me, you know that.'

'I've come to square you for Tommy Bonnar.'

'Ah-hah, yes. Poor owd Tommy, eh?' McGuire said. 'Never did have much luck about him. God rest him, though, it was a heck of a way to die. I knew those ciggies would kill him one day but I never did think it would be like that.'

'How much was he into you?'

'Nah, nah. I wouldn't dream o' takin' money from a dead man. I'll be happy just for to write it off.'

'Tommy would not have wanted it,' said Dominic. 'He

might not have been much good at picking winners but he was punctilious when it came to paying his debts. Did you not find that?'

'Punctilous?' McGuire laughed. 'There's a word you'll not be hearin' much of round the midden-head. I never found owd Tommy much of anythin', to answer your question, Dom. I never had much by way of dealin's with him.'

'Did he not owe you money?'

McGuire lifted his hand and gave it a little mid-air shake. 'I took somethin' from him now an' again. God knows why he came to me. It wasn't much at all, though. Twenty, twenty-five. Somethin' like that. I'll write it off.'

'I would rather you did not,' said Dominic. 'How much?'

'Call it thirty, that'll be doin' it.'

When Dominic put his hand into his overcoat pocket McGuire stiffened slightly. He could not help himself. He raised his shoulders from the chairback and wriggled his broad bottom on the padding. He watched the hand emerge and ogled the sheaf of brand-new ten pound notes with relief not greed. He watched Dominic peel three notes from the sheaf, then three more, then five after that, glancing up from the Italian's hands to his face now and then, frowning.

'What's this?' he said.

Dominic said, 'I think you have made a mistake.'

'Nup, no mistake, Dom. This is too much.'

'Well, better too much than not enough,' Dominic said. 'It's the way Tommy would have wanted it. It is the least I can do for him now.'

'Well, you're a generous man. I wouldn't be doin' this for any o' my boys, dead or alive, I can be tellin' you that. I'm certain Tommy's soul will be restin' all the easier for knowin' that his debts have been paid.'

'I am sure it will,' Dominic said.

He placed the banknotes upon the desk, balancing them on top of the stubby little radio. McGuire did not reach out for them, did not grab. He left them where they were, stood and offered a handshake which Dominic accepted.

'You're a real gent, Dom,' he said. 'Peace to poor Tommy then.'

'Peace to us all.'

'Is that what you want?' McGuire said.

'Of course. Isn't that what we all want?'

'Sure an' it is,' said McGuire. 'Sure an' you're right as usual.'

There was no sign of either of the runners on the landing or the stairs. Dominic did not hurry. He picked his way carefully, not looking back. He knew that McGuire was above him, leaning against the angle of the stairhead. Just before he reached the street he heard the bookmaker shout, 'Don't be a stranger now, Dom. Don't be a stranger.'

Dominic gave a little wave of acknowledgement, went out into the grey daylight and walked unhurriedly to the motorcar that was parked at the street's end. He climbed into the passenger seat and the car took off.

Tony, at the wheel, said, 'Well?'

And Dominic said, 'Take him out.'

Chapter Eighteen

On the day of the night of the murder of Charles Henry McGuire — a Friday — police throughout the city had been occupied in the exasperating task of escorting a horde of demonstrators from Argyll Street, up into Renfield Street, along Sauchiehall Street, and back again; two or three thousand men marching abreast, shouting slogans and chanting songs of a derogatory character aimed against the forces of law and order.

The forces of law and order, none too chuffed, had been culled from several different divisions to flank the army of the unemployed and smother on the spot any outbreaks of violence that might happen to occur. Behind the demonstrators, like a buffer, came another wedge of the boys in blue and behind them again a rank of beautiful mounted horse any one of which — horse not rider — would have made a grand centrepiece to a family dinner, served with peas, potatoes and a dash of gravy browning. The intention of the marchers was to disrupt traffic, make a whale of a noise and draw as much attention as possible to the fact that there were a hundred and twenty thousand men out there whose wives and children were slowly starving to death on the Westminster dole. The coppers were not unsympathetic to the cause but they, the coppers, had seen just too much of the underside of life to be entirely free of cynicism and knew that no matter how tough things got for the wives and kiddies back home publicans and bookmakers would continue to grow fat on the crumbs that fell from the table not of the rich but the poor.

Sore heads and aching feet did not make for vigilance late that Friday night, particularly as the pubs were packed, the shebeens doing a roaring trade and not a tart between Scotstoun and Saracen Cross was left stranded for long without the attentions of a gentleman friend. The brawling brown wind that blew warmth and a false taste of spring up the valley of the Clyde may have had something to do with it, but the consensus of opinion under the blue lamps was that the buggers were simply making hay before – to mix a metaphor – the roof fell in with a vengeance and the government cracked down again.

What then was one corpse more or less, another stabbing, another victim of the senseless sectarian rage that no right-minded citizen could properly put a name to, that was just part of the unholy game that the Glasgow keelies played one with the other and all for one.

If Charles Henry McGuire had been found hanging on the monument at Gorbals Cross or face down in a pool of blood at Eglinton Toll then a wee bit more fuss might have been made, more attention paid to the nature of the crime and the apprehension of the criminal. But McGuire was not found on his own patch. He was found at half past five o'clock in the morning huddled on waste ground behind the Marine Social Club in Vine Street across the river in the former burgh of Partick. Naturally the constable who found him hadn't a clue who he was. The detectives who were summoned to the scene were no wiser but, given that the corpse had been stripped of all means of identification, surmised that the motive was probably robbery and nothing more sordid or sinister.

What the bookmaker had been doing in Partick on a blustery Friday night in January was a mystery that was never solved. Perhaps he had been taking bets on another bookie's turf or sampling the rare vintages that were offered in the pubs west of the river. Perhaps he had a secret love nest in that part of town, though neither his current girlfriend nor his wife would wear that theory and were all for elevating Chick to sainthood as far as the interrogating officers were concerned.

Nobody could explain how McGuire travelled to Vine Street. No witnesses came forward to place him on a bus or tram, no cabby willing to swear that he had taken him on as a fare. Nobody in the pubs remembered him; which wasn't really surprising since Friday night did tend to induce amnesia in a lot of folk, a condition somehow exacerbated by the appearance of inquisitive police officers, in or out of uniform.

Certainly nobody had noticed the Singer Senior Six that had prowled into the bottom end of Vine Street at approximately five past midnight or had seen the driver and his companion open the upright boot, or what the boot had contained, or what had been done with what the boot had contained. There had been no cry, no groan from what the boot had contained to catch the attention of the citizens of Vine Street, for what the boot had contained had been dead for an hour or more and had bled all over the tarpaulin in which O'Hara and Tony Lombard had wrapped it back over the river in the vicinity of Chandler Street where, in fact, the deed had been done.

Poor old ostentatious Chick: he lay unclaimed on a slab in the Marine Division mortuary for the best part of forty-eight hours during which period the medical examiner concluded that death was due to a series of eleven stab wounds to chest and neck, specifically a penetrative intrusion deep into the plural cavity and a slash that had all but severed the internal carotid artery thereby causing the victim to drown in his own blood. Lacerations to hands and wrists, together with tearing to the sleeves of overcoat, sports jacket and shirt suggested that the victim had endeavoured to defend himself and may even himself have been armed. The point was moot. No weapon connected with the murder was ever traced. The chap was dead and that was that.

Martha, McGuire's wife, reported him missing late Sunday afternoon, identified the corpse mid-morning Monday and tearfully provided enough detail for the CID to decide that this was an opportunist murder and that theft was the only motive; a natural error given that Mr McGuire's wallet, fountain pens and wristlet watch were missing and that he hadn't so much as a brass farthing in his pockets when found.

At the request of officers west of the river, Southside Division made a few enquiries among the Gorbals lads and grilled the amiable John James Flint, Chick's second-in-command. No charges were forthcoming, however, not even in respect of illegal bookmaking, and the case was handed back to where it properly belonged, out of sight and out of mind in dear old distant Partick.

If any of McGuire's boys nurtured funny ideas about who might have done the dastardly deed they prudently kept their mouths shut. 'Flinty' Flint had let it be known that it would be business as usual in the old homestead and no more nibbling away at the Italians' territory. In fact, Flint was installed in Chick's squeaky swivel chair in the office off the Paisley Road before the first greyhound leaped from its trap on Monday evening. And that was more or less the end of the story – except that on the following Friday Tommy Bonnar and his two little 'nephews' were buried side by side in the Southern Necropolis, official victims of nothing more dramatic than a tragic accident.

Sober and solemn in dark suits and black alpaca over-coats, most of Tommy's friends and acquaintances attended the committal.

Afterwards they solemnly shook hands with Tommy's father who had taken time off work to be there and to thank them all, especially young Mr Manone, for looking after Tommy down through the years.

It was all rather moving, really, though nobody quite managed to shed a tear; nobody except Alex O'Hara who, for some odd reason, found that without his boyhood rival to browbeat, bully and bait, the world was curiously empty and by no means a better place.

Patsy Walsh knew nothing of this. He had departed from Glasgow Central on the night train to London at ten minutes past eleven o'clock on Friday, January 9th, which, as it happened, was almost exactly the moment when Charles Henry McGuire was breathing his last. Patsy was in Paris, installed in a flea-bag hotel in the Marais, before McGuire was identified and, passport stamped and papers in order, was tramping the streets in search of honest employment at precisely the time Tommy Bonnar's coffin was being lowered into the ground.

The Hallops, on the other hand, knew about everything, and understood practically nothing. They hemmed-and-hawed about turning up at the funeral, were still hemming-and-hawing when the first clod hit the coffin lid, still tucked away in the windy heights of the Sunbeam Garage trying to decipher what it all meant and how it would affect them and deciding, ostrich-like, that if Mr Manone didn't actually see them then Mr Manone might forget that they had ever existed and that the whole thing would blow over once and for all.

Lizzie Conway and her girls had more to occupy them than the rumours that tripped through the Gorbals, though Polly at least harboured a few dark thoughts about the nature of coincidence apropos the murder of the bookmaker and what role, if any, Dominic Manone might have played in it.

Lizzie was still on cloud nine, still dazed by love.

Appearances by Bernard Peabody were no longer confined to Friday nights, nor were the girls shuttled out of the kitchen when Mr Peabody arrived, for he, Bernard, seemed to regard them with something of the same fondness as he regarded their mother. His injured right hand had been stitched and was healing well and, in the interim, he had all but mastered the tricky art of filling out forms with his left and would, when Lizzie pressed him, demonstrate his cleverness by making neat little drawings – a house, a mouse, an apple tree – with his rent-book pencil on the back of the *Evening Citizen* for which he received by way of reward a big bosomy hug from the woman and enthusiastic applause from Rosie and Babs.

Against the grain of the times, there were indications that things were showing signs of improvement for the Conways.

Mr Feldman had arranged an interview for Rosie in a famous Glasgow bookshop, the sort of establishment that lay so far beyond Lizzie's ken that it might have been situated on the moon. Far from putting up an objection, as Mr Feldman had feared she might, Rosie's mother was delighted and gave her whole-hearted approval and support.

Babs too had been elevated, moved out of the CWC counting house into an office on the second floor where, on a brand-new Underwood typewriter, she hammered away at letters rather than invoices.

At first Babs could not imagine why she had been promoted or why Miss Crawford and Mrs Anderson suddenly began to treat her if not as an equal certainly with a measure of respect. She was even permitted to enter Mr MacDermott's office now and then and saw with her own eyes the big new Hobbs safe, identical to the one that reposed at the bottom of the Clyde, and a newly glazed window protected by four stout iron bars through which not even Patsy Walsh could have squeezed himself.

Naturally she reported her promotion to her mother and discussed its implications with Polly and eventually concluded that Dominic Manone was responsible and that he had arranged it not to reward her personally but, rather, to please and impress Polly.

Polly was not so sure.

Polly was in a low state, not depressed, not even bored, just curiously restless and impatient. She had expected more attention from Dominic Manone. She was disappointed that he had not been in touch with her again and could not help but feel that somehow she had been used and had become more embroiled than she might care to admit in Dominic's cloudy affairs.

The fact that she had turned into a thief and had pilfered money that her daddy had stolen from the Manones did not trouble her. The fact that she had lied and engaged in several small, almost random betrayals did not even enter her head. She was caught in an eddy and as she waited for something novel and exciting to happen, something to do with Dominic, she trundled through the days in a state of inexplicable agitation.

And the year, as years will, moved on.

It had been a busy Wednesday evening in the Conway household.

Rosie's Sunday-best skirt had been sponged and ironed, each separate pleat rendered sharp as a knife blade. Her blouse was brand-new, best quality, purchased with fifteen shillings that Polly had voluntarily donated to the communal chest, money taken out of her savings, so she said; a claim that only Babs had reason to doubt.

There was a new hairband too, a mottled brown ribbon that Lizzie had bought for herself some months ago but that so lent itself to the image that she envisaged for an aspiring bookseller that she insisted on giving it to Rosie and insisted on her daughter wearing it to the interview at Shelby's in spite of the fact that Rosie thought it made her look like the Lady of the Lake.

Babs had come through with shoes; nothing fancy but a reasonable fit after a knob of newspaper had been squeezed into each toe.

Rosie's hair had been washed, dried, brushed, titivated into this style then that, inspected, rejected and recast until, at long last, Lizzie was satisfied that her youngest was an object to be proud of and that whatever other reasons Shelby's might find for rejecting her it would not be her appearance.

It was after nine, a late hour mid-week for the Conways, before a knock sounded upon the landing door; a tentative knock, seemingly quite timid.

Babs wondered if Jackie had come out of hiding and had cooked up a valid excuse to lure her away from Mammy's apron strings and engage in a bit of what had best be designated as 'courtship' down in the back close, a procedure that would take about five minutes if Jackie's previous performances were anything to go by.

Lizzie wondered if it might be Bernard dropping in unexpectedly, although he had told her that he wouldn't see her again until Friday. And Rosie, who hadn't heard the sound, of course, but had noticed the family's alertness, became tense, for she hadn't forgotten that night not long since when O'Hara had barged in and threatened them or what O'Hara had done to her down in the backs, or – come to that – what she had thought of Alex O'Hara before she had been taught a lesson in common sense.

It was left to Polly to answer the door.

She had no thoughts, no agenda of her own, no reason to suppose that the late-night caller would have anything to offer her by way of diversion.

'Auntie Janet? What are you doing here? Is it Gran? Is Gran poorly?'

She came in from the landing with jerky little steps, turned to her right and entered the kitchen as if travelling on a wire. She wore her workaday overcoat, an old tartan scarf and a clam-shaped felt hat. Her frizzy red hair stuck out from under the hat like flames from a broken gas mantle and her normally pallid complexion was mottled not with face powder but by tears.

Rosie, who had been basking in front of the fire in bodice and knickers, hastily covered herself with a shawl and

Lizzie, astonished, stood frozen by the table, a towel in her hands.

'Janet?' she said. 'Janet, dearest, what's wrong?'

The tears that had apparently flowed freely not too long ago had dried up and Janet's manner was dry and hot now, like an ungreased griddle left too long on the stove. 'I've been robbed,' she said. 'I've been stolen.'

'Stolen from, surely?' said Rosie, not intending to be heartless.

'Stolen, stolen from?' Janet said, her voice rising. 'What does it matter what way you put it? I've been robbed, it's all gone, every penny, every pound scrimped an' saved over the past twenty years, nothin' left but a few coppers in the bottom o' the tin, all the rest of it has disappeared.'

'Robbed?' Lizzie put down the towel and moved to comfort her sister. 'Did somebody break in? Did they hurt Gran or . . .'

'She's fine. She doesn't know. I didn't tell her. Questions. Questions. It would only have led to questions, more questions. I'm sick o' questions. *I've* been robbed an' *I* know who done it.' She elbowed Lizzie aside, and pointed. 'She done it, your precious daughter done it. She took it. I seen her.'

'Get bloody stuffed, Auntie,' Babs said. 'I never touched your cash.'

'Cash! See! She knew it was cash!'

'Well, it would hardly be soddin' stocks an' shares, would it?' Babs said.

Rosie piped up. 'Maybe it is just lost.'

'Lost! It's not lost. *She* took it, that bitch stole *my* dowry money.'

'Dowry money!' Babs and Polly exclaimed in unison.

The girls exchanged glances. Janet, quick as a viper, saw it. She pulled out a kitchen chair, perched herself upon it, folded her hands over her handbag and straightened her spine, trying for dignity.

Lizzie said, 'Are you gettin' ... I mean, have you actually got a man?'

'No, I don't have a man right now. That doesn't mean t' say I'll never have a man again. When the right man turns up I'll have the money for to marry him. I'll not be losin' *my* chance because I'm in debt.' She closed her fists on the handbag. 'Go on, laugh if you like. Daft Auntie Janet, her an' her dreams.'

'Nobody thinks you're daft, dearest,' Lizzie, said soothingly.

Babs grunted, 'Naw, not really.'

'Twenty years it's taken me t' save that money. Doin' wi'out this, denyin' myself that. Twenty years an' now it's all been taken from me.'

Crouched beside Janet, plump knees spread, Lizzie said, 'I'm sorry for your loss, but what makes you think my girls know anythin' about it?'

'Saw them in the cupboard.'

'You did not,' said Babs.

'So that is what was hidden in the cupboard,' said Rosie.

'As well you know,' said Janet.

Rosie propped her chin on her hand, fascinated by what her aunt had divulged. 'How much was there?'

'Three hundred an' twenty-four pounds.'

'My God!' Lizzie sat back on her heels.

'If ever anythin' happened to our tenement,' Janet said, 'it would have bought Mammy an' me a place for to live.'

'Unless your dream-boat came along first,' said Babs. 'Fat chance!'

That was the key, the catalyst, the detonator, the very last straw.

Janet jerked her head. 'What do you know about it? What do you know about livin' in that house wi' that woman an' never havin' a man? Aye, you'll have a man, no doubt. You'll have plenty o' men chasin' after you, wi' that blonde hair and those – those things stickin' out on your chest. All I ever had was what was left after Lizzie went off wi' her flash Harry. Never a thought spared, never a thought spared for me.' The hat slipped, releasing a spray of coarse hair that bobbed and chivvied on her brow. '*Where's my money? Why've you taken my money?*'

'Babs didn't take it,' Polly said. 'I did.'

'You?'

Polly got to her feet. She felt no guilt just the dead weight of retribution lying upon her and weariness at the prospect of having to explain to her aunt why it had been necessary to have cash and why she had thought that the money was rightfully hers. 'Yes,' she said. 'I discovered it by – by accident one day a month or so ago. I thought, I honestly thought it was cash that my father had hidden away.'

'Frank?' said Janet. 'What does he have to do with it?'

'Nothing, apparently,' Polly said. 'If I'd known they were your life savings I wouldn't have touched them.'

Janet blew out her lips, jerked her head in her sister's direction. 'Do you believe that, Lizzie? Do you expect me t' swallow such a cock-and-bull story?'

'It might be the truth,' said Lizzie.

'Frank's money?' Janet shook her head, and uttered a croak of mirth. 'Frank never had any money, not a tosser of his own. Frank Conway? Hoh! I'll tell you about Frank Conway. He didn't steal from the Eye-tie. He didn't join up to escape Carlo Manone. He joined up for to escape *you*, Lizzie. To escape you an' that litter o' babies that was takin' up all your time an' attention so there was none left for him, poor soul.'

'You liar!' Babs said. 'Daddy would never leave us.'

'Would he not, but?' Janet went rattling on. 'Frank's money under the floorboards? Don't make me laugh. He came t' me for money. He came t' me up at the house an' I gave him everythin' we had, every penny we had. Precious little it was but it was his for the askin', all his for the askin'.'

'He went to you?' said Lizzie. 'Why did he go t' you?'

'Because he knew I'd do anythin' for him.' Janet tilted her

chin. The hat slipped, almost fell off. She would not spoil her moment of triumph by snatching at it, however. 'He knew I loved him.'

'You?' said Lizzie, without scorn.

'Aye, an' I proved it too. Proved it plenty o' times.' Janet tugged the hat from her head and, waving it as if it were a grenade, swung towards her sister. 'All those times when you were swelled up who do you think kept Frank happy? Eh? Do you think he stayed wi' you because he loved you? God, he never loved you. He loved *me*, Lizzie. It was *me* he loved an' it was *me* he'd have come back for.' Her lips pursed in a bitter little pout. 'That's who I was savin' for. He's the one. He's the man. I never gave up the hope he'd come back an' take me away. I never gave up hope.' She got up, small and shabby but with swagger. 'Now, where's my money, girlie? I want it back.'

'You can't have it back,' said Polly. 'I've spent it.'

'Lyin' bitch,' said Janet.

'You leave her alone,' said Lizzie, rising too. 'You can say what you like about me but I'll not have you sayin' those things to my girls.'

'Thieves, that's all they are. Thieves an' whores.'

Lizzie's blow was more of a punch that a slap. It rocked Janet but did not silence her. She staggered, crumpled against the edge of the table, and went on talking, her voice not dimmed but strengthened.

'My man, he was,' she said. 'My man. My money.'

'Prove it,' Babs shouted. 'Yeah, prove it, you stupid old cow.'

'I believe her,' Rosie said.

'What the hell d' you know about it, dummy?' Babs shouted.

'Alex O'Hara told me about Dad.'

'O'Hara, that — that toad!' Babs shouted. 'I suppose he's been up this old hag an' all.' She leaped towards her aunt. 'Did you take O'Hara to your bed an' all? Aye, an' who else, I'd like to know?'

'None else,' said Janet, very still now. 'Only him. Only Frank. There was never any other man to match him. I wisht he'd come back.'

'Well, he isn't comin' back,' Babs yelled. 'He's dead. He's dead an' thank God for it.'

Lizzie sighed. 'Don't say that, dear.'

'Right, my money?' Janet said, holding out one thin, hard hand.

'I haven't got your money,' Polly said. 'I told you. I spent it.'

'Not all of it,' said Babs, scowling.

'Yes, all of it,' said Polly. 'I gave it to someone. I gave it to him just the way you say you gave it to Daddy. To help him get away.'

'A likely story.' Janet rubbed her cheek, for the flesh had begun to swell a little and had turned bright red. 'It'll have gone to Manone. Manone. Hoh! He took you t' the fair, Lizzie, didn't he? Payin' him money all those years when there was nothin' to pay for.'

'An' you let her,' Babs said. 'Dear God, you let her.'

And Polly said, 'Yes, I gave it to Mr Manone.'

That stopped her, that brought her up short. Smugness vanished from her eyes in an instant. 'What?' Janet said. 'What are you tellin' me?'

'Paid back to Dominic Manone,' said Polly.

'But you said . . .'

'Ah, yes, but I'm a born liar, Auntie Janet, aren't I?'

'You said . . .'

'I gave it to Manone, all of it.'

Babs laughed. 'So why don't you ask *him* to give you it back?'

Janet turned. 'Is this true, Lizzie?'

'I don't know. I expect it is,' Lizzie said. 'If the girls say it is then . . .'

'Bye-bye nest egg,' said Babs.

'But – but it's my money.'

'Not any more it ain't,' Babs said.

'I'll – I'll – I'll report you all t' the polis.'

'No, you won't,' said Lizzie. 'You can't.'

'Aye, but I can.'

'And tell them what?' said Polly. 'Tell them about Dominic Manone?'

'I wouldn't do that if I were you, Janet,' Lizzie said with an odd, almost protective note in her voice. 'It wouldn't be sensible to drag Mr Manone into our family squabble.'

'My money, my savin's . . .'

'Gone,' said Rosie, very distinctly, 'like my daddy. Gone for good.'

'And,' Polly said, 'you've only yourself to blame.'

It had been years since the three Conway girls had clambered into the niche bed beside Mammy all at one time. It seemed a natural thing to do, though, after the crisis that Aunt Janet's visit had incurred and the doubts that trailed in the wake of her revelations; a sign of unity that Lizzie hadn't the heart to reject.

She wore her nightgown and had stuck a few paper curlers in her hair. Rosie too was dressed for bed but Babs and Polly had only kicked off their shoes before, rather sheepishly, they slid on top of the blankets and settled themselves at the foot of the mattress.

'Now,' Lizzie said, 'I want the truth. Where's Janet's money?'

Polly said, 'I gave it straight to Patsy Walsh.'

'Why?' said Lizzie.

'Because I thought the Manones might try to kill him.'

'He robbed the warehouse, I take it?'

'Yes,' said Polly, 'but got away with nothing.'

Lizzie said, 'Did O'Hara threaten him?'

'No, not exactly,' Polly said. 'After what happened to Tommy Bonnar, though, I was afraid the same thing might happen to Patsy.'

'How did you stumble on Janet's savings?' Lizzie asked.

Polly hesitated. 'Pure accident.'

'Tell her,' Babs said. 'It's all out now in any case.'

'I was looking for a place to hide Babs's – our share of the robbery.'

'Your share?' said Lizzie.

'My share,' said Babs. 'She never had a share.'

'When I discovered money hidden under the boards in Gran's house,' Polly said, 'I naturally assumed it was Daddy's.'

'So you just took it?'

'Yes.'

Lizzie heaved a sigh. 'Has he gone now, this boy?'

'I think he's in Paris.'

'You just wanted rid of him, didn't you, Polly?' Lizzie said.

'I suppose I did.'

'Did you give him all Janet's money?' Lizzie asked.

'I bloody hope not,' said Babs.

'Half,' Polly said. 'I put the rest into a bank account.'

'You didn't tell me that,' said Babs. 'Where's the bank book?'

'I've hidden it.'

'Where?'

Polly gave an embarrassed shrug. 'Back of the wireless set.'

Rosie giggled. 'And I thought it was just Victor Sylvester.'

Lizzie said, 'You'll have to give it back.'

'Like hell we will,' said Babs, 'not after what Janet done to us.'

'Janet didn't do anythin' to us,' said Lizzie.

'You don't seem very surprised at what Auntie told us,' said Rosie.

'I'm not. I knew he had someone else,' said Lizzie. 'I'd a

notion it might be Janet but I didn't want to have to face up
to the truth.'

'She's a right cow,' Babs interrupted. 'Imagine lettin' you
pay the Manones for all these years an' never sayin' a word.'

'How could she?' said Lizzie. 'She was waitin' for Frank to
come back.'

'Alex O'Hara says somebody else took the Manones' money,'
said Rosie.

'You an' O'Hara seem to have been very bloody chummy,'
said Babs.

'It was a while ago,' said Rosie, 'when I still thought he
liked me.'

'Well,' Lizzie said, 'I'm relieved things are out in the
open at last.'

'For all the good it'll do us,' Babs said.

Lizzie put an arm around Rosie, and said, 'I'm goin' to marry
Bernard. He loves me an' I love him. I've been feelin' guilty about
goin' off an' leavin' Janet to cope wi' Mother – but I think I've
got over it all of a sudden. So that's one problem solved.'

'One problem?' said Babs. 'What about us?'

'Will we go with you,' said Rosie, 'to Knightswood?'

'You will,' said Lizzie. 'Your sisters won't.'

'Wait a bloody minute,' said Babs. 'Are you sayin' that Polly
an' me are to be kicked out in the street just because you want
to marry this guy?'

'It's not goin' to happen right away,' said Lizzie.

'I mean, are you punishin' us?' said Babs. 'Anyhow, why can't
we come with you to Knightswood? Bernard wouldn't mind.'

'No, but his mother would,' said Lizzie. 'The house isn't
big enough for six of us. Besides, I'm sure you wouldn't want
to leave your friend.'

'What friend?' said Babs, frowning.

'Your friend downstairs,' said Lizzie.

'Jackie? My God! Jackie's not ...' Babs paddled her legs in
frustration. 'You are, you're punishin' us, for God's sake.'

'I'm not,' said Lizzie. 'I'm just doing what I want for a change.'

'And the debt to Dominic Manone?' said Polly.

'There is no debt,' said Lizzie. 'Never was a debt.'

'Dominic doesn't know that,' said Polly.

'He will,' said Lizzie. 'He will when you tell him.'

'Me?'

'Aye,' Lizzie said. 'You.'

Early on Thursday afternoon, Miss Fyfe gave her a whisk over with a clothes brush, Mr Feldman issued a few last-minute instructions, wished her the best of luck, and waved her off to her appointment at Shelby's.

Rosie was at an age more selfish than sensitive. Most of the unpleasantness that Aunt Janet had stirred up was almost forgotten in her excitement. She had been looking forward to the great adventure — her first interview for a job — ever since Mr Feldman had arranged it. She had even persuaded Polly to accompany her into Glasgow one evening and lead her to Mandeville Square so that she wouldn't get lost when the day came.

The building had been impressive but the shop's narrow ground-floor windows had revealed little, except some expensive-looking books with tinted plates laid open on a velvet cloth and, at the back, three or four shelves of leather-bound volumes. Rosie had been a mite disappointed. Shelby's was not the jumbled, jam-packed sort of bookshop that she had envisaged and had an air of austere gentility that made it seem just a wee bit stuffy. A job, any sort of job, was not to be sneezed at, however, and come Thursday she put her doubts behind her and rode the tram into Glasgow feeling more alert and nervous than she had ever done before.

As soon as she pushed through the heavy swing door and stepped into the shop, all her doubts vanished and her nervousness was replaced by a kind of awe. Sixteen or not, a Gorbals girl or not, she knew that this was the place for her. It was quiet, so very quiet that she could almost hear the silence; not the muffled silence that she was used to but the sort of silence you could feel on your skin, tranquil, soothing and pleasantly warm, with a faint plushy odour that words couldn't adequately describe – the aroma, the effluvia of books.

Books in profusion, more books than were held by the public libraries in Norfolk Street and Scotland Street put together, more books than carelessly crammed the barrows where Babs took her when she had a spare shilling to spend. Books here were treated as more than commodities and were granted a respect to which Rosie instinctively responded They were stacked on floor-to-ceiling shelves, individualised on wooden stands, housed in stately glass-fronted cases and laid open in display cabinets. There was hardly a soul in the long reach of the shop, as if the books themselves were the inhabitants, the citizens of Shelby's rooms and admitted acolytes only reluctantly and in penny numbers.

One elderly gentleman in an old-fashioned Chesterfield lurked in a corner, head bent as if in prayer, a little volume bound in card open in his hands. One younger gentleman with a shock of curly brown hair down to his collar and a Raglan overcoat flung open leaned gently against a display case, carefully inspecting a huge calf-bound tome that lay open on top of the glass. And, though Rosie failed to notice him, a boy in shirt-sleeves and a canvas apron was perched on a tall ladder so far above her that he was almost lost in the shadows of the ceiling cornice.

It wasn't consideration or a suspicion that she might be hard of hearing that brought the shop-boy down to floor level. He knew better than to raise his voice within the precincts of the bookroom. He had learned the hard way to restrain his natural exuberance and pretend that he was as well mannered if not as well bred as most of Shelby's customers. He nipped swiftly down the ladder and was at Rosie's side almost before she realised it.

'Yass,' he said in a throaty whisper, then, just in case he had misjudged the age and class of new arrival, added a reluctant, 'madam?'

Rosie turned to face him. She arched her tongue against the roof of her mouth then, fighting a nervous slur, said, 'I am here to see Mr Shuh – Shelby.'

'Which Mr Shelby 'ud that be?' the boy said.

'Mr Oswald Shuh – Shelby?' said Rosie, uncertainly.

She had no trouble reading the boy's lips but she could not make out the sneering, jumped-up working-class accent that rang as false as a fourpenny bit. She would have felt more comfortable if she had, for she would have known, as Polly would have known, that he was no more socially exalted then she was, just a tad more experienced in patronage.

'Is it fur work?' the boy said.

He had a thin, gutter-ground face, sallow and severe.

'I have an appointment,' said Rosie, voice rising; so much so that the elderly gent in the corner turned and peered at her, not disapprovingly but with an air of sympathy. 'Where is Mr Shelby to be found?'

'Didn't know he wus lost, darlin',' the boy said, then, spotting higher authority, added hastily, 'However, if you'll step this way, miss, I'll see if I can ... Ah, there you are, Mr Shelby. Young lady here claims she's got an appointment with Mr Oswald.'

'She has, Gannon,' the higher authority said.

'I thought he was still in London, sur.'

'He is. I'll do the honours. Now scuttle along, please.'

'Sur,' said Gannon, and was gone.

Rosie looked up at the higher authority and felt better immediately.

He was tall but not so tall as to be intimidating. He had a square-ish sort of face, a prominent chin with a cleft in it, dark wavy hair, and sported a pair of heavy tortoiseshell spectacles. Coupled with the fact that he wore no coat, the specs lent him an air of informality. His waistcoat, Rosie noticed, was ink-stained and the cloth, though expensive, had frayed a little round two of the buttonholes. His shirt sleeves were fastened with rolled gold links, however, and she guessed that he must be one of the Shelby clan.

'Rosalind Conway?'

'Yes.'

'I'm Robert Shelby. My father sends his apologies. He's been detained elsewhere on business. He's asked me to put you through your paces and report back to him.' He smiled, taking the sting out of it. 'Can you make me out?'

'Yes, sir. I can read your lips fine.'

'Surprising. Everybody tells me I'm a fearful mumbler.'

'I do not think you are, sir.'

'Well, that's gratifying.' Looking down at her he seemed momentarily at a loss, then he said, 'We won't bother with the office. If you come with me, I'll take you directly to the catalogue desks and we'll see how your penmanship shapes up.' His put his hand against her shoulder, very lightly. 'This way.'

She walked by his side down a carpeted aisle between display cabinets and waist-high bookcases, looking up at him.

He said, 'I believe you come with Mr Feldman's recommendation.'

'Mr Feldman is my teacher, sir.'

'Mr Feldman was my teacher too.'

'You?' said Rosie. 'But you are not deaf?'

'Abe Feldman taught me to play chess.'

'Oh!'

'Do you play?'

'No, Mr Shelby, I am afraid I do not.'

They had reached an alcove towards the rear. It was protected by a carved wood arch but the shop was clearly visible from beneath it. Behind the barrier, however, were two long tables, each top inlaid with fine, pale green leather. Books were piled up on them and on the floor between. On each table were three big brass ink-stands and a rack containing pens, blotting paper, envelopes and other assorted stationery. On one table was a typewriter – an antique Oliver with keys like a spider's legs – an embossing press and a device that Rosie recognised as an automatic numbering machine. Seated at the table was a man of about sixty. He wore a threadbare suit, a rumpled shirt, and had a small moustache the hue and texture of badger's bristle. He glanced up and winked at Rosie through a pair of thick gold-rimmed spectacles.

'Mr Briggs, our researcher and cataloguer,' Robert Shelby told her. 'If we do decide to employ you, Rosalind, it's Mr Briggs who will train you. What do you think of that, Albert? Can you cope with a female apprentice?'

'Male, female; can't hardly tell the difference these days,' Mr Briggs said. 'Are you the deaf lassie?'

'Hard of hearing,' Rosie answered.

'Huh!' Mr Briggs said. 'One deafie, an' one half blind. What a pair that'll be, eh, Mr Robert? Hardly worth more than one wage between us?'

'I wouldn't tell my father that,' Robert Shelby said. 'You might give him ideas.' He opened a drawer in the base of the table, took out a sheaf of lined foolscap paper, placed it on the table, drew out a chair. 'Now, Rosalind, I'm going to ask you to copy a piece from a book, a rather odd book written in Latin several hundred years ago. It's called *Novum Organum*, by a chap named Francis Bacon.' He reached to the pile by the table, plucked out a book. 'It's not a first edition, of course, but it's early. Bound in vellum, this funny waxy sort of stuff. Put one of our ebony rulers across the pages to hold them down and copy the whole of the page with the tape marker in it. Can you can do that?'

'Yes.'

'Perhaps I should relieve you of your coat and hat?'

'Please,' said Rosie.

She slipped out of her overcoat and gave it, her hat and scarf to Mr Shelby. She was already studying the book's wrinkled pages and unfamiliar type. She understood the nature of the test: her ability to make an exact copy of a page written in a language she didn't comprehend. It was a good test, fair if difficult and indicated something of what would be expected of her if she got the job. She seated herself, selected a pen, opened one of the ink-wells. The pen-nib was brand-new, steel with a fine point. She licked it to make the ink stick.

'I think, Mr Briggs, we should let the young lady get on with it.'

'Aye, I think you're right, sir,' Albert Briggs said, then leaned over, put his moustache almost against Rosie's ear and in a soft, tobacco-smelling breath, added, 'Dot your *tees* an' cross your *eyes*, lass, an' you'll do fine.'

Rosie hardly heard him; she had already begun to write.

Chapter Nineteen

Polly was aware that ominous changes were taking place in the Conway household. By her own account Rosie had fared well at her interview. She was optimistic that she would be offered the job at Shelby's and would soon be earning twenty-five shillings a week and stepping out on the rocky road to independence. At the same time, Polly realised, Babs and she were being made to assume responsibility for their own mistakes and that, while she would never abandon them, Mammy would never again treat them as prized possessions.

They had let her down, had failed to live up to her high expectations. Mammy had every right to punish them. But, Polly reckoned, it wasn't spite or selfishness that had prompted her mother to shift the onus of responsibility, but that she, Mammy, had fallen in love. While Babs might mock that excuse or consider it no excuse at all and dismiss the reality of loving as so much sentimental twaddle, Polly was intelligent enough not to condemn what she did not understand. She had an inkling, just an inkling, of what had possessed her mother, what had changed her.

She recalled very vividly indeed what she had felt that night before Christmas when Bernard Peabody had proved himself more of a man than any of them would ever have suspected, more brave and daring than Patsy Walsh could ever be; that plain, ordinary, honest man with his hand closed round an open razor, refusing to let go in spite of the pain. She wondered if that was what love was about, an acceptance of the pain that went with the responsibility of loving someone; wondered too how it must feel, that sort of responsibility, that intensity, that constant need to be worthy one of the other, and if she would ever find a man who would make her feel that way.

On Friday morning she stole time from office routine to type out a letter to Dominic. She signed it, sealed it and put it away in her handbag. As soon as she was released from work that evening, she caught a tram to Molliston Street and delivered the letter at the door of the Rowing Club, gave it into the hand of an Irishman who promised to see that it reached Mr Manone without delay.

On Saturday afternoon Polly left the Burgh Hall at five past one o'clock.

She hurried out into the street in a state of nervous expectation. There was no sign of the Italian motorcar.

She felt a stab of anger that Dominic had not obeyed her summons and, almost in the same heartbeat, a sudden sense of loss at a promise that had never been made. She had been wrong to expect him to drop everything and rush to be with her, to put away his own concerns to attend her. She remembered Rosie's silly assumption that Alex O'Hara was her 'boyfriend' when patently he was nothing of the kind; had she also made a fool of herself by believing that Dominic Manone was attracted to her when in reality he couldn't have cared tuppence?

The Alfa glided up behind her as she stalked along the pavement. He brought it in against the kerb and, leaning, opened the passenger door.

Polly hesitated, tied by a vestige of annoyance that he had not been stationed right at the doorstep, had kept her waiting, kept her guessing even for a couple of minutes. There was also relief, though, and a surge of pure breathless pleasure at seeing him again. She slid into the passenger seat as if it were the most natural thing in the world.

'Thank you for coming,' she said.

He fashioned a little gesture with his right hand, a gesture that she would come to know well. He was smiling, and his smile seemed to reflect feelings that were hidden within her too, pleasure at meeting again.

He put the motorcar into gear and drove off, eased the Alfa around the corner into Eglinton Street and swung left, heading for the Glasgow Bridge. He sat low in the leather seat, almost as if he did not want to be seen. He wore the soft woollen overcoat, the red scarf, no hat. He looked younger, almost boyish. A curl of dark hair had strayed on to his brow and Polly was tempted to touch it, to tease it back into place. She laughed for no reason, and felt her concentration scatter, the whole weary weight of accusation and negotiation, the dreadful necessity of putting herself in this man's hands vanish as the motorcar crossed the river into Glasgow.

She said, 'Where are you taking me?'

'For lunch,' he said. 'I imagine you won't be expected home for a while.'

'No,' Polly said. 'I told my sisters—'

'Your sisters?' Is it a conspiracy I have to deal with?' Dominic said.

'No conspiracy,' Polly said, 'just me.'

'I think I may be able to cope with just you,' Dominic said.

'Did I do wrong?'

'I don't know,' Dominic said. 'Did you?'

'In sending you a letter via the Rowing Club?'

'Oh, that,' Dominic said. 'No. It gave the lads something to gossip about.'

'Gossip?' Polly said. 'About you, about – us?'

'My aunt thinks you're dangerous,' Dominic said.

The Alfa was locked at the junction of Jamaica and Great

Clyde Street, trapped by a brewer's dray and a tram. The tram loomed large by Polly's side. She was conscious of four or five men hanging on the platform, peering in at her as if she were a fish in an aquarium. She could hear them shouting remarks in a friendly sort of way. Babs would have given them an unladylike sign of displeasure or would have mouthed swear words at them. Polly simply looked away.

A moment later the tramcar lurched like something in a fun fair, dodged away from the Alfa, and rattled out of sight.

'Dangerous? Why would your aunt think that?' Polly said.

'She thinks that you sent me a letter of romance.'

'How ridiculous!' Polly said, pleased. 'Didn't you show it to her?'

'No,' Dominic said. 'I prefer to let her think that's what it was.'

'Well, it wasn't,' Polly said.

'I know,' said Dominic.

The Alfa nosed along the busy riverside through carts and drays. Polly could just make out the slabby grey shapes of ships moored at Custom House Quay and then, with another spin of the wheel, they were heading into an area of warehouses and tenements at the back of St Enoch railway station.

'Where *are* you taking me?' Polly asked again.

'Goodman's,' Dominic told her. 'Okay?'

'Okay,' said Polly.

Summer, winter or spring, Saturday half-day was a thing of joy for Bernard Peabody. He did little that was constructive with his free time; escaping the confines of the city brought him pleasure enough. He had a strip of garden at the back of the terraced cottage and had begun to tinker with improvements soon after his mother and he had moved in. In a veiled, patient way he had plans for an Alpine rockery that ran contrary his mum's demands for a vegetable patch.

Gardening, however, was not on Bernard's mind that mild January afternoon; nor was football, nor strolling a favourite route through the new public park; nor was anything very much except getting himself ready for a twilight ride back across Glasgow to the Gorbals to pick up Lizzie soon after she got home from work, to take her out for a quick fish tea and on to the pictures; the Coliseum probably, where Syd Chaplin was starring in *A Little Bit of Fluff*, which he'd heard was a priceless gem of reckless adventure.

He just prayed it wouldn't be too reckless for Lizzie's taste, or that she wouldn't think he was trying to take advantage of her, though what Bernard envisaged by that euphemism would have made Jackie Hallop and even young Babs chortle at his naïveté. It wasn't that Bernard wasn't a man of the world – he had seen more nastiness in his lifetime than most men – he simply lacked experience with the opposite sex. He still tended to regard them, Lizzie in particular, as somehow morally superior to anything in trousers. 'Taking advantage' then would be a wee bit of hand-holding and an experimental nudging of knees under cover of darkness in the back row – no, not the back row, the middle row of the balcony if, that is, the Coliseum even had a balcony.

So he pondered on Lizzie and balconies while he scraped away at his chin with a safety razor and, without vanity, studied his face in the oblong mirror that was propped above the sink.

He tried to imagine what a woman like Lizzie could possibly see in him. He wasn't square-jawed and handsome, broad in the shoulder or strong in the arms – God, there were fifteen-year-old apprentices who had more muscles than he had – but the run-in with O'Hara had increased his confidence and the kiss, that tender, muffled kiss under the Sunday lights, had given him such a boost that he'd felt invincible for days afterwards.

He was, so he believed, a practical chap and had devised a sort of strategy. He wouldn't try to sweep Lizzie off her feet with his masculine appeal. Instead, he would go about things in a down-to-earth manner, to bring about the desired result – the result he desired, that is – in the not too dim and distant.

He glanced at his right hand, unbandaged now. The diagonal scar across the palm was still plainly visible and even tended to bleed just a little when he gripped anything too tightly. But he had healed quickly and whatever aches and pains the drying wound incurred were easily ignored.

He scaped the safety razor carefully over his Adam's apple and then, for absolutely no reason he could think of, began to sing.

He didn't even know what he was singing – 'One Alone' from Sigmund Romberg's *The Desert Song*, as it happened – or why he suddenly tossed down the razor and, spreading his arms, filled the cramped little room with the sound of his voice, lifting and lilting, laying it on thick, as if he were centre-stage at the Alhambra. He sang for himself, not for the entertainment of the neighbours through the wall, or for his mother, or even for Lizzie, drudging away at the tubs in the Sanitary laundry on the other side of the city.

He sang because he was happy, because he hadn't sung for himself or anyone for many years: he hadn't lifted his voice, except in kirk, since he'd marched down to the quays with the other lads, kilts swinging and rifles shouldered, with the whole damned town turned out to see them off, waving and cheering; he had sung then, by God, had sung lustily and gladly, a hero among heroes: 'Madamzelle from Armentieres', and 'Tipperary', and 'Till the Boys Come Home'. But after that day he had sung very little: after a month in the field he had sung not at all – until now.

'Bernard, stop makin' that awful noise.'

'I'm singing, Mum.'

'Then stop it.'

'Why should I?'

'I don't know what's got into you these days.'

'Sure you do, Mother, just think about it.'

'I prefer not to think about it,' his mother said from outside the door.

'By the way,' Bernard said, 'I'll be out tonight an' I might be late. Don't wait up for me, please.'

Silence: then, 'Late?'

'I'm goin' to the pictures with Lizzie.'

Silence: 'I see.'

He dismantled the razor and wiped the blade clean, dried it and the razor's separate metal parts and put them into the tin box where they were kept. He rinsed out his shaving brush – waiting. He knew his mother was still hovering outside. He gave a mischievously little shrug of the shoulders, put his brow against the wooden door, and said in a sonorous tone, 'Last tram.'

Silence: 'I hope you're not goin' to do anything foolish, Bernard.'

'You mean, anything you wouldn't do?'

'You know what I mean.'

He opened the door suddenly. She was loitering in the attenuated little corridor, already wearing her broad patterned coat and floral hat. He had no idea where she was going and did not much care. Some church or Guild outing. Some collective shopping trip. Why she regarded her social life as more interesting and important than anything he chose to do was beyond him. She took no pleasure in his pleasure. She grudged him his happiness because it was none of her doing. If he had been going out to a concert with one of her friend's dismal daughters then she would have been egging him on. She would have been sure of him then, certain of retaining her place on the moral high ground.

'No, Mother,' he said, grinning, 'what do you mean?'

'That woman,' Violet Peabody said.

He was too relaxed to let her annoy him, to scratch at his guilt.

He laughed. 'I'm goin' to the pictures not the altar, Mum,

and "that woman", as you so delicately put it, is quite safe —
fairly safe — with me.'

'I really don't understand you, Bernard.'

'I know,' Bernard said. 'You never have,' then breaking into
song again, flipped the towel across his shoulder and sauntered
into the bedroom to dress.

If you walked across the iron suspension bridge that links
Carlton Place with Custom House Quay, turned right then left,
you would have stumbled into a neighbourhood that even the
most informed Glaswegian could not properly define and that
Polly, Gorbals born and bred, knew hardly at all: a conglomerate
of old commercial and domestic properties bearing down on
queer little shops that peddled everything from second-hand
suits to wigs and bird-seed, accordions to cheap false teeth; beer
cellars impregnated by the smoke of locomotives shunting in and
out of St Enoch's and the scaly stench of the fish market that lay
beyond the Bridgegate; plus a couple of eating-houses cherished
by the *cognoscenti*, dingy little places that served wonderful lunches
and dinners without breaking the bank. Goodman's was one
of these.

Goodman's was favoured by small-time businessmen, lawyers from the Justiciary Court, newspaper reporters, and policemen who had something to celebrate, like a birthday or a
promotion or, now and then, a hanging.

It was not dauntingly formal. In addition to oysters, jugged
hare and venison it served quite homely dishes like pork chops,
liver savouries and beefsteak pudding. Twenty-six tables packed
the ground-level room. On weekdays it was impossible to find
space between noon and half past two. On Saturdays it was a
little, just a little, quieter. In any case, Dominic had booked a
corner table in advance. To her surprise Polly did not feel out
of place. She certainly did not appear out of place in her 'office'
outfit, for there was a distinctly commercial air to the clientele

and she was by no means the only young woman being treated to Saturday lunch.

She studied the handwritten menu, selected broth, a beef pudding to follow, and only when the waitress had gone, glanced around the room.

'No signs of a trade slump here, I see,' she said.

'Is that a Communist sentiment?' Dominic asked.

'Just a passing remark,' Polly said.

'Our friend Walsh would not care for this place.'

'Patsy? I doubt it.' Polly brought her attention back to Dominic, something not difficult to do. He was seated back in his chair, forearm resting on the table, right arm folded across his chest in a manner that Polly thought just a wee bit Napoleonic. 'If you're fishing for information about Patsy Walsh,' she said, 'don't bother. I'll tell you what you need to know.'

'Has he left Glasgow?'

'Yes. Last week.'

'On what day?'

'Friday, I think.'

'Night train to London?'

'Probably,' Polly said. 'I don't know where he is now, however. Somewhere on the Continent.'

'I have no intention of searching for Patsy,' Dominic said. 'I've nothing against him, you know. I am glad he's gone, to tell the truth.'

'Really?' Polly said. 'Why would that be?'

'Because I would not be here with you otherwise.'

She was startled by his directness – or what seemed like directness. She thought about it for a moment, long enough to read ambiguity into the compliment, then said, 'I don't belong to Patsy Walsh. I'm not especially attached to him. In fact, I'm relieved to see the back of him too.'

'He is not for you?' Dominic asked.

'No, he isn't for me.'

'Did you give him money?'

'How did you ... Yes, I gave him some money.'

'How much?'

'I don't think that's any of your business.'

'Perhaps not,' Dominic said, 'except that I'd like to make it up to you.'

'What do you mean?'

'Pay you back.'

'At everlasting interest?' Polly said.

Dominic shook his head. 'Not a loan.' He sat forward, coming closer. He didn't look round, didn't seem furtive, or embarrassed to be discussing money with a woman. 'I will give you back what you gave to Walsh. In full. No hidden charges, Polly, no interest due.'

'Why would you want to do that?'

'Because I can afford it and you can't.'

'I didn't persuade Patsy to leave because you asked me to,' Polly said.

'I know.'

'Are you paying me to keep my mouth shut?' Polly said.

That surprised him. He drew back, frowning. He might have allowed some of the persuasive softness to go from his voice if, at that moment, the waitress hadn't returned with the broth. She placed the bowls before them and offered a pepper-pot. Dominic waved her away with a polite motion of the hand.

He lifted his spoon, weighed it in his fingers for a moment, deliberately not looking at Polly. Still not looking at Polly, he said, 'About what?'

'The reason I wrote to you, asked you to meet me today.'

'So it was not a letter of romance after all?'

'Anything but,' Polly said.

'How disappointing,' Dominic said.

'I'd never have found the nerve, never have had the cheek to do that,' Polly said. 'It's business, just business.'

'Concerning Patsy Walsh?'

'No,' Polly said, steeling herself, 'concerning us.'

'Us?'

'Your family and my family,' she said. 'Your father and my father.'

His surprise was palpable, a kind of alarm.

He said, 'My father lives in America. What does he have to do with us?'

'My father didn't steal from your father,' Polly said. 'My daddy had nothin' to do with the money that went missing. You know it. You've known it all along. I know it too now.'

'If he – why did he run then? Why did he enlist?'

'Because somebody accused him and he was afraid.'

'Afraid?'

'Afraid that your father would do to him what somebody did to Tommy Bonnar. Afraid for his life, and my mother's life too, probably. He took the blame and ran away, just like Patsy, only with more justification.'

'This is all – all news to me.'

'Oh, don't pretend,' Polly said. 'You've taken money from my mammy for years for no reason. There was nothin' to pay back, no debt, honourable or otherwise. I think you knew it. I'm *sure* you knew it.'

'I was only a boy when ...'

'I thought you'd say that,' Polly told him. 'You weren't a boy at all, Dominic. You were a young man. Old enough to understand what was going on. I've heard you talk, I've heard talk about you. Precious little goes on that you don't know about. You make it your business to know things. You knew that my daddy was innocent. I think that's why you looked out for us. Took our money with one hand and looked out for us with the other.'

'Where did you pick up this story?'

'It isn't a story,' Polly said. 'It's the truth. I can prove it, if necessary.'

'Prove it? How?'

She did not answer that question. 'What's more,' she

continued, 'I think you've had a bit of a conscience about it, which suggests to me that you know who stole the money in the first place.'

'How could I possibly . . .'

'Who pointed the finger at my dad.'

She had kept her temper admirably – so far. Beneath the table, she pressed her knees together and squeezed her fingers tightly into fists.

She was still in command of the situation. At any moment, though, she expected Dominic to say something that would raise her hackles and sweep away her self-control. She would have preferred to talk of things other than the past, matters other than betrayal and deception and extortion. But this was the substance of his life and she could not blink the fact that it was also the bond that had brought them together, that link and nothing much else.

'I do not know who pointed the finger at your father,' he said. 'My father may know that but I have no intention of asking him.'

'What about your uncle?'

'Guido? What about Guido?'

'He would know. He's bound to know.'

'Polly,' Dominic said, 'that part of it, you have to let it go.'

'Why should I?'

'It's too long ago.'

'God!' Polly said, scathingly. 'Too long ago! We're still paying for it.'

'All right,' Dominic said. 'Eat your soup.'

'Eat my . . .'

'Eat your soup and we will talk about it rationally.'

'I'm not upset.'

'You have every right to be upset,' Dominic said. 'Please. Eat.'

'Talk about what rationally?' Polly said.

'How I can best make amends.'

'I see,' said Polly.

She lifted her spoon and began to eat.

Dominic smiled and began to eat too. They ate in silence for a moment or two then he looked up at her and said, 'Good?'

'Yes,' Polly agreed. 'Very good.'

On her way from the tram Babs encountered Dennis. She had in fact come up behind him as he'd been staggering back from Brady's where he'd been drinking the last of the profits on the sale of the two motorcycles. He had turned the short journey into an epic – at least the alcohol had – and had covered God knows how much territory, reeling from one side of the Calcutta Road to the other in great ragged loops and half-circles so that it seemed like a miracle that he had wound up in Lavender Court at all.

Here whatever was left of his senses – mere homing instinct, perhaps – had kicked in and he had put himself into intermittent communication with the tenement wall, rolling and rubbing along it, guided by the iron works' eternal flame. Babs came clicking round the corner at her customary fast lick and spotted her lover's brother at precisely the same moment as he came into opposition with empty space – a close-mouth – and, deceived by darkness, leaned heavily upon it, leaned and leaned, listing and reeling into the close so that by the time Babs reached him he was lying in an astonished heap on the horizontal stone amid cat pee, crumpled newspapers and crushed cigarette butts.

'Dennis, for God's sake!' Babs said. 'Get up.'

'Canny.'

'Get' – a toe to the tail-bone – 'up.'

The mumbled mouthful was not flattering to womankind; Babs didn't take it personally. She leaned over, grabbed Dennis by the lapels and hoisted him to his feet. He lolled against her, burping, his gaze fixed on some translucent will-o'-the-wisp that danced across the backs, that skipped and shimmied over the black pools like sunshine on fresh asphalt. He watched the sonsy fairy dance and felt the lassie's breasts against his back and, though Barbara knew it not, had one of those odd laxative visions that come upon drunks and poets from time to time, a moment of love for all mankind, a woolly, welcoming epiphany that told him what it meant to be a man.

Babs too knew what it meant to be a man.

She side-stepped neatly as Dennis, with surprising ease, chucked up his breakfast and an ocean of brown beer.

'You are,' she said, 'disgustin',' and stomped off out of the close, leaving Dennis swaying like a mountain ash and wondering if he should topple forward or backward or if he might somehow make it home to bed.

Babs exited from one close, walked thirty paces, entered the close at No. 10 and, without sympathy for anyone who might be sleeping within, battered on the door of the Hallops' flat until Billy opened it.

Babs was in no mood for sauce. 'Your brother's lyin' blind drunk in the close next door,' she snapped. 'Tell Jackie t' go an' fetch him.'

'Jackie's in bed, but.'

'Then get him up, sonny, get the bugger up.'

She stomped upstairs to the top-floor landing and rapped on the glossy brown door. No answer; no one, apart from Rosie, was at home. Mammy was at work, of course, and – now she remembered – Polly had told her that she intended going into Glasgow straight from the office and wouldn't be back until late afternoon. Babs toyed with the notion that Polly might be out there with a chunk of *her* money – Auntie Janet's money, technically – stuffed into her handbag, shopping like a mad woman. But that wasn't Polly's style; whatever had taken Polly up town it wouldn't be that, wouldn't be larceny.

Babs let herself in with her latch-key.

She lobbed her hat on to the lady-lamp and went into the

bedroom. No Rosie. She took off her coat, tossed it on to the bed and went through the hall to the kitchen. Still no Rosie, no sign of Rosie.

Babs experienced a slight spooky shiver; the deserted kitchen, all clean and tidy, reminded her a little of Lon Chaney's basement in *Street of the Damned*. Anger melding into apprehension, she pulled back the curtain on the niche bed. Rosie's body was not sprawled upon the quilt, however, and Babs, with a little snort at her own stupidity, soon found her sister's neatly printed note upon the table, propped against the bowl that covered the plate that supported the cold pork pie that was supposed to be her, Babs's, lunch.

Gone to the library. Back at four. Love Rosie.

Babs sighed, put on the kettle and, unbuttoning her jumper and blouse as she went, returned to the front bedroom to change.

She felt isolated in the empty apartment, not lonely, certainly not threatened, just – cut off. She'd been feeling that way for several days. She suspected it might have something to do with what had happened with Aunt Janet or maybe with the fact that Rosie was about to land a job in the city, for a job in Glasgow was considered better than a job in grimy old Govan. She was a wee bit envious of Rosie, envious of Polly too. She didn't have her sisters' natural good looks or refinement, the collection of articulate little habits that lifted them, albeit only an inch or two, out of the pack and made them different. She wasn't different. She was much the same as other girls in other closes; not starving, not sick, not ambitious. She didn't want a big house, fancy furniture, fur coats – well, maybe one fur coat: all she wanted was to have an easy time and, now and then, some fun, lots and lots of fun.

Knock-knock.

'Who's there?'

'Jackie.'

'Jackie who?'

'Don't be a clown, Babs. It's Jackie, from downstairs.'

She had peeled down to her Twix wool-silk vest and drawers, had loosened but not removed her stockings and her elastic pull-on brassiere.

She didn't know why she'd changed or what she was going to change into, what she was going to do for the rest of the afternoon let alone the evening. She had taken her clothes off just to be comfortable and would have munched her pork pie with the plate on her lap and her feet propped on the side of the range, toasting her bum like a bread roll.

She padded into the hall, not dishevelled but — what was the word Polly used, that naughty French word? — *déshabillé*. Yep, she knew what the word meant now, standing there, not even shivering, with Jackie just outside the door. Her niggling sense of isolation departed, erased by Jackie's Hallop's presence.

Suddenly she was herself again, her own sweet, adorable self.

'Bab-sey, open the bloody door, eh?'

She opened the door.

She struck a pose, one arm raised, hair fluffed out.

'Hello there, big boy,' she drawled. 'Whut cain I do faw you?'

'Jez-zus!' Jackie said. 'What's this?'

'What does it look like?'

'Jez-zus!'

'Are you just gonna stand there like a dooley?'

'What? Nah, I'm ... I found Dennis.'

'Good,' Babs said. 'Now, come *in*.'

'But you're not decent.'

'That's because nobody's home.'

'Aye, aye!' said Jackie, grinning, and skipped eagerly into the hall.

'I've one question for you,' Polly said, 'one question to begin with: how long did you intend to let my mother go on paying?'

'Until you no longer had need of my protection,' Dominic said.

'Oh, that's rich,' said Polly. 'That really is rich.'

'It is, however, the fact of the matter,' Dominic told her. 'How shall I put it? I inherited not only your father's debt—'

'There was no debt.'

'All right, I accept that,' Dominic said, placatingly. 'I inherited what I thought was a genuine debt from my father and with it a certain obligation to look out for your welfare.'

'You sound like a damned politician,' Polly said. 'Trust me, pay your taxes, and I will protect you. You may not like it but I know what's best.'

'That is a very harsh judgement on our system of government.'

'Never mind the government,' Polly said. 'What are you going to do to make amends? You won't be getting your monthly screw from us from now on, that's for sure. A few shillings may mean nothing to you, Mr Manone, but it means a lot to us.'

'Polly, my business is built on shillings.'

'Some business!' Polly said.

She wasn't angry with him. In spite of having consumed a substantial lunch she was clear-headed and sharp, enjoying the thrust and parry, gratified to be standing up to a man who had had such a shadowy existence on the periphery of her awareness for so long, who had had such an influence on her life and whom she had blamed, willy-nilly, for every bad thing.

'I will tell you this,' Dominic said, 'for it's no great secret: it is not my business at all. It is still my father's business. He keeps a close watch on what I do here in Scotland. He also takes a lion's share of our profits.'

'How is that done?' Polly asked.

'By credit transfer,' Dominic said.

'I mean, why do you do it?'

'What choice have I?' said Dominic. 'He is my father. Everything I have I owe to his enterprise, his industry. He gave me everything.'

'And takes most of it back,' said Polly.

'Well.' Dominic shrugged. 'Since the market crashed he needs every penny just to keep his head above water.'

'Is he a gangster?'

'No.'

'Are you a gangster?'

'What do you think?' Dominic said.

'My daddy was – only they didn't call it that back then.'

'Not everything I do is strictly within the law,' Dominic admitted. 'You know that already, of course. Walsh must have told you.'

'I didn't need Patsy to tell me,' Polly said. 'I've *been* to the Rowing Club. I've *met* O'Hara. I'll tell you something, I used to hate you. Really. I used to loathe and detest you.'

'Used to?'

It was far into the afternoon now. Clamour from the streets had quietened. In an hour or so men would come pouring into the city from the football grounds, pubs would open and Glasgow would be possessed by other Saturday sounds, all raucous and belligerent. Within Goodman's the tables had begun to empty, waitresses were clearing and re-setting for dinner. On the table in front of Polly nothing remained of the meal except a heavy silver coffee pot, little cups and a dish of sugar cubes.

'I don't know what to make of you,' Polly said quietly.

'Is that why you are so reluctant to ask me for what you want?' Dominic said. 'Or do you not really know what you want?'

'Oh, I know what I want,' Polly said. 'I want money.'

He frowned and nodded at the same time, as if the

banality of her request had disappointed but not surprised him. 'How much?'

'One hundred and fifty pounds, in cash,' Polly said.

He nodded again, but said nothing.

'And,' Polly went on, 'final settlement of the debt that never was.'

'The hundred and fifty,' Dominic said, 'is that by any chance your estimate of what your mother has paid to my family over the past dozen years?'

'No,' Polly said. 'I'm prepared to write that off.'

'That is very generous of you.'

'I take it you're not quibbling?'

'No, I'm not quibbling,' Dominic said. 'But I am curious about the exactness of the sum.'

'All I need,' Polly said, 'is enough to settle our debts and to be free and clear of any further obligation to you or your family.'

'Ah!' Dominic said. 'And then what will you do?'

'I think,' Polly said, 'my mother intends to get married again.'

'So she told me,' Dominic said.

'You disapprove?'

'On the contrary,' Dominic said. 'What about you?'

'What about me?'

'Will you marry?'

'I might,' Polly said, 'if someone asked me.'

'Someone, not just anyone?' Dominic said.

'No, not just anyone.'

'So you have no one particular in mind?'

Polly said, 'Aren't we drifting off the subject, rather?'

'The money? That is not a problem. I will see to it that you have your hundred and fifty pounds in cash no later than Monday afternoon. I will have it delivered to you personally at the Burgh Hall. I take it you do not want your mother to know where the money comes from?'

'That's right,' Polly said. 'And our so-called debt to the Manones?'

'Written off,' said Dominic.

'In that case,' Polly said, 'I doubt if we'll see each other again.'

'That,' Dominic said, 'is my one regret.'

'I can't believe,' Polly said, 'you've grown so attached to us that you'll miss us for one moment. Surely you've enough "obligations" to keep you occupied without bothering about some scruffy lot from Lavender Court.'

'If,' Dominic said, 'if we do meet again, Polly, neither one of us will be in debt to the other or under any obligation.'

'What do you mean?'

'It would be just you, and me.'

'I still don't see what you—'

'I think you do,' said Dominic.

'Dear God!' Polly said. 'Don't tell me you only agreed to my terms because you think I'll—'

'No obligations,' Dominic said. 'None.'

'Am I supposed to feel grateful?'

'I was hoping for something other than gratitude.'

'Huh!' Polly could think of no other reply, no honest reply. 'Huh!'

Dominic said, 'If I happened to be waiting outside your office next Saturday at one o'clock would you ignore me?'

'Of course not. I'm not that impolite.'

'Would you have lunch with me again?'

'I – I might.' Even to Polly's ears, it sounded lame; worse than lame, it sounded coy. She had never thought of herself as a flirt and had no intention of letting Dominic Manone put her into that position. She squared her shoulders. 'What would be the point?' she said. 'Look, what do you want from me?'

'I think I want to marry you,' Dominic said.

'*What?*'

'I would, however, be prepared to settle for another lunch engagement.'

'Are you ... is this the beginning of a courtship?'

'Probably,' Dominic said. 'Lunch? Next Saturday?'

And Polly, without hesitation, said, 'Why not?'

Chapter Twenty

Late night in the parlour of the house beside the park, the room lit only by the rays from a standard lamp and the embers of the coal fire in the grate, a thick, ectoplasmic haze of cigar smoke concentrating the light in the region of the hearth where Dominic and his uncle were seated, one in a Georgian armchair, the other, less at ease, on the sofa.

Guido had removed his waistcoat and shirt. He was clad only in trousers and an undervest, his long, skinny arms fungus white, his chest shrunken, his throat criss-crossed with turkey-neck wrinkles. More frustrated than angry at Dominic's recalcitrance, he had been wheedling away at his nephew for the best part of an hour and he was tired now and wanted only to go to bed.

Dominic had also shed his waistcoat and had unbuttoned his shirt. He lay in the armchair, somnolent as a drunkard, still as a snake, watching his uncle, waiting for it to dawn on the old man that he, Dominic, was master of his own destiny and that he, Guido Manone, had finally met his match.

'For the last time, Uncle,' he said, 'I am not going to feed Walsh to the coppers. I have no intention of making an anonymous telephone call to some detective in the CID to inform him that Patrick Walsh fled the country on the night that McGuire was murdered. In any case, the coppers don't know Walsh from Adam. Patsy has no record of arrest.'

'But the set-up—' Guido protested.

'There is no set-up. There is only coincidence,' Dominic interrupted. 'The case is dead, closed – or soon will be. If the coppers were sniffing around the Rowing Club or had O'Hara or Tony under surveillance then I might be tempted to divert their attention to Patsy Walsh, but there's no need. Do you not understand? No need.'

'What if he comes back to Glasgow?'

'What if he does?' said Dominic. 'There is no possibility of him doing work for us again. Walsh is well aware of that. He's not one of your hooligans with fewer brains than a grasshopper. If and when he comes back here, he can work for Flint, or for Deasy over in Possil. We have nothing to do with these gentlemen. We are above that now.'

'If that is what you think why did you deal with McGuire?'

'I dealt with McGuire because he overstepped the mark. I had him taken out because of the children.'

'Children?'

'Tommy's children.'

'None the less . . .'

Dominic spoke softly, using the same seductive tone that he might have used to Polly. 'No one is gonna grieve for Charles McGuire, Uncle, not even his wife. Flint will see to it that she continues to get her share, and that will be the end of it. Do you not remember my father's golden rule? No trouble, make no trouble, and the police leave you alone. How long have you been in this country, Guido? Twenty-four, twenty-five years?'

'More.'

'How many times have you been in a court of law? Never. Not once. Do you think that is because we are lucky? No, it is because we are clever, clever and unassertive.'

'McGuire had to be got rid of.'

'I know it,' Dominic said. 'That is why I made it happen.'

'Because of the children?'

'Yes, mainly because of the children.'

'And this other thing?' Guido asked.

'What other thing?'

'Concerning the girl.'

'If you mean my liking for Polly Conway,' Dominic said, 'I have no reason to explain myself to you.'

'Your aunt and I are . . .'

'I have respect for both of you,' Dominic said, 'but when it comes to marriage it is up to me to make the choice. I am not going to be herded into the bridal bed like some bovine girl from a Tuscan hill village.'

'She is not Italian. She is not a Catholic.'

'Am I?' Dominic said. 'I have never set foot in the old country. And you know where I stand on religion.'

'What is it about this girl that attracts you?'

'I want her.'

'Then take her. You do not have to talk of marriage.'

'I want her for my wife.'

'You hardly know her,' Guido said.

'I know her well enough,' Dominic said. 'I thought you were keen for me to marry and settle down?'

'But this girl . . .' Guido shrugged. 'Not to this girl.'

'Because she is Lizzie Conway's daughter?'

'She is . . .' For an instant it seemed that the old man would let that sentence trail off too. He was riled by his nephew's refusal to listen to sense, though, and snapped, 'She is beneath you.'

'Beneath me?' Dominic said. 'Is she any more beneath me than the girls that Teresa has been throwing in my direction? Those poor, bewildered immigrants with their family connections trailing behind them like withered vines? I will tell you what the attraction is: I am not required to feel pity for Polly Conway, that I am favouring her. Quite the contrary, in fact.'

'Then you do not understand what it is to be a Manone.'

Dominic stubbed out the little cigar that had been smoking in his fingers. He ground it thoroughly into the big glass ashtray on the carpet beside the chair. He looked up at his uncle, studying him, still waiting for that moment when frustration would change to apprehension.

He said, 'I understand what it is to be loved.'

'Loved? She does not love you.'

'Perhaps not yet, not quite yet. But it will come.' Dominic straightened and sat upright. 'You would not be making this fuss if I told you that I was interested in Lina Pirollo, would you?'

'She is a nice girl. She would suit you well.'

'And, of course, if I married his daughter we would soon be able to get our hands on Pirollo's business?'

'Which is something that your father would be grateful for.'

'I am sure that is so,' said Dominic. 'But what good would the pretty Miss Pirollo be to me afterwards?'

'She would bear your children and look after your house.'

'But would she *understand*?' Dominic said.

Guido looked up, his chin tilting away from his chest. 'Understand?'

'What I am? What I do?' Dominic said. 'I do not want a wife who lives in the kitchen and keeps her mouth shut. I want a wife I can talk to, a wife from whom I don't have to keep secrets.'

'I am tired,' Guido said. 'We will talk of this another time.'

'No, we will talk of it now,' Dominic said. 'We will talk of it now so that you may have an opportunity to prepare Aunt Teresa for what is about to happen. And to cook up your excuses.'

'My excuses?' Guido said. 'I have no need for excuses.'

'Frank Conway did not steal from my father,' Dominic said.

'I do not know what you are—'

'Did he?'

'What nonsense has this girl been telling you?'

'*You* took it,' Dominic said. '*You* spirited it away. And as if that was not bad enough, you accused Frank Conway. But he fooled you, did he not? He joined up and died in the fighting in Flanders not to protect you but to protect his family.'

'This is untrue. This is fantasy.'

'Why did you need so much money so desperately? Did you get a girl into trouble? Did you have to bribe some woman, or buy off her husband, perhaps? What *was* the reason, Uncle Guido? Why did you not just ask my father to bail you out? Will you not answer me?'

'There is nothing to answer.'

'Were you too ashamed to talk to your own brother? So ashamed that you would steal from the family rather than admit what you had done?' Dominic said. 'What was it? It *was* a woman, wasn't it?'

'What if it was?' Guido said, sullenly. 'It is a long time ago.'

'Conway's wife?' said Dominic.

'What are you saying?' Guido roused himself. 'I would not touch that fat slut. I have too much respect for myself. You think I took Carlo's money to give to a woman, do you? I did not. I took it because he twisted it out of me. Conway. Frank Conway blackmailed it out of me. He knew what happened.'

'What did happen?'

'I thought she was willing.'

'God in heaven, Guido! You raped someone?'

'What if I did? She was nothing, dirt, sleeping with her sister's husband, screwing her sister's husband.'

'You raped her,' Dominic said. 'Then you paid her to keep quiet.'

'I did not pay her. I paid Frank Conway. He fixed it.'

'Where is this woman now?'

'I do not know.'

'You do, damn it,' Dominic said. 'What is her name, Guido?'

'I do not know. I cannot remember.'

'Guido, what is her name?'

'Janet.' He hesitated. 'Janet McKerlie.'

'Lizzie Conway's sister?'

'Yes.' He stood, looming, big carpenter's hands folded at chest height. 'Now do you understand why you must have no more to do with Polly Conway?'

'No, Uncle, I don't,' Dominic said.

'But what if she finds out?'

'I will make sure that she does not find out.'

'How will you do that?'

'By making her one of us,' said Dominic.

Janet said, 'He gave it to you, didn't he? What did you have to do t' get it, that's what I'd like to know.'

'Look,' Polly said, 'the whole thing was a mistake. Here's your money, every last penny. Just take it and put it away safe.'

'Where did you get it?' Janet said. 'If it came from the Manones . . .'

'It didn't. The guy I lent it to,' Polly said, 'paid it back.'

They were alone on the landing at the top of the turret steps.

The wind moaned in the stairwell. Two floors down the gush of a lavatory hung suspended in the half-dark. The leaning old tenement smelled fresh tonight, though, its saturated odours swept away by a dry east wind. Polly was well wrapped up, a scarf cowled over her head and knotted beneath her chin. Janet, however, had slipped out in a thin dress and looked, Polly thought, even more shrunken than usual.

'I can't leave her for long,' Janet said. 'She'll wonder what's goin' on.'

'Take it then,' Polly said. 'It's all there.'

She had withdrawn the money from the new bank account and put it together with the money that Dominic had had delivered to the office in a plain manila envelope. The notes were high denomination, and the packet seemed remarkably slender for the amount it contained.

'Count it, if you like,' Polly said, as her aunt accepted the envelope.

'I'll take your word for it,' Janet said. She hesitated. 'I don't suppose I'll be seein' Lizzie for a while?'

'I doubt it.'

'I should never have said what I did.'

'No,' Polly agreed. 'It wasn't very wise.'

'Will she come back?'

'Mammy?' Polly said. 'Oh, I expect so, once she calms down.'

'I don't know what to tell Gran. She's not as daft as you might think,' Janet said. 'She knows somethin's goin' on.'

'I'll come in, shall I?' Polly said. 'I'll tell her Mammy's under the weather and won't be round to see her for a week or so.'

'I wish you would.'

Janet held the envelope as if it had no more value than yesterday's newspaper. She was, Polly thought, remorseful but lacked the ability to display anything but bitterness. When she turned to step back into the apartment, Polly laid a hand on her arm. 'Did you really imagine that Daddy would come back to you, or, for that matter, come back at all?'

'Frank? Nah. He was too frightened.'

'Frightened of what?' said Polly. 'Carlo Manone?'

'Responsibility,' Janet said, 'that's what our Frank was afraid of. But I don't suppose you know what I'm talkin' about.'

'Oh, but I do,' said Polly. 'Believe me, Aunt Janet, I do,' and followed the woman indoors.

Everything was happening so quickly that Lizzie had no idea whether her life was at last coming together or was finally falling apart.

Rosie had been invited 'to take up a position' with Oswald

Shelby, Sons & Partners and, heeding Mr Feldman's advice, had accepted, even though it meant leaving school in mid-term. She had bidden a tearful farewell to the Institute on Friday afternoon, had put off her uniform and, looking quite the little lady, had gone off on Monday morning to catch the tramcar into Glasgow with all the other shop-girls and clerks.

Lizzie had not been there to wish her well on her first day of employment. She had been off at her usual early hour to begin her shift at the laundry and it had been left to Polly to ensure that Rosie ate a hearty breakfast, washed her face, combed her hair and had enough money in her purse for tram fare and a bite of lunch.

It had also been left to Polly to mend fences between Mammy and Janet. Once Janet had her money back, though, and Lizzie had been coaxed round to Laurieston to offer the olive branch, Janet's confessions soon sank down into the silt of habit and, within a week or two, were lost in banal revelations about the state of Grandma McKerlie's bladder and bowels.

There was also no doubt that young Jackie Hallop was 'courting' Babs and that Babs, for all her hoity-toity airs, had developed an affinity with the boy downstairs, an affinity, Lizzie suspected, that had more to do with sex than with planning a future together. Lizzie did not dislike Jackie. He had qualities that reminded her of her late husband. While she would have preferred Babs to take up with someone as honest and reliable as Bernard she couldn't deny that Jackie's exuberance did have a certain appeal. Besides, the motorcycle repair business seemed to be flourishing and the Hallops were seldom short of cash.

What she objected to was that Jackie, Dennis and young sister Louise had all but taken up residence in her kitchen. They would appear at all hours to play cards, listen to the gramophone or simply chew the fat. It was all that Lizzie – with a little help from Polly – could do to persuade them to leave before midnight.

Jackie would tell her, 'I fair like your house, Mrs Conway. Bags o' room, bags o' room, an' nobody for to nag us.'

'Aye, an' it disnae smell neither,' Louise would put in, as if that in itself was a compliment.

What disconcerted Lizzie was not so much the appearance of these unlikely cuckoos in her nest as the fact that her chicks seemed to enjoy the Hallops' company. Rosie, for instance, who spent her days in the unimaginably quiet atmosphere of Shelby's antiquarian bookshop, would throw herself wildly into the card games, would whoop and clack with the best of them. Even Polly, usually so sensible and reserved, would be lured into Chasing the Ace or taking on the bank at Newmarket.

Two or three nights a week – always on Sundays – there would be a houseful; French toast sizzling in the pan, teacups on the table, bottled beer, a great, hovering, throat-catching pall of cigarette smoke that even a wide-open kitchen window could not dissipate.

Expecting sympathy, Lizzie complained to Bernard.

'Cards?' Bernard said, neutrally. 'Well!'

The following Sunday evening Bernard turned up at Lavender Court bearing a bunch of flowers for Lizzie, a box of dates for the girls, and – just by chance – a pocketful of loose change which, by the time he had finished showing the Hallops what an old soldier remembered about the art of Pontoon, was considerably heavier than when he'd arrived.

A life coming together, or a life falling apart?

Lizzie had no idea.

All she could be sure of was that routine upon which her existence had been based six months ago now had to be squeezed into days that seemed to grow ever shorter. In addition, she was bored by elements that had once seemed crucial, among them the daily grind of sanitising infected garments and labelling poor folks' intimate possessions, of trudging up to the backlands of Laurieston to engage in guarded chat with Janet and help her ailing mother undress. If it hadn't been for Bernard she might

have envied her girls their blossoming, might have cried herself
to sleep at the realisation that they were off and running and
would soon leave her behind.

Her trust in Bernard allayed such fears, however, and she
was forced to concede that her restlessness stemmed mainly from
the fact that too much was happening too soon, and that she
couldn't for the life of her predict just where it was all going
to end, or, for that matter, when.

'Patience, dearest,' Bernard would say when, on those rare
occasions when she had him to herself, she would shed a little
tear and try to explain how adversely progress was affecting her.
'What's for us will not go by us.'

'What does *that* mean?' Lizzie would snivel.

'Lord knows,' Bernard would tell her. 'It's a sayin' my
mother's very fond of – so it probably doesn't mean anythin'
at all. The Italians have a similar sort of sayin', but I can't think
of it offhand.'

'The Italians!'

'You're just unsettled. It's the time of year.' Bernard would
put an arm around her. 'Here, have a hug, that usually does
the trick.'

Lizzie would not resist the hug – having more or less fished
for it – but she was sometimes just a little disappointed that her
wonderful man could not make everything come right, could not
quite usurp the phantoms of her past or bring the future to pass
right there and then. It was unreasonable but she could not help
it; what she wanted was too much of a tangle in her mind for
her to understand, let alone for poor Bernard to fix.

If anyone possessed a magic wand that person was Dominic
Manone. He had waved it to find Polly and Babs decent jobs
when decent jobs were scarcer than apples on a fig tree. He had
protected them from the likes of O'Hara. Sure, he had charged
sweetly for the privilege, but he had always been there and had
never let them down. Lizzie had no idea why she should be
afraid of him now.

Worry, like a sudden jab of pain, would draw her up while she stooped over the reeking tubs or bent over a garment with her needle, would cause her breath to catch in her chest as she climbed the stairs in Laurieston or fried eggs in the pan for all and sundry in the kitchen at home. Worry about Polly. She would watch Polly flick out cards at the kitchen table, watch her smile as she raked in the coppers and small silver that skill or luck had brought her – and would wonder what Polly was keeping to herself, what secrets lay within her daughter that she, Lizzie Conway, had not put there and had not nurtured.

She was deceiving herself, of course. She knew perfectly well why she was afraid of Dominic Manone and why she could not confide in Bernard.

Polly and Dominic: Polly stepping out with Dominic Manone, stepping out of the black Italian motorcar that she, Lizzie, had never once set foot in; her Polly stepping out with an ease, a style, a confidence that she had never possessed. Where had it all sprung from, this grooming, this poise and coolness, this apparent acceptance of all that had once seemed so gloomy and intimidating? How could she stop it? Or should she stop it, or was this just the price that had to be paid for security?

All coming together or all falling apart?

Only time would tell, Lizzie supposed: God help us, only time will tell.

It was two weeks before Easter when Babs dropped the bomb-shell. She told Polly first. She told Polly for the simple reason that she had to tell someone and Polly these days seemed to be the only person she could trust to offer the sort of advice that a girl in her situation required.

The curious thing about it was that Babs was not dismayed when her condition was confirmed by the lady doctor in the little shopfront consulting room at the far end of the Calcutta Road.

So far she hadn't found sexual intercourse all it was cracked up to be and did not regard conception as one of nature's great mysteries. As she walked home from her second consultation, though, she felt quite joyful, and rather fulfilled. There had been something inevitable about her connection with Jackie Hallop and nothing mysterious about how the damned thing had happened, only which of the dozen or so acts of union had actually put one up the spout.

Naturally she was tense and a wee bit anxious but she didn't doubt that Mammy would know how to fix it, that Mammy would settle everything for her and her baby, and that once she got over feeling rotten in the morning everything would be all right.

'Pregnant,' Polly said. 'Dear God! Are you sure?'

'Had a test. Didn't need a test but had one anyway.'

'You don't seem very upset.'

'I'm not.'

'I would be if I were you,' Polly said. 'I'd be scared to death.'

'Aye, but you're not me,' Babs said. 'Anyway, there's nothin' to be scared of. Heck, it happens a hundred times a day, a thousand times a day. Mammy had four of us an' it never did her any harm, did it?'

'Have you told Jackie yet?'

'Haven't told anyone. You're the first to know.'

'Thanks,' said Polly. 'But if you think I'm going to tell Mammy, think again. You'll have to do that yourself.'

'Wonder how she'll take it?' Babs said.

'Not well,' said Polly.

'Well,' said Babs with astonishing stoicism, 'there's nothin' any of us can do about it now. Maybe I should tell Jackie first, eh?'

'Maybe you should,' said Polly.

✼   ✼   ✼

'Jeez-*zus!*' Jackie exclaimed. 'A baby! Are you sure, Babs? I mean, how d' you know? I mean, you're not havin' it right away, are you?'

'Don't be so bloody daft,' Babs said. 'Not till October.'

'How ... how ...'

'Think about it,' Babs said. 'Think about it *verrry* carefully, Jackie, see if you can figure it out.'

'I don't mean that,' Jackie said. 'I mean – eh – how're you feelin'?'

'Okay.'

'Sick?'

'Queasy in the mornin', but I'm nearly past that stage.'

'Heartburn?'

'What're you, a doctor?'

'My mam always got the heartburn.'

'Jackie?'

'Uh?'

'I'm waitin', Jackie.'

'Waitin' for what, but?'

'The magic words, Jackie.'

'What magic words?'

'Will – you – marry – me?'

'Oh, that!' Jackie said. 'Sure, I'll marry you.'

'Is that it?' said Babs.

'What more d' you want?'

'A kiss would be nice.'

'No problem,' Jackie said and, rather tenderly, took her into his arms.

Dominic gave Polly no opportunity to devise an excuse; not that she would have done so in any case. She was distracted, though, wondering how Mammy would react when Babs broke the bad news. In Bab's book it wasn't bad news at all, simply something that had to be dealt with as a consequence of the fun she'd had with Jackie Hallop.

Polly found her sister's carefree attitude to motherhood quite bewildering. There should have been embarrassment, shame, penitent tears, denial of responsibility, a shoving of blame on to the guy; the standard response of every pathetic little heroine in every romance that Polly had ever read. But Babs had never been a dreamer. She was a realist, not a romantic. She had never subscribed to the moonlit vision of, say, *Breathless Surrender* that made other girls so vulnerable. Polly often wished that she could be more like Babs, less sophisticated and more adaptable.

She was preoccupied when Dominic picked her up outside the office on Saturday afternoon and it took her a good five minutes to realise that they weren't heading into Glasgow for the usual pleasant lunch at Goodman's.

Eventually, Polly said, 'You're taking me to your house, aren't you?'

'Yes.'

'You're taking me to meet your aunt?'

'Yes.'

'Why didn't you warn me?'

'I was afraid you would take fright.'

'Is that what a nice Italian girl would do, take fright?'

'If you were an Italian girl,' Dominic said, 'there would be no need to introduce you to my aunt. She would know who you were, who your father was, and your grandfather, and just how much servility it would take to impress you.'

'Or vice versa?' Polly said.

He glanced at her, not quite smiling. 'Yes, or vice versa.'

'I'm not the servile sort, you know,' Polly said.

'I know that.'

She looked from the window towards the walls of the mineral terminus, at the cranes that lofted themselves into view and the mean tenements that cowered beneath them. She spotted a little band of ragged children huddled against the wall of a public house, a girl of just nine or ten with a baby sister or brother cradled in her skinny arms, her face scalded by the cold spring wind, her feet and legs bare and dirty.

She had never had to go barefoot, none of them had, not even when things were at their worst. She had never had to suffer biting poverty like that poor wee lass. Mammy had protected them, had saved them, had lifted them up; yet they had been shaped by the poverty around them, by knowledge of their own salvation, hardened, not weakened by it.

The children whipped out of sight as the Alfa accelerated.

Polly said, 'This thing between us, Dominic, is it serious?'

He glanced at her. 'On my part it has never been any-thing else.'

'You're seeking your family's approval, aren't you?'

'I do not need their approval.'

'What would your father say if he knew about – about me?'

'He already knows,' Dominic told her. 'I wrote to him last week and told him that I had fallen in love with a young woman and that, with or without his permission, I intended to marry her.'

'Oh!' Polly said. 'What if she doesn't want to marry you? Don't you think it might have been a good idea to write to her first?'

'I am not one to rush things,' Dominic said, rather stiffly.

She could not be sure whether she had insulted him or merely increased his uncertainty. He was more nervous than she was about the meeting and suspected that his declarations of indifference as to what the family would think of her amounted to little more than bravado.

'Would you like *me* to write to *you*?' she said.

'Polly. Please.'

'Please?'

'Please don't tease, not today.'

'You want me to behave myself, is that it?'

'Yes.' He was startled by his own vehemence and, after a moment, burst out laughing. 'Yes, for the love of God, behave yourself.'

She put on a little act, sitting erect in the leather seat, all prim and prissy, lips pursed, eyelashes fluttering, hands folded upon her handbag, neat and prudent and discreet. Inside, though, she was whirling with excitement, anything but calm and controlled. It had just dawned on her that in the last few seconds Dominic had asked her if she would consider becoming his wife.

'Dominic?'

'What is it now?'

'Have I just been proposed to?'

'After a fashion, yes, I suppose you have.'

'And did I give you an answer?'

'You did not,' Dominic told her. 'But at least you did not say No.'

'Will that do for now?' Polly said.

'You will need a little time to consider it, I imagine.'

'Yes,' Polly said. 'If you don't mind.'

'I don't mind,' said Dominic.

'Thank you,' Polly said.

'For what?'

'For asking me anyway,' said Polly.

Chapter Twenty-One

If thirty-five months of active service had taught Bernard anything it was how to wield a spade. He had never been called upon to lay down a line of trenches but he, like many an infantryman, had lived with a rifle in one hand and a digging implement in the other. He had excavated latrines, scraped out gun emplacements, levelled the tops of redoubts and had even been rounded up for burial detail when there was no one else to do the job. He was adequate with a rifle but better with a spade for, like swimming, bicycling or rolling a cigarette, digging, once learned, was a skill never lost.

Once he had set his mind to it, therefore, Bernard's rockery made rapid progress. It might even have been finished before Good Friday if only the weather had held, and the Conway girls had not decided all to go daft at once.

He had gone to the pictures in Glasgow with Lizzie on Saturday evening, an early showing of *The Cockeyed World* which was definitely on the racy side but which Lizzie had seemed to enjoy. It was the first time Bernard had really liked a 'talking picture' and hadn't found it stilted. In fact he had been too engrossed in the badinage between the characters, especially when Lili Damita was on screen, to do more than clutch Lizzie's hand and pinch the odd chocolate bon-bon from the box on her lap.

Lizzie had not been her usual self, though. He had noticed it after they had come out of the cinema and were seated in a booth in the New Savoy fish restaurant eating haddock and chips. She had seemed not just tired but 'down', and worryingly disinclined to confide in him. When he had asked what the matter was she had been evasive. He had asked her again as they had waited at the tram stop before going their separate ways.

'I don't know, dearest,' Lizzie had said. 'I just don't know what's wrong with me these days.'

'You're not ill, are you?'

'Nah, nah. I'm fine.'

'Is it the girls?'

She had shaken her head, without much conviction; a moment later her tram had come rattling down Renfield Street and he had kissed her and helped her on to the platform with a feeling that he had somehow let her down. He had loitered on the pavement, tempted for one silly moment to hare after the vehicle, but it was too late. Instead he had caught the last west-bound tram out to Knightswood, puzzled and gloomy and teased by a nameless guilt.

He had intended to spend Sunday afternoon gardening and make the long trip over to the Gorbals in the early evening. When he had told his mother of his plans, she had sniffed disapprovingly, had left a plate of sardine sandwiches for his lunch and had gone zipping off to take part in a special afternoon Daffodil Service for Guild members in Whiteinch Parish Church.

Bernard worked patiently with spade and riddle, sieving the earth that would bed the rockery. He had already put down two drainage channels and layered them with stones that he had gathered and lugged back from a building site at the back of the old Muttonhole Farm. He laboured diligently, shaping the mounds of soft brown earth that made him think of Lizzie, though he could not imagine why. Somehow it did not entirely surprise him when, at about half past two, Lizzie turned up at the cottages.

He had been on the point of quitting. He was already looking forward to a sandwich and a cup of tea when he heard knocking upon the front door. He had left the kitchen door open but did not dare walk through the house, trailing mud. He went along the communal pathway that backed the cottages and down the narrow lane, looked out into the street and saw her there at the door.

She wore a loose donkey-brown overcoat, a vagabond hat and an unmistakable air of harassment. Bernard called out to her and beckoned. She came to him, not quite running. He wiped his hands on his trousers, took her in his arms, gave her a welcoming hug, then led her back down the lane and along the path to the garden.

There were other folk about, neighbours enjoying the spring sunshine and some of the wives had even risked the wrath of God by hanging out washing. There were babies in prams, small children playing at tea-parties on the sparse grass, cats dozing on doorsteps and window sills, all very peaceful and settled.

He seated himself on the top step at the kitchen door and reached down to remove his boots. Then he stopped. She was standing close, looking down at him, and she was crying.

Bernard said, 'I knew there was somethin' wrong. It's one of the girls, isn't it?' Lizzie shook her head.

'Two of the girls,' she said.

'We'd best go inside,' said Bernard.

Perhaps it was tea or several sardine sandwiches that calmed Lizzie down. More likely, though, it was sheer relief at having someone with whom to share her woes. Woes they were too – Bernard did not belittle them – but they weren't insoluble and he saw at once that they might work to everyone's advantage in the long run.

'Both of them,' Lizzie said. 'Why did it have to be both of them? I shouldn't have left them so much by themselves.'

'Lizzie, Lizzie,' Bernard said soothingly. 'They're not wee lassies any more. You did your best. You can't go blamin' yourself.'

'I was selfish, Bernard. Selfish.'

'You're hurt because they're goin' on with you.'

'I wanted somethin' for myself, somethin' left for me.'

'You still have that.'

'I don't. I'll have to take them in, look after them.'

'What?' Bernard said. 'Look after Dominic Manone?'

'Don't make fun of me.'

'I'm not making fun of you, sweetheart,' Bernard said. 'I'm just askin' what it is you think you have to do?'

'Try to ... try to ...'

'Tell me again,' Bernard said, firmly.

'Tell you what?'

'Exactly what happened when you got home last night.'

'Well, they were there, waitin' for me. Babs an' the Hallop boy ...'

'Jackie.'

'Aye, Jackie.'

'Tell me exactly what was said.'

'That she was expectin' his baby an' they were gonna get wed.'

'An' Jackie didn't put up an argument, didn't run for the trees?'

'He seems as keen on marriage as Babs,' Lizzie said. 'Keener, in fact.'

'So,' Bernard said, 'let them get spliced. You're not goin' to stand in their way, are you, Lizzie?'

'How can I?' Lizzie said. 'But they don't know what they're gettin' into. They don't know what marriage is like.'

'Then they'll just have to find out,' Bernard said.

'It's all very well for you, you won't have to look after them.'

'Nor will you,' Bernard told her.

'I will. I will. I can't leave her now, Babs an' the baby,' Lizzie said. 'I can't have her livin' downstairs wi' that crowd, not wi' that crowd, not wi' a brand-new baby.'

Bernard said nothing for a moment. He lit two cigarettes and passed one over the table to Lizzie who took it and inhaled, absently.

The sun had shifted into the west. The front of the cottages lay in shadow, the soft, blue-grey, unrepeatable shadow of early spring. But across the road the trees behind the railings of the estate were filled with sunlight, gnarled trunks gilded, buds and unfolding leaves trembling not with a mid-afternoon breeze but with the thrill of the light itself.

Lizzie stared out at the painted scene, and smoked her cigarette.

Bernard said, 'Tell me about Polly.'

Lizzie spoke without meeting his eye, like a person in a play whose words were meant for the audience.

'Polly,' she said. 'That's even worse.'

'Why is it worse?'

'He took her to the house. He took her there in his motorcar. To meet his relatives. She says he wants to marry her.'

'An' does she want to marry him?' said Bernard.

'She says she does.'

'You knew nothin' about this romance?'

'I had an inklin',' Lizzie said, uncomfortably. 'But I never thought it would come to anythin'. I mean, I thought Polly was far too sensible ever to get mixed up wi' a man like Dominic Manone.'

'Because he's Italian?'

'Because he's a crook.'

'Polly knows that, of course,' Bernard stated.

Lizzie jerked her head, frowning. 'She does. She must.'

'An' loves him in spite of it?' It was on the tip of Bernard's tongue to add '*Or because of it,*' but he had too much savvy to let it slip out.

'I don't know if she loves him,' Lizzie said. 'I never know what Polly's thinkin' or what she feels about anythin' these days.'

'You know she still loves *you*,' Bernard said.

'If she did, she wouldn't . . . God!' Lizzie exclaimed, desperately. 'How can I stand up to a man like Dominic Manone?'

'Do you want to, Lizzie?' Bernard asked. 'I think that's the question you've got to ask yourself. Do you really want to?'

'I can't let her do it, can't let her throw her life away.'

'Would you rather she married someone like Patrick Walsh?' Bernard said. 'From what I gather Polly got rid of *him* pretty quick when he showed signs of gettin' serious.'

'Are you suggestin' that Dominic Manone's the right man for her?'

'Polly seems to think so,' Bernard said.

'She's too young to . . .'

'She's not too young,' Bernard said. 'She's — what? — two or three years older than you were when you had her.'

'That's got nothin' to do with it,' Lizzie said.

'It's got everythin' to do with it,' said Bernard. 'She's your eldest, Lizzie, more like you than you might care to admit. In my opinion, for what it's worth, Polly could do worse than hitch up with Dominic Manone.'

'How can you possibly say that? He's a criminal.'

'Well,' Bernard said, 'there's a lot of those about these days, Lizzie, in and out of jail. Look around you. What do you see? Councillors linin' their own pockets, coppers takin' bribes, members of the parliament up to their armpits in trickery and graft. Look at the street corners, dearest, an' tell me truthfully if you'd rather your daughter married one of those louts, one of those shiftless, never-work-again types than Dominic Manone.'

'That's not fair,' Lizzie said. 'There are plenty o' decent folk in the Gorbals, thousands of honest, hard-workin' men for Polly to choose from.'

'Aye,' Bernard said. 'But it seems she prefers Dominic Manone.'

Lizzie put down the cigarette. She folded her arms across her breasts and hugged herself, rocking a little from side to side in the chair. 'I never thought I'd hear this from you, Bernard,' she said. 'I thought you'd tell me how to stop her, how to turn her away from this marriage.'

Choosing his words with considerable care, Bernard said, 'I notice you're not askin' me to step in an' stop Babs marryin' *her* young man.'

'That's different. It's too late to do anythin' about Babs.'

'Do you think Manone will put Polly on the streets?'

'Don't be so daft.'

'Do you think he won't protect her?'

'No, he'll certainly do that.'

'I don't want to sound callous,' Bernard told her, 'but Polly will be safer with Manone than with anyone else. He won't let any harm come to her. He won't let anythin' from outside touch her. He'll keep her safe an' well provided for, whatever happens.'

Thoroughly confused, Lizzie shook her head.

'I thought you were honest, Bernard,' she stammered. 'I thought you were against all that stuff.'

'I'm honest,' Bernard said, 'only because I have to be. Most times I'm happy to be the way I am. But I may as well tell you, now an' then I wish I wasn't so damned honest. I wish I had just a wee bit more *grab* in me, a wee bit less conscience. Never more so than now. There are no premiums paid out on honesty these days, Lizzie, an' things are not goin' to get much better. Soon it'll be every man for himself, an' take what you can get.'

'An' will you do that, will you take what you can get?'

'Nope,' Bernard said. 'The only thing I want, dearest, is you.'

*   *   *

It was rare, very rare, for Guido and Teresa Manone to be seen out together, walking not hand-in-hand but hand-on-arm like any elderly couple from the big houses in Manor Park Road.

Teresa had insisted upon dragging her husband from the lunch table to take her walking in the park. She had already dragged him from the breakfast table to accompany her to church, for Guido was indrawn and compliant these days, chastened by she knew not what. While he was still prone to grumble he no longer dismissed her claims upon him out of hand; an improvement in relations that Teresa put down to Dominic's up-and-coming engagement to the Conway girl who, even if she were a Scot, seemed to have taken Dominic's measure well enough to want to marry him.

Unfortunately Teresa had no yardstick for measuring the Scots girl. She knew that Polly was the daughter of Lizzie and Frank Conway but she had no intimate knowledge of what had happened to Frank, apart from the fact that he had embezzled a large sum of money from Carlo and had gone off and got himself killed in the war.

She had no curiosity about Lizzie whatsoever, had never once enquired why the big, rather blowsy woman would turn up from time to time to engage her nephew in conversation or why she, that woman, enjoyed a privilege denied to most of Dominic's clients. She was not even sure that Lizzie Conway was 'a client', or even what that word meant. She had consciously courted ignorance of the Manones' affairs since that night – a hundred years ago, it seemed – when she had relinquished her virginity to Guido and with it all rights to individuality.

If she had been blessed with children she might have made her mark through them, ensuring that they were her soldiers, her warriors in the matrimonial war, and through them have reclaimed some of what had been lost to her. But she was old now and her husband, whether he would admit it or not, was old too. All she had to call her own was Dominic, and he had never been hers in the first place. Soon the girl, the stranger, would arrive in her house and steal away the last crumbs of her usefulness.

She walked slowly by Guido's side along the curving path under the plane trees, leaning upon him, obliging him to match his long, creaking stride to her dainty steps.

Sunday in April, a warm afternoon; crocuses fading and daffodils spraying from the grass, children and dogs and courting couples, old couples too, and single men, poor men, spread over the green acres. On the horizon reared the steeples, cranes and scaffolding of industrial Clydeside, a region and a culture about which Teresa knew little.

In silence they strolled half the circuit, a sedate, almost stately couple. She had fur on her hat and collar. He sported spats on top of his hand-lasted shoes. His black alpaca overcoat was buttoned up to the throat, for although the breeze was warm and the young girls were already bare-armed Guido's blood was thinning and the cold was all inside.

Then Teresa said, 'I want to go home.'

'Very well,' Guido said. 'If you are tired we will turn about.'

'Home,' Teresa said, 'to Italy.'

He stopped in his tracks and looked down at her. A frown creased his forehead like the imprint of an axe. 'When did this fit come upon you, woman?' he said. 'Home? Scotland is our home.'

'Dominic has no need of us now, Guido.'

'He will always have need of us.'

'He will have a new wife to look after him.'

'You do not like her, do you?' Guido said.

'I like her well enough.'

'Because she is not Italian, you do not like her.'

'Guido, I just want to go home.'

'Phah!' he exclaimed, not loudly. 'Italy? What is there for us in Italy? What would I do there? Would you have me pretend I am still a soldier and go marching down the Via

Roma waving a flag for the new emperor? Besides, Carlo will never let us go.'

'If you ask him, if you tell him that you are old and tired ...'

'Old? I am not old, and I'm certainly not tired.'

'Look at you,' Teresa said. 'You cannot walk round the park with me without stopping every twenty paces to catch your breath. No, it is time to go home, Guido, to put all this behind us and sit together in the sun.' She hesitated. 'There are pretty girls in Genova too. If you pay them enough they will provide you with company.'

'I have no interest in girls.'

'Write to Carlo. Tell him we want to leave.'

'I will tell him no such thing.' Guido drew her after him, pinching her sleeve. He found a bench and pushed her on to it, folded himself down beside her, big hands hanging between his knees, shoulders slumped. 'We cannot go back to Genova. Carlo still has enemies there. He has enemies everywhere. Why do you think he forbids Dominic to visit his motherland? Why do you think he refuses to let Dominic visit him in America?'

'What do you mean?'

'Dominic is safe here. In Italy or America he would be in danger.'

'This is nonsense,' Teresa said. 'The stories that men make up.'

'Why does Carlo have to make up stories?'

'To seem more important than he is,' Teresa said. 'He does not want you near him, that is the true story. He does not want you on the same piece of land that he stands on. Apart from that, he does not care about us. We have done everything he has asked of us for forty years. Now it is Dominic's turn. He will take care of his wife and she will take care of him. She knows what he does and what he will continue to do and, like me, she will accept it. If she is sensible she will not question him. He must have settled that matter or he would not be proposing marriage.

So' – Teresa sighed gently – 'there is nothing to keep us here, Guido. It is time for us to go.'

'Jesus and Joseph!' Guido said, shaking his head. 'Jesus and Joseph.'

'Do not blaspheme, if you please.'

'I will blaspheme if I feel like it,' the old man said, sulkily.

'If you are afraid to write to Carlo and ask him to let us go home then talk to Dominic. He will write to his father on our behalf.'

'I do not need Dominic to do my dirty . . .' Guido's frown deepened. 'I mean, to communicate with my brother. I will write to Carlo myself.'

'That's good,' said Teresa, as if the matter were closed.

'If,' Guido said, '*if* and when I decide that we are no longer wanted here.'

'Or needed,' Teresa added.

'I suppose we could probably afford to purchase a little place down the coast,' Guido said.

'Where?' said Teresa. 'Viareggio, Livorno, Piombino per-haps?'

'I was thinking of Saltcoats or Largs,' said Guido.

'Italy,' the woman said. 'Italy. I want to go home. I want to go home.'

She got up and walked away from the bench as if she intended to start her journey back to Genoa there and then, with or without his sanction.

At first Guido did not move, nothing that is except his head which rolled on his scraggy neck so that he could stare after her. He cursed softly and savagely under his breath.

She had told him nothing that he did not already know: that he was finished here, that his work was done, that it was indeed time to go sit in the sun. But he did not feel finished, did not feel that he had accomplished what he had set out to do, that he had escaped the shadow of his own folly, that loony half-hour when he had taken Frank Conway's mistress for himself. He had nobody to blame but himself for the fact that Carlo had cast him off or, rather, had left him behind.

Guido, old Guido, glowered at the retreating figure of his wife.

If he listened to her, if he allowed her to nag him into leaving Scotland, who would construct the deal with Pirollo, who would keep the managers up to scratch and ensure that honour money was paid on time; that ruthless men like McGuire or the incumbent Flint or others who had not yet shown themselves would not reach out and snatch what belonged to the Manones?

He did not need his wife to answer those questions. He knew the answer in his heart: Dominic would.

He stared bleakly along the path through the bands of spring shadow.

She was right, of course. He hated her for being right.

She was right in urging him to bow out, not to become some carping old nuisance tucked away in a villa on the Clyde coast, close enough to interfere but too far away to exert much influence. What he hated most, though, was the idea that he would be stuck with Teresa in a country that he no longer cared about or even remembered very well. He could not tell her that, however, in case he needed her to look after him tomorrow or the next day, whenever old age struck.

The fact that Teresa had thrust upon him was that he was no longer necessary. Dominic had Tony to advise and support him. Plus the new wife, Janet McKerlie's niece, the girl with the solemn oval face and serious brown eyes who might have been an Italian but, of course, was not; the girl, the woman who not only claimed to love Dominic but who probably understood him better than anyone, since she was part of that strange, new generation that was not — not in Guido's book at any rate — lost at all, but that knew precisely where it was going and how to get there.

Guido rose ponderously, as if the years had suddenly caught

up with him. He held the collar of his overcoat tightly against his throat with one large, carpenter's hand and, walking as quickly as he dared, hurried after his wife, seeking not reconciliation but the crust of authority that she had left him.

'Teresa,' he said, catching her by the arm. 'Teresa, wait.'

'What is it you want from me now?'

'I will write to my brother tonight.'

'About Italy?'

'Yes, about retiring to live in Italy,' Guido said.

'And Dominic?'

'He can damned well do as he pleases.'

'You must not be bitter about this marriage, Guido.'

'Bitter?' he said. 'Bitter? I am not bitter, woman. I am tired, that's all.'

'See,' said Teresa, without a smile. 'I told you so.'

The first time that Dominic kissed her was by the seaward side of the old salthouse on Headrick sands. He had picked Polly up in Lavender Court at half past eleven o'clock, long before Guido and Teresa had returned from mass, and they had motored down into Ayrshire on all but empty roads. They had stopped for lunch at a hotel near Prestwick golf course and had driven on afterwards, nosing south, with the Firth of Clyde dark blue beside them and the high peaks of Arran accompanying the Alfa on the distant horizon.

Dominic avoided Pirollo's territory. He did not even consider calling in at any of the Italian-owned cafés that dotted the coastal route. There would be time enough to introduce Polly to his friends and acquaintances. He had more important matters to attend to that pleasant April afternoon.

To Polly it was all new, all novel: a first sight of the sea, a first taste of salt air, limitless distances, colours that shifted and changed in unceasing variety, the texture of the sky, the soothing tones of the worn little sandstone towns through which they drove, down to the old square by Headrick harbour where they left the car to walk a while.

It was a simple matter for Dominic to head out of the city on Sunday. It did not occur to him that the excursion might bring enormous pleasure to a girl who had been raised in the grime and stench of a Glasgow slum. Polly had never been further from home than Greenock. There had never been enough in the kitty for Mammy to take them away for a full day's outing let alone a holiday. Without connivance then, Dominic offered Polly a taste of what might be and, defined by the great, breezy candour of sea and shore, a suggestion that their life together would be as clear and open as the April sky.

He had been to the salthouse before, long ago. His father had brought him here before the war, together with Guido Pirollo and another child whose name Dominic had forgotten. Uncle Guido had been with them too and a couple of young women; again the names were lost. They had been packed into the back of an open-topped Siddeley that his father had picked up somewhere. The journey over the back roads had seemed interminable. He remembered that one of the young women had sung and had tried to teach Uncle Guido how to dance the Grizzly Bear on the spit of sand that ran down to the sea and that everyone had laughed and it had all seemed innocent. Out of selfishness, or shyness perhaps, he chose not to share that memory with Polly.

In the lee of the salthouse he kissed her, tentatively at first. Kissed her without haste, but not insistently. He held her hand.

They walked a few steps together. Then she turned and kissed him, pressing him back against the salthouse wall, leaning into him, one leg raised behind her as if she were dancing. He tasted her lipstick. He could feel her body pressing against his, not innocently.

They broke, walked again, saying nothing. Only two or three tense steps. He put his arm around her waist. He stopped. She waited. He kissed her two, three, four, five times. The tip of his tongue brushed her lips. His breath and her breath mingled. A soft breathless excitement mounted between them so that when he released her he felt as if he were floating in the air like a gull. He drew breath and let it out again. He looked at her, smiling, and saw that Polly too seemed to be floating. He reached for her once more and, floating among the gorse bushes with the waves lapping nearby and the wall of the old salthouse warm behind them, they kissed again.

Polly was no longer rational. It did not matter what Dominic was or what he had done or what he would do in future. There was no room in her heart for the cautions that her mother had laid upon her. In that moment she was loved *and* loving, without the slightest notion of how love should be expressed or even how it had come about.

Dominic pushed her away just a little, just enough to suggest that there could be no parting between them now that would not bring hurt. He pushed her away and then, with a little moan, brought her back, not to kiss but to hold, to hold so close that she felt as if nothing could ever separate them again.

'Polly,' Dominic said. 'Polly, will you marry me?'

And 'Yes,' she said. 'Yes. I will. Yes,' before he could change his mind.

A head count revealed eleven Hallops resident in the ground-floor flat in Lavender Court, a fact that surprised not only Lizzie but Sandy Hallop too, since that gentleman had spent so much time in bed that his family seemed to have grown up around him without his being aware of it.

On the pavement Sadie Hallop, Jackie's mother, was indistinguishable from a thousand and one wee Glasgow wifies. She had bottle-bottom spectacles, a tartan shawl and a permanent list to starboard brought on by carrying heavy shopping bags or reaching down to hold a toddler by the hand.

Sadie, though, was sharper than appearances suggested. At one time in her pre-marital past she had been an infant-school teacher, an educational connection that seemed quite at odds with the great dumb lumpkin whom she had elected to marry.

There was certainly nothing much left of the girl that Sadie had once been, of the proud teacher, the lover, the blushing bride. Every role had been subsumed into raising a family that had seemed to grow numerically larger every time dozy old Sandy had opened an eye and blinked. Dennis was twenty-seven years old, wee Angela four; a breeding season that appeared to Lizzie to be not so much irresponsible as almost miraculous but that spoke volumes for Sadie Hallop's ability to cope with new arrivals.

The 'family gathering', though, was a bit of a nightmare. Sadie insisted on conducting discussion of the wedding arrange-ments – which had at one time seemed so simple – over the supper table in her kitchen. Eleven Hallops, four Conways and, lost somewhere in the steam, poor patient Bernard, set about the destruction of a steak pie the size of a battleship, a rice pudding as deep as the Kingston dock and enough bottled beer to float one in the other.

Kiddies perched on the bunker lid, toddlers squabbled on the bed, young girls – Rosie among them – were relegated to eating off a shoogly folding table in the lobby and an air not so much of sober discussion as chaotic celebration prevailed, for Sadie Hallop saw no shame in a shotgun wedding and was eager to embrace not just Babs but her very first grandchild too.

It was left to Bernard to extract Jackie and brother Dennis from the bedlam – Sandy had already gone to bed – and walk them down to Brady's for a quiet pint and a quiet word.

'What's the deal then?' Dennis said. 'I mean, what're you offerin'?'

Bernard's head was not quite so clear as it should have been. In fact, he was slightly less sober than Jackie who had drunk nothing all evening but ginger beer and whose attitude to marriage seemed to be that of any randy young man and took no account of the fact that his bride would be several months pregnant when she tripped into the registry office.

'The Conways' house,' Bernard said.

'Aye,' said Jackie. 'I thought we'd settled that, but.'

'Not quite.' said Bernard. 'If you become the householder you'll have to pay the rent every month. Can you manage that?'

Dennis snorted.

Jackie nodded.

'Speakin' now,' Bernard went on, 'as the agent of the factor I can recommend a change in tenancy only if I regard the incoming tenant to be solvent an' of reliable character.'

'Solvent?' said Jackie.

'Got money,' said Dennis, and snorted again.

'I've got money,' Jackie said. 'What's more, I'll even look after the old dear an' the sisters, if you like.'

'That won't be necessary,' Bernard said. 'You'll have the house all to yourself, Jackie. Mrs Conway an' I will – ah – we'll be gettin' married too very shortly, and we'll be goin' to stay in Knightswood.'

'What about Rosie an' Polly?' Jackie said.

'Polly's engaged to be married.'

'Jesus!' Dennis said. 'Did Patsy come back then?'

'I'm surprised Babs hasn't told you,' Bernard said. 'Polly's got herself engaged to Dominic Manone.'

Jackie chuckled and dug his brother in ribs. 'By God, we're gonna be related t' the Eye-tie. Think o' that, Dennis. Sky's the limit now.'

Bernard said, 'What about the flat, Jackie? Do you want it transferred to your name, or don't you?'

'I do,' Jackie said. 'Sure, I do.'

'Yeah,' Dennis said. 'May as well go the whole hog while you're at it.'

'I'll be at it okay,' said Jackie, grinning again. 'Night an' day.'

'Manone, eh?' said Dennis.

'Yeah, old Dominic – my brother-in-law,' said Jackie.

'Can't lose now,' said Dennis. 'Can't bloody lose.'

'I wouldn't count on it,' said Bernard, sadly.

Dining with the Manones was a different experience. Dominic appeared anxious to impress his future in-laws, though why this should be Bernard couldn't quite fathom – and if Lizzie had an explanation she kept it to herself. She undertook a manoeuvre of considerable subtlety, however, to ensure that Babs and Jackie found themselves excluded from the invitation and that Bernard was drafted in their stead. He then had to go through all the palaver of having his best suit dry cleaned and the expense of pur-chasing a new necktie and black shoes which, fortunately, would also do for his own wedding in the not too distant future.

He changed at Lizzie's house and looked, Lizzie said, like a million dollars, an opinion endorsed by Rosie who bounced on to his knee, took the cigarette from his mouth, and kissed him on the lips.

'Oh, Bernard,' she said. 'Why don't you marry me instead of Mammy?'

Bernard was no longer embarrassed by the Conway girls. He had come to realise that flirtatiousness was common in young women and reflected his primness as much as anything else. Besides, he was filled with desire for Lizzie, desire and curiosity, but had lost his fear of that aspect of matrimony and the urgency that went with it.

He retrieved the cigarette from Rosie and, facing her squarely, said, 'You're far too skinny for me, kiddo.'

'I am not skinny.'

'No, you're not,' he said, relenting. 'In that dress, you look ...'

'What?' she said, giggling. 'What?'

'Almost human.'

'But you still do not want to marry me?' said Rosie.

'Sorry,' said Bernard. 'I'm spoken for.'

At half past six o'clock the Alfa, driven by Tony, arrived at the close and Bernard, Lizzie, Polly and Rosie sailed down the stairs and into it to cheers and jeers from assembled young Hallops and a sulky scowl from Babs who still did not understand why Jackie and she had been left out.

Dominic had pulled out all the stops. The dining-room table had been drawn out to its full imposing length and set with a baffling array of spoons, forks, knives and crystal glasses and, as in the best restaurants, had fat linen napkins shaped into pyramids beside each place.

What really took the cake as far as Lizzie was concerned were the silver candlesticks that crowned the tablecloth, each installed with a pure white wax candle that burned with a slender yellow flame. There was something not just elegant but grand about it all and she, even she, was lost in admiration for all that her eldest was being offered. What impressed her most of all, though, was the commanding ease with which Polly handled herself, as if she had already become mistress of the house and used to this manner of living.

The Rowing Club, the cafés, pubs, warehouses and corner shops, bookies and shuffling down-at-heel runners all seemed very far away, so remote that it was almost impossible to believe that they shared the same existence as the handsome young man who presided over the dinner party and who, at an appropriate moment, presented Polly with a little red-leather box containing an engagement ring: a fine, three-stone diamond cluster set in platinum and gold, but not too ostentatious for its meaning to be lost.

With Dominic at her side, Polly slipped the ring on to her finger. It fitted perfectly, which was not entirely surprising given that she had chosen it herself a week back on Saturday.

She looked up at Dominic and smiled. He stooped and kissed her brow.

They were obviously in love, Lizzie thought, but rather too calm and cool about it, as if the emotion had been rehearsed beforehand and had lost its spontaneity. She wondered if they were lovers yet or if that pleasure was still to come; if it would be as it had been between Frank and she, hot and groping and sweaty, marred by a furtive kind of urgency as if, even within marriage, there were no time for any other kind of commitment.

On her daughter's behalf, she shed a few sentimental tears.

Champagne in fluted glasses, a reticent toast; then the door opened and two young maids brought in the soup in a huge silver tureen.

It was only then that Lizzie realised what was wrong, what was missing.

'Where's your uncle?' she asked. 'I thought he'd be here.'

'Guido had business to attend to,' Dominic said. 'He sends his regrets.'

'An' your auntie?' Lizzie said, glancing up.

'In the kitchen. She may join us later — if she's not too tired.'

Lizzie nodded, and let it go.

She was piqued at the absence of Dominic's family, though, just a wee bit insulted, more for Polly's sake than her own. Then it occurred to her that perhaps Dominic's relatives were not at the table because Dominic wanted to present himself just as he was, his own man, without Guido and the shadows of the immigrant generation lowering over him.

Polly said, 'Dominic's aunt and uncle are thinking of going back to Italy.'

'Retiring,' Dominic said. 'After the wedding, of course.'

'What'll you do then?' said Lizzie. 'Who'll take care of your house?'

'I will,' said Polly, firmly.

And at that moment Lizzie knew that Polly too had gone.

Chapter Twenty-Two

The spring season brought Lizzie no relief from harassment, though she had little to do with organising the first of the three weddings or the celebratory supper that took place in the Co-operative Society Halls after Jackie and Babs had said their piece before the registrar. Although he had politely declined an invitation to attend, Dominic had sent the bride a gift of twenty-five pounds which, given the circumstances, Babs saw no reason to refuse and which more than covered the cost of the reception.

Jackie had displayed more responsibility than Lizzie had anticipated. In the closing weeks of April he pitched himself into a frenzy of wheeling, dealing and motorcycle repair that kept Dennis and he busy at the garage far into the night; so much so that Babs, growing stealthily larger day by day, saw little of him and whined and swore a lot in a manner most unbecoming to a blushing bride. She remained employed at the warehouse, of course, and would continue to work there until June, for however casual Jackie's attitude to income might be a wage was still a wage and Mammy still had to pay the household bills during those last disintegrating days in Lavender Court.

Babs and Jackie Hallop were married on a Friday afternoon in May. The bride, in a mauve costume, looked radiant if just a tiny bit on the plump side, but the groom in a brand-new electric-blue suit stole much of her thunder. He was manic, gleeful and tearful by turns, and Lizzie was thankful that her new son-in-law wasn't fond of strong drink or God knows what sort of a fool he would have made of himself.

As it was, the wedding supper was a loud and strenuous affair, with ribald speeches, dancing to an accordion band, the serving of hot meat pies, sausage rolls and vast quantities of beer. There were even a few scuffles among the Hallop boys before the ritual departure of groom and bride for a two-day honeymoon in a boarding-house down the coast.

The happy couple rode off in a taxi-cab to the railway station festooned in paper ribbons and peppered with rice and confetti. Lizzie cried. Bernard comforted her by reminding her that their own wedding was only weeks away and assured her that it would be a much quieter affair.

On their return from their brief honeymoon Babs and Jackie took up temporary residence with the Hallops. They were constantly in and out of the Conways' flat, however, popping up and down stairs like squirrels in a cage, until Lizzie hardly knew whether she was coming or going and felt that she had lost not only her daughter but her home as well.

The patience and strength that had sustained her for so many years seemed to drain away as May crept into June and dispossession gave way to depression. She saw less of Polly, more and more of Babs and Jackie who were already planning how they would 'gut' the house, what they would keep by way of furnishings and what they would gaily discard, until Lizzie began to wonder if she was doing the right thing in marrying Bernard Peabody at all and wish that she'd never stepped out on the road to matrimony.

The only fixed constants at this time were work, obligatory visits to attend her mother – and Bernard. Naturally, poor Bernard bore the brunt of Lizzie's uncertainty and was called upon to supply even more hugs, kisses and reassurances than usual.

Janet refused to attend Babs's wedding. She claimed that she didn't approve of the Hallops, whom she had never in fact met. She also refused point blank to be a witness at Lizzie's wedding or take any part in it at all. When Lizzie appealed to her mother to intercede with Janet on her behalf she met with implacable hostility and a stream of insults which if they had not been so banal might have wounded her even more deeply.

'Aunt Janet's only jealous,' Rosie assured her mother. 'And Gran is annoyed because we are going to live in Knightswood and you will not be able to dance attendance on her three times a week.'

'Do *you* think I'm lettin' them down, dear?'

'You are not letting anyone down, Mammy.'

'What about you?'

'Me?' said Rosie. 'I am going with you and Bernard, am I not?'

'Aye, of course you are. You'll have to sleep in a cabinet bed, though. You won't have a room of your own.'

'I do not mind that,' said Rosie, cheerfully. 'I have never had a room of my own. I will not miss what I have never had. And it is not much further from Knightswood into the shop on the tramcar.'

Shelby's bookshop had become the focus of Rosie's life. It was all she could do to disguise how much it meant to her to sit secure in the quiet, faintly dusty depths of the shop listening to booksellers' talk and handling rare old volumes as affectionately as Babs would cradle her baby, as tenderly as Polly would kiss her husband-to-be. Everything about Shelby's appealed to Rosie, from its eccentric clientele to the sheaves of catalogue copy that she helped prepare and the rackety old Oliver upon which she typed out quotations.

Most of all she liked the men she worked with, Mr Albert and Mr Robert, especially Mr Robert, who treated her with more consideration than she probably deserved. She confided in no one how happy she was, no one except Mr Feldman, who popped into the shop now and then. Only he could understand how an ordered life could be so satisfying and how, at last, she had finally left the silence of the streets behind.

Sometimes, though, she wondered if Alex O'Hara still loitered outside the Rowing Club on Saturday evenings, a ciggie in his mouth, pint glass in hand, his eyes turned towards Paisley Road and if, in that violent heart of his, he nurtured any regrets at the realisation that he would probably never see her again.

Somehow she doubted it.

There were no such lingering sentiments in Polly. She was Dominic's fiancée and, come September, would be Dominic's wife. The past was a closed book, a door she did not intend to reopen. She had no regrets whatsoever at the direction her life had taken. Even if she had not been captivated by love she would have felt nothing but faint scorn when the postcard from Paris flipped into the letterbox; a cheap postcard showing a view of the gardens of the Tuileries upon the back of which Patsy had printed in pencil, '*Wish you were here*,' a prosaic little greeting that made Polly glad that she was not.

There was no romance in poverty, no poetry in aimlessness. Patsy in Paris would be the same as Patsy anywhere, an adventurer struggling to find adventure, a rebel in search of something to rebel against, a lover who did not know where to look for love. For all that, she did not tear the card in half and toss it on to the coals. She stuck it into the cardboard carton in which she had already begun to assemble her trousseau or, rather, that collection of bits and pieces that she did not wish to discard.

Polly did not know why she kept that first and only communication from a man who had never been her lover and whom she had never loved: perhaps, she thought, because arrogance demanded it, the qualities of patronage, forgiveness and self-assurance that she had already begun to learn from Dominic and that, in the years ahead, would surely become their bond.

Then waiting was over and it was their last night together in Lavender Court. Tomorrow Lizzie would step up before the altar in Knightswood New Church – Mrs Peabody had insisted on a church wedding – and marry Bernard Peabody. She had already given up her job at the laundry. She had been accorded a rousing send-off by her workmates and presented with a painted vase by which to remember them. Most of her clothes – Rosie's too – had been transported across town in brown-paper bags and Babs and Jackie had already assumed possession of the wardrobe and closets.

The lady-lamp was still in place in the lobby, all the furniture, cushions, curtains, crockery and cutlery, even the wireless set, were just where they had always been, except that, caught in a limbo of transition, they no longer seemed to belong to anyone at all. It was still 'her' house but it was no longer her house. Next time she entered it Lizzie would be her daughter's guest. Everything would be different, even the smells, and it would be Babs and Jackie Hallop who were shaping a life for themselves within these four walls.

It would have been more practical for Polly to marry before her mother but Dominic preferred to wait until September when Aunt Teresa and Uncle Guido would depart for Italy and Polly and he would be free to choose a new cook and a new housekeeper to look after them. Meanwhile, Polly would lodge in the house in Manor Park Avenue, an arrangement much less scandalous than it seemed. Although they would share the table and the parlour and Polly would learn from Teresa what would be required of her, they would not share a bedroom. On this point Dominic was adamant.

It was not, he said, that he did not wish to make love to her but simply that some stripe of traditional morality remained within him, stemming from he knew not where. Mainly, though, he did not wish to offend Aunt Teresa's Catholic sensibilities by jumping the gun and creating more awkwardness in a situation that was already awkward enough.

There was more to it than politeness and morality, however, and Polly reckoned that Dominic still nursed a faint, fond hope that his father would bring the family across the Atlantic to bless and be with him on his wedding day.

It was not to be. For whatever reason, vain or valid, Carlo Manone stubbornly refused to return to Scotland no matter how often Dominic wrote and begged him to change his mind.

An odd but not uncomfortable arrangement would pertain tomorrow in Knightswood New Church: Bernard had asked Dominic to be his best man and Dominic had agreed. Polly would be her mother's maid. There were, it seemed, no others suitable, only family and family-to-be; a strange alliance, Polly realised, a necessary compromise that linked them all, sisters and strangers, into a unity, however temporary. There would only be a dozen of them, all told, plus a nosy little audience in the back pews, Mrs Peabody's friends from the Guild.

Afterwards the family would dine together in the room in the Ca'doro that Dominic had booked and that Dominic would pay for, then they would all go their separate ways: she to Dominic's house, Babs back to the Gorbals, Rosie to Knightswood, Mammy and Bernard off for a three-day honeymoon on the Isle of Arran. And the Conways would no longer be the Conways. They would belong to some larger clan that, in due time, would spread and expand until all that was left of the girls that they had been were memories clouded by a host of new experiences too unpredictable to name.

On wire hangers in the rumpled bedroom wafted the afternoon dress and tunic overdress that Mammy would wear tomorrow, the silk dress with the cowl neckline that she, Polly, would wear, Rosie's summer dress with a skirt flared from the knee; all new, all fine and fashionable, a line of fabrics that had cost more than any of them would have believed possible just half a year ago. And more to come at the time of her wedding, her quiet, elegant September wedding to the Italian, to the *bête noire* of her childish dreams.

Rosie lay asleep beside her, her breath purling softly.

Propped against the pillows, Polly watched the filmy garments float like ghosts in the half-dark and felt for the first time a little tremor of apprehension at the irony of what she had committed herself to and what she had done. She sat up suddenly, and because she could not bear to be alone padded barefoot through to the kitchen.

'Polly, is that you?' Lizzie asked.

'Yes.'

'Can you not sleep, dearest?'

'No.'

'Me neither,' Mammy said. 'Come on, slip in beside me an' give me a cuddle. You're not too old for that, are you?'

'No,' Polly said. 'I'll never be too old for that.'

She could just make out her mother's nightgowned figure in the pale pre-dawn light that filtered through the curtained window above the sink. She felt her way towards the niche bed and slid beneath the covers.

When she felt her mother's arm about her, tucking her in, she recalled those winter nights not so long ago when they had all slept together on one mattress on the floor, all gathered in together, shivering at first, until Mammy, by some trick that she, Polly, had yet to learn, had made them all warm.

'Is Rosie . . .'

'Fast asleep,' said Polly.

'Do you want t' talk?' Lizzie said.

'I don't mind,' said Polly. 'I'm wide awake.'

'I want you t' tell me somethin',' Lizzie said. 'Since it's just you an' me, Polly, an' we won't be like this again, I want you to tell me the truth.'

Polly felt a prickle of doubt in her stomach, a tiny stab of the guilt that she'd lived with since before she'd had a memory, a premonition that Mammy knew everything about her, every thought, every feeling that she'd tried to keep to herself. Secrets were adult things, though, things that had to be earned and cultivated and she had recently come to realise that her mother had acquired some secrets that could not be shared, even with a daughter.

'Do you love him?' Lizzie said.

'Dominic? Yes, I love him.'

'Are you sure?'

Polly drew herself away a little, not in haste.

She didn't want to have to face such a question and felt aggrieved at her mother's failure to understand that there *was* no answer, no truth, that she could not explain or rationalise how Dominic affected her.

She knew only too well what lay at the back of her mother's concern, a fear that she was marrying not for love but for gain, that she had somehow managed to deny to herself that Dominic was a criminal. Did Mammy imagine that she was still naïve and innocent? How could she possibly explain that part of what she loved in Dominic was just that dangerous contrast between what he was and what he did? She had no desire to change and reform him. On the contrary: she wished to share his life in all its parts, to understand all his complexities and ambiguities, not to have him hide from her.

She said, 'I might ask you the same thing, Mammy.'

'Aye, dearest, but it isn't the same thing.'

'Are you sure that you love Bernard?'

'Absolutely sure.'

'You thought that about Daddy too, didn't you?'

Lizzie was quiet for a moment. She sighed. 'I suppose I did.'

'But you took a risk, right?'

'I took a risk, aye.'

'Well, that's what I'm doing,' Polly said. 'I'm taking a risk. We're all taking a risk. No, I don't mean just you, just me. I mean Dominic, Dominic and Bernard as well. Do they know what they're getting into when they take *us* on for better or worse? I doubt it.'

'A fat, middle-aged widow,' Lizzie said, with a wry chuckle.

'That's not what Bernard thinks, that's not how he sees you.'

'Nah,' Lizzie said, 'I know it isn't.'

'That's the difference between us,' Polly said. 'I think Dominic knows only too well what he's getting, what I am, what makes me tick.'

'An' what's that?' Lizzie asked.

'Ambition,' Polly answered; then, suspecting that she had revealed too much, quickly added, 'I mean, I want to feel safe. Isn't that what we're all supposed to want these days, to feel safe and protected?'

'An' loved,' said Lizzie.

'Yes,' Polly admitted. 'And loved.'

Polly felt her mother's arms grope for her again and because she was still a dutiful daughter, at least for a little while longer, let herself yield, let herself sink against the softness of her mother's breasts, brow against her mother's cheek. Tomorrow, though, it would be a man that her mammy held in her arms, another man, Bernard, not Daddy.

Come September she too would know what it meant to share that kind of love. She didn't think she knew what love meant: yet she did, of course she did.

She turned her head on the pillow and saw that the blind had lightened and knew that under the pall of brown smoke that hung over Glasgow the June sun had peeped over the horizon, that the time of transition was almost over and that her mother's wedding day was just about to begin.

'No matter what happens to you,' Lizzie said, very softly, 'you'll always have me behind you. Now an' always.'

'I know, Mammy,' Polly said. 'I know.'

She felt herself yielding, more than she would have wished, guilt and restlessness and uncertainty smoothing away until, soothed and comforted, secure in her mammy's arms, she fell asleep at last.